DRAKE THOMAS

-BOOK 2-

DECEPTION OF MERDERICK

TYLER SVEC
JORDAN SVEC

CITIOFBOOKS, INC.
3736 Eubank NE Suite A1
Albuquerque, NM 87111-3579
www.citiofbooks.com
Hotline: 1 (877) 389-2759
Fax: 1 (505) 930-7244

Ordering Information:
Quantity sales. Special discounts are available on quantity purchases by corporations, associations, and others. For details, contact the publisher at the address above.

Printed in the United States of America.

ISBN-13:   Softcover   979-8-89391-589-1
                        Hardback   979-8-89391-590-7

Library of Congress Control Number:

Other works by Tyler Svec

The Kingdom

I. Alliance

II. Rebellion

III. Redemption

DRAKE THOMAS

I. Rise of Grimdor

Super Hero Stories

I. Crunch

II. Boom

More at svecbooks.com

To Dave,
You've faithfully proofread every book we've
written...and we still don't have any clue what your
favorite kind of book is.

Thanks for all you've done!

DRAKE THOMAS

-BOOK 2-

DECEPTION OF MERDERICK

TYLER SVEC

JORDAN SVEC

DRAKE THOMAS
DECEPTION OF MERDERICK

Chapters

<u>SYNOPSIS</u>

Drake Thomas woke by the side of the river. After a few moments, it became clear that he had no memory of his life prior to that moment. The only thing he had to his name was an unusual mark on his hand. His new companions thought that the mark might indicate some ancient legend and pertain to a certain prophecy.

Within a matter of days, Drake and his companions found themselves on the run from people who seemed to be looking or hunting for Drake. Under the leadership of their friend Rohemir, in a desperate attempt to flee the enemy (known as the Sorcerer), they tried to take a shortcut through the nation of Grimdor.

Grimdor, which had long been the ancient home of their enemy, proved to be a perilous journey and only resulted in almost being captured again.

They fled to the town of Revly where they met a man named Aiden. With his help, they escaped the clutches of the Sorcerer and finally made it to the Elven nation of Ariamore.

After being pursued by the Sorcerer to the borders of Ariamore, the threat of war was inevitable. Misinterpreting the mark on Drake's hand, they put him and his companions in charge of the battle. That decision proved disastrous, though they did achieve victory.

Some days after the battle they met a strange shopkeeper named Isabel, who seemed to know many things but never revealed how she knew them.

The enemy's power grew and in the middle of the night, Gwen was kidnapped.

SHAVROCK

Drake wished that it had been longer until the morning had arrived, but before he knew it the sun had peaked over the horizon. His eyes were heavy and bags were under his eyes as he tried to find the strength to climb out of bed.

He Ellizar and Lily had stayed up talking about everything for nearly an hour after the excitement. He had hardly slept since Gwen had been abducted, and he could tell by the condition the others were in that they hadn't slept well either.

Drake thought the situation through again and again, trying to come up with some kind of a theory as to why Gwen would be kidnapped instead of him. It didn't make logical sense to him and if he had known that this was going to happen he would have gladly let himself be captured just so they would leave her alone.

Drake dressed and then made his way to the dining room where he found that he was the second person to arrive. Aiden sat at the end of the table, quiet for the most part, as if contemplating some great feat that was going on inside his head.

Rohemir arrived moments before Atruss and Gabrielle gracefully entered the room. They took their seats and began eating. Drake didn't say anything, too tired to break the silence.

Lightning chased itself across the sky and thunder crashed, shaking the city of Belvanor. A red sky filled the horizon to the east, while the skyline to the west was filled with thunderheads of reds and purples. Though they were intimidating, the sky was filled with sparkles as the sunlight lit the distant droplets.

"Looks like you are going to have quite a storm to go through. Are you sure it'll be safe for you to fly?" Rohemir asked.

"We have a choice. You don't get stronger without storms," Aiden replied. "With each second that passes we make it easier for the Sorcerer to catch us. We know that the Sorcerer is capable of creating storms. This could be from him to keep us here, which is why we have to try even harder to get away and reach our destination."

"Agreed," Atruss replied. "We can't afford to have you four in the open any longer, you have to go somewhere you can't be found."

"Remnda correct?" Rohemir asked. The others nodded. Aiden caught Drake's eye for a moment or so, instilling a sense of security and trust that Drake hadn't felt before.

The conversation died and they disappeared to their rooms for a few minutes, grabbing all the necessary supplies that they needed. It wasn't much, just an extra change of clothes and whatever weapons they had acquired over the past two months. Within the hour they were standing in an open clearing just outside the castle walls. They looked to the west, the storm clouds growing ever closer. The Taruks were waiting in the clearing, patient as ever. Aiden was the last one to join their company, walking forward with several leather straps.

"Okay, who's riding and who's not?" Aiden asked.

"Excuse me?" Lily asked in reply. Aiden smiled weakly.

"Usually there's only room for two on a Taruk and that's maxed out and there's five of us," Aiden explained. "Which means that someone is going to have to be flying the whole time."

"And just how are we supposed teh do that?" Ellizar asked.

"I have a special harness. We will tie you to one of the Taruk's feet and you'll fly along quite peacefully. I suggest that Ellizar is the one flying."

"Of course yeh would suggest that all yeh elf kind do is pick on the dwarf. Poor little Ellizar can't do anythin' the way he would want teh."

"Cry me a river," Lily replied, with a laugh. Ellizar shot her a look and half smile.

"Do yeh have any logical reason fer hangin' me from a Taruk or are yeh doin' it merely fer entertainment sake?"

"Skander's a little large to hang from a Taruk," Aiden said. Ellizar looked at him knowingly.

"You tellin' me a great beast like a Taruk, can't carry a Gigantor amount ov weight?"

None of them could suppress a chuckle.

"The way I see it you're lighter than anyone else which will put less strain on the Taruk," Aiden explained. "Plus, the only harness I could find for this sort of a thing was one for a dwarf. It took me forever to find one."

"There's a reason fer that!" Ellizar exclaimed. "It's not natural fer people teh hang from a Taruk."

"That's not the only thing that's unnatural," Lily remarked. Ellizar threw his axe on the ground.

"Do yeh have a problem elf?" Everyone laughed, including Ellizar himself.

"Of course not Ellie, I'm just trying to play with your head."

"I'd say it's working," Skander said. Within a couple of minutes, they had helped Ellizar into the harness and then tied it to Destan's leg. Drake and Lily went on his Taruk while Skander and Aiden rode Elohim. The Taruks flapped their massive wings and they gently rose into the sky, Ellizar screamed like they had never heard.

"What do you think is going to happen to us?" Lily asked.

"I'm not sure," Drake answered, looking ahead to the storm, which accurately depicted what he was feeling inside. "I feel as though a piece of my heart has been ripped out. I can't even try to help her because I don't know enough to do anything."

"We can always do something," Lily encouraged. "But in this instance, I too feel hopeless and discouraged. Our enemy is so strong I'm not sure how anyone will stand against them."

They fell silent noting that for the first time, the Taruks had changed their course slightly, heading more to the north than the northwest. Drake wondered for a moment if the Taruks were lost but Destan's thoughts and emotions said that they were heading in the right direction.

Drake still found it strange that he had ended up with a Taruk. For reasons that he couldn't explain he found himself getting more and more involved in a crisis that he couldn't even remember until that day by the river. Who had he been before that? What had his life been like?

Soon it became clear that they were headed straight into the storm and that they weren't headed towards Remnda like they had been told. Drake didn't worry about what lay ahead and instead focused on putting on the heavy cloak that he had been given a couple of days earlier. He laid part of it over Lily and tried to shield them from the rain that was ahead of them.

They entered the storm and watched as the sun disappeared. The further they flew the darker the clouds became. The rain pounded on them. The wind whipped at their clothes, eventually ripping the heavy cloak from their grasp.

They flew for hours without any rest from the weather. Finally, Aiden ordered them to put down in the storm, able to pick out a clearing from up in the sky, which proved that they had better eyesight than Drake did.

They unstrapped Ellizar from the harness he had been in all day and then took shelter underneath the trees. The shelter did them no good as the leaves had been blown off.

When the dawn came Lily found an inch of water covering the ground where she had laid down to sleep. She stood up, and changed into her other set of clothes, which really weren't any drier due to the thundering rains that had come down on them last night. The leaves were gone from the trees, leaving the forest bare and desolate. The trees were silent, ready for the winter that would soon be coming.

Aiden sat up against a tree, facing away from her and the rest of the camp. She walked up the small hill, standing just behind him. His clothes were wet and his hair was matted with mud as was her own. He stared into the forest. She sat down a few feet away from him, resting her back against another tree.

"Good morning Lily," Aiden greeted.

"Good morning. That was quite a storm yesterday wasn't it?"

"You can say that again. Although from what I understand you and your friends had a similar experience in Grimdor?"

"Yes, it was worse than this one, but not by much."

Aiden grunted. "Our enemy is not as strong as he would like."

"He isn't?"

"If he was, this storm would have killed us. He is powerful, yes, but not all-powerful. He never will be."

"I don't see how he could be, Drake has the mark and that means that Sherados is here among us right?"

"Yes it does, but the world does not know that yet! They are blind to the truth that is right in front of them. I'm not sure how else to put it, but until the time is right, Sherados cannot come forward."

"Why not?" Lily asked. "If Sherados came forward now why wouldn't people believe him?"

"The way things are working in this world right now, they would likely think that he was the Sorcerer. After all, no one has ever seen the Sorcerer, and only a handful of people know they have seen Sherados. They would have no reason to believe that the person who said he was telling the truth wasn't lying. Sherados must wait until people know in their hearts who the Sorcerer is. Only then will he be accepted by people."

"It's sad really," Lily replied. "Lathon was the greatest ruler the world had ever known, and now the heir has to wait until the correct time to come forward."

"It is sad," Aiden admitted. "But if that's the way it must be done, then it must be done. Evil does not rest and therefore neither can Lathon."

"Do you think Gwen is okay?" Lily asked. "I have a hard time believing that us running will help her."

"We're not running Lily," Aiden started. "We are never running. We are preparing our hearts and souls for the battles that lie ahead of us. If we don't take the time to train ourselves and teach ourselves the necessary disciplines and practices to survive a war, then we would be fools to run into battle unprepared. That's what he wants us to do! The Sorcerer wants us to run in and attack him. He would take great pleasure in leaving us barely alive and destroying us slowly. We are doing the right thing."

"I'm probably asking you a lot of questions, but why did only Gwen get mauled when they came out of that mirror?"

"I've been hoping an explanation would come, but I haven't been able to come up with any answer."

"Maybe the reason she was mauled was so that person in the hospital could take her."

"It's a possibility. The world works in strange ways, and if on a deeper level, this is a plan by the Sorcerer, then it is a well-thought-out plan. Hard to say, the future is always in motion, so it is useless to try and predict what will happen."

"So nothing is for certain?" Lily asked.

"The only certain thing is that the world is changing and that the word of Lathon as written in the ancient scrolls is true. Other than that there is nothing that can be trusted to stay the same throughout the ages. This world throws a lot of curve balls at you, and if you don't have a conviction about what you believe, and know to be true then you'll be swept out to sea as easily as a grain of sand." Lily didn't answer.

"Where are we headed?" Lily asked. "Somehow I get the feeling that we're heading in a different direction than we were originally supposed to."

"That's because we are heading in a different direction. You seem to not trust Rohemir and this will be our chance to test it. We've told him and everyone else except Atruss that we're heading to Remnda. Best I can figure, we're roughly two hours from our final destination, which isn't far from the castle that Drake and Gwen ended up at."

"Do you think it's safe to be so close to that place?"

"I want to keep an eye on it. Something is going on beneath the surface that I can't see. I'm not sure how long we are going to be able to train, but I have a feeling that while we're here something's going to happen that will alter the future of this war."

"We just can't have a couple months of rest can we?"

Aiden laughed. "Not likely."

They were silent for the next couple minutes as Aiden closed his eyes seeming to be asleep but Lily knew he was likely just listening for any sign that there were unexpected visitors in the area. Lily opened her mouth to speak but Aiden held a finger to his lips. He opened his eyes, carefully moving his hand to the knife strapped to his side.

The silence pounded in her ears, but finally Lily heard the faint noise that he had. Footsteps.

Aiden turned, throwing his knife at an incredible speed. The dagger found its target, lodging itself in their opponent's throat. The Borag collapsed on the ground.

"You have good ears," Lily complimented.

"If a person listens they can hear many things," Aiden replied, removing his knife from the Borag. "Orange pieces on his shoulder armor. He's a scout. Looking for those who are loyal. If he's here you can be sure more are nearby."

Lily readied her bow, seeing something from the corner of her eye. She hastily strung an arrow and fired it striking another Borag in the chest.

Aiden raised his eyebrows. "Nice shot."

They pulled the arrow from the Borag. Aiden looked at the vile creature as if looking for something specific.

"Such a waste of a life," Aiden said. "They came all this way just to fall into the traps of their evil ways and are lost from all that is good."

"Is there any chance that any of them might be able to change their ways and become good?"

"People can always change their ways, but it is a struggle of the heart and soul. The soul wants to, but the heart has been deceived and fights them at every turn. Every day they have the choice, and many will never choose the right thing. If they do, they will be saved, but until then they will wander in their darkness, hoping they are doing the right thing. We know better though."

"Think there are more of them?" Lily asked. Aiden looked around, studying the landscape. He pointed to the west where a group of unsuspecting Borags were coming over the top of the hill.

Neither of them moved as the Borags looked in their direction.

"Wake the others and get to the Taruks!" Aiden exclaimed. Lily began running. A dozen arrows were loosed, and all of them missed their targets.

Lily loosed an arrow in return, as she ran into their camp. The sound of the Borags' armor had already awakened the others, who were on their feet with their weapons drawn.

"Get to the Taruks!" Lily exclaimed. The others didn't question her, making their way over to Destan and Elohim. Drake and Lily helped Ellizar into his harness and then climbed onto Destan. A moment after they climbed on, the Taruks were airborne, swooping low over the forest.

Lily felt her heart drop, realizing that hiding from any enemy with the leafless trees would be impossible. They watched from above as Aiden ran from the remaining Borags.

Destan and Elohim both flicked their tails, sending brilliant streams of white light to the ground below. The area that the light struck was destroyed, leaving piles of debris. There was one path between the wreckage, and Aiden was coming right towards it.

The Borags picked up the pace, hoping to catch him before the Taruks could land. They succeeded. Aiden turned around, sword in hand, engaging the Borag closest to him. He pulled back his arm to swing again. In an instant, the Borag was defeated, but not by Aiden's sword.

A strange creature appeared out of its hiding place and chased the Borags into the forest hunting them down with speed and power. When the Borags were no more, he came back to the circle of debris where the Taruks had landed.

Drake dropped from the Taruk and ran towards Aiden. The creature, which was bigger than they had realized, raced towards Aiden who didn't seem to be concerned.

Lily fired an arrow, but it never hit its target as it was dissolved in a small puff of flames. Aiden turned to face them, keeping her from shooting another arrow.

"There's nothing to be afraid of," Aiden told them. "He is on our side."

"He is?" Lily asked.

"That's what the man said elf!" Ellizar yelled from the Taruk. He managed to get himself out of the harness and make his way over to the rest of them. The beast stood ten feet tall and was all muscle. The skin was dark grey and covered with a slimy oil that gave off an aroma that Drake wished he could forget.

Spikes ran up the spine, and there were also several spikes in each shoulder although those were only an inch or two high as opposed to the ones on the back which were a foot or two long. Two large swords were strapped to his back and several more daggers and knives were strapped to him.

Ellizar mumbled something to himself, finally standing next to Lily and looking up at the creature standing in front of them. "I don't know what kind of creature this is, but he's pretty tall."

"We're known for being tall dwarf!" the creature bellowed. Ellizar's face washed white and the rest of them tried to keep their mouths from dropping open. The voice had been dark and eerie, even if it hadn't been intended.

"Time for formal introductions," Aiden started. "Everyone, I would like you to meet Shavrok. I know you're probably wondering what he is, and I can tell you only what I know, the rest you're going to have to learn from him. He is a Gog."

"I've never heard of a Gog before," Drake admitted.

"Most people haven't," Shavrok replied.

"They are thought to be extinct," Aiden explained. "However, as we all know, in this world there are things that are not like they seem. Only a handful of people have seen their kind in the past hundred years."

"I can't say I'd want teh cross paths with yeh anytime soon," Ellizar replied with a laugh. Shavrok laughed, his voice echoing throughout the whole forest.

"You have nothing to fear as long as we are on the same side," Shavrok replied.

Aiden started to follow the creature.

"Where are we going?" Skander asked.

"I am taking you to Negev instead of Remnda," Aiden announced. "You will be very safe there. No one would dare attack a Gog city. They are deadly in battle, and more than secluded enough to hide us without raising suspicion. If there's anyone who can best help us at this moment it's the Gogs."

"I've never heard of Negev," Skander stated. They started walking through the forest. The Taruks took flight as if they knew where to go.

"You won't be able to find any map with the name on it. At least not a current one, which works things to our advantage. Like I said, there are only a few people in this lifetime who have seen a Gog, because they go to great lengths to keep themselves hidden. Myself and Atruss are the only ones that I know of, actually I amend that. There is one woman who has seen them before."

"Who?" Drake asked.

"Isabel," Aiden answered. They walked through the forest, following the Gog who seemed even larger and more dangerous than he had previously.

His head darted from side to side. and the spikes on his back seemed to shift as if though he could sense something that they couldn't. His ears were tucked back into his head, nearly invisible. They all took notice of the Gog's knuckles that also had spikes protruding from them.

"You should feel very honored," Shavrok told them. "There have only been three people to ever see and dine with us, but you are the first who will get to live with us. We have gone to great lengths in preparation for this day."

"How far is it to the village?" Drake asked. Shavrok shook his head.

"Not village; city. Not far, maybe three more hours of walking, Destan and Elohim are probably already there and resting by now."

"How'd you know the Taruk's names?" Lily asked.

"Aiden told me so I could send them to the city with my thoughts," Shavrok explained. "I did not want to risk saying the message aloud in case some of those vile little devils should be near."

"You mean the Borags?" Drake asked. The Gog shook his head.

"Vile is vile no matter what form it takes," Shavrok pointed out. "Many deceptions are in this world, my friends. The form of evil is one of them. People look at the Borags and the Spirits and say *that* that is what evil looks like. Others look at me and say that I look like I'm evil, and others still look like you do, but no one believes that they are evil. All evil is evil.

"So can yeh tell us a little bit about yer race?" Ellizar asked. "We've never heard anythin' about yeh, except maybe in ancient stories and songs, and even in my memory I can't recall one mentionin' Gogs."

"In ages past, the far parts of the world used to call us the Gongorai," Shavrock began. "Thousands and thousands of years ago, there were a great number of Gog's that roamed ancient earth. At that time it was a free land and a free world. Then there came a great war, with a very powerful Sorcerer at the head of the Borag army as I'm sure you've heard of?" They nodded.

"We allied with the enemies of the Sorcerer and fought the most ferocious battles you can imagine. Next to a Taruk, nothing is more destructive than a Gog. We were too dangerous for our own good and the Sorcerer picked our race of people to be the first that he was going to exterminate. The war raged between our two races and finally, the Gogs were defeated, the few of us that were left withdrew from the world altogether and made a city that we now call home.

"Ever since then, we have stayed in hiding, choosing to never put ourselves in a position that would lose so many Gog lives. We have remained hidden, waiting with our army so that someday when the time was right we could step forward and set the record straight."

"Is the time right now?" Skander asked. "What about the wars that have ragged in the past? Why did-"

"The time was not right then!" Shavrok boomed. "The time has come for us to declare our existence to the Sorcerer and fight that little demon until he is crushed into the ground. We seek to make a war."

"How do you know that the time is right?" Drake asked. "People tell me a lot of things, but some of them I'm not sure I can believe."

"When your heart is quiet and you are truly at peace with everything in your life, and you listen real hard to the silence and everything around you. You will hear many things. The world has changed and it is about to do so again. The time of the end has begun."

"The end?" Skander asked. "You mean the world is going to be destroyed?"

"The end of one age is near and the beginning of another is about to begin. Sherados is among us even now and it is because of him that we are making plans to enter war."

"But what if Sherados doesn't come forward for a couple of years?" Drake asked. Shavrok stopped in his tracks and looked him in the eye.

"Sherados has come forward, if he hadn't then we wouldn't be doing any of this. We would still be in hiding, building our strength and waiting for the time to be right."

Eventually, the hills ceased and open fields stretched far in front of them. A few minutes later they could see water in every direction, with a distant band of land that wrapped nearly all the way around. Far to either side, hidden among the trees, the water entered and exited through a river, which the large bay sat right in between.

A worn footpath became visible in the dying weeds and grass. A chill wind came in off the water, but the sun was still shining offering them a little warmth. The path soon became stone and they passed by several more Gogs. standing guard for the city which must certainly lay ahead of them. Drake followed the others blindly noticing large siege towers sitting in the distance.

The path slowly meandered down, while the cliffs continued to grow. Soon they were deep within the rock. The air became warmer and the wind ceased, they could now hear the sound of a city.

Their descent ended when they reached the coast and turned to the left heading down the beach only a little ways until the city of Negev came into view. Drake's mind struggled to wrap his mind around how large the city in front of them was. An entire city sat on the coastline, built on rocks that appeared to have been put there for the sole purpose of building the city. The rest of the city was carved out of similar rocks, except these were red.

The city reached a hundred feet above them and the top of the cliff they had been on was even further up than that. The city reached down the coastline as far as the eye could see and beyond that Drake wasn't sure that it even ended. Ships sat in the water, and large stacks of logs piled nearly sixty feet high were lying on the beach waiting to be used.

"Welcome to Negev, home of the Gogs and the secret force that no one knows about," Shavrok said. The spikes on his back retracted, disappearing into his skin. The oil on his skin dried up and the stench vanished.

"What just happened?" Skander asked.

"We don't look as scary when we're not on the lookout, but if we're in a dangerous situation those spikes will return," Shavrok told them. "It would make it impossible for us to lay down if we had those spikes on our back the whole time."

"I was goin' teh ask yeh about that one," Ellizar said.

"Yeah sure you were," Lily replied. Ellizar smiled.

"There will likely be several hours until the main supper meal so I'll assign you a guide so that you may see the city. I have things to attend to," Shavrok explained.

They approached the front gate which was entirely made out of stone. They stopped as the guards motioned to them and Shavrok proceeded to talk to them in their language.

They were allowed to enter and the massive gates were closed behind them. Drake couldn't imagine how anyone, short of using magic, would ever break through these gates. They were two feet thick and at least twenty feet tall.

They were brought through the city, receiving some stares from the citizens of the city but most of the Gogs smiled and waved at the company. They passed forges, with black smoke pouring out of the chimneys before being swept out to the bay. Weapons lay in piles as well as some armor, although there seemed to be twice as many weapons as opposed to armor.

"Why is it that you don't have very much armor made up?" Skander asked. "Did you just start making it?"

"No, we made it the same time we started the weapons," Shavrok began. "You will find that the skin of a Gog is stronger than most chain mail and for that reason, Gogs don't usually wear armor. Some elite groups of Gogs don't even use weapons. I am the leader of that group, which is why even though I carry swords with me I only use them as a last resort."

They walked through the city until they thought they had reached the other side, between them and the lake was a wall that had openings to the wharf which had been built out.

"We dug out the shoreline so that we could put our ships close to the city," Shavrok pointed out, leading them out onto the wharf. In each opening was a ship, standing nearly fifty feet above them, far larger than any other ship that they had seen up to this point. The masts reached into the air and Gogs of every shape and kind walked the decks which were docked perpendicular to the wharf.

Some of the ships had special designs built into them. Drake quickly took notice of special openings that were to either side of the bow, near the water level. There were also large ramps that were on the decks of other ships. The city wall finally came to an end but the line of ships didn't as they continued. On the beach there were hundreds and hundreds of landing barges that were being built.

"How many Gogs are there in this city?" Skander asked.

"The last count we did we were near seven hundred thousand of us. Not all in this city of course. We got too big for our city long ago and now we have secretly built a dozen other cities not far from here. When the Gogs finally march to war we will strike a devastating blow to the Sorcerer and his army."

"I still can't believe that this has never been discovered," Drake concluded.

"We are very thankful. Although I think the Sorcerer will be very disappointed."

They continued walking past the landing barges. Beyond that, there were large siege towers and ramps. The city wall started again, this seeming to be a separate part of the city as they had to go through another gate and set of guards. Once inside they noticed how similar the two sections of the city were.

Fields opened up in front of them, with different flags in them. A shooting range lay before them as well. On the other side were hundreds and hundreds of smaller buildings only eleven or twelve feet tall. They were the main barracks, and in the middle of the barracks, a central tower, thirty feet tall stood in front of them. They were led into the barracks, noticing that both Elohim and Destan were sitting in the open fields.

The Gogs stood at attention as Shavrok approached. They entered the central tower where a large spiraling staircase stood in front of them. Everyone climbed the stairs until they came to the main floor, which consisted of beds as well as wash basins for all of them.

"These will be your sleeping quarters for the next three months, or however long you wish to stay," Shavrok told them. "I hope they are to your satisfaction. We had them built specifically for your arrival here. Supper will be in four hours and when the time is right I will send a guide to escort you to the dining hall. As our honored guests we have made this first dinner a special dinner. I will leave you to get ready and I will see you later."

He wished them farewell and then left them. They wasted no time in cleaning up the best they could. They got dressed and waited for what felt like an eternity as they struggled to fight off the sleep that so badly wanted to overtake them.

At long last, a guide came to their door.

They were led back into the main section of the city where everything looked far different than it had just a little while ago. The streets were silent of Gogs and the shops were closed. Festive music filled the air.

They came to the grand hall in the middle of the city. Both doors were opened and they were led inside to a well-lit chamber. Drake had heard only a little bit about the other races of the earth, but already this dining hall reminded him of something that Dwarves might have built. The walls were cleanly cut, showing off their dark marble color, and the light from the torches caught every facet of the crystal. Drake knew that this building was underground and stretched into the cliff that hid them.

The talking stopped and every head turned to look in their direction as Shavrok strode into the room. He spoke in their language introducing the guests. When he was finished speaking they were seated at their table. The Gogs that had gathered broke out into cheering. They gave thanks for the food that had been prepared and then wasted no time in beginning the feast.

Their table was waited on by some of the Gogs who knew their language. Some of them even knew Elvish and spoke to Lily and Aiden in the language, leaving Ellizar looking more confused than Drake had ever seen him.

"Maybe you should learn to speak Elvish, then you'd know what they were saying," Drake suggested to Ellizar.

"I'll pass on that. I find it a little weird when they are talkin' in Elvish."

"Why's that? Speaking their language would be helpful, maybe then you'd know what they were saying about you?"

"Oh come on now Ellie, you speak perfect Elvish with me all the time," Lily chided.

Drake gave an amused look.

"You know Elvish?"

Ellizar shrugged.

"I may have picked up a thing or two," Ellizar said with a childish smile.

"You know Elvish?" Drake asked again.

"And I know a large amount of Dwarvish," Lily said. "It was the only language he knew when I met him."

"I'd like to know more of this story someday," Drake said.

"I'll tell it to you in Dwarvish," Lily chided.

The feast continued and their drinks and food were refilled until they couldn't eat or drink anymore.

"We will begin your training tomorrow," Aiden announced when the meal was nearly over.

"What are we going to be working on?" Lily asked.

"A little bit of everything. I'm going to give you some fighting lessons and then I'll teach you a little bit about the customs of the world and then I'll let you do as you wish once supper is over. I will have a special task for Ellizar and Skander in the days to come."

"What is it?" Ellizar asked.

"We'll talk about it tomorrow," Aiden answered. "I can't let all the secrets out right at the beginning, can I?"

Ellizar frowned. "Normally, I would say no, but right now, I wouldn't care if yeh did. I need to be able teh mentally prepare fer what yeh want us teh do."

Lily laughed. "Like you need to mentally prepare for anything, as I recall any time you've said that is when you were eating."

The time passed and finally, it came time for them to excuse themselves. They walked out of the large dining hall. Aiden stayed behind, saying he had some business details to discuss with the Gogs. The moon was now high in the sky and the stars were visible, their light shining down on the bay in front of them. The ships floated in the water, and the waves quietly lapped up against the floating fortresses. Silence covered the city.

They walked back to their sleeping quarters and talked long into the night. They finally fell asleep, slipping into their dreams. Drake dreamed of him and Destan flying, a woman was riding with him but even though she was right next to him he couldn't make out any of her features. Her identity was a mystery. The dream changed after a little while and he was looking down at another woman who was sleeping in her bed.

He recognized the woman immediately as Isabel. He watched her with interest and looked around the room at all the unusual knickknacks. She was certainly different from everyone else he had met, but maybe that was part of her charm.

WEAPONS OF WAR

The sun had risen high into the sky by the time Drake and the others woke. They dressed and picked up their gear, making their way to the training field. The fields were wide open and surrounded by trees. Flags were set all across the fields. Large numbers of Gogs marched in the opening and sparred with each other. They spotted Aiden and Shavrok on the other side, patiently waiting.

"Good morning," Shavrok greeted.

"Good morning," Lily replied. "Sorry, we slept so long."

"Just don't let it happen again," Aiden started. "We have much work to do and only a little time in which to do it. If we waste any time then we'll pay for it dearly. The first thing that we will teach you is simple swordsmanship. You fight well, but you have to have the endurance to fight all day if it comes down to it, otherwise you might as well surrender now."

He reached behind him, grabbed a couple of swords, and handed one to each of them. Even Ellizar got a sword, but his was much shorter than the rest of the others. They looked at the swords they had been given and then the ones they had brought with them, giving Aiden a confused look.

"Blunt blades. You don't want to kill your best friend when you spar with them do you?" They quickly changed their weapons and laid their real weapons in a pile on the ground. They drew the swords and moved them around trying to adjust to the difference in the weight and style of the blade.

"Swordsmanship is one of the most important skills you will learn. You must know how to handle one no matter what kind of job you're assigned to do. Lily is gifted with her bow. But should you run out of arrows or get directly attacked you have to have at least a basic understanding of swordsmanship.

"I have seen you fight and I know that you already have many of the skills needed. This is not meant to re-teach you anything, but it's a way of improving the skills that you already have. Drake, you are first."

"What do I do?" Drake asked. Aiden drew his sword. Drake quickly let a breath of relief escape him noticing that Aiden also had a blunt blade.

"Attack me."

Drake hesitated and soon found himself fighting off a dozen blows Aiden sent at him. Drake spun, trying to bring his blade through Aiden's defenses and across his chest. The blade was easily swiped away and moved to Drake's side where the sword hit him. Aiden stopped and pulled away. Drake looked at the impact point forgetting for a moment that the blade had been dulled.

"Rule number one. You don't hesitate. If you hesitate your enemy has all the time in the world to figure out a way to get at you and get under your skin. You have to strike hard while doing so in a way that doesn't leave you putting all your energy into every move. You have to learn control. This can be the hardest thing to learn.

"You have to control your energy, your mind, and your emotions. Failure to do any of the above and you will become a puppet to your enemy. They will read the thoughts in your head and figure out your next move. Lily, you're next."

Lily drew her sword and stood staring at Aiden. Their contest lasted only a few seconds before she took the advice that Aiden had just given Drake and lunged at Aiden's shin. Aiden quickly leapt backward and then moved to his left, missing another strike that had been aimed at him.

Lily twirled and soon found her sword flying through the air and clattering on the ground, as Aiden's blade struck her hand. Aiden picked up her sword and handed it back to her.

"Not bad. Why do you hold your sword like that?" Aiden asked mimicking how she had been holding it. Lily looked at it, never having given thought to how she held her sword. "You've got a one-handed sword, but your grip on it is at the end of the pommel and not at the top. The only reason I was able to defeat you so easily was because I had observed this before so I figured out your weakness. You must hold your sword firmly and do not let it go, otherwise you will fall to the enemy." He moved onto Ellizar who stood just as short as ever, his helmet pressed onto his head.

"Your turn."

Ellizar pulled out the blade and frowned at it.

"Do yeh suppose I could have my ax?"

"You have to be skilled with a blade just as you are with an ax, it makes you harder to predict."

"Very well. If it must be done then it must be done." Ellizar swung his sword repeatedly while Aiden easily defended himself. Ellizar swung it over his head bringing it down on Aiden, moving towards his head. Aiden moved out of the way and the sword struck the ground, giving Aiden all the time he needed. Aiden put a foot on Ellizar's sword, keeping it on the ground, and then kicked him back from the sword. Ellizar fell to the ground.

"That was just the way I planned it!" Ellizar exclaimed.

"Sure you did Ellie," Lily replied.

"You did good Ellizar, but there are a few things that could be improved. Your footing needs some serious help for one. You walk as if you're wearing solid bricks on your feet. When it comes to fighting, your feet have to think it's a dance. The lighter on your feet you are, the quicker you can avoid attacks and so on. You have to be able to adapt to your enemy's advances, and you can't do that with lead feet. Also, you were getting reckless at the end with that last attempt. This goes back to the control thing I was talking about. The more you can keep your cool and fight well, the more your enemy will be angered and perhaps lose their cool, giving you the advantage. Your turn Skander."

Skander slowly drew his sword and stood holding it up in the air. Aiden studied him for a moment. Skander took the hesitation and slashed at him. Aiden blocked it and spun to the left slashing at Skander's waist and striking him. Skander stepped back and lowered his blade.

"Have you ever been trained with a sword?" Aiden asked.

"No, I haven't. Only copied what I've seen other people do. Even though Lily is my sister, because I was an elf giant they didn't treat me like their child. I never got taught anything unless Lily taught it to me."

"That's why you're here," Aiden started. "First of all, your opening stance wasn't very good, at least not if you want to live. You had yourself exposed to anything your enemy could throw at you. Your sword does you no good if you put it on a shelf way up out of your reach. When you brought your sword down like you did, it was the same sort of deal. It was like a book falling off a shelf. Easy to dodge, and then easy to strike at you because your sword was still going the opposite direction." Aiden stepped back and looked at all of them.

"You did well in your first lesson, and if there's one more piece of advice that I will give to you today it's that you need conviction. Why do you do the things that you do? What's the reason behind all of them? The way you hold your sword, the way you swing it, the way your feet move. You need to know why you do things a certain way. If you don't know why you're doing them, you'll be swayed from your path more easily. Find conviction. Think about that as you duel today. I've got a little bit of preparing to do for tomorrow's lesson so I'll leave you to duel with Shavrok and some of his friends. I'll see you this evening and I'll tell you what we're going to be working on next."

"Aiden I have a bone teh pick with yeh!" Ellizar yelled as Aiden began walking away. Aiden looked back and Ellizar shot him a face of concern and then pointed at Shavrok who was nearly twice the height he was. Aiden smiled.

"How did you manage against those giants?" Aiden asked.

"I had an ax, not a sword."

"It should be no different for you. By the time you guys are done with your training you'll be trained with so many different weapons you'll be a walking armory. We will get to the axes when you master the sword. Do the best you can and remember everything that I told you. I'll see you later."

They said their goodbyes and then began the sparring, drawing a crowd as they fought the best they could making sure to take into consideration everything that Aiden had pointed out. Drake improved as did the rest of them giving them all a sense of hope that they hadn't felt before.

The day faded and they took a break for lunch and then continued into the afternoon working on the same things they had been working on in the morning, as well as anything else that Shavrok pointed out.

At first, they found themselves finding new energy as the day wore on, seeming to get stronger and stronger and not feel the fatigue that was coming over them. Soon however they were tired beyond tired, much to Shavrok's amusement. He let them leave and call it quits for the night. They made their way back to their beds and fell asleep.

The next day came and went and they found themselves doing much of the same thing that they had done the day before. They had sparred throughout the morning, trying their best to show that they had used the advice that Aiden had given them and that they were becoming better at swordsmanship. Still, even though they had made great progress they found themselves doing the same thing for the rest of the day.

Unlike the day before, they sparred with several Gogs, not just Shavrok. They were told this was so they could all work at once and could better build up their endurance. Drake noticed how sore he was from the day before and every movement he made ached, but still, he pushed through.

They went to the dining hall and ate their lunch and then went back to the training fields, sparring again and continuing to improve upon their moves and endurance. Finally, during mid-afternoon, they were allowed a break when

Aiden started taking them somewhere else.

They made their way to the ships that sat in the harbor. Drake almost had to laugh at the size difference between Ellizar and the ship. The size and magnitude of these ships never ceased to amaze Drake or the rest of them. They were twice the size of any ship they had seen up to this point, giving them the impression that they could run a regular ship over if they wanted to. They were given a tour and were educated in the building and engineering of the ship.

The ships on the inside were just as large as the outside. The ceilings were at least twelve feet high and there were also three levels instead of just two.

There were several doors on the second level which caught Drake's attention. They were large and sealed with pitch. The more Drake looked at them the more curious he became until he finally asked what they were for.

Shavrok explained that they were for land invasions. If they wanted to they could run the ship aground and open those and their troops would be able to jump out. Even if they didn't run the ship aground, they could load onto the landing barges and load quicker than having to climb down the ladder.

"Shavrok, what's the other sail for?" Lily asked. She pointed it out to him and he smiled.

"That is what makes these ships truly unique and superior to any other ships. There are times when the wind that is down here is not very strong and certainly not as strong as we need. When that is the case, we put out an extra sail which will rise twenty feet further into the air. You may have noticed when you were flying with Elohim or Destan that the wind is very different up there. It's light and strong at the same time. We call it magic wind."

"Wow," Skander concluded, walking to the bow of the ship where a harpoon sat loaded. "What's this?" Without meaning to Skander hit the release and sent the massive arrow towards the city wall in front of them. It struck the wall, a large crack running through it.

"What are these things made out of?" Ellizar asked walking up to the next harpoon which was sitting on the deck. Shavrok moved forward and easily picked up the harpoon.

"These are no ordinary harpoons," Shavrok started. "The projectiles are made out of rock and iron, forged and strengthened in fire until they are harder than any material in the world. These are designed specifically to take down castle walls so we will be able to get into the city more easily. You can see what one of them did to the walls of our city. If this were to be fired at the city gate or even the inner wall, they would shatter."

"Do you have these for the ground army as well?" Lily asked. Shavrok smiled weakly.

"We originally wanted to have some of them with our ground army, but we ran into a slight problem. The weight is too much for the animals to carry at speed for such a long distance. For the ground army, we have regular ballistae, which still pack a powerful punch. Come now, there is one final thing we must discuss about the ship's design before you are free for the day."

"I see you've finished your tour?" Aiden asked, joining them at the front of the ship.

"Yes, we have."

"As you can see, there is a lot of open deck space due to these ships' enormous size and length. With that in mind, we would like to do large amounts of damage to the city before we reach a seaport," Shavrok explained. "We want to put catapults on the ship. Ellizar and Skander this is the secret job that I was telling you about earlier. I want all of you to try and figure out a design that will work to fire projectiles at the city from the ships without damaging the ship and its crew. You will have three Gogs to assist you in the construction. Take your time and make sure it's a good design.

"For the rest of the week, your training will consist of sparring in the morning and working on your design the rest of the day. If we can get it perfected, the Gogs will build the rest of them while you are educated in other manners," Aiden said.

"Can't you just take a catapult from the land army and put it on here?" Skander asked.

"The one to sit on the ship has to be a part of the ship," Aiden answered. "If it's not anchored correctly, it could fall off the ship or fall through the deck. The idea is to have it built strong enough that it can do its job without breaking and make it to the city wall, or in the city. When you get to testing, however, you might want to do it on one of the ships further down, where there isn't a city. The last thing we need is to damage more buildings and walls."

"How long do we have until supper?"

"About an hour. You don't have to start working on it until tomorrow if you don't want to," Aiden told them.

"We'll at least start it," Skander said. "Even if nothing gets built today, we can still come up with an idea of what we want to build so we're not unprepared tomorrow."

"Very good. Learning to plan ahead will save both your head and your feet. In that case, I'll leave you for now I've got some other business details to attend to. Just don't destroy the ship and don't miss supper or else you'll be very hungry tomorrow morning."

"A dwarf never misses a good meal!" Ellizar exclaimed, laughing. Lily rolled her eyes.

"That's right, a dwarf thinks with their stomach."

"At least we eat as opposed teh the race ov Men and Elves who look like twigs in the desert."

"Shows how much you know," Lily fired back. "There's no trees in the desert therefore there can be no twigs."

"Let's just get workin' and then get teh the meal that *we* all are lookin' forward teh." They began working on a design and Aiden left them. The night faded and the sun dipped into the horizon.

The fluttering of wings woke Atruss as an owl landed on the window sill.

DECEPTION OF MERDERICK

Atruss opened his eyes, focusing on the dark surroundings that made up his room in the palace. Below them, in the other levels, lay the sleeping city of Belvanor, completely unaware of the visitor that had flown to his window.

He threw the covers off him, careful not to wake his wife. The moon was out and the stars shone down on the city. He reached the open window and looked at the owl that had landed on the window sill. It flew back a couple of feet to a large balcony, resting on the railing. Atruss opened the door and walked out, the cool air greeting him.

The owl turned and looked off into the distance. Atruss followed its gaze seeing another large owl coming toward him. This one was black with yellow eyes that seemed to bore holes into everything that they looked at. It flew over the city, slowly and methodically as if trying to find something that had been lost. The bird finally looked in his direction and flew towards him landing on the railing next to the other bird.

In the owl's mouth was an envelope. Atruss retreated inside, lit a lantern, and was finally able to see what was written on the outside of the envelope. He could read none of it at first, as it was written in a language that had been forgotten by the world long ago. Then as if it understood that he wasn't able to read the writing it changed, shifting within itself until it read his name.

He opened the envelope, unfolded the piece of paper, and looked upon the writing that was the same as the writing on the outside of the envelope had been. Soon though it became written in the Elvish language.

Greetings leaders and citizens of Ariamore;

Allow me to introduce myself first, seeing as how we haven't met each other yet. My name is Merderick, I am a person of no importance to some and a person of great importance to others. As I understand, it's all a point of view and I cannot guarantee that my view is the same as yours, therefore let's just say that I'm a concerned citizen of the world, and have discovered terrible secrets.

I was walking through the woods the other day when I stumbled across a group of men, six of them to be exact. In their possession, there was a woman, taken captive and kidnapped from your city for reasons that I do not know. I had some men with me at the time. I attacked the company and overtook them and am now in the possession of the woman.

I mean her no harm, and as she will tell you my men and I have not done anything to her. That is not in my character and I wish to return the woman. She doesn't know where she is and I don't know where she came from, so I seek to help her find her way. She is the one who gave me your name so that I might ask permission to enter your city without any harm coming to me or my men. Our minds are not filled with ill intentions, only with intentions of goodwill as we seek to help this woman.

Also I might ask a small favor of you. I understand that on the same night that the woman was taken from your city there was one of my men captured and is now in your dungeon. His name is Tremin and I would like to offer a trade of the woman and the man. Tremin is my dearest friend and I'm sure that he would not have tried to harm anyone unless there was a reason beyond my reckoning.

If you would agree to my request I would be very appreciative. Just write a reply and send it back with the owl that brought it. It's still waiting for the reply and then it'll come back and find me. At earliest reckoning I shall be at your doorsteps in three days, should the weather and our supplies hold up.

Faithfully yours,

Merderick

Atruss folded the note and sat on the edge of his bed. His wife had woken up.

"What's wrong?" his wife asked.

"We need to have an emergency meeting, the three of us."

"Rohemir's room I take it?" Gabrielle asked.

"Any room as long as it's not this one. Let's get to one of the inner chambers, where there are no windows. No one can be eavesdropping on us."

"What's wrong?" Gabrielle asked.

"I'm not sure, but we need Rohemir to figure out the mystery that surrounds this note." He moved to the balcony again and looked into the eyes of the black owl, becoming enthralled in them, unable to look away. The bird looked at him and seemed to tell him through his thoughts that he would be waiting when they were done. He moved to the hallway that was filled with the distant glow of a lantern as Gabrielle went to prepare the room they would be meeting in.

Atruss reached Rohemir's room and didn't take the time to knock, barging through the door and opening the blinds to let in the moonlight. Rohemir squinted as he woke up.

"We have had an interesting visitor and an even more curious note that arrived just minutes ago."

"A note?" Rohemir asked. Atruss nodded.

"I will speak of this no more until we are in one of the inner chambers. Come!" Rohemir quickly threw on a robe and followed Atruss out into the hallway.

It was only two minutes before they reached the inner chamber that he had been talking about. This particular chamber was unique from the rest of them in Belvanor. The walls were thick, twenty feet at the thickest and fifteen feet along the far wall. It was a smaller room and was only used for situations like this.

Atruss entered first and then Rohemir followed, locking the multiple locks on the inside of the door. They were now in another small hallway that would lead to the main room. When they had gone ten feet Atruss closed another door and also locked it, making it impossible for anyone to listen in on what they were saying.

They exited the hallway and entered into the ten by ten room which was filled with one lantern that hung over a small table and four chairs. Gabrielle was waiting for them.

"Gabrielle, would you look at this note and tell me what you see?" Atruss asked holding the piece of paper out to her. She grabbed it and unfolded it, her eyes showing mystery and surprise at what she saw. "Can you read anything?"

"What kind of language is this?" Gabrielle asked. "I can't make out a single... wait a second. I can read it now. I can read it as clearly as anything that I've ever read. Like a book I've read a thousand times. What is this?"

"That's my question I have a hunch and it's one I'd rather not confirm until it's confirmed by Rohemir." Rohemir's eyes showed surprise.

"You think I can read it?" Rohemir asked. Gabrielle handed the note to him. "Why would you think that I could-?"

"Because you once worked for the people in Grimdor. I think you might be able to recognize the script." Rohemir looked at the paper, his eyes showing surprise, but a different surprise than Gabrielle's had.

"This is no ordinary script," Rohemir confirmed. "This is far worse than I wish to speak of."

"Try."

"When I was working in Grimdor I managed to get myself into the old libraries to further my knowledge of the Borags and their beliefs in hopes of better understanding them, thinking that might give us some insight and a leg up on them. I stumbled across a restricted section of the library and found that all the scripts in it were exactly like this.

"Later on I learned that this was the script that the Sorcerer himself wrote in. By doing so he could write something and no one would be able to understand it. As you pointed out though, after several moments the script changes so that we can read it."

"What do you think that means?" Atruss asked.

"Perhaps it means that the letter was intercepted and tampered with?" Gabrielle tried.

"It's a possibility, but if it came here by owl then it's unlikely. In the libraries of Grimdor, several books and scrolls and letters did this very same thing. If they were all written by the Sorcerer then maybe he knows how to write in nothing else but this dark and vile language and has to put a spell on it for others to be able to read it."

"You think that this letter is from the Sorcerer himself?" Atruss asked. Rohemir shrugged his shoulders.

"We all know that someone has united the Spirits and Borags. Up until now, we haven't known if the force that had united them has grown strong enough to appear in physical form. To say that this was written by the Sorcerer himself is to admit the unthinkable."

"What do you think we should do?" Atruss asked.

"According to the story he told, he rescued Gwen therefore he can't be the Sorcerer because he wouldn't do something like that. There's a chance he's telling the truth," Gabrielle concluded.

"I say we permit him to enter the city, the only thing I'm unsure about is the prisoner that he wants to set free. There has to be a bigger reason behind it. Unfortunately, we can't ask Gwen any questions because she isn't here, however, Aiden said that Tremin was part of the group that was trying to kidnap Gwen," Atruss concluded.

"Whatever decision we make we should make as soon as possible so we can prepare one way or the other," Rohemir started. "The fact of the matter is one of our people has been kidnapped and is now trying to be returned by a polite man who has asked permission to enter our city. I say we give him clearance and take all the precautions that need to be taken."

"I agree with Rohemir on the last part, although I am still wary about letting him pass into our city," Gabrielle answered. "If we are to let him through then we really must call Drake, Aiden, and the rest of them home. In case it is a spy of the enemy then they will think that they are still being kept in the city, making us the target and keeping where they are completely hidden."

"If we're all agreed on this I'll send out a reply to this letter immediately and then send out another to Aiden telling him to get back here as quickly as possible. I will also want the guards doubled. Our visitor won't realize that it's doubled because he's supposedly never been here before. Also, I want the word spread and I want to make sure that no harm comes to him and his men. I want this to be a safe crossing for him. There's too much at stake for it to be anything but."

"I just hope it's not the Sorcerer that's going to be marching into our city," Gabrielle answered. "If it is, he'll be able to see our entire defense."

"It's a risk we have to take. As soon as Merderick and his people are gone we'll send them all back to Remnda to continue their training."

"It's decided then," Rohemir concluded. They all remained there while they wrote the two letters, Rohemir wrote the reply to Merderick, and Gabrielle wrote the letter to Aiden. When they were both done, they were sealed in envelopes and they left the inner chamber, undoing all the locks and finally entering back into the hallway.

They walked together until they reached Rohemir's room where he split off from them saying his goodnights as the door closed. Atruss still wasn't completely at peace about the choice that had been made and he knew Gabrielle was feeling the same thing.

They got back to their room and found the owls still waiting patiently, they gave one of the envelopes to the black one and the other to the white one which was his own. The owls took off without a moment's hesitation and then vanished into the night sky. Gabrielle and Atruss climbed into their bed but were unable to sleep, instead choosing to talk long into the night.

III ACQUAINTANCES

Elohim and Destan sped towards Belvanor. Fear and anticipation gripped them all, while Drake dwelled on the uncertainty of the situation. They weren't entirely sure why they were headed back, but Aiden had said Gwen was involved.

Before long they saw the fortress of Belvanor on the horizon, surrounded by the large forest and grass canyons. The trees were empty and lifeless, but the sun managed to break through the grey clouds.

A woman waited with horses three hundred yards out in front of the castle wall, her hair glistening in the sun. Curiosity began to stir in Drake's mind as he realized that it was Isabel waiting for them. The Taruks swooped down toward the ground and gracefully landed. They climbed off and helped Ellizar out of his makeshift harness that they had rigged up and were quick to run to the horses.

They passed through the gates and countless levels of the city until they entered the main courtyard, directly to the front steps. They continued inside, while Isabel took the horses away, tying them up to a nearby hitching post where they could graze on the grass that remained. After that, she walked away. Drake watched her as she faded from view.

"I'm not sure what you fed those Taruks this morning, but I think it worked; you have made incredible time," Gabrielle said. They all smiled, doing a half bow, before being stopped. "You do not need to bow to us. We are nothing more than normal people who lead a group of people."

"Why have we been called here on such an urgent note?" Aiden asked. "A message arrived to me, but it was a bit vague."

They quickly told them of everything that had transpired.

"Who is this Merderick?" Rohemir asked. "He seems to be in the right place at the right time, does he not?"

"We are unsure about him, to say the least," Atruss said. "Do you have any thoughts on the matter?"

"I was in Iscariot a couple of weeks ago," Aiden explained. "When I was escaping, a man was walking towards me and the Korazin. I did not see the man clearly, but there is no doubt in my mind that this man who is coming here is, in fact, the Sorcerer himself."

"A bold claim, don't you think?" Rohemir asked.

"I'm not claiming anything. I'm telling you that he is the same person."

"You are saying that not only is the Sorcerer strong enough to take human form, but that he will soon be walking through the gates of this very city?" Gabrielle asked. Fear was evident in everyone's expressions. "Are you certain of this?"

"Lathon is speaking to me as clearly as I am speaking to you. This is no mere friendly exchange of prisoners."

"If he is the Sorcerer as you say, wouldn't that be a strange move for him?" Atruss asked.

Aiden shrugged. "Depends on what Merderick would hope to gain by having Tremin released to him."

"Should we tell anyone else?"

"No. Speak of this to no one. Not yet. Where is Tremin? If Merderick is interested in Tremin, we need to find out why."

"You are free to speak with him if you wish," Atruss stated. "I'm not sure what good it'll do you."

"You will have to remain here for at least two days after Merderick leaves, in case there are any spies around. We need them to think that Drake and the others, yourself included, are training here."

"I understand."

They said their goodbyes and parted ways with Gabrielle, Atruss, and Rohemir remaining in the great hall. The rest continued back to the outside world, which was the same as it had been, unchanging in the darkening day.

"I think it would be best if you ran along and did something else for the day. I have a bit of work to do in the prisons and I'm not sure if being in Tremin's presence could be harmful to any of you," Aiden explained.

"How could it be harmful to us?" Lily asked.

"We can't risk anyone finding out a lot of information about you, and if you came with me there is a chance of that happening. The enemy can find anything they want on me. They won't find anything they can use against me."

Aiden climbed on his horse and waved as he trotted off into the city leaving the four of them. The rest of them mounted their horses and rode through the streets, which were now a flurry of activity. Now that all the recruits for the army had arrived, the city was full of life. They exited the castle wall and to the left a half mile where recruits were trying their skills at fighting.

They dismounted and drew their weapons, having to force Ellizar to use a sword like Aiden had instructed and not an ax. He grumbled to himself for a moment or two, but then he was fine as they sparred and tried to defeat each other. For the most part, it was Skander and Drake going against each other and Ellizar and Lily going against each other, which Drake thought was one of the more hilarious things he had seen.

"Blasted elf kind! I've had just about enough ov yeh!" Ellizar exclaimed, standing to his feet after having been beaten for the tenth time in a row. "Attack me again! I can promise yeh this time yeh won't beat me."

"I love a good challenge," Lily replied, holding her sword to the side. Ellizar did the same, both of them trying to guess the other's first move. Lily moved first, lunging towards Ellizar with her blade, all the while keeping the same poise and control that had been frustrating Ellizar up to this point. Ellizar took a swing at her, but it was easily blocked and then countered by Ellizar who stepped back and threw his sword to the ground.

"Yeh leave me no other option, but teh resort teh tactics that have worked fer as long as people have roamed ancient earth."

"I hope they're better than you at debating because you don't have me convinced," Lily replied, giving him a wink. Try as hard as he could, even Ellizar couldn't help but let a smile stretch across his face. Lily rushed forward and smacked him across the chest with the blunt blade and smiled at him again.

"I win," Lily replied lowering her weapon. Ellizar let a battle cry escape him, tackling Lily to the ground and pinning her down until she finally gave up.

"Ah and what do yer precious fightin' moves have teh say teh that?" Ellizar asked. "Let it be known that there are other ways teh fight rather than with swords."

"Then maybe you should learn some of them," a voice echoed from behind them. They turned around to see Isabel standing there. Her dress was pink this time and her hair was dark brown, her eyes sapphire blue. Drake studied her with each step she took. She seemed to show up at just the right time, in just the right place. She was both innocent and guilty Drake concluded. The more he was around her the more he wanted to know more about her.

"Would you like to know some moves?" Isabel asked. None of them spoke, each exchanging their thoughts through glances they made within a couple of seconds.

"Do you know any?" Skander asked.

"I know quite a lot about some aspects of fighting, and very little about others. In hand-to-hand combat, I know a lot though. Unless you're my enemy, in which case I appear to know nothing, when in fact I know something."

"Sounds confusing," Skander replied.

"It can be, but then there's time's where-" Drake didn't get the chance to hear any more of what she had said as he was knocked to the ground. By the time he came too, he noticed that the only one standing was Isabel who did a slight bow. Drake held his gut where her foot had connected with him. Isabel laughed and snapped her fingers. All the pain that they had felt or were feeling vanished from their bodies.

"As I was saying. It sounds confusing but then there are times when their confusion is the split second I need to gain the upper hand. You see, hand-to-hand fighting takes a little more skill in some instances, depending on how well-trained your opponent is. They will look at you, first with a stare." She connected with Drake's eyes, not moving away. Drake tried to stand tall and proud but soon found himself afraid of the woman who stood in front of him.

"The more you can stare and intimidate someone, the better off you'll fare in the battle. Why? Because when you are staring them down you can learn a lot about a person. You can predict their first move and once you get that one right, you'll know you can outsmart them again and again. The first thing you have to do is learn how to not think when you're fighting.

"You might think about your technique but as far as your reflexes and your actions are concerned they have to think for themselves, otherwise the training is useless. You have to learn to trust in something greater than yourself to protect you from the danger that is rushing towards you."

"Sounds hard," Drake concluded.

"It is hard, but well worth the struggles if you can master it. Now, let's get started. Do you at least know the basics of hand-to-hand combat?" They took turns showing what they knew and trying their best to learn a few simple moves that Isabel showed them. They practiced their moves and tried to spar against her, but they found that she was far too great to be taken down by moves as simple as theirs.

Isabel moved like a cat. She would be there one second and then gone the next. By the time they followed her movements, she had already sprung into another attack and it would finish them off. As always though, if she had injured them too badly, she snapped her fingers and their pain vanished.

She corrected them and then they continued until finally the day had disappeared and they were nearly the last ones to leave the training field. Isabel said her goodbyes and then disappeared into the city, leaving them to find their way back to their quarters. They began walking and the longer they walked the more Drake's curiosity was beginning to get the best of him.

When it became possible he slipped away from the others, making up an excuse about where he was headed, and then went out into the city. He wandered to the east side of the city, quickly locating *The Wingy Wares*, Isabel's shop, which was still being built. Drake walked up to the front porch, noticing that the building didn't look as if it was finished, but Drake remembered she would have wanted it that way.

He reached to knock on the door and it swung in by itself and then closed itself behind him. Drake thought for a moment that his mind was playing tricks on him. The inside looked as if it hadn't been harmed at all. Instead, it looked the way it had a week ago. The only different thing was a thin cloud of fog that hung an inch or two off the floor.

He walked further into Isabel's house, and the fog became thicker, allowing him to see no further than an arm's length in front of him. He noticed that the plants and flowering vines that covered the walls seemed to be sleeping, all curled up in themselves.

"You're wondering about the flowers aren't you?" Drake flinched when he heard Isabel's voice. He searched the fog for her and finally spotted her standing against the railing of an upper level.

"I'm wondering about a lot of things these days. I'm not sure where to start," Drake replied. She began coming down the stairs towards him, once again with her dress and her hair looking completely different.

"How about at the beginning? I always find that's a little helpful," Isabel replied. They both chuckled. "If you're wondering about the insides of the building that isn't finished yet, that's an easy one. I bought this place from a wizard gone bad. Even though he went bad, there was plenty about this beautiful place that must have been important to him, and he had protected it with enchantments. Unlike most people he allowed the building and everything in it to be destroyed, but it would rebuild itself stronger and faster than the first time; if anything just to infuriate his enemy.

"Though they would try to destroy his house, they couldn't. They could try to break him down by destroying all that was dear to him, but they couldn't do that either."

"Whatever happened to him?" Drake asked. Isabel shrugged her shoulders.

"I don't know. I think there might be a way to find out but I'm not sure if it'll work or not. I've been working on it for years now."

"Do I dare ask what it is?" Drake asked. "I hope it doesn't blow up like your owls do."

"This *thing* doesn't blow up. It could be very dangerous to use though. A different kind of dangerous."

"What it is?" Drake asked unable to stifle his curiosity. She motioned for him to follow her. They went up the set of stairs and then unlocked a door and stepped into the room that waited for them. To the left and the right were different tables, all with assorted weapons of every kind. Drake's curiosity began to rise even more as he pondered Isabel's mysterious past.

At the head of the room, there was a large cloth that covered an object. The object stood eight feet tall and went all the way to the floor. They approached, with Drake being more cautious than he had been up to this moment.

"This is a great weapon that could be used against the Sorcerer in the days to come. I only finished building it this last week and I haven't had any chance to make it 'safe' if you take my meaning." She pulled back the cloth. Drake panicked. In front of them was a mirror that was large and dark.

"Isabel? Isn't this the same sort of mirror that hurt Gwen?" Drake asked. She shook her head no and let the silence hang in the air for a couple of moments. His eyes moved to the carvings around the mirror noticing that some of them were different from the ones that he had seen days ago.

"This isn't the same mirror, but it looks rather convincing doesn't it?" Isabel asked. "I've been working on it for what feels like forever and now it's finally done. It's made to duplicate the mirrors that the Sorcerer has. The only difference is no one can see you when you look through it. Hopefully. Care to give it a try?"

"How does this work?" Drake asked.

"Just the way the other mirrors worked. You control them with your mind and that will give you a clear image of what's going on in the world. Just think of the place your heart so desires to see and then you'll see it."

Drake's heart beat wildly as he stood in front of the mirror. Everything in the mirror changed to the area he was thinking of. He hadn't thought of any area specifically, but instead of Gwen. He saw a company of men walking through the forest and also laid eyes on the soldiers who were marching in rank behind the party of people.

Drake's anger raged within his soul when he finally spotted Gwen, crammed into a small long box that didn't even give her enough room to turn over. Guards were to both sides, and the forest in front of them, Drake realized was in Ariamore.

The vision faded and the mirror glazed over leaving him to look at nothing but the silvery surface in front of him. He looked over to Isabel, noticing a tear sliding down her cheek. Isabel looked at him and then without speaking left the room and closed the door.

"You alright?" Drake asked. His heart cried out for answers and broke as Isabel's sobbing made its way throughout the shop and house.

Drake turned back to the mirror and looked into it again. At first, there was nothing, and then just like before, the mirror showed him a picture of what he wanted to look at. He had thought of the seaport of Revly and now it was before him, having fallen into war and destruction.

People lay in the streets. Some took cover and some were dragged into the streets, questioned by a few of the Borags, and then killed before they had the chance to answer. Smoke rose into the sky and fires burned everywhere he looked. His heart broke and anger filled him.

This is what he was training for. He would make sure when this war was over, that he had done everything in his power to free the people of the world. He knelt on the ground and hung his head, wishing for a strength that he didn't have.

There was no way that he would be able to do any of this on his own. Drake looked away from the mirror and then smelled the air, thinking for a moment that he had smelled smoke from the picture in the mirror. The picture changed again and this time Drake found himself looking at dark mountains. Rain poured down and then a flash of light filled the sky.

The image before him was covered in darkness but he could see two faint figures blending in and moving with the rock. Drake wished that Isabel was here to tell him what he was seeing but the vision faded as soon as it had come. Drake looked away from the mirror and then looked into it one last time, striving to learn something about Isabel if it was possible.

Isabel came into focus. She lay face down on her bed in the next room, sobbing into her pillow, instilling a greater curiosity in Drake than he had felt up to this point. What had she seen in the mirror that had caused such a storm of emotion? Had she seen the same thing as he had?

The mirror changed the image. The area he was now looking into was rocky and barren, without a doubt he knew that it was Grimdor. Drake studied the scene, seeing a city in the distance, smoke rising to the sky. Isabel walked towards him in the mirror, her appearance just the way it was now.

Thousands of questions filled his mind but Drake couldn't answer any of them and finally gave up trying. He looked around the house and shop for a while longer hoping to talk to Isabel when she came out of her room.

He waited for nearly an hour, listening to her crying and sobbing, which seemed to be easing. Finally, the crying stopped and he was left to stand in the silence. Isabel had cried herself to sleep and Drake's heart longed to help her. Drake moved towards the room that Isabel had entered and reached for the doorknob, wondering if he should enter or not.

Finally, he convinced himself that he should. The dark skies were seen outside the window, allowing some pale grey light to enter. Drake moved around to the other side of the bed that Isabel had cried herself to sleep on. She lay on her back now, her face still wet with her tears.

She clutched a book in her hand and it was laid across her chest. Drake gently reached out and grabbed the book out of her hands and flipped through it noticing that it was a journal. He held it to the window and opened it to the last page that had been written on. The page was soaked with tears, which had made the ink run and smudge making it nearly impossible to read. Drake looked at the letters for a few seconds, only able to make out a few words.

I know – mine. After that Drake could understand nothing else due to the ink having run. Drake looked at the three words and the smudged spaced between them. Guilt swept over Drake and he put it back in her hands, feeling as if he had invaded her privacy. He grabbed a blanket from the end of the bed and pulled it over her. Drake left the room and then left the building.

He stepped out into the city, remembering everything he had seen in the mirror. The mirror in itself was enough to make him suspicious of Isabel, but he doubted he had to be afraid of her. Then again everyone else in the city seemed to be.

Drake walked aimlessly down the streets until finally, he came to a large stairwell that would take him up to the top of the wall. He looked out over the open field and then the grass canyons.

A longing to help people filled him and Drake began to truly believe in the scar on his hand. Ever since he had awakened on the side of the river, people had told him that the scar on his hand would change his life and he would do things that he had never imagined he would do.

Drake had doubted them, but the more time that passed the more he realized that it was true. He believed that something greater than himself had given him the scar and now it was just a question as to which person he was. Was he Sherados? Or was he the one to make the way for Sherados?

He made his way back to the sleeping quarters on the top level of the city. He laid down in his bed and fell to sleep, dreaming of everything he had seen in the mirror and also of Isabel who was still mysterious to him.

IV — CURSES AND SHADOWS

The rising of the sun was bittersweet for Atruss. The sun's light was cool and distant; fall had come and now winter was thinking about entering. A few snowflakes drifted through the air and landed on the balcony.

"You're worried aren't you?" Gabrielle asked coming forward. She put her arm around him and he around her as they both stared into the sunrise.

"I feel as if though what is going to happen in this city today will change the outcome of the war. I don't think this is just any traveler that's coming to us. What his business is with the prisoner Tremin I can't begin to guess."

"Perhaps it's not for us to know," Gabrielle replied. "Don't let your heart be troubled over something that you don't know the answer to. If you are meant to know it then you will know it at the right time."

"The horizon is clouded to me," Atruss admitted.

"Clouded perhaps, but there is hope. Someday soon Sherados will come forward and lead us to victory. For even the darkness of night is shattered by the light of the morning."

"I know, but the darkness is long and gloomy. It dampens my spirits. Though I try to see the good in things, I fail, left only to see the gloom and despair that is in front of us. Our soldiers are not trained, and we can't hope to defend ourselves at this point."

"I think Aiden's right when he says we have to reach out to the other nations and try to help them. By doing so we'll gain their allegiance, and we might just find that they think and believe the same things we do. They just don't dare to stand, until they stand with someone else."

"I guess someone has to have the guts to make the first move don't they?" Atruss asked. Gabrielle nodded her agreement.

"People can stand better against a common foe if they unite themselves. It's exactly what our enemy doesn't want. He seeks to remove the name of Lathon from history and kill the prophets. He wants to divide us and conquer us, so he can rule the world as he sees fit."

"I have no intentions of letting this nation fall into ruin," Atruss told her. "We will do what we can to help the other nations, although it might take us all winter just to train our troops; by that point, the Sorcerer may have attacked all the surrounding nations and we will stand no chance."

"But we will still stand, and that's more than other nations will have been able to say!" Gabrielle replied. They donned their robes and then made their way to the main hall where everyone was eating their breakfast.

Drake, Lily, and Ellizar all sat together at a table in a corner, while Skander and Aiden sat across from them. Atruss looked at Drake and watched him as he interacted with the others. Funny how one person could have so much of an effect on the world. It would be easy to blame all of this on Drake but he wouldn't allow himself to do that. He had been given that mark for a reason.

He searched around the room wishing that he could look out into the people of the world and know which one was Sherados, or if Sherados was even with them at all.

"Aiden, could I speak with you for a moment?" Atruss asked.

"Of course," Aiden answered. He excused himself and Gabrielle sat down and began eating breakfast with them, Atruss and Aiden meanwhile joined up with Rohemir on the far side of the room.

"Did you find anything out from Tremin?" Atruss asked. Aiden shook his head.

"I got nothing out of him. The only way to figure out anything about him would be to set him free and watch where he moves, although I think he would likely be on to us by that point."

"I agree, besides with the sor-Merderick coming today we have to have him to do the exchange. Without him Gwen will be as good as dead," Rohemir replied.

"I wish there was something else we could do. It feels too easy. Am I the only one who feels like that?" Atruss asked.

"We both feel the same way," Aiden answered. "We can't let Tremin go and then follow him because he'd know we'd be following him, but what if we sent him with Merderick and then tried to have them followed."

"Who can we trust to follow them and not give away any secrets if they get caught?" Atruss asked.

"As it just so happens the Farsees and I had been discussing such a scenario and we think that Aiden should be the one to go," Rohemir answered.

"The Farsees?" Aiden asked. "Maybe I'm out of line, but is something like this really something religious leaders need to be burdening themselves with? This is a decision for the council, not the Farsees."

"You sound as if you oppose the Farsees?" Rohemir asked.

"I do if they twist people's words and put their nose into an area that is not theirs.

"How about Rohemir?" Atruss suggested. "Aiden's already busy and my wife and I have to run the city. I think you would be able to do the job and not be found out. Don't you?"

"Yes I probably can do the job just fine," Rohemir replied. "I did work as a double agent many years ago, which, the way I see it, makes me a prime candidate. If I get caught they will likely go easy on me and believe my story."

"It's done then, once Tremin and Merderick leave, Rohemir will follow them and see where they end up. Make sure your messenger bird is with you."

"You don't have to worry about that," Rohemir replied. Even as he finished his statement a young man came running forward. He came to a stop in front of Atruss. He did a bow and stood silent for a minute.

"What is it?" Atruss asked.

"A man and a group of other men were seen entering the grass canyons twenty minutes ago. They had a woman with them, thought you ought to know."

"Yes, very good. Tell all the men stationed in the grass canyon to pull back to the city and take their posts," Atruss said. The young man nodded and took off running to the city gates and out to the grass canyons. The three of them exchanged looks.

"Looks like our schedule's going to be a little different than we thought. If they're in the grass canyons, we have maybe an hour before they arrive. I want all the men stationed as if this place was going to be attacked. All troops who aren't at the wall or lining a path on the outside of the castle will be lined up in formation on the inside of the gate, leaving no escape options should Merderick or Tremin try anything."

"As you wish sir," Rohemir replied, leaving to carry out the orders. Aiden stood silent, as did Atruss.

"Keep Drake and the others in sight, but not directly in sight. The last thing we want is for Merderick to figure out who he is. As soon as the exchange is complete and they're a fair distance away I want you to take all of them and get out of here and get back to Negev as fast as you possibly can. We need everyone trained by spring at the very latest. I can take care of things here just fine. Hopefully, Rohemir will be able to dig up some information that will prove helpful to us."

"I hope everything works out the way we want it to," Aiden replied.

"So do I, because our next move is determined by this one. If this move gets screwed up we'll never be able to mount a good offense."

"I have a feeling that this nation will be divided in the end, and not necessarily by the Sorcerer's doing."

"What are you saying?" Atruss asked.

"I'm saying that this war is going to be larger than any of us. The nations will be split among themselves. Once that happens, we will have to not only join forces with the nations of Men, but also with the Giants, Dwarves, and anyone else who has been exiled from their nations."

"I'm not sure how much war this world can take. Having to fight a war while trying to deal with a civil war is almost too much for a nation to stand against," Atruss remarked.

"Which is why the Sorcerer wants that to happen. The weaker we become the stronger he gets. We just have to stand true to what we know and believe. If we do that then we'll be just fine."

"It should be very interesting to see what lies ahead for the nation of Ariamore," Atruss replied. Aiden nodded and they went their separate ways. Aiden went off to get everyone ready for the arrival of their guests while Atruss was left to ponder the meaning of things by himself.

Soon Gabrielle came to his side and they made their way down to the main level of the city where everyone was gathered and waiting. The troops had lined up just as he had told them to, creating a path that would lead up to an opening in the street in which Atruss and everyone else of importance were gathered.

The guards on the top of the wall kept watch on the edge of the grass canyons where their guests would soon be appearing. The minutes passed, each one feeling longer than the first.

A horn called out in the distance, drawing the guards' attention. To the left, they could see six horsemen riding towards them, a thin trail of dust rising from the ground.

"Hold them at the gate and ask them a few simple questions!" Atruss ordered. The guards nodded and then turned their attention to the party that approached.

"We are about to have a guest in our city! Be careful though, there are certain things about this guest that we aren't quite certain about. We are not saying there are ill intentions, but there could be. Be ready for war should he attack with a hidden force, and also be ready to celebrate if his only reason for coming is to bring Gwen back. Is Tremin here?"

"Yes he is," Aiden answered as several guards moved him into the clearing.

Behind Aiden, Drake and the others stood side by side, all dressed in their nice clothes. He looked through the throngs of people. Rohemir stood on the outskirts of the crowd, a horse casually tied up to a post.

The horsemen could be heard riding up to the gates. They rode to a stop and the sound of the guards talking to them reached their ears. At once, the city became so quiet that Atruss could hear his nervous heart, beating in his chest.

"May I have your name sir?" the guard asked.

"My name is Merderick, my good elf. I am expected. This is Gwen of Fiori, I freed her from a group of renegades and I wish to return her in exchange for a friend of my own."

"Your business is known and you are expected. You may enter the city. We are generally cautious of new faces so don't try anything."

"That is a wise thought my lad; for these days the world is filled with dangerous people who mean only to deceive you, let there be no doubt in your heart that I am someone that you can trust."

The gates opened and they were let through, escorted down the path that had been created by the armed guards standing on both sides. Every eye was fixated on Merderick as the company approached. Atruss watched, most carefully, noting Merdericks' calm and pleasing demeanor. His clothes were well put together and, if anything, he looked more like a wealthy merchant than a person to not be trusted. His head was bald and he had a grey beard that came neatly down to the middle of his chest.

The clacking of the horse's hooves ceased and Merderick dismounted and then helped Gwen down. Gwen remained standing for several seconds before rushing off into the crowd and jumping into Drake's arms. The crowd cheered. Merderick smiled.

"As promised, one Gwen. Safely returned," Merderick said, his words were strong and fluent. Pleasant to the ears and the heart.

"We are most grateful," Atruss replied. "What of those who were part of her abduction?"

"I killed the lot and left their bodies for the vultures."

"On that note, I would like to thank you. If you have done what you have said then we are most grateful."

"I wouldn't have said it if it wasn't true," Merderick defended.

"I can see you are a man of integrity!" Atruss complimented. From the corner of his eye, he could see Drake and Gwen. Gwen seemed to buckle and become weak. Drake kept his arm firmly around her. He shifted and kept her standing upright.

"Your honesty is appreciated," Atruss replied. "We have the prisoner Tremin. Admittedly, we are hesitant to release him because he was suspected to be in on the plot to kidnap Gwen in the first place."

"I understand your concern well. My only motive in acquiring his freedom in any respect, is that I wish to keep peace in my family. You see Tremin is my nephew. I know his mother and his father would hate to see him murdered. Although I know there's no way for me to prove one way or the other that he did or didn't help. I would not be able to live with myself if there wasn't peace in my family. It is for the good of my family that I am doing this."

"If he is your family, then I understand perfectly why you would want him back," Gabrielle answered. "You may judge him as you see fit." Tremin was led forward and then released. He slowly walked over to Merderick who turned his attention back to everyone else.

"I thank you from the bottom of my heart," Merderick replied. "You don't know how much this means to me. I would not want to see my family in such pain and turmoil as they likely would've been. Even though he is my family, I will judge him as he should be judged."

"That is all that we ask," Atruss said. "Now would you care to join us for a meal so that we can further discuss certain happenings that are better left for chambers and meeting rooms?"

"I'm afraid that I must be on my way. I have been away for many months on business and I still have many days of traveling if I am to make it to my home and I would not want to keep my family members waiting any longer."

"In that case, I wish you all the speed you can ride with," Atruss replied. Merderick bowed and then mounted his horse, pulling Tremin up as well. They turned and rode out of the city, followed by the rest of his men. The city gates were closed as they rode into the horizon.

No one spoke until the city gates had been sealed and then the crowds erupted into cheers, all of them rushing towards Gwen as though she was some kind of a celebrity. The crowd was chased away by Aiden who stepped in and sent them back to their posts.

Gwen whispered her thanks to Aiden and he nodded in reply as Atruss and Rohemir approached. Rohemir had a horse next to him, the same white horse he had been riding the first time they had met.

"Welcome back Gwen!" Atruss greeted, embracing her. "It feels like forever since you were taken captive."

"It feels like forever since I was here," Gwen answered.

"I'm glad to see you," Lily said.

"Why don't we start by findin' ourselves somethin' teh eat?" Ellizar suggested. "It's early in the mornin' and it's a good time fer a feast!"

"That's a dwarf for you, always thinking with your stomach," Lily replied. Ellizar shot her a look. "But this is one time that I agree with you, my friend." Ellizar laughed an infectious laugh which eventually brought smiles to all of their faces.

"Enjoy your meal, I must leave now. I can't let them get too far ahead," Rohemir said. Gwen's confusion was only temporary as Rohemir explained himself. "I'm going to follow Merderick and Tremin and hopefully dig up some useful information on them. Is there anything I should know about them, Gwen?"

"No, there's nothing you should know," Gwen said after a moment.

"Very well, in that case, I shall be on my way." Rohemir mounted his horse and then waved goodbye. The sound of the city gates being opened was heard and he vanished from their sight.

"Aiden, why was he sent?" Lily asked.

"There are many things we're unsure of. I figured by sending him away for a little bit the answer, one way or another, will reveal itself. But enough talk about this, we'll be leaving in only a few hours so Gwen tell us everything that happened?"

"What is there to say?" Gwen asked in reply. "It's all a blur, really. All I know is that I was kidnapped and then returned."

"We are glad that you're safe, now if you'll excuse me I have to have a little chat with certain people," Aiden explained. He disappeared into the thinning crowd, leaving them to be by themselves. They all embraced her and welcomed her back, nearly bringing tears to Gwen's eyes.

Even though the display of affection wasn't much, they could see in her eyes that it was as if she had been given the world. She embraced Lily last and then noticed Isabel had approached them.

Isabel stood in the distance, her hair red and her dress a dark blue color. They held eye contact, and for a moment the world faded away until they were the only two people that existed.

"I'm glad to see that you've made it back safely Gwen," Isabel greeted. Gwen just smiled and nodded. "It's a lucky thing we made it through today without any injuries, being in the presence of the Sorcerer and all that."

"Are you saying that Merderick is the Sorcerer?" Drake asked.

"Yes, I am."

"Well yeh can't just say somethin' like that without proof," Ellizar replied.

"The only reason I speak of it dear Ellizar is because I have all the proof that I need," Isabel answered.

"And what proof would that be?" Skander asked.

"I'm related to him."

Drake stared at the stars on the cold autumn night. They were back in Negev to live with the Gogs and continue their training. They had been back for a week and still nothing had been explained further.

Isabel may have revealed part of her past but she hadn't told them any more than that, preferring to keep it to herself for the time being. As much as Drake respected one person's right to their privacy he found it deeply disturbing.

Not even Aiden had tried to explain why Isabel hadn't explained what she had said. There was a chance that Aiden didn't know the answer, but Drake's heart told him otherwise. Aiden seemed to know everything that went on and happened, even when he wasn't around.

When Drake looked at Aiden, he saw a glimpse of the person that he wanted to be. He didn't desire power and control, but he wanted to be able to help people and to know what to do when problems arise. Aiden had that and Drake didn't.

He threw another log on the fire and watched the sparks fly into the night and then vanish a few feet later. His mind wandered in and out of everything that it could drift to, finally coming to rest on Gwen.

She along with everyone else were asleep in their quarters, which were now well guarded by the Gogs. He couldn't even begin to describe how grateful he was that she was back and that he could talk to her. His heart had been a storm of emotions when she had been kidnapped, giving him an indication of how strong his feelings for her were.

Still, for whatever reason she seemed unusually quiet and withdrawn since she had returned. Often he would find her by herself in some far-off place of Negev. She always smiled and seemed to be happy to see him, but something in her had changed.

"Mind if I join you?" Drake's mind was pulled out of his thoughts as he looked to see Aiden standing next to him.

"Campfire's lit," Drake answered. Aiden sat down, leaning up against a lone tree that stood on the beach.

"What's keeping you up?" Aiden asked.

"I could ask you the same thing."

"So you could, and after you answer me perhaps you can ask me that question."

"Couldn't sleep."

"I gathered that much. Why couldn't you sleep?"

"Bad dreams."

"Dreams you say?" Drake nodded. "You want to talk about it?"

"Not really."

"It helps to talk about things Drake. Keeping things inside does nothing but torture you and alienate you from the people who want to help you through a tough time. That's what friends are for."

"I guess there's no arguing with that explanation is there?" Drake asked, Aiden smiled. "They're not dreams as much as they are unknowns. They make me nervous and get me thinking at night. I can't sleep because of them."

"Anything particular?"

"Isabel."

"Ah yes, the enchanting shopkeeper! Never met a woman like her before, anywhere in all my travels. She is an unusual sort, quite a past. She has a heart for Lathon though."

"You know her past?" Drake asked.

"Yes. I know many things about her that a normal person does not know. That's usually because the normal person writes her off as a nutcase and doesn't care to ask about her past."

"What is it?"

"Intriguing."

"That's what I'm starting to conclude. The way she fenced with us on the practice fields was something that I would have never would have thought of her."

"People are full of surprises, that's why it's best to get all the facts before you make up your mind about someone."

"I suppose. Would you tell me about her past if I asked it?"

"No, I figure you can ask her yourself."

"Like I'll make it back to Belvanor anytime soon?"

"I didn't say you'd have to make it back to Belvanor. She's coming here, to meet with us for the next week. There's much we can learn from her and little time in which to do it."

"She's coming here? How does she know where this place is?"

"I told you there were three people who have been gifted the honor to dine with the Gogs, me, Atruss, and Isabel."

"Didn't see that one coming."

"I suspect that you've come to some conclusions about Isabel."

"I'm not sure if they're right or not. But I suppose I don't have all the facts," Drake asked. "A flaw of mine I suppose."

"There's nothing wrong with having flaws Drake Thomas, but do be more careful about it in the future. After all, you may write someone off as whatever you think they are, only to find that they are different, or that they have changed. You must learn to be a good judge."

"Isn't that what everyone said Lathon was?"

"Yes they did, and they didn't say it without good reason. You see a good judge looks at all the evidence, not just part of it. Only then can they make a good judgment on people."

"Good advice," Drake admitted. They were silent for several moments.

"What else is bothering you, Drake?" Aiden asked.

"Does Gwen seem different to you?"

"Why do you ask?"

"I feel like she's hiding something from me. From all of us. I can't make certain of what it is. Whatever it is...she's not the same."

"I can't say that I've particularly noticed anything strikingly different. It might be something as simple as it is the effects of being kidnapped. We never know what they did to her."

"I wish she'd tell us. It would make me worry a lot less."

"I'm sure if she was ready to tell us, she would," Aiden reassured. "You can't rush people, if you rush them they tend to run in the other direction."

Drake grunted and pulled a few blades of grass from the ground and threw them into the fire.

"What else is bothering you, Drake?"

"Everything. Life just seems to never stop. One moment you think you're in the clear and the next moment you're stuck in a storm so overwhelming that you don't think you can ever get out."

"I have felt that way many times Drake, but you mustn't worry about the future. You must be content to be your own person. The person that you are called to be. If you're worried about the future or about the people or things around you, you will end up on a road that you can't get off. Trying to impress others; it's a futile road let me tell you. In the end, they die the same as you do."

"I wish I could have all the answers like you do Aiden."

"Answers? I don't have all the answers Drake, but I make sure to listen to the world around me to hear them. The answers are everywhere you look. When you look at people, some of them have the answers you don't. I learned many things through stories and watching people."

"Stories?"

"Stories are my favorite way to learn things, Lathon used many stories to get his point across to people. I guess in some way, people can connect to stories more easily than they can connect to someone just telling them what to do. In it, they find their questions and then the answers."

"So you're saying if I want to have *more* of the answers, I have to listen."

"That's right. It goes right along with being a good judge." They both stared into the fire, watching it consume the logs until there was nothing left but the ashes.

"Well, I think you'd better get some sleep Drake Thom-"

"Can I ask you one more thing?"

"Anything you wish."

"I guess, it's not so much me asking as it is telling you what happened when I saw Merderick. The world ran cold and my blood nearly stopped. My scar was filled with an icy sensation to the point that I thought I couldn't live. Then some images came to me. Water. Rushing water. Nothing more came to me than that, but my heart was in turmoil at the image. Who is Merderick?"

"We'll find out tomorrow, but this certainly does add another interesting dimension to the puzzle. Strangely, enough I think that Gwen might have been feeling the same sort of sensation before she returned."

"What makes you say that?"

"Her eyes were the same as yours were then. They were blank and expressionless, filled with a fear of something that haunted you."

"Do you think there's a connection between Merderick and these pictures?"

"Perhaps, but then again we don't know all there is to know. Even if he was the one responsible, what would be his purpose behind it?"

"I guess we'll just have to have all the facts before we decide anything," Drake replied. They both laughed.

"Indeed we will." Aiden stood. "Now I'm going to get some sleep. Isabel usually likes to arrive early in the morning and even now it's not far off. Goodnight Drake."

"Good night Aiden."

Aiden left the fire and within a few minutes, Drake had as well. Drake lay down in the bed, finding that his troubles and worries were easily forgotten and sleep came over him, allowing him to rest peacefully.

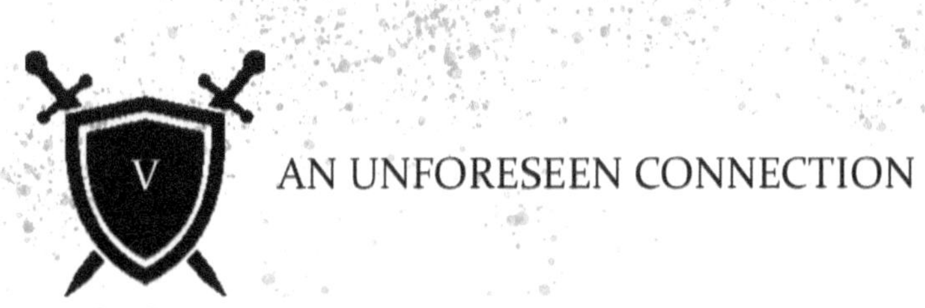

AN UNFORESEEN CONNECTION

Everyone woke and found their way down to the breakfast that had been prepared for them. The Gogs talked all around them, most of them in their own language, though many made efforts to converse with their guests. Drake could tell Gwen was adjusting to the Gogs, he perceived that she seemed to be struggling with something else.

"Good morning everyone," a voice greeted them. They turned to see a woman in a long black dress. Her hair was greying and came down past her shoulders, her eyes were full of life and excitement, glowing a bright sapphire color.

"Good morning," Drake greeted. "How can we help you?"

"May I sit?" the woman asked. Drake looked at the others who all shrugged their shoulders.

"Have a seat," Drake motioned.

"Have you had anything to eat yet this morning?" Lily asked.

"No, I haven't. Do you think I could still get some food?" the woman asked. As if Shavrok had read her mind, he set a plate of food in front of her. The woman thanked him and then casually began eating the food, seeming to forget about the people around her.

"What brings you here?" Gwen asked. The woman looked up from her food and smiled.

"I came here to help with the training of five particular people," the woman answered.

"Five people?" Drake asked.

"Yes, two humans, two Elves, and a dwarf. An unusual group, but then again nothing is normal these days. After all, I'm sitting here." She laughed and took another bite of her food.

"You seem to know who we are, but we have yet to learn your name," Lily replied.

"This isn't the first time we've met."

"What's your name?" Ellizar asked.

"My name's Isabel." They looked at the woman in front of them, who looked nothing like Isabel.

"I'm not quite sure I believe you," Skander replied.

"It's the truth whether you believe me or not," Isabel answered. "Let me finish my breakfast and then we'll go off somewhere and I'll try to explain everything that I possibly can." Aiden came up to them and Isabel stood from her spot, gracefully bowing to him.

"Glad to see you could make it," Aiden said, turning towards them. "I know there are many things that you are wondering about. They will all be explained shortly."

They small-talked, waiting for Isabel to finish her meal. When finally she was done they walked back to their quarters and found themselves sitting in front of a roaring fireplace with cups of tea.

"I suppose I should probably get started explaining myself and my history to you, seeing that I look nothing like you are used to," Isabel said. As if she had merely thought the command, her skin and hair changed and she looked exactly like the Isabel they had known for the past several weeks. "Is that better?" She laughed to herself and then her appearance went back to the way it had been previously.

"I found this little charm bracelet in an old trunk when I was a youngster," Isabel said. She pulled a small simple bracelet off her wrist. Again her appearance changed to the aged woman they had met earlier at breakfast.

"That isn't natural," Ellizar stated. Isabel laughed.

"It's a little freaky actually," Drake said. "Where did you grow up?"

"The Dead Mountains," Isabel said. Immediately everyone became silent. "Surprised?"

"Just a little," Lily said.

"As you must imagine, growing up in such a place, my bracelet has come in handy when hiding over the past years."

"Okay, I'm dying to know, how are you related to the Sorcerer?" Gwen asked. Their eyes were all focused on Isabel who took a sip of her tea and then set it down on the table next to her.

"I'm not directly related to Merderick, who is the Sorcerer. I was married to his brother for quite some time."

"His brother! The Sorcerer has a brother?" Ellizar asked.

"It's a well-kept secret but he *does* have a brother. I met a man many, many years ago and I fell in love with him. He was everything to me. We were married at a very young age. I had just turned seventeen. We had a baby together, a boy. His name is Tremin."

"Tremin?" Skander asked. "The same one who just left Belvanor?"

"For a while, we lived happily ever after. Then I started to notice a change in my husband until he was no longer the person that I had fallen in love with or married. My husband turned extremely violent towards me; even Tremin started to become more aggressive and violent. Eventually living with them was becoming a threat to my life.

"One day my husband showed up with a man and said that he was his brother. During all the years of our marriage, I had never heard of a brother before. His name was Merderick."

"I never would have guessed you were related to the Sorcerer or Tremin for that matter," Lily replied.

"There's often more to people than meets the eye," Isabel told them. "When I was married to the Sorcerer's brother I couldn't help but notice that there were a few things that my husband seemed to treasure more than any others. Above all were a set of mirrors, hidden deep within a castle, and then a staff that he called the *Wizard's Staff*.

"As time passed I grew afraid of what might happen. Throughout the years I had heard many conversations and picked up on many tidbits of information I probably wasn't supposed to know. Fearing for my life as well as everyone else's, I did the only thing I could do. I tampered with everything that I possibly could.

"I read things I hadn't been allowed to read, learning all I could about my husband and his obsession with the Borags. I read hundreds of papers, written in every language, and when I was done I burned them. My husband never figured out where they went. I'm sure I would've been killed if he had.

"The years passed and I finally decided that I had to get out and never come back. I did two things to both guarantee my safety and to hopefully put a kink in my husband's plan. I went to the Sorcerer's mirrors and I tampered with them, putting a curse on them that no one would realize until they walked through it. It was a curse that would brutally attack any family members of the Sorcerer who tried to walk through the mirrors.

"Then I grabbed the Wizard's Staff and I took it. If I had known then how important it was to the Sorcerer I would have destroyed it, but I didn't know, and it was allowed to exist for many more years.

"I left in the middle of the night and never went back. As you now know, my bracelet changes my appearance. I added one more feature that made it so my appearance would change every few minutes so I wouldn't be recognized. That is why so many people are uncomfortable around me.

"Once I was free I created a copy of the Wizard's Staff. A copy that was so good that I couldn't even tell the difference between the two of them. A year later, I returned to Iscariot and then I threw them through the mirrors so that they landed in the other nations. To this day I still don't know where one of them is."

"You mean someone found the other one?" Drake asked. Aiden nodded.

"One of them was discovered and is hidden with some friends of mine."

"If the Wizard's Staff is hidden then we don't have anything to worry about do we?" Gwen asked. "The Sorcerer won't be able to rise to his full power."

"Except we don't know which one is real and which one is fake," Aiden reminded. "I've seen both of them and I don't have a clue which one is the real one. All I know is, if we want to end this war quickly we have to find it and then destroy it. We can't let the Sorcerer find it."

"If he finds it before us then there's no hope is there?" Skander asked.

"There is always hope, as long as we keep our hearts on the right path. We can win without destroying it, but the world will be a much darker place if we do not," Aiden said.

"How do you mean that?" Drake asked.

"My husband discovered the Wizard's Staff. After that, the man that I loved disappeared from my life." Isabel started. "He slowly faded until he was a shadow to me. He was different. I think if the Sorcerer was to get his hand on this weapon, the citizens of the world would find themselves in a similar situation. They, too, would slowly fade until they were no different from the Sorcerer."

"So if we try to find it, we can save people from this threat?" Gwen asked.

"Yes, but taking on such a burden? There are several things that you don't know in life until you reach the moment of truth and this is one of them. You will not know until the moment comes if you have the strength to destroy it," Isabel answered.

"There is only one way to find out, and there's only one way to shorten the war and that's to find the Wizard's Staff," Aiden explained.

"I take it we're going to be setting out on some quest to find the Wizard's Staff?" Drake asked.

"Eventually. It doesn't make very much sense to go looking for it right now, with winter so close. We could practically walk right by it and not see it. Plus we have to get some kind of idea of where the Staff actually is. We'll have to wait until spring."

"Do you think the Sorcerer will attack in winter?" Lily asked.

"It wouldn't surprise me," Isabel answered. "We have to double the training in case something should come up."

They fell silent looking at each other and then at Aiden who seemed to have a light in his eyes that they hadn't seen before. It glimmered with a knowledge that they didn't have.

The next few weeks were nothing short of exhausting for the five of them as they were trained with every kind of weapon. They didn't hear anything of the outside world, instead, they focused all their attention on what Isabel and Aiden were telling them.

They were trained with bows, and then with axes which made Ellizar's' day as he normally poked fun at the others who were struggling to catch on. They fired the jokes back at him and watched him as his face was more humorous than they intended.

Along with the training and handling of weapons, they found themselves doing an exhaustive amount of reading. Aiden had insisted that they read up on all the nations and their history as well as the typical characteristics of each race. Drake couldn't deny that he found it interesting, but he had yet to see what it had to do with the battles they would face.

The atmosphere in Ariamore had changed from when they had first arrived several months ago. Where once a peaceful feeling had taken the forefront, now anticipation and unease were felt. The army that Ariamore had assembled was far larger than Drake had expected it to be and was fairly well trained for the short amount of time they had been preparing.

Atruss and Gabrielle had come to visit them on several occasions. Still, to Drake's surprise, they chose to keep the existence of the Gogs a secret. Based on what Drake had learned over the past couple of months about the Farsees and the council, it was probably for the better.

The Gogs seemed to not care about the outside world and were planning for war daily. Drake often watched the Gogs as they practiced and sparred with each other, already scared to think of what it would be like to see a Gog in war. He almost felt sorry for the army that would have to face them.

Machines of war were built, and then dissembled and put on the ships which were getting closer and closer to actually being ready, despite all the setbacks they had faced during the final days of building the catapults.

"Is everyone ready fer the grand event?" Ellizar asked, a smile beaming across his face.

"That's why we're here," Lily remarked.

"Well, prepare teh be amazed at this incredible new invention that will aid us in the war! Fire when ready Shavrok!" The catapult was released. The projectile flew towards the open water. The arm of the catapult snapped from its frame crashing through the deck of the ship and sending the catapult crashing to the second level. They all looked to Ellizar who was standing with his mouth open in shock.

"Shuckers!" Ellizar exclaimed.

"Shuckers?" Lily asked. Ellizar looked at her.

"That's right, I said it!"

"I know you said it I'm just wondering what on earth it means. I'm not even sure it's a real word."

"Oh trust me it's a real word because I just used it. Although I do find it a great accomplishment that the Dwarves came up with a word that the Elves don't understand. The Elves are supposed teh be the smartest and wisest in the land are they not? Therefore this must mean that the Dwarves are the smartest people in the land."

"I'm sure it's a word that the Elves have used in the past, but we quit using it because we didn't want to be like the Dwarves."

"What's that supposed teh mean?"

"If we used strange words like 'shuckers', then we might end up short like you and we don't want that to happen, Ellie."

"Blasted elf kind! I don't know how yeh always manage teh turn a perfectly good insult back on me!"

"Now that's what makes the Elves truly superior."

"I'm not goin' teh talk teh yeh anymore!" Ellizar asked. "Yeh always make fun of poor Ellizar."

"Was it not your design that just sent the catapult through the deck of the ship?"

"I'm not answerin' that! I'll have yeh know that the test went perfectly fine. We know now that this design needs teh be fixed if we're goin' teh get it teh work the way we want."

"Good observation," Drake commented. Ellizar looked at him and shook his head.

"Yeh guys are all alike. I don't know why I hang out with any of yeh."

"You do it because you love us," Lily replied. Ellizar smiled but didn't reply, and instead turned his attention to Shavrok who was coming towards them. The catapult was already being pulled out of the ship so it could be repaired.

"That's better than the first test that we did," Ellizar said.

"Yes but we still ended up destroying part of our ship," Shavrok replied. "If it's not working by the first sign of spring we'll have to abandon the project. The world cannot sit by and wait for us forever."

"Well said," Aiden replied. "Everyone go get something to eat and then head off to bed. Our enemy will not rest in the winter and we have maybe a month of true winter left."

They did as he said and made their way off to their beds, eventually leaving Drake to think and ponder the situation at hand. The night brought him rest but not nearly enough as dreams of what might be plagued him constantly.

Gwen woke in the middle of the night, her mind in torment. Searing pain in her mind had not only taken hold of her but was getting worse, keeping her awake for hours during the night. This was the tenth night she had felt this pain. Unable to subdue the pain, she often found herself at nighttime wandering off into the forest without knowing that she had done it, until finally, she woke up from the daze that she had been in.

Her mind was being slowly taken over by something that she couldn't control and it was changing who she was. Her heart cried out, but no one heard her as she fought and struggled with herself. She threw the covers off and then put on one of her dresses, but nothing else.

A couple of inches of snow had fallen on the ground, but she was unable to prevent herself from going out into the snow. She wandered around and her mind floated in and out. One moment she knew what she was doing and the other she was driven mad.

She walked for hours, hardly remembering one step from the next. At last, she came to a stop in the middle of a large valley and fell to the ground. Her heart raced and her breathing was hard and labored as she struggled with herself.

She muttered unintelligible words and crawled on her hands and knees, and eventually collapsed, her strength leaving her. When her eyes opened again she saw two wolves standing in front of her. Her mind cleared as she looked about her and shivered in the cold.

Fear consumed her as she had no idea how she had gotten here or what she was doing. Willard and Miles came to her and sniffed at her, looking at each other with concern in their eyes. Gwen stared at the sky, unsure how to explain what was going on.

'Gwen!' Merderick's foul voice entered her head and then left just as quickly. She silently cursed herself for allowing this to happen.

Noises were heard from somewhere in the forest, and when she looked she realized that only Willard was standing next to her now. How long she had been out she didn't know, but Miles had slipped away.

"How much further?" Isabel asked, having trouble keeping up with her four-legged friend.

'Not far!' Miles encouraged. They continued their way through the snowy forest until at last they came around a large oak tree and saw Gwen. She lay on the ground, her hair and clothes were a mess, and she stared ahead blankly, muttering unintelligibly to herself.

Isabel dropped to one knee, quickly checking Gwen's pulse. Gwen didn't react to her touch.

"What was she like when you found her?"

'Muttering to herself, crawling on all fours like an animal. I've never seen anything like it. What do you think it is?'

"She's under a curse," Isabel concluded.

'I've never seen a curse do this,' Willard noted.

"Her heartbeat is erratic. Breathing irregular. You can touch her, wave your hand in front of her face and she doesn't even blink." Isabel quickly demonstrated. "Any time I've come across a person like that it usually means they're under a curse. When you look at who she was with for a couple of days it would make sense."

'She was with the Sorcerer right?' Miles asked. Isabel nodded.

"Knowing Merderick, he put a curse of some kind on her."

'Can't we wake and ask her?' Willard asked.

"Merderick's too smart for that," Isabel explained. "He'll have some protection against her answering such a question."

'What do you mean?'

"Merderick could have made the curse in such a manner that if she were to answer that question, the curse may kill her."

'Which means all we can do is sit back and watch?'

"Sadly," Isabel admitted.

'We'll hope and pray to Lathon that when she comes to her senses, we can find a way past the curse,' Miles said. Willard nodded in agreement.

"Take heart, my friend. There's always a way around a curse, though it may take time to figure out the loophole that Merderick missed."

They were silent for some time, as Isabel watched and studied any movement of Gwen's. She had seen many curses in her time, but so far this one appeared to be the most extreme.

Isabel quickly stood and went into the forest returning with snow-covered sticks and logs. Soon there was a roaring fire going at Gwen's feet, and Isabel covered her as much as she could.

'If we could bother you for a moment,' Willard started. *'We discovered something you may wish to see. A secret that must remain between us.'*

"It's not the secret stash of food you showed me yesterday is it?" Isabel answered. Miles glared at Willard.

'Secret stash of food? It's the middle of the blasted winter and you're keeping food from me? You're a miserable little thief!'

'Oh come on Miles, it's not like I was hiding it from you, I was merely guarding it for you.'

'And you didn't tell me about it, why?'

'Because I wanted to make sure it didn't disappear too quickly.'

'You're hopeless,' Miles replied. *'To answer your question, Isabel, I don't think it has anything to do with food.'*

"In that case, I'm interested in seeing it," Isabel answered.

'Come with us,' Willard replied. Leaving Gwen for a moment, she followed the two wolves into the forest. They walked for many minutes without seeing anything other than the snow-coated forest in front of them.

They came to a large cliff that dropped off suddenly. To their left, there was a roughly hewn staircase that led down to the ground below, but they didn't go near it. Instead, Willard and Miles crept towards the edge and then lowered themselves to the ground completely.

At first, Isabel could hear nothing but their breathing and a few of the squirrels that scampered around in the snow. They listened harder and finally, she heard what Willard and Miles wanted her to hear. Voices. They were faint and distant and sounded as if they were in a tunnel, but they seemed to be steadily growing.

"Who's doing the talking?" Isabel asked.

'Look at the clearing closer!' Miles urged as quietly as he could. Isabel strained her eyes to see what wasn't there and then eventually she did see shapes. They appeared as though they were nothing more than air, but shapes *were* moving on the ground below them. They crept away from the clearing and waited till they were back at their camp before they said anything.

"What were those people?" Isabel asked.

'Remember that castle we took Drake into?' Willard asks. *'It's the same people. We're not that far away you know. We've never been able to see their outlines before unless we were at the city gates. They're growing stronger,'*

"We don't have much time."

Isabel kept watch the entire night, careful to make sure that no harm came to the four of them. Willard and Miles were to either side of her. Willard was fast asleep, but Miles sat up and also watched the surrounding forest. In front of her, Gwen lay, wrapped up in a few of the extra layers Isabel had put on when Miles had come to get her.

She observed Gwen with interest, keeping a close eye on her breathing and her pulse, noticing that it varied at times. She often moaned and cried out in her sleep.

The sky was slowly starting to lighten in the east, showing the signs of a coming dawn. Snow still fluttered down on all of them. Isabel kept Gwen swept off and made sure that the fire was burning hot enough to keep her warm.

Gwen began to stir, and immediately, Isabel dropped her mug of tea on the ground and rushed to Gwen's side. Isabel took her head in her hands and ran her fingers through Gwen's tangled hair.

Gwen opened her mouth to speak but nothing came out. Isabel helped Gwen sit up and move to a fallen log and poured a mug of a special drink she had brewed, and handed it to her. She put it to her lips and drank the liquid.

It would feel as if a fire was going down her throat, burning its way toward her heart. Once it hit her stomach her body would come alive, feeling as though a great energy was now at her disposal. Gwen drank the tea and visibly came alive, her eyes coming out of the fog that had overtaken them.

"Good morning Gwen."

"Good morning Isabel."

"Do you know where you are?" Gwen studied the surroundings carefully.

"Where am I?"

"About ten miles west of Negev. You've been doing some traveling. Do you remember any of it?"

"I'd like to say I did, but I don't."

"Thought so," Isabel said. They talked for a minute or two, and with each reply Isabel's suspicions were being proven true.

"Has anything that happened in the past couple of weeks that you haven't told us?" Gwen hesitated.

"Once again I'd like to say there wasn't."

"A curse was put on you?" Isabel asked. Gwen remained silent, appearing as though she was unable to speak even though she wanted to. "You can tell me, Gwen."

"A riddle comes, a riddle goes, yet still the answer seems hidden."

Isabel pondered the words. "So you can't answer anything about a curse that might have been put on you, correct?"

"One hears many things, whether the truth is among them is uncertain, I can lie but I can't tell the truth."

"I see," Isabel replied, thinking hard for a few minutes. "This might not be as bad as it seems Gwen. I had a curse put on me once years ago. With every curse there's a way to get around it, it's just a matter of finding it. The curse that was put on me was that I would not be able to leave the city that I was living in. The only way to get around it was to change my appearance."

"Your charm bracelet?" Gwen asked.

"It was the only way to get around it."

"How do we get around a curse that's placed on someone else?"

"Like yourself? I can ask you questions if you're unable to speak the truth, lie, or give it to me in riddles depending on what the curse will allow you to do. Ready?"

"No," Gwen answered. Isabel smiled lightly.

"Did Merderick put a curse on you?"

"He would have no reason to put a curse on me."

"Why would he put a curse on you?"

"A flicker of light in the distance must mean there's a flame somewhere. He found a light and now he's searching for a flame."

"He's looking for the Wizard's Staff, and he seems to think you can find it for him."

"You put a curse on the mirror preventing him from looking into it."

"He wants you to look in it for him so that he can know the location of the Wizard's Staff. Am I correct?"

"No. You couldn't be further from the truth," Gwen lied.

"Do you know what mirrors he's talking about?"

"I've seen many mirrors, most of them show me my reflection."

"Most do, but not all of them. Did he give you a time limit?"

"There are twelve full moons in the year, eleven of them don't count."

"You have one month left to find a mirror and look in it?" Isabel asked, Gwen remained silent.

"What's going to happen if you don't meet the time limit?"

"The seasons change for real just as they change in life. Should I not meet the one full moon it will forever become winter for me, and I will be left to lie alone, to wander the wilderness naked."

"You'll die, or something close to it?" No reply came. "Was there anything else?"

"Wolves travel in packs. Large packs. They seek to destroy those who oppose them."

"He's going to attack somewhere then...Belvanor?"

"No," Gwen lied. Isabel let a sigh of relief escape her, glad to at least have an explanation for the way she had been acting lately. Isabel played the events of the past week or two in her head, putting all the pieces of the puzzle together. It all made sense now, and her heart leaped for joy.

"Did Merderick tell you he was the Sorcerer?"

"No."

Isabel fell silent and Miles watched with interest, carefully pondering each word that had been said. They lay there for some time, asking questions and decoding the riddles that were returned, trying to learn further information about the Sorcerer and what he may have in hiding. The longer they talked the more she was filled with fear about what the upcoming war would look like. She had always known it would come down to this day, and now that it was nearly here she was more afraid than ever.

Isabel's mind drifted back to the events that had transpired years ago, replaying all of them in her head. Was there something that she could have done to prevent the situation before her now?

"Don't worry Gwen, there are more forces at work in this world than evil. Everything happens for a reason. Maybe this is part of something greater. Drake has a scar on his hand and you have a unique past, as do I. If one thing was meant to happen to one person then you were meant to have this curse put on you and I was meant to figure out what it all means. There is a purpose behind everything if only we seek to know what it is."

"I wish I knew why I was suffering so much," Gwen stated.

"We must trust that Lathon works everything together for good, even if we can't see it from where we are."

"My past haunts me like a bad virus," Gwen admitted. "I don't remember my parents. Do you remember yours?"

"Yes," Isabel answered. "I remember yours as well."

"You knew my parents?" Gwen asked.

"I knew both your mother and your father. I loved them both dearly. You have the same face as your mother. I can see it in you every day. Your eyes shine with the same light that once filled hers. You are very much like your mother."

"And my father?"

"A charming handsome man, who worked hard for a living. I don't think I see any of him in you. You are your mother's child."

"What happened to them?" Gwen asked. "That's one of the things that's bothered me most. They just dropped me off on Lily's doorstep and took off... did they love me at all?"

"Yes, there was much love Gwen. Your father was already dead when your mother dropped you off. She was on the run from some very dangerous people and she knew she would never be able to give you the life that you deserved. She left you on the doorstep of Lily's house and left. It broke her heart, but she had to do it. A life on the run is no life at all."

"I wished I could have met them, or at least my mother," Gwen admitted. "Is she still alive?"

"Perhaps. One day she just vanished and I haven't seen her since."

"Can we find her?" Gwen asked.

"We can't find her now. Not with a war brewing on the horizon. I have guesses of where to look for her though. I promise you Gwen that when this war is over...if your mother hasn't sought you out, I will find your mother; for I desperately wish to speak with her as well."

"I'd like that," Gwen answered in a whisper that was nearly overcome with emotion. "For years I've dreamed of meeting her, to even have a chance to meet her is a dream come true."

"I understand," Isabel asked. "I wish I could see my parents again, but they are far from my reach and would not hear me if I called them."

"What do you know about Drake's family?"

"He looks like his mother, he has so much of his father in him though. Children are the legacy of every parent. They get to leave a piece of themselves in a living being to carry on. It's a tremendous gift and so many people throw it away and don't realize what they have."

"What's his family like?"

"They're very kind-hearted, always seeking to help others. His cousin has had a big impact on me."

"He has a cousin?" Gwen asked. "How many people know about this?"

"Only a handful if I remember correctly."

"It'll be quite a day when we finally get to all meet our families," Gwen noted. "It'll be like a whole new life has just begun. It's one change I could get used to."

"Many are afraid of change. But change must happen, otherwise, the world would go nowhere and people still wouldn't know the name of Lathon. I look forward to seeing Sherados coming forward and revealing himself to the people."

"Sherados," Gwen said, thinking for a moment. "Isabel, you seem to know more than some people, so maybe you could answer this question for me. Is Drake Sherados? He has the scar and his skills are unmatched by the untrained."

"Whether he is or isn't Sherados is not for me to say. I only say that at the right moment, Sherados will step forward. No one knows when that moment is or what it'll be like. He could come forward and declare himself right now if he wanted to. Yet he holds back and waits for the time to be right."

"I wish the time *was* right now, so we didn't have to fight in a war."

"Wars are unpleasant, no doubt about it. However, there are many good things about hard times. Through them, we grow and become stronger. We learn to be thankful for what we have, instead of lusting after what we don't. If there's anyone who's learned this, it's me. My life certainly hasn't been free of hard times."

"Care to elaborate?" Gwen asked.

"It's more complicated than I care to go into at the moment, but one day everything will be out in the open. It will be both terrifying and relieving."

"Do we have to tell the others? About the curse I mean."

"If you want their trust."

"Why can't I go far away, where I don't have to face them."

"Because that's what the Sorcerer wants," Isabel said. "The Sorcerer wants you alone, because if you're alone...you're not much of a threat. He can more easily get under your skin and drive you mad."

"I'm scared to tell them," Gwen admitted. "Scared that they won't understand. Scared that if Drake loves me, he won't see me the same anymore." She anxiously played with her skirt. "How can I face them?"

"With Lathon by your side!" Isabel encouraged. "They already feel as if you were hiding something. I can see it in their actions. The truth will set you free. Come."

Gwen nodded, consigning herself to the decision to tell them the truth. They put out the fire and without further hesitation, they turned and left.

VI UNDER SIEGE

As had become normal, their morning had been spent training. Drake could hardly believe how much they were learning in such a short amount of time. They could now effectively fight with almost every kind of weapon. Every day they sparred with Aiden or with a Gog and now Drake found he could hold his own and wasn't as easily beaten.

Pretty soon a war would be upon them and he would likely be put in charge of a part of the army. Drake wasn't sure if he was glad to have that responsibility or not. However, he had learned so much since the last time, Drake was certain the outcome would be different.

The catapult design that Skander and Ellizar had been working on, now worked and was copied and placed onto the deck of every ship in the harbor. The Gogs prepared their troops, scaring Drake a little bit. He had never seen a Gog in battle, and he hoped he never had to go up against one. With their towering, muscle-filled bodies, and spikes that ran up and down their back they were a foe the enemy wouldn't easily defeat.

"Has anyone seen Gwen lately?"

"No I haven't," Lily answered. "Maybe she just went out for a walk, or is in another part of the city."

"Or maybe she's been kidnapped like she was last time," Drake suggested.

"She wasn't kidnapped, she's right here."

They turned around to see Isabel and Gwen walking across the field, Willard and Miles followed behind the two of them. "There's much to talk about."

"Is everything alright?" Ellizar asked.

"Willard and Miles, go find Aiden and bring him here immediately. He should hear this." Willard and Miles disappeared and everyone exchanged concerned glances when they laid eyes on Gwen, who stared blankly into the space in front of her.

They moved inside and a few minutes later Aiden came in with Willard and Miles following right behind. Aiden took a seat at the table and Willard and Miles sat next to the fireplace, all looking towards Isabel.

"Has anyone here noticed anything different about Gwen here the past month or so?"

"Yes," Lily answered. "I just didn't know what to think or if I should say something." They all nodded in agreement.

"She is under several curses that prevent her from coming out and saying what really happened when she was with Merderick. She can't say what's going to happen. However, unless she does his bidding, she will die from the curse.

"She has been told to find the Wizard's Staff by locating it in one of the Sorcerer's mirrors. As I told you, years ago I made a copy of it and I don't know which one is real and which one isn't. The Sorcerer wants the Wizard's Staff, but due to the spell that I put on the mirror when I left my husband, he can't look into the mirrors for himself. At least not the one he would want to look through.

"He wants Gwen to find it for him. By her looking through the mirror he would be able to invade her mind and figure out from her memories what she saw in the mirror, allowing him to see the location of the Wizard's Staff. Unless she looks through the mirror she will die from the curse eventually, or at least from what I gathered she would go insane and end up alone in the wilderness. I believe also that the Sorcerer is planning to attack Belvanor as a way of forcing Gwen to go to the mirrors."

"We can confirm that," a voice replied from behind them they turned to the voice seeing the Korazin walking in. They looked in worse shape than they were usually in. They walked into the room and stood along the outside wall with

Rade standing at the other end of the table, bowing respectably.

"You have news?" Aiden asked.

"Yes," Rade answered. "We have just come from Grimdor where we were surveying things, trying to estimate the number count of Borags and Spirits that are at the Sorcerer's disposal. We are unable to get a count, many more come every day."

"The weather patterns throughout different parts of the world have been catching our attention as it hasn't rained or snowed anywhere but *here* in the past month," another of the Korazin said.

"The rest of the world is a barren wasteland, dry and not improving. We believe that the Sorcerer is affecting the world's weather patterns to make it easier for him to attack the cities and towns he desires," Rade said. "Large numbers of Borags have been entering Giahon for some time. We estimate their numbers at one hundred and eighty thousand Borags, and Lathon knows how many Spirits must be in those ranks." Everyone's jaw dropped open in shock and they cried out in unbelief.

"The Sorcerer controls Giahon now?" Skander asked.

"Not surprising," Isabel interjected. "Giants have always been in the ranks of the vile. With them as his allies, he could strike at any moment." Rade nodded his agreement.

"Even as we speak there is a storm of immense size making its way along the southern coast of Giahon," Rade continued. On the other side of the storm, the sea is frozen. If we are right, the hosts of Grimdor will walk on the frozen sea and circumnavigate the Grass Canyons, so as to not repeat their last failure.

"Are you sure of this?" Aiden asked.

"There is no doubt in our mind," Rade replied. "If he does as we expect he will enter Belvanor from the sea and use the Grass Canyons against you, trapping you within your own defenses."

"He must think we are still there," Ellizar concluded.

"Do not be deceived about his intentions," Isabel warned. "He seeks the Wizard's Staff. Nothing else. He seeks to harm Gwen to the point she cannot resist his curse."

"Should we take Gwen away?" Lily asked. "Far away where the Sorcerer can't find her?"

"It matters not where I am," Gwen admitted miserably. "His voice calls to me in the dark hours of the night. I can feel his presence, be he here, or a hundred miles away. Nothing will cure my misery."

"How long do you think until the hosts of Grimdor arrive?" Aiden asked.

"Two days at most," Rade said, thoughtfully.

"Is there no way that Gwen can look into the Sorcerer's mirror, to find the Wizard's Staff without the Sorcerer finding out?" Skander asked. "Even if he does find out, as long as we beat him to it we're okay, right."

Aiden raised an eyebrow. "It would be risky, but I suspect he would still attack anyway. If anything to use it as a distraction so that *we* wouldn't be able to leave to go find it. I think if we look for it, we'll go to the mirrors after the battle, right now though we have no other choice but to head back to Belvanor immediately and help prepare," Aiden replied.

"How are we supposed to fight a battle against such a large force?" Drake asked.

"We take our troops and attack them," Aiden answered plainly. "The walls of Belvanor will not easily fall. The Gogs will not aid us in this attack, but they will be very important in the days to come."

Isabel stood decidedly and wrapped a coat around her. "Then, let's not waste any more time."

It was nightfall of the first day when they arrived at the Belvanor. The Korazin had taken the forms of Taruks, speeding them all on their way. They landed at the palace gates and then were graced with the humorous sight of Ellizar trying to push his way through three feet of snow. The Korazin wished them goodbye and took to the sky, heading out to spy on the armies of Grimdor.

Gabrielle and Atruss, though alarmed with the news that they brought, immediately began making preparations. The citizens of the city who were unable to fight were sent out to the *House of Refuge*, which was a large cave system that filled the Grass Canyons to the north.

Though it was not a perfect solution, it would keep the woman and children alive. If it was needed they could follow the caves to the north for many days and from there they could escape into the wilderness.

The dawn of the second day came and Rade returned with news that did little to cheer their hearts. Tremin led the armies of Grimdor, which were coming over the sea, just as the Korazin had predicted. The army brought with them siege towers and other weapons of war, as well as a single cart with Rohemir chained to it.

Over the two days they had been back at Belvanor, Isabel worked on many things, though she hardly stepped foot in the palace. Often Isabel and Drake would conveniently run into each other in the street, or in some strange place.

Gwen, on the other hand, became harder and harder to manage. Often she would wander off alone, only to be found somewhere by herself. Sometimes still she would burst out in anger and then collapse into tears as soon as she came back to her senses. Drake hated having to see her in so much pain, but he tried to comfort her to the best of his abilities.

By nightfall of the second day, Belvanor was silent. In all that time, the snow had not stopped and now they found themselves buried beneath several feet of it. Though the snow dampened their spirits, it did little to slow the advance of the approaching army. The snow melted and dried up moments before the hosts of Grimdor would put their feet down.

The soldiers of Ariamore waited patiently, watching the procession of torches move toward the waiting city. Their catapults were ready and the barrels and projectiles were waiting to be launched over the wall and into the opposing army.

For the moment only the silence could harm them.

The black banners of Grimdor, which were fitted with red trim and the mark of the Sorcerer in their middle, seemed to glow in the night. Tremin rode proudly at the front with two others flanking him on each side.

Meanwhile, Lily was still trying to catch up with the fact that Isabel was his mother. Everyone was full of surprises, reminding Lily once again that you could never judge a book by its cover. Isabel was more than an eccentric shopkeeper. Just as Lily was more than just an elf.

Her thoughts were drowned out as the army stopped just out of bow range. They stood there for an amount of time that no one cared to measure. Whether they were daunted by the sight of Belvanor, being ready for the battle, or waiting for the order from the Sorcerer to attack, Lily didn't have a clue.

Tremin made no move to speak to any of them and instead, the night was filled with the sickening cry of Borags, calling out their chants and taunts in their hideous language.

Aiden came close to her. "Get ready."

Lily nodded and descended the stairs to her left. She ran through the street for fifty feet, until an opening in the ground was before her. Lily entered into the chasm, which descended sharply into the ground. Originally for supplies, this shaft now boasted a brand new addition.

The tunnel continued to the left but another branch had been recently dug (in the past couple of months) by the Dwarves who lived in Belvanor. This one was only four and a half feet tall. Ellizar stood at the entrance, holding a torch.

"Are you ready?" Lily asked. Ellizar smiled and laughed a far more jovial laugh than she would have expected, seeing the danger that was present.

"Ov course I'll be careful! I'm a dwarf after all. Yer the one who needs teh be careful."

"Be careful," she reminded.

"Don't you worry Lily, I'll be out to join yeh soon. I can't let yer life be borin' now can I?"

"Listen for the horn, Ellizar." She smiled and gave him a wink as she went back the way she had come. She came alongside Aiden, looking out at the sea of Borags.

"Everything good?" Aiden asked. Lily nodded. Tremin yelled something in the dark and hideous language of the Borags, to which they replied with thunderous cries, which pierced the hearts of everyone present.

As if a spell had been cast upon them, the soldiers of Ariamore shrank back, and in their hearts, they began to despair. They eyed each other warily as if suddenly thinking ill of their brothers in arms.

Sensing this Aiden stepped forward, and faced the men atop the wall. He spoke loud and clear as if a different spell was cast. The shadows and doubts were moved from the minds and hearts of those present. A great cry went up from the walls of Belvanor, and the horns of Grimdor echoed loudly. Aiden turned to Lily, somehow instilling the same hope in her as had been instilled in the soldiers behind them.

Lily grasped a horn from her belt and blew a single note loudly.

"Here we go!"

Ellizar could hear the shouts of the army and the pounding of their feet which shook the ground. Several other Dwarves were with him. The tunnel continued to the left and the right with multiple shafts that went straight away from the city.

Ellizar had never been tasked with building such a tunnel in such a short amount of time, but the Dwarves of Ariamore had proved to be hardy and worked quickly, despite the odds. Now each of them stood at the head of their shafts, a lit torch, waiting to fall to the trail of powder that had been put down.

Though not a part of their original plan, strange visitors during the night of the second day had come with carts of the strange mixture and instructed them on how to use it. They had given the visitors beds and food for the night, but by the time morning came they had gone.

The cries of the soldiers in Belvanor encouraged him, The horn was called 'Elan', and where it had been crafted neither of them knew. Not long after, the silence was broken by a note that had never been known in that part of the world.

Though Lily had carried the horn for as long as he had known her, she had never blown it. In the moments that followed he heard the strong, sweet sound of Lily's horn.

All the Dwarves in the tunnel looked in his direction and on his nod, began counting loudly in the native Dwarvish tongue. The footsteps of the Grimdorian army thundered on the frozen ground.

"Thorogard!" Ellizar called. The dwarf dropped his torch and ran in his direction.

"Grimkil." Ellizar yelled. The farthest dwarf on the other side of the tunnel dropped his torch. As each one reached the next, another torch was dropped. They all came to him and Ellizar dropped his torch, lighting the trail of powder that caught fire with frightening intensity.

They ran back up to the main city, joining with the other Dwarves on the wall, just in time to see the ground rising beneath the Borags in a stunning display of fire and smoke.

VII · FIRE & ICE

Everyone atop the wall dropped to the ground as an explosion greater than any they had ever seen filled the area in front of Belvanor. Machines of war, Borags, and supplies that had been over the stockpiles of the strange substance were sent into the air.

"Wow!" Lily said, hardly able to get the words out. Aiden stood, and Isabel came running up to them as the smoke cleared. Where once had been an open field, now only a massive crater and wreckage remained. Hundreds, if not a thousand Borags had been destroyed in a matter of a second.

To their wonder and astonishment, Tremin was still standing. He glared at them from his place, which had been unaffected by the inferno. The Borags who had not been destroyed, remained where they were, seeming afraid to continue.

"What power has kept him alive?" Lily asked.

"Spirits, Mage's, Enchanters. The Sorcerer has legions of them in his ranks," Isabel answered. "This is the moment of truth. Now, we'll find out how many Magicians he has with him," Isabel explained.

The wind and snow stopped and within seconds the ground was dry. Lily watched in horror as the ground and bits of dust, piece by piece, began to shift and move until land bridges over the crater had been formed.

"Okay, he has a lot of Dark Arts people," Isabel said, plainly.

"How can we stand against this?" Lily asked, beginning to despair. Already the land bridges were done and Tremin was calling to his troops in the horrid tongue that only they knew.

"By remembering who we serve!" Aiden declared, yelling loud enough to be heard by anyone within earshot. "Stand your ground!" Siege towers, which had been destroyed, reassembled themselves. Eagerly the Borags poured onto the ramps that led to the top of the towers. Giants came up through the ranks and pushed against the siege machines. Slowly the giant structures began inching over the land bridges, towards Belvanor.

"Get ready!" Aiden yelled. Lily repeated the command. The men on the wall stood to arms finding the necessary courage to face their enemies. "Catapults, release on my command!" The soldiers atop the wall, stood next to the release, watching and waiting. Aiden looked at Lily and nodded.

Once again she blew powerfully on the horn, its note ringing into the night.

Immediately, the catapults were released. Rocks and projectiles of immense size sailed through the air. The night sky hid the flying objects, leaving the Grimdorian army to panic in anticipation.

At the same time the archers, fired upon the Borags, taking out many.

"The Spirits are giving his troops unnatural stamina." Isabel pointed out the Giants who had been peppered with arrows continued to move as though nothing had happened.

"What do we do about this?" Lily asked.

"I'll be back," Isabel said cryptically. She hurried off into the city, leaving Lily and everyone else to stare at the siege towers which were inching closer.

Drake watched from his hiding spot, within one of two supply tunnels. Built in an age long past, the entrance by the sea had been made in such a way that it was invisible to the untrained eye.

The tunnels ran underground, from the sea to the city square of Belvanor. The passage had been little used in the recent decade and very little, if at all in the past year or two. They were hopeful that Tremin would not know about it, and so far that seemed to be the case as regiment after regiment of Borags passed them by.

The sea was ice and, despite the losses from explosions, the end of the army didn't seem to be in sight. Rade stood alongside Drake, while some of the Korazin were with Skander who was in the other supply tunnel across the battlefield.

"How long do we wait?" Drake asked, his nerves starting to get the best of him.

"Rade!" a voice called out. Drake jumped in surprise, as Isabel appeared next to them. "Where would the Sorcerer place magicians or Mage's?" Rade thought for a moment.

"I'm honestly surprised he hasn't just sent Spirits to level the city," Rade commented.

"Isn't he just trying to send Gwen insane?" Drake asked. Rade and Isabel nodded. "If we can take out the Spirits then we may gain the upper hand."

"There's only seven of us," Rade reminded.

"Yeah, and there's a lot of army sitting on the frozen sea."

As if Rade had come to some kind of realization, the purple ring on his hand began to glow brighter.

"All you've got to do is break the ice," Isabel said.

"Exactly!" Drake exclaimed. "The Spirits will be so busy fighting you, that they won't be able to focus their energy on us."

"I like the sound of this," Rade said. He looked to one of the other Korazin, who nodded in approval. "Drake, get back to that second door and do something to hinder the siege ramps. My brothers and I can take care of this."

"Is someone going to tell Skander?" Drake asked.

"Don't worry, we can get word to him," Rade said with a smile. Somehow Drake sensed that it was the first time he had done so in several years.

"Yes sir," Drake said, urging his company back to the second entrance to the tunnel. Once they exited, they would be two hundred yards from the walls of

Belvanor.

They quickly reached the second door and then waited, watching the slow progression of the siege towers and the army. Under the command of the Spirits in Tremin's charge, the ground was still rebuilding itself. But it was slow and muddy (now that all the snow had melted), making it difficult for the giants to push the siege towers forward.

"I need to go check on Gwen," Isabel said. "What are you going to do about the siege towers?"

"I'm thinking," was Drake's only reply.

"Think quickly." Isabel turned and left, and the elf in his command, Toross, came up.

"What is the plan, sir?"

"We need to stop the siege ramps."

"Yes, I know that, but how? The giants have already taken many arrows and yet they do not slow."

"If I asked how many soldiers you thought were on top, what would you say?"

"Twenty at least," Toross replied. The silence hung in the air. The elf looked at him in bewilderment. "You're not serious?"

"Oh, I most certainly am!" Drake replied with a mischievous smile. Toross's face was still showing his shock. Drake stifled a laugh. "Tell the others."

Toross quickly did as he had ordered and soon everyone was waiting for Rade.

In an instant curses and shouts of exclamation rose from the back of the army. The Korazin rushed in, staying low to the ground and leaving a trail of fire on the ice.

Tremin and the company halted and Drake and his men seized the opportunity and ran out into the cratered ground, unnoticed. For the moment all eyes were on Rade.

Drake and his men ran to the front of the siege ramps and began climbing the gridlocked pattern of logs until finally they decisively overwhelmed the unsuspecting Borags.

The sea to the south was filled with fire as the remaining portion of the Grimdorian army was surrounded. Cries came from within the flames as the Spirits and Magicians tried desperately to defeat the continuing harassment of the Korazin.

A minute later the Spirits and Magicians were defeated and the ice broke beneath the Borags and they drowned in the sea.

Drake spotted Tremin, who had been blind to the fact that every siege tower was now not in his control. Slowly the procession began moving forward as the trolls, who had also been blind to everything they had done, resumed their task of pushing the heavy machines.

"I must say I did not think this would work!" Toross exclaimed, a smile on his face. "Should we signal the soldiers on the wall so they won't shoot us?"

"No. Stay down and out of sight. We need them to keep shooting, so no one suspects," Drake replied. Toross nodded.

"Won't they be surprised!"

"Towers!" Aiden yelled. "Lily! You take that tower and I'll take this one!"

"Alright!" Lily yelled in reply. Turning her attention from the scores of Borags that were now beginning to gather at the gates. "Men to arms!"

The bows that they had been using were slung on their backs, and each soldier drew their sword.

"Be ready!" came Aiden's cry as the siege towers came to a stop. They waited impatiently and when the gate was opened it revealed Drake Thomas and ten other men all crouched down out of sight. Everyone smiled and chuckled as the sight was repeated everywhere a siege tower had come to rest.

"Good to see you, Drake!" Lily greeted. Ellizar came running up for only a moment, laughing heartily at the sight.

"Yer the best lookin' Borag I've ever seen!" Ellizar exclaimed.

"Thanks, I think."

Aiden came up to them. "Split in two groups. Half of you are now being sent into the battle outside the walls, the other half will remain here and be ready should they break through our defenses!" Lily and Ellizar were the first to go down the ramp.

The battle continued for hours and hours until finally, the skies began to lighten, though dark grey clouds warned of another coming storm. The ground, muddy and cratered made fighting difficult and getting anywhere quickly, cumbersome.

The sword of a Borag struck Lily across the chest, but the impact did nothing but put a dent in her armor and his sword. The Borag lunged forward and took hold of her. Lily tried to break free of his grasp but failed to do so. Lily gasped for breath as her strength began to fade.

Gwen cursed to herself as she walked mindlessly down street after street. She wasn't supposed to be here. Her mind slipped further and further away from her, driven mad by the curses placed on her.

A powerful urge had taken control of her as she no longer had the strength left to fight the curse. She had to look for the Wizard's Staff. She *had* to try and put an end to this. The only reason that any of this was happening was because the others had convinced her that she shouldn't look in the mirror. She had made the wrong choice.

The sounds from the world around her faded and a whisper echoed inside her head. She cried as, step after step, she was driven mad by the man who had done this to her.

Isabel came around the corner, looking at Gwen strangely. They held eye contact for only a few seconds before Gwen turned and began stumbling her way to the south walls, where she knew the siege towers would be.

The siege ramps even hours later were still well-defended, allowing people who needed a break from the battle, to rest as they needed to. Gwen pushed her way up the ramps, hoping to lose Isabel in the crowds. Her venture failed and she soon found Isabel walking only a few feet behind her.

"Don't do it, Gwen!" Isabel yelled.

"I am going to do it!" Gwen yelled back. "I'm going to look in the mirror and get us all out of this battle."

"You can't believe anything Merderick says," Isabel warned.

"I just want to be free...that's all. I want to have a normal life and if looking into a mirror is all it takes then I'll do it in a second!"

"Don't do this Gwen, don't throw yourself away! There's a better way. You just have to trust me."

"I can trust no one right now!" Gwen replied, nearly screaming from the pain she felt. "I can't even trust myself. I have to do this or I'll die. The life is fading from me."

"Gwen, I won't let you do this."

"I'm doing it anyway," Gwen snapped, walking away. Isabel shifted.

"Guards, bring her!" Gwen took off running and a group of five soldiers began chasing her. They caught up with her, pressing her up against the wall. Isabel strode forward, a different light in her eyes.

"You're not going to the mirrors Gwen," Isabel said. "You're coming with me." Isabel grabbed her by the arm and the soldiers followed.

VIII   DOUBLE CROSSED

Drake rolled out of the way, the sword barely missing him. He leapt to his feet, only to be knocked backward, falling onto one of his fallen comrades. He had fought dozens if not hundreds of people throughout the night and he knew this Borag had a weakness, he just had to figure out what it was.

Time faded until they were the only two people in the battle, each one willing his mind to win the stare-down contest that they had started. The Borag's eyes narrowed. Drake widened his eyes and let his mouth open as if something was behind the Borag. Drake knew that the Borag had believed his rouse because his expression lightened. Drake seized the opportunity and lunged forward with his sword.

His enemy blocked the attack and kicked Drake in the side. Drake stumbled, trying to keep his footing as fallen Borags and soldiers covered the ground. The beast swung again. Drake dropped low and swept his foot along the ground.

The Borag was swept off his feet sending the sword flying. Drake pulled an arrow from one of the fallen and struck his enemy down. The Borag struggled for a moment and then went still.

Drake rose to his feet, unable to understand a hatred that was so deep. Each person that he killed, made him hate war. He had heard stories of the Borags raiding towns on their way to a battle and killing everyone and everything in sight. In their wake was a wasteland, left to rot away until it was no more.

Lathon had called them to be different from the rest of the world just as he had been, and he had warned that it would come at a high cost. Every day was a battle and although the past couple of months had been peaceful, Drake knew that someone would have to stand against their enemies. Even now, Drake didn't hate his enemy, he simply wished to live.

Drake carefully worked his way towards the center of the battlefield, searching. His job had been to save Rohemir. His thoughts and feelings on Rohemir were still confused and complicated, but now he had every reason to believe that Rohemir was on their side.

He ran as fast as he could, slaying several Borags along the way. The scar on his hand turned to ice, warning him of a danger that he could not see. The world faded and he was forced to stop as something held him against his will.

The sound of the battle subsided from his mind and he heard a foul voice instead. Even though Drake couldn't understand the words he knew they were filled with ill intentions. As if the voice gave up trying to control him, his mind came back to normal and he found himself standing in the middle of the battle.

One moment faded into the next and how much time passed, he didn't know. A few minutes later Drake finally spied a small wooden cart.

Rohemir.

Drake sprinted towards the cart, which was nothing more than a simple flatbed cart with shackles and chains around his ankles and wrists. Drake's heart warned him of a threat that he couldn't see. He rushed forward, his fears confirmed when a flash of steel came from his right. He tried to twist out of the way but was unable as a sword grazed his arm.

Drake quickly regained his composure and rushed towards him, and Tremin easily blocked the attack and then proceeded to unleash his own. Weariness consumed Drake as everything Tremin had done in the past couple of months flashed through his head. Drake secretly wished for the opportunity to destroy the man who had kidnapped Gwen several months ago.

A roar was heard in the sky above and Drake stole a glance at the grey skies, which were now filled with the pale light of the morning.

A Taruk flew towards them, red in color, instilling a sense of fear in Drake's heart. It wasn't Destan or Elohim. Drake called for both of them with his mind and continued to fight Tremin.

The sound of Taruks echoed through the battlefield. Destan and Elohim decsended on top of their enemy. The Sorcerer's Taruk fell onto the ground rolling and crushing troops beneath.

The Taruk was quick to get to its feet and take flight again, heading directly towards the gates of Belvanor. Destan and Elohim gave chase and at once were within striking distance of the Taruk. Destan reached out and grabbed the Sorcerer's Taruk by the tail throwing the beast off balance as he flew.

Destan released the tail, not leaving the red Taruk enough time to adjust his flight path. The Taruk crashed into the wall of the castle and then fell to the ground. In surprise, the red Taruk took flight with the others pursuing him.

Drake darted to the left to avoid a blow that had been sent at his chest. Instinctively, Drake spun around and swung first, reversing his direction.

Tremin was up to the challenge and easily deflected Drake's attack as they went faster and faster. Tremin snarled and thrust his sword out at Drake's face. Drake moved out of the way, but not before a stinging sensation filled Drake's cheek.

Drake leapt forward but found that by the time he had reached his destination his enemy had moved and Drake was sent flailing forward. He landed on his feet but then fell to his face as Tremin tripped him. Drake's sword scattered to his left ten feet. Drake scrambled to get to the sword but stopped when a dagger entered the ground near his hand. He looked up to see Tremin gloating.

"Nice try Drake Thomas, but if you try to grab that sword again, I can promise you that the next dagger won't land in the dirt...Admit you're defeated and let me kill you. I'll forever be known as the one who killed Drake Thomas, Sherados."

Drake froze, his mind going numb with fear as Tremin pulled back his sword and prepared to swing. Drake's hand twitched, waiting for the moment to make his move. Tremin began to swing and Drake rushed to grab the dagger which had embedded itself in the ground near where his hand had been.

He threw the dagger at Tremin, but it was easily swiped aside by his sword. Tremin drew his sword back but never got the chance to swing it as his arm was pulled back and twisted around until it snapped. A moment later, Tremin's limp body fell to the ground.

Drake looked to the person who had saved him. He stood tall and proud, but at first glance, Drake couldn't tell if he was human or elf. He was dressed as a soldier would be, but even with that, it was difficult to tell what color it was or which army he belonged to. He held Drake's sword out to him.

Drake took his sword that the man held out to him. The longer Drake looked, the more Drake was overwhelmed by a sense of familiarity.

"Thank you," Drake said.

"You're most welcome Mr. Thomas," the man answered. Chills ran up and down Drake's spine as he recognized the voice but couldn't manage to place it. "It would be useless to try and get this man free Mr. Thomas." As if reading Drake's thoughts the man continued. "The chains that hold him are linked to the life force of the army. Only when the army surrenders or decides to retreat will Rohemir's chains be released."

"What is your name?" Drake asked.

"My name does not matter at the moment, all that matters is that we end this battle and end it quickly! The more time that passes, the more danger we're in." Without offering another word of explanation the man vanished into the battle.

"Drake!" A voice called out. Drake drew his sword and swung to his left. A frightened yelp came from a wolf that scurried out of the way. His heart was filled with relief as Willard and Miles came up to him.

"That almost ended badly," Willard said.

"Sorry."

"So Tremin's dead?" Miles asked. Drake nodded his answer. *"I'm sorry to hear that. I can only imagine how Isabel will take the news."*

Drake silently kicked himself, having forgotten that Tremin was Isabel's son.

On that note, however, we came to find you!" Miles exclaimed.

"Is something wrong?"

"Maybe. Have you seen Gwen lately?"

Drake thought for a moment. "She's with Isabel."

"We saw her being forcibly led through the city streets by several guards and Isabel."

"Are you certain?"

"She was tied and gagged," Willard informed.

"Isabel's a traitor?" Drake asked, his anger and fear rising.

"We only know what we saw," Miles started. *"We don't know any more of the story than what we told you."*

"Where do you think she was taken?" Drake asked. Willard gave him a look.

"Only one place that I can think of."

"The Wingy Wares?" Drake said aloud. Willard and Miles nodded their agreement. Drake replayed the events of the past couple of weeks, noting that the curse that had been put on Gwen would force her to look into the mirror for the Wizard's Staff, the one thing the Sorcerer needed to crush the world beneath his feet.

He also knew that Isabel had one.

All the mysteries that had been unsolved about Isabel were now rushing into his mind and occupying every last second of it. He had been wrong and now they would end up paying for it.

"We need to get to the Wingy Wares."

The three of them left at once, as they entered back into the supply tunnel that he had been in at the start of the battle. A few minutes later, they exited the tunnel and entered into the city.

Much to his dismay, Borags filled the streets, attacking and killing anyone they pleased. The horrors of war were everywhere. They had held the siege towers under their control for hours, but now it looked like they had failed.

They passed by alley after alley and street after street and then rounded the last corner and came to the street of Isabel's shop.

The street was empty. Drake looked first to Willard and then to Miles and then listened to the silence that consumed the alley. Even the sounds of the war were out of their reach from this part of the city.

In the silence, they could hear crying and each of them knew it was Gwen. Miles yelped in surprise as flowering vines broke free of the alleys and buildings to either side of them and wrapped themselves around Willard and Miles pulling them to the sides. Drake drew his sword and slashed at the vines, but found that they were hard as iron and would not break.

Suddenly, a vine began to wrap itself around his ankle, but before it had a chance to tighten its grip Drake was gone. The vines turned in his direction, growing with a speed that was unnatural in every respect. The vines closed in all around him, and the alley behind was filled with a blanket of green and flowering blossoms.

He leapt towards the porch on the front of the shop. Landing with a thud, he scrambled to his feet and closed himself inside the shop. The vines hit the door and seemed to hiss, before recoiling to the street.

Drake took a moment for his eyes to adjust to the lack of light. A cloud of fog hung low around his feet and rain poured from the ceiling. Drake tried not to dwell on the rain too much. He knew Isabel's shop (The Wingy Wares) was different from any other he had been in, but he hadn't imagined it would actually be raining inside a building.

His heart warned him of danger and he flinched several times as a couple of owls fluttered through the air, some of them just above his head. The sound of Gwen crying became more evident as Drake moved to the stairs, cautiously taking one step at a time.

Each step felt like a mile as the rain continued to fall. At last, he entered a room at the end, gradually bringing back the memory of several months ago. A large object remained covered at the end of the room, and Drake knew that it was a mirror like the Sorcerer's mirror.

Drake looked along the wall and spotted Gwen tightly bound by the same vines that had been chasing him. The rain still poured down and Gwen looked up and into his eyes.

Drake rushed forward, trying to cut the vines that held her. Gwen was gagged and looked as if she had been in there for a thousand years. Her skin was pale and dried and her eyes appeared hollow and empty.

"You won't free her Drake Thomas."

Drake tried to hold his emotions in line as he turned and faced Isabel who was standing at the other end of the hallway. Drake grabbed his sword but found that it was ripped from his grip, lost to the fog at his feet. Drake's heart sank, knowing that there was no way he would be able to find his weapons in time to protect himself.

"I've taken extra precautions to make sure that no one would be able to set her free," Isabel answered.

"Traitor!" Drake exclaimed, looking at Gwen and then at Isabel again. "What are you doing? Free her?"

"I can't do that Drake. This is for the good of everyone else. Remember what Aiden said about getting all the facts before you make up your mind."

"No. I don't have to do that because I already know that you're a traitor. You've kidnapped her and as soon as you have a moment-"

"You think you have it all figured out?"

"I don't think I have it all figured out, I know I have it all figured out. I will set her free and I will be coming to get you."

"No you won't," Isabel answered with such certainty it scared Drake. He started to move but was unable as the vines on the walls reached out and grabbed him, pulling him back towards the same wall that Gwen was held to. "I was hoping I wouldn't have to do that Drake, but you left me no choice. I'll be leaving you now, when the battle is over I'll be back. The more you try to escape the tighter the vines will get and the more you try to scream the more the sound will not be heard. If you know what's good for you, you won't try anything." She turned and left, leaving both him and Gwen tangled in the vines. The rain poured down and outside he knew the battle still raged.

Evening was upon them and Ellizar was weary of all the fighting that was associated with battle and war. He might be better off than he used to be, but that didn't mean he enjoyed fighting for his life. Each person he struck down, left a scar on his heart and mind.

The devastation in front of the castle was overwhelming. Fallen soldiers from both sides lay everywhere. Fires burned all around, some of them had been started by the Taruks, The sun, though it was setting, seemed far warmer than it should have been for this time of year. Ellizar didn't have to think twice to know that it was the Sorcerer's doing.

For most of the day, the southern sky had been filled with clouds that were dark and grey as the Sorcerer had tried to conjure up another storm to freeze the sea back over, likely to send reinforcements, but the Korazin had done everything in their power to make sure that it didn't happen. As a result, a normal-looking sky graced the sunset.

A great shadow fell over the part of the battlefield where Ellizar was standing. Elohim flew overhead and Aiden slid off Elohim and ran over to Ellizar.

"What news do ya bring?" Ellizar asked.

"It's almost over," Aiden said. Ellizar sighed, noticing for the first time that the battlefield was strangely quiet now. Few Borags were left alive and those who were fought carelessly

"Where are the others?" Ellizar asked. "I've been fighting for hours, and I haven't seen anyone. Not Skander, Drake, Gwen, Lily. None of them. Where are they?"

"I'm here!" Skander yelled from the distance. "Though I can't speak for the others."

"I'm sure we'll find them, but first we must finish this battle," Aiden directed. Together they went around and fought the last few Borags, and when the last one had fallen, Aiden pulled a horn from his belt and signaled that the battle was over.

Skander and Ellizar both collapsed to the ground, gratitude washing over them like water on the rocks.

"I can't believe we survived," Skander said.

"I had my doubts," Ellizar said.

"We were lucky today."

"Luck has nothing to do with it," Aiden replied.

"How else do you describe what happened here today?" Skander asked.

"The will of Lathon is how I describe it. Luck is just a loser's explanation for winning. There is no luck and no fate in this world, to believe in either of those is to say that you have no ability; to say at the end of the day nothing matters. We did pull off an incredible feat, but it was not luck, it was something greater than all of us watching from above."

They fell silent for a moment before Ellizar finally spoke. "I always have said I believe in Lathon, but sometimes I find it hard to believe that someone created all of this. The way people are wired these days they seem to not want to believe. The pagan religions of the world worship all sorts of gods but they never thank them for creating them. They teach that they all look over certain things, you know crops, weather, love, stuff like that. I know Lathon's real, but sometimes my doubts get the best of me."

"As they do any person," Aiden said, beginning to walk down the streets. "Everyone wants to think that someone is watching over them or else they wouldn't have wanted to create all those *gods* in the first place. In their hearts, they *want* to believe in something greater."

"How are we supposed to prove to them what we believe is true?" Skander asked.

"Out of all the gods that people have created, have any of them had prophets? Sure they all claim to have prophets but you know as well as I that they are all bogus. When you look at the prophecies about Lathon and Sherados and then you look at the two of them you can see how they match up to what was said about them and that's what makes it true."

"Who is Sherados?" Ellizar asked. "Is he among us now?"

"He's been among us for quite some time, and it'll only be a little longer before he comes forward. The world is about to change."

"Do you know who he is though?" Skander asked.

"I've done much research and I know for a fact that everyone here has met him, but beyond that, I cannot say."

"I hope he comes forward soon or else people might begin to lose faith." They walked through the city, and Ellizar became more and more concerned with each minute that passed. Nearly everyone else they knew came up to them and greeted them. Atruss and Gabrielle, but still Lily was nowhere to be found. He eagerly searched the battlefield, looking for any sign of Lily.

IX FRIENDS AND ENEMIES

Ellizar finally caught a glimpse of long black hair. Lily lay under a heap of Borags, with her face pressed into the muddy ground. Ellizar let out a cry as he pushed the Borags off her. He rolled her over fearing the worst.

His heart stirred and his hopes soared as he noticed her chest gently rising and falling with her breathing. He looked into her face. One of her eyes twitched. Ellizar wiped his eyes and gently put a hand against the side of her head.

She flinched from his touch and her mouth opened up in a silent groan. She raised her head for a moment and then laid it back down. A large bruise was over her left eye, but she opened them both and looked at him.
She gave him the only weak smile she could muster. Her breathing became a little more labored as she started to laugh.

"What are yeh laughin' about elf kind?" Ellizar asked, smiling wider than he had in a long time.

"Either I'm alive and being discovered by a weird, short, bad-tempered dwarf, or I've died and am being greeted by the ugliest angel I've ever seen." They laughed and he helped her sit up straight, finally embracing each other. They held each other for several moments.

"Out of all the faces that I hoped to see if I was to wake up, that was the one I wanted to see," Lily whispered.

Aiden and Skander quickly came running across the battlefield to where they were.

"I was starting to wonder where you had gotten to," Aiden said. Lily blinked and tried to get her eyes to adjust to the light that was all around her. She reached for her hand and pulled it away when she felt the touch of blood.

"I'm not sure I even remember what happened," Lily answered.

"So does anyone know where Drake is?" Aiden asked.

"I haven't seen him for a while, last thing I know he was fighting Tremin to free Rohemir," Lily replied.

"Rohemir," Aiden said. They quickly found the cart that Rohemir had been tied onto. Rohemir's chains were now undone and he sat on the edge of the cart looking as if he had just woken up from a long nap. Aiden quickly ran to his side, helping Rohemir to his feet.

"Good to have you back, did you find out anything before you were captured?"

"I don't remember anything. The last thing I remember is leaving here on horseback," Rohemir said.

"It doesn't matter what we remember or don't remember, Drake and Gwen are both missing," Aiden replied.

"The last time I saw Gwen she didn't look very good. She looked weak, as though a great sickness had come over her and the will to fight had left her," Lily answered.

"We know where she went then don't we?" Aiden asked. "Rohemir we need a favor of you."

"Anything you wish."

"While you have been captured there have been some developments and we believe that Gwen may be on her way to a fortress about three hundred miles northeast of here. I don't know what the city's name is, but she might be looking for a chamber that none should look for. One with mirrors."

"In that case, our time is short indeed. As soon as I can get a horse I will be on my way."

"You can take a little time to rest if you need it, seeing that you've been captured for so long."

"If you won't rest then there's no reason I should be able to.

They walked with Rohemir to the stables and got a horse. He mounted up and rode into the city streets and eventually out the gates and into the Grass Canyons, his horse having to take its time going through the large battlefield which would likely be strewn with corpses for a while.

Once he was out of their sight Aiden rested his hand on his sword.

"Where exactly do yeh plan on lookin' fer Gwen and Drake?" Ellizar asked.

"The only place that makes any sense," Aiden answered. "If my guess is correct, she is in the city and so is Drake. We just have to make our way to the east side."

"Isabel?" Skander asked confusion tainting his voice. "If you knew where she was, why did you send Rohemir on a wild goose chase?"

"The only reason I sent Rohemir to the fortress is because I'm not certain I'll find *her* in the city."

Aiden led them through the city and to the east side. Isabel's shop was up near the left and large vines stood to either side of the street. They were motionless and still, but Aiden watched them closely as if he expected them to do something.

Willard and Miles stood in the middle of the street, looking like they had seen a ghost. Aiden ran up to them with the others close on their heels. To their left and their right, they saw that the plants had been badly damaged by something or someone.

"It's about time you made it here," Willard said. "We've been trapped by these plants for quite some time."

"What kind of plants are these?" Ellizar asked.

"They're like none I've ever seen. They grow like wildfire and chase after you down the street. We accompanied Drake here as he searched for Gwen, but we got caught up. He managed to make it into the shop. He hasn't come out since."

Ellizar wasted no time, breaking into a mad dash towards the shop on the right. The others were quick on his heels, warning him to be careful in case there was some hidden danger. Ellizar ignored all their warnings.

Aiden ran up the stairs to the porch first and held a hand up to stop Ellizar and the others in his track. He turned towards the door and reached out to knock on it. Before his hand even reached the door it was opened, swinging inward and revealing Isabel standing in front of them.

"You look as if you've just seen a ghost," Isabel commented plainly.

"Maybe we have," Lily replied. "Have you seen Drake or Gwen?"

"Yes I have, they're right in here. I've had them tied up for several hours. For their own good." Isabel left the door open and began leading the way into the strange and mysterious shop. The door swung shut behind them and they were left in the darkness until their eyes adjusted to the lack of light.

A low bank of fog had settled into the shop, staying a few feet off the floor, clouding their vision of what was beneath. The air felt moist and damp, chilling them to the bone. They looked at the walls and everything else, their minds burning with curiosity as they noticed that it looked as if it had been raining. A moment later as if the rainstorm had suddenly vanished, sunlight began to break through the dark clouds that were overhead.

At the end of the room was a large object which was shielded from their sight, and to their left tied and held up by the flowering vines on the wall were Gwen and Drake.

Drake's eyes focused in on them, a new hope sparkling in his eyes while Gwen's were grey and clouded. Isabel waved her hand and the vines that held them in place released them and withdrew back to their place on the wall. Drake and Gwen fell onto the floor, nearly vanishing into the fog before Drake climbed to his feet.

Drake opened his mouth to speak but never got any words out as Gwen groveled on her hands and knees like a wild animal. She mumbled and muttered to herself, frantically looking from side to side.

"What's happening to her?" Drake asked.

"The curse is taking hold of her mind," Aiden answered. "I don't know what else we can do for her. We can't have her look into the Sorcerer's mirror, because otherwise the Sorcerer will know where the Wizard's Staff is."

"But if it would save her?" Drake asked, sounding hopeful.

"We cannot hope to believe anything that the Sorcerer says, Drake. His words are poison, dripping and blurring things in our minds until the very evil we sought to destroy is the very one that consumes us. Meddling with anything the Sorcerer makes or says, is dangerous. I know there must be a way to find the Wizard's Staff and release her of the curses, but at the moment I cannot see the light at the end of the tunnel."

"I wish there was something we could do," Lily said.

"Then let us all put our minds together and not rest until we find a way."

Nightfall came and still, they hadn't come any closer to coming up with a solution to their problem. Drake looked around the dark shop, having chosen to stay here for the night instead of joining the others back at the palace. His body ached and groaned with every movement he made, sore from the battle as well as being held in place by the plants that Isabel had commanded to wrap him up earlier in the day.

Gwen was still muttering and mumbling to herself, held to the ground by the flowering vines and breaking Drake's heart with each second that passed. Gwen meant so much to him and to see her like she was caused him so much pain he wished for nothing more than to go to the first mirror he came to and find the Wizard's Staff himself.

Drake climbed up from his spot and then moved to the door, stepping outside for a little bit of fresh air. The air was crisp and cool, but to Drake's surprise it was nothing like winter should be. This time yesterday there had been a couple of feet of snow covering the ground, now the ground was bare and the air was cool, feeling more like autumn.

The Sorcerer's power struck fear into Drake's heart. It seemed every day the Sorcerer was doing something to make life harder for his enemies. He could control entire weather patterns. With that kind of power, Drake's courage and determination withered.

Drake's mind drifted; Sherados was supposedly among them now. Drake had been paying extra close attention to the people he interacted with in the past couple of weeks, but the answer still eluded him.

Tremin had told him that he was Sherados and Drake was half tempted to believe him. If that's what Tremin had thought then there was a good chance that the Sorcerer thought that, which gave Drake more enemies than he cared to think about.

Drake's attention was diverted from his thoughts as music interrupted the silent night. He listened, noticing it was someone humming. The music put a smile on Drake's face but also sparked a little bit of curiosity as he carefully stepped off the porch and began moving to the sound.

It only took a matter of minutes before Drake rounded a corner and came into a small alley where a campfire was burning. Isabel sat at the side of the fire in a chair with an easel and a paint tray before her.

The smoke from the fire drifted into the sky, whisked away by the slight breeze that moved through the city. Isabel seemed not to notice him as she painted and hummed to herself. Eventually, she stopped painting and turned to look at him.

"Welcome Drake Thomas. What are you doing up at this time of night?"

"I could ask you the same thing," Drake replied. To that, Isabel just smiled.

"I'm painting of course. I would've thought that would be obvious."

Drake couldn't hide a smile. "I know you are painting, but it's the middle of the night...that's a little unusual."

"No, what's unusual is painting during the middle of the day. I find painting relaxes me and is a good release for the troubles and sorrows that I've faced during the day, or my life. I sometimes can't sleep during the night, so then I paint. I can do it outside during the nighttime because anyone who is normally afraid of me is asleep. I can walk through the city without anyone caring at all."

"That makes sense I guess," Drake concluded. "What tune were you humming?"

"An old tune that my father sang to me when I was falling asleep. Never understood it as a kid," Isabel commented. "But it's been heavy on my mind lately."

"Does it have words?"

"Yes, but they can be hard and confusing. With talk of Vemroliet trees, one can hardly expect it to be a good conversation." She laughed.

"Are Vemroliet trees even real?"

"It matters not right now. Come see what I've been working on." He came around and looked at what she was painting. The colors melted into each other creating an abstract picture.

"I hope you don't mind me asking, but what is it? I know it's a painting but I can't seem to make out what it's supposed to be."

"This is called a Trayven," Isabel answered. "Or at least it's my version of a Trayven. Before Lathon sent us prophets, the Elves were very skilled at these particular paintings. They would change their picture every day, often foretelling of things that hadn't happened yet. It was a way for us to see into the future and if we didn't like what we saw then we would do what we could to change the future."

"Where did you learn to paint like this?" Drake asked.

"My mother taught me. She was a very busy person, but she always managed to make time for me, which meant so much inside my heart. Some people never get that."

"Do you think that this painting might help us figure out how to help Gwen?"

"It's a possibility, although a Trayven usually won't tell you anything specific about the future and not necessarily about you. The first one I ever painted as a young child, told me what day of the week would happen tomorrow. Not the most useful, but for my age I was very proud of it. To answer your question though, I think that help is on the way."

"You do?" Drake asked. Isabel nodded.

"I've sensed that there's someone in the city who's waiting for the right moment. When the time is right, he'll have a solution to our problem."

An hour or so passed before Drake found himself awake and then saw that Isabel was sleeping next to the fire. He stood and brushed himself off, moving over to the painting that she had been working on.

He sat in her chair and stared at the blurred blob of color, doubting that the painting had any sort of unique qualities about it. After a minute or so the colors began to shift and form different shapes which caught Drake's attention and held his gaze for several minutes. He had no idea what he was seeing but the sight was enough to put chills on his spine.

Eventually, the vision that the painting had created, changed and turned nearly all black. Drake noticed the surroundings as Isabel's shop. Gwen was still tied up to the wall and a man entered and walked briskly through the shop.

Drake's heart nearly leapt from his chest and his mind raced, wondering if he was seeing things as they happened or if this was something that would happen in the future. Unable to help himself he bolted from his spot and ran towards the house. Isabel meanwhile remained asleep by the undying fire.

As far as Drake could tell the vision he had seen in Isabel's Trayven the previous night had been something that wouldn't happen immediately. He had run back to the shop just as fast as he could, only to keep himself awake for hours and hours on end and find that no one was coming.

He had fallen to sleep, wondering who the man was. Drake had seen him somewhere, but as hard as he tried he couldn't place the man's face. Isabel had come back in the morning, bringing her picture along with her.

Drake looked at the picture, again fascinated by it. If they always showed him something of the future he would be painting night and day in hopes that he would learn who Sherados was, or who he was for a matter.

The second option was one that Drake was struggling with every day. Who was he, really? Except for the past four or five months, he had no history and he didn't expect to ever remember anything before that.

For a little while Drake amused himself with wondering what might happen in the future. After the war was over what would he do with the rest of his life? Would he be serving some great king, or would he be a king himself?

Maybe he would travel around to the different nations and see and learn all that he possibly could. Maybe he would become a Tarukai and try his hand at that. Maybe still, he would find a nice little town and settle down and live the 'normal' life.

As much as Drake wished to do all of those things there was one thing he wished to do more than any other. He wanted to find his family and he couldn't think of any better way to spend the rest of his life. He may not be able to remember anything about his family, but there had to be someone, somewhere who would remember his parents and the lives they had lived.

He wanted to meet them and find out who they were and try to piece together the pieces of the puzzle that at the moment were eluding him. His mind and his heart failed to agree on this one thing, his mind not sure if he would want to know. What if he found out his parents were friends of the Sorcerer, or had been killed by him? How would Drake live his life then?

He sat up from his spot on the floor and moved to the small kitchen. Isabel was already making a small breakfast and the smell of it certainly aroused Drake's senses and cleared his mind of the fog that had occupied it.

Soon there were plates of hot food waiting to be eaten. As soon as the last plate had been set on the large dining room table Aiden entered, with Lily, Skander, and Ellizar right behind him. They released Gwen from the wall for several minutes trying to convince the mumbling and muttering woman to come eat the food that had been made.

Gwen barely heard them and continued wandering through the house on all fours, convulsing as though someone had been torturing her for hours and hours. Drake turned away and ate his food, trying to block out the sound of her voice.

They finished their meal and sat watching and looking at Gwen who was acting more like a wild animal with each second that passed, the curse now taking a large toll on her. She cursed herself and ripped at her clothes. She pulled at her hair and smacked the floor with her fist.

"What are we supposed to do?" Drake asked. The others watched but didn't reply.

"Perhaps I might be of assistance!" a voice said from behind them. Light flooded into the shop for several moments before the front door was shut. Drake shivered and looked at the others knowing that they didn't recognize him. Drake had only met him on one other occasion and that was during the battle. He walked confidently and with an authority Drake felt was unmatched by almost everyone in the shop. As if it had been commanded all hints of darkness left the room.

His face was just as it had been when Drake had seen him during the battle, but still, there was something about the man that was unnerving. Drake still couldn't tell if he was human or elf, but maybe it didn't matter.

"You're the one who killed Tremin during the battle yesterday," Drake said. He watched the other's faces light up with the revelation. The man looked at him, his bright green eyes piercing Drake's soul.

"Yes, I am the one who killed Tremin during the battle yesterday, but it is not the first time you and I have met. It's a shame you can't bring yourself to remember."

"The first time was-"

"We met nearly five months ago in a little town that is no more. A town called Fiori. Perhaps you remember a particularly narrow escape where I woke you up and urged you and your friends to leave!"

"How did I not see it before?" Drake asked.

The man's expression softened and a smile tugged at his lips. "Let this be a moment of learning for everyone!" As Drake listened to him speak, he couldn't deny there was something about the man that was powerful. His words were comforting. "You may know me as Michael," the man said. "But it is not I who am here to help you, rather I bring a person who may be able to help."

He stepped aside and another person came forward. He was tall and lean, with long black hair.

"Have we seen you before?" Skander asked.

"We have met in Fiori."

"Fiori?" Ellizar asked.

"Yes. I was sent to kill Mr. Thomas. I took the form of a woman to do so. However, Rohemir stopped me."

"I don't believe it," Ellizar said.

"I wouldn't expect a dwarf to understand," the man said. A cloud of blue mist appeared for a short second and then it took the form of the beautiful woman that they all remembered from that night so long ago. "Now do you believe me?" In an instant, he changed form back into the man. "My name is Cerin."

"You're a Spirit," Ellizar concluded.

"Your intelligence astounds me," Cerin replied.

"It astounds us at times too," Lily said. Ellizar gave her an amusing look but for once let the matter go.

"How is this possible?" Skander asked. "I thought all Spirits served the Sorcerer?"

"Tremin, was my master since I was first discovered. Whatever you may have been told about Spirits, we are bound to the Sorcerer by certain curses. However, there are a few exceptions to the rule.

"We were once people of Grimdor, but we wanted away from it. We tried everything we could think of, but the Sorcerer was too strong for us to stand a chance. He killed our bodies and used his dark arts on our souls, making us who we are today. Unless we wish to stop living entirely we must fight for him, or someone else."

"How can you help us?" Drake asked.

"It seems that I am the leader of the Spirit nation of Vernal," Cerin started. "A powerful position. To this day I am the only one of our kind who has ever been allowed the privilege of seeing the Sorcerer face to face, years before he would return to the Earth. Seeing I had this special privilege, the Sorcerer for whatever reason, thought that he should redo my curse and make it slightly more flexible since he would be spending more time with me than the rest of my kind."

"When he said the spell he made a mistake, although it took me until just recently to understand the implications of his mistake. The long and short of it is this...the spell states that I must fight for him and the nation of Grimdor, but only if he specifies that before the battle or war, he wants me to fight."

"So you can fight for us?" Lily asked.

"For the moment. The rest of the Spirits are likely not aware of this small loophole. If the Sorcerer catches on to this mistake then I will be of no help to you. He is too busy planning his revenge on the world and the people of Lathon. Too blinded by his anger and hatred to see the small mistake at the moment. Until he figures it out I will help you in any way that I can. I can tell you everything he's doing and everything he's planning on doing. We must start with Ms. Gwen.

"The Sorcerer has put her under a curse correct?" They all nodded. "I thought so. Another fortunate thing about the spell the Sorcerer put on me is that we can now share thoughts and information through our minds. He can give me orders from anywhere he wishes no matter where I am. Usually, when humans try to do magic they cannot reach someone's mind unless they are nearby, which shows you how powerful the Sorcerer is.

"With this connection, I was able to know of this spell before you did. In the past couple of weeks, I have spent my spare time looking for a weakness in the spell that might allow us to free her of it without the Sorcerer knowing. I was not successful in this venture, but I do have another idea that might do the trick."

"It's not going to hurt her will it?" Skander asked.

"No," Cerin replied. "As it is, she's in more pain than she knows what to do with. Anything, I'm sure, would be an improvement."

"What do you have in mind?" Aiden asked.

"I think Isabel has an object that might help us answer that question." Isabel looked at Cerin "You know what I'm talking about?"

"I was doubtful. I had never seriously considered it."

"What is it we're talking about?" Lily asked.

"Ms. Gwen is under a spell that torments her until she looks into one of the Sorcerer's mirrors and locates the Wizard's Staff. He believes he needs this relic if he is to be successful against Lathon and Sherados. The closest one is in the chamber of a particular castle, several hours flying from here. But Isabel has constructed an almost identical lookalike. It might have just the right combination of differences to keep the Sorcerer from finding out, and free Gwen of the curse."

"How will he not know?" Ellizar asked. "Especially if you and his thoughts are connected."

"I have become very good at blocking him out. Isabel, I believe, created the mirror so that no one else would see what they were looking at. Gwen will still suffer greatly when she's looking in the mirror, but perhaps the Sorcerer won't be able to see what she sees. I cannot guarantee anything, let that be clear."

"Should we wait for her to be in her right mind before we have her look in it?" Skander asked.

"Any postponement will kill her. She may look like she's insane right now, but her mind is still good. Her mind is driven mad by one thought and desire and that is looking into the mirror, having her tied up like she is, it is only harming her. Uncover the mirror and have her look into it and I'll read her thoughts and see what she sees."

"Won't we be able to see what she sees in the mirror?" Drake asked.

"If this was a normal mirror yes," Isabel answered, "But I made this one different so that every person, even if they were looking in the mirror at the same time, would see different things." Drake nodded, remembering the day that Isabel and himself had looked into the mirror.

"Take her to the room with the mirror," Cerin replied. Isabel and Aiden moved towards Gwen and grabbed her by the arms, struggling to contain her strength as she fought them. She kicked and flailed, forcing Drake and Lily to grab her feet and hold her as they carried her through the house to the next floor.

Drake dreaded each step that brought them closer to the moment of truth. Gwen could be nothing more than a pawn. Something used to distract them while the Sorcerer plotted his next move. Drake's eyes scanned either side of the hallway, looking for anything that might help his unease, but he found nothing.

Instead, all he found were strange knick-knacks and things that only Isabel would know what they were. Several doors lined the hall catching Drake's attention, having not remembered seeing them before. He looked at each of them as they passed by, noticing that one of them was open. The sun shone and the walls were covered with a different plant than the flowering vines which covered everything else. As if the door had noticed he was seeing inside it, it slammed shut and locked itself.

SEEING STONES

They released Gwen. The mirror was still covered and Cerin stood at the head of the room, looking at them and then at Gwen who walked muttering and mumbling to herself as she tore at her hair and clothes.

Isabel walked to the side of the mirror and pulled the cloth off. The mirror was just the way it had been the first time Drake had seen it. The reflection, grey and veiled, not allowing a person to see anything at first. As if someone had immediately changed something in Gwen, she stood upright and looked towards the mirror, cocking her head slightly as she looked at it.

She muttered to herself for a moment and then intently looked at it. They also looked in the mirror, hoping to catch a glance at what she might be seeing. Cerin stood with his head bowed and muttered a spell to himself. Gwen's expression was one of pain at first, but it soon lightened and it seemed as if she was learning something that she hadn't known previously.

Within a minute Gwen's strength had left her and she fell to her knees, still looking to the mirror. Cerin's eyes flashed concern as he looked at all of them and then back to Gwen.

"Cover the mirror now!" Cerin exclaimed. Isabel threw the cloth back over the mirror. Gwen fell backward, the pain that had been evident on her face now gone. Drake ran forward and helped her sit up, holding her as she looked around at all of them.

She trembled slightly and her skin was pale. She looked up at Drake and then up to the mirror that was now covered. She clung to Drake and then looked to the left where Isabel stood. They held eye contact for a moment before she looked at Cerin.

"Welcome back Gwen," Drake greeted, a smile on his face. Gwen looked at him with confusion racing through her eyes.

"Was I gone?" Gwen asked. The others exchanged glances.

"More or less," Aiden answered. "Don't you remember?"

"No. The last thing I remember is being kidnapped," Gwen replied.

"Do you remember what you just saw?" Isabel asked.

"No. I'm not even sure I remember who everyone is." She looked towards Cerin. "Do I know you?"

"It's alright, he's a friend of ours and he's on our side," Ellizar said. They turned their attention towards Cerin. "What did she see? Did everything work like you thought it might?"

"She saw many things in the mirrors, including the place where the Wizard's Staff is located. Unfortunately, the location was a little bit vague, but we'll have to work with what we have."

"The staff was lying on the ground on an island that is feared by most people. An island where heat and suffering become one," Cerin answered. "Do you know which island I am talking about?"

"You're talking about Calamar, or the Island of Fire," Aiden replied. Cerin nodded. "I was there a few years ago, not much to tell about it though."

"Island of Fire?" Drake asked. "That doesn't sound very inviting."

"It's home to the largest wild Taruk herds in this part of the world. Very dangerous. There are a few cities on the islands but that's about it. For the most part, Calamar depends on their fishing industry for their food and water, due to the dry conditions on the island."

"Is that all the mirror showed you?" Isabel asked.

"The staff will be found by someone before you can reach its shores. Beyond that, I'm not sure what the future holds. I couldn't tell by what she saw if the Sorcerer would find it or if it would be someone else. Either way, time will be running much shorter than you would like it to."

"What else is new?" Lily asked, getting a slight chuckle from all of them. "Do we have any idea of where it is on the island?"

Cerin shook his head. "I only saw the ground. I have no other way for us to find a more specific location unless there's some great secret that I don't know about in this house."

They turned and looked at Isabel who smiled weakly and shrugged her shoulders. Without speaking she turned and walked back down the hall, motioning for them to follow.

Gwen was able to walk by herself now, although she still appeared weak and pale. Drake walked close by her side and the others weren't far away as they stopped outside the door that had shut itself when they walked by the first time.

The door opened and quietly swung inwards, letting a massive amount of light escape from the room. One at a time they entered and stood along the nearest wall, which Drake quickly noticed was covered with a Trayven. Drake looked at it, noticing that just like the one he had seen Isabel painting earlier, it first appeared as an abstract shape and then shifted and brought the image into focus.

He watched as first his face appeared and then changed to Aiden's, and then Gwen's, and then two other people that he didn't know. They were in a cave. Their faces were disfigured and before long Drake wondered if he was even seeing a cave at all. The image faded and the wall went back to normal. Drake reached out to touch the painting and pulled his hand away when paint dripped on it.

Putting the mystery aside for the moment, he turned to look at the source of all the light. Small orbs floated in the air. Each of them emitted a bright light. They slowly floated around the room which was once again much larger than Drake would've thought, easily five hundred feet in every direction including up. The orbs floated by him, sounds emerging from them. Some gave sounds of conversation, others fighting. Drake almost thought he could see a picture in one of them.

A staircase stood in the middle of the room and spiraled up to a landing at the top. Isabel led the way up the stairwell, looking out at the orbs as though she was looking for a specific one.

"What are these?" Skander asked, reaching out to touch one. It changed its course and flew up next to the wall keeping its distance from him.

"These are seeing stones, or at least that's what I call them," Isabel answered. "They're not influenced by magic. They're real living things. They can hear and they are very careful about who they associate themselves with. If they don't trust you they won't tell you anything."

"Where did you get these?" Lily asked.

"After I escaped from my husband in Grimdor, I felt that I had to go back. The seeing stones showed me how to get out of Grimdor without being detected, so I made dozens of return trips and stole all of them from the Sorcerer. With these, we might be able to win the war because we know where he's headed and what he's doing. He's not safe from spying like he might think."

"How do they work?" Drake asked, also trying to touch one. It acted the same way the one Skander had tried to touch, flying to the wall.

"Each one will show you a different part of the world. It'll only show you that part of the earth though. We just have to find one of them that shows Calamar, or the Island of Fire, and see if it'll show us the island in any greater detail, hopefully it will."

They slowly climbed the staircase for several more minutes as Isabel, who had clearly won the allegiance of the seeing stones, grabbed one after the other and then released it when it wasn't the one she wanted. Finally, she grabbed one and looked into it for several minutes a smile coming to her face.

"It's on the southwestern part of the island," Isabel answered. "It's undiscovered, but it will be found by someone before we get there. Beyond that, it doesn't know anything."

"Do you know if the Sorcerer's presence is on the island?" Aiden asked.

Isabel looked back into the seeing stone.

"He's not there yet, but I see a great host of ships leaving from a seaport. I don't think they've left yet, but they're certainly getting ready. It's Revly, I can see that now. Lots of Borags. More than could fit into Revly."

"What does that mean?" Gwen asked.

"It means that the Sorcerer is diverting most of his troops and pulling them from other cities to take over the island. He wants the Wizard's Staff more than anything. If he has it then he knows he has power," Isabel answered. "Our enemy may be strong, but he's certainly not the smartest person in the world. He's left himself vulnerable."

"He thinks that we don't have any kind of a force," Ellizar reminded.

"As Isabel said, our enemy is smart but he doesn't know everything," Aiden answered. "You are certain that the Wizard's Staff is on the southwest part of the island?"

"Yes."

Aiden slipped into deep thought for a few minutes.

The rest of them wandered up and down the staircase or looked at the paintings on the walls, which showed them many things. As Isabel had told Drake some of the paintings were simple, showing him his favorite color or type of food.

"I think we need to speak with Atruss and Gabrielle," Aiden told them. "We have many things to do and plan and I'm not sure how any of it is going to unfold."

They left the house and all the strange things inside as they walked through the city. Destan and Elohim flew up in the sky, helping in the cleanup effort, grabbing the dead enemy soldiers and carrying them away to a large wasteland a couple of miles from the castle.

They entered the palace and were ushered into the throne room where Atruss and Gabrielle were waiting. They were greeted with smiles and hugs as they came forward and eventually took a seat at a table in a small room to the side where they filled them in on the recent happenings.

"You know where the Wizard's Staff is?" Gabrielle asked. Aiden nodded.

"We at least know the general location, we also believe that the Sorcerer is going to send all available units to attack Calamar, emptying the cities on the mainland. I say we use this mistake on his part to attack him and attack hard. Take back some of the cities that he has persecuted or destroyed," Aiden answered.

"I agree," Atruss replied. A smile spread across his face. "However it's not going to be quite that easy. First of all, we must think about what's going to happen when we get to the island. If what you say is true about the number of troops the Sorcerer is sending, then you will be hopelessly outnumbered. I don't see how you'll make it within a hundred yards of shore without being spotted or killed."

"Need to have faith about these things," Aiden answered with a smile. "I've thought about that and I have every intention of giving the island a little surprise when we get there."

"Surely you're not thinking that this army will be able to attack the island. You know the council and the Farsees don't like that island. They will never support us in this endeavor," Atruss answered.

"They don't need to send the army to the island. I think it's time we unveil the allies that no one knows about," Aiden replied. "The Gog's time for war has come. They can attack the island, causing a sufficient distraction along the northeastern shore. Upon their arrival I'm sure all of the Borags will be pulled to that shore, leaving us to walk wherever we want."

"I'll admit it's a good plan," Atruss answered. "But the council won't like that we've kept this secret from them for so long, and the Farsees I'm sure will only make it harder for us to carry it out."

"I thought they were the religious leaders?" Drake asked.

"You should remind them of that sometime," Aiden said with a laugh. "They think that they are the kings of the land. Their idea of religion and mine is completely different, therefore we don't always see eye to eye."

"That's putting it mildly," Gabrielle interjected. "If they had it their way they would have Aiden's head on a platter."

"I'll back you in this because I believe that the time for war has come and politics are now dead," Atruss answered. "We must speak to the council though, and the Farsees and at least give them a chance to get on board."

"I understand," Aiden answered. "We'll send the Gogs to attack the Island of Fire and then I'd like to send select regiments to counter-attack the seaport of Revly and several other key cities nearby. Also, I believe Willard and Miles can be of some use to us as well."

"Willard and Miles?" Lily asked. "They're wolves; what can they do?"

"Everyone can do something Lily," Aiden answered. "It's just a matter of conviction and belief. Lathon doesn't just place concerns and dreams on our hearts for nothing. He wants us to act on them and rush forward and do something about it instead of assuming someone else will do it. The next great idea on how to save the world begins with each of you. If only you will believe in yourself."

"I still struggle to believe that I have any kind of real purpose in this world," Drake started. "I know I shouldn't but I do."

"Sometimes our worst enemy is ourselves," Aiden answered. "So often, even though everyone else might support us, we are bound by our fear of failure or the fear of getting out of our comfort zone to do something. Still, we must push ourselves to move beyond, because otherwise, we'll never grow as people. We must take control and silence the voice in our heads that tells us we can't do it. You can climb a mountain and it'll look big from the bottom, but when you get to the top you'll see how small everyone else is because they didn't make the climb."

"So we need teh take a step of faith?" Ellizar asked. Aiden nodded.

"Only you know what your step of faith is going to look like. Everyone is different. For some people, the step of faith is going to be rushing into battle even though the odds seem severely slanted, and for others, it'll be helping a stranger even though they're afraid."

To that they had no reply as they separated and went in different directions. Finally, Gwen and Drake found themselves alone in the setting sun.

"It's good to be back," Gwen said, staring at the sunset.

"It's good to have you back," Drake answered. "I may not have said anything before, but I noticed when you were gone just how much I missed you."

"Really?"

"Yes, it's a little hard for me to explain, because it's not like we've ever spoken about this before, but I felt as if a part of me had died when you were gone. Does that sound crazy at all?"

"Yes," Gwen answered. "But I think love is crazy. Look at the world around you and you see examples of it over and over again. People are willing to go to war for the people that they love. This world is full of love and I think that's what Grimdor and the Sorcerer are missing. They have no love in them, they don't know what it's like and so they seek to destroy us because of their hatred and jealousy."

"I had never thought of jealousy before," Drake replied. "It makes sense though. They hate that we have; what they can't have. They regret the choices that they've made that have put them in the situations that they're in and now the only way they can validate anything they've done is to destroy everything different from them."

"Well said Mr. Thomas," Gwen said with a smile. "The world doesn't know a love like the one that Lathon has and will demonstrate for us. A love that would drive a person to do the unthinkable and come into our war-torn world and save us."

"I believe in the prophecies, I've just always had this part of me that wonders how this great king Lathon could have an heir if no one's heard from him in hundreds, maybe thousands of years. How is that possible?" Gwen shrugged her shoulders.

"I don't think that's for us to figure out Drake," Gwen answered. "He's Lathon, and he was, and I believe he still is the most powerful king in the world. It was always said that with Lathon anything was possible. I think that's the only explanation that's needed."

The dreaded hallway stretched out before them, leading them somewhere they didn't want to go. The battle that lay beyond the doors would be far harder than any battle they had fought with swords thus far. Aiden walked tall and confidently as did Atruss, their steps echoed through the empty hallway. The meeting chamber, filled with the council and the Farsees lay ahead of them.

Atruss grabbed the door handle, leading the way. The small talk and light chatter that filled the room fell silent when they entered. The Farsees sat up in their chairs, the leader of the Farsees looked towards Aiden for only a brief moment and then looked at Atruss.

"Now that you are here we may start the meeting," the leader of the Farsees said. "However, are you sure you want someone sitting in on this meeting who does not follow the religious codes and rules?"

"He's got just as much a right to be here as you do," Atruss started. "There have been several new developments in the past twenty-four hours and I insist on him sitting in on the meeting."

"If you must insist, then you must, although I don't see the purpose of having him here. After all the council and the Farsees are quite capable of governing this land and making decisions by ourselves," the leader of the Farsees answered.

"We do not doubt that nonetheless, he is my choice to sit in on this meeting and give input because he is responsible for our latest victory."

"Victory?" the Farsees leader asked, a strange smirk on his face. "What kind of a victory do you call that? From what I understand nearly a thousand of our soldiers were killed in the battle. That is no victory."

"It's war! If you expect everyone to come out alive then you're mistaken,"

Aiden replied. The Farsees and the council looked at him, anger in their eyes. "Maybe next time you should pick up a sword and stand in front of the coming army. Maybe then you would understand what loss is like. It takes far more bravery and courage to do what every member of our army did than it does to sit up here in a robe all day."

"How dare you speak to us that way? Who do you think you are? It is said in the ancient scrolls of Lathon that violence is not permitted and that we are to cleanse ourselves of the terrible sins we have committed."

"Terrible sins?" Aiden asked. "I think you misunderstand the ancient scrolls. Wouldn't Lathon want his people to protect themselves against such reckless hate?"

"He will protect us, but first he will send Sherados to us. Only when that moment comes can we achieve victory and pick up swords."

"Maybe Sherados is with us right now?" Atruss suggested. The response seemed to silence the Farsees for the moment.

"If you're going to suggest that we use our little force to attack the other cities and fight against the Sorcerer, I will have to object!" one of the council members answered. The Farsees all nodded their heads in agreement. "We cannot hope of defending ourselves if we're out incurring the wrath of our enemies."

"We cannot hope to win by sitting on the sidelines," Aiden pointed out. "We have to attack or else we'll all be destroyed."

"Whether we attack or not doesn't matter. According to the laws and religious code, we must wait a month before we attack, due to cleansing ourselves."

"Fools," Aiden muttered, everyone looked at him. "That rule was never in the original text and you know it. All you do is create hundreds of rules and make it impossible for anyone but yourselves to believe in Lathon. Furthermore, you, yourselves don't even follow the rules. I've watched you. You stay in your palace and put on a good face when you're out in public, but, here, you are like a tomb. Nice from the outside and nothing but rotting flesh and bones on the inside."

"Gentlemen, before you retaliate against him, let's get down to business," Atruss told them. "I agree with Aiden that we have to do something to fight the Sorcerer effectively. If we don't I'm afraid we'll all die and then all the possessions that you hold dear to you will be destroyed.

"Through a strange turn of events we have figured out the motive for the Sorcerer attacking Belvanor. It seems he wants to acquire the Wizard's Staff. The last thing that he needs to rule this earth and destroy all that's good. He, as well as us, have learned the approximate location of the Wizard's Staff and we now propose that we send an army to the island and try to find it."

"Why should we send an army?" One of the council members asked.

"We need something to distract the troops that are on the island to allow us to search for it freely."

"And I suppose that you would want to send our army to attack the island? Which island do you think this Wizard's Staff is on?"

"The Island nation of Calamar is where the staff is located," Aiden answered.

"You expect us to send an army to Calamar?" one of the council members said with a laugh. "You do realize that the nation is a wasteland? There's nothing worth fighting over there. The entire land has been destroyed by the Taruks who occupy the land. Attacking it would be useless. I think I speak for all of us when I say that I do not think that our army should do this."

"Gogs will certainly be a useful ally against the forces of Grimdor," Aiden replied. Laughing followed.

"We have never considered you very bright Aiden, but now we think you're just delusional. The Gogs have been extinct for longer than we've been alive. You're losing your mind! You see Atruss, we told you that he would never amount to anything." A knock came on the door.

"Enter!" Atruss exclaimed. The doors were opened, revealing Shavrok and twenty Gogs behind him. Aiden and Atruss both watched everyone's faces as they laid their eyes on the muscular, intimidating beasts in front of them.

Weapons of every kind were strapped to their bodies. The spikes protruded from their backs and their knuckles matched their hardened face.

"Hail Atruss and Aiden!" Shavrok greeted. The Gogs bowed. They stood up and looked at everyone else who was at a loss for words.

"How dare you raise an army without us knowing?" one of the council asked when finally he found the courage to end the silence. "This is a plot to kill all of us and overthrow us. We should have these two arrested immediately!" the others started nodding and shouting their approval but all of them were stopped when Shavrok moved towards them.

"Touch either one of them and you will be the first to experience the wrath of the Gogs. Long have we waited to fight the evil that we've seen growing on this earth and now that time has finally come. All the Gogs will go to battle against our enemies. Decide now what side you are on."

"You hear that everyone, that's blackmail!" one of the Farsees exclaimed. They started shouting out but were silenced by a roar from Shavrok.

"We have not come to blackmail people!" Shavrok boomed. "We have come to stand up for what is right. Sherados is about to come forward and we wish to stand with him."

"You cannot possibly follow the codes of Lathon," one of the Farsees answered. Shavrok let a low growl escape him.

"Why not?"

"Because you are a Gog, and only the Elves can truly be followers of Lathon!"

"That's true, after all, no one can be as perfect as they can," Atruss replied. The Farsees and council members hardened their faces. "For years, you have let Dwarves and Men live in this nation as well. Are you saying now that Gogs shouldn't be allowed to live here?"

"They can live here, but they can never be true followers of Lathon. In the end, only the elf kind can be saved."

"I disagree," Aiden replied. "Gogs have just as much of a right to fight for Lathon as anyone else. If we follow the law as you say we should we are all going to end up dead. The Gogs will help us take the nation of Calamar and liberate it from the forces of evil which are probably running ashore right now."

"Attack if you wish, but there are few who believe that the Wizard's Staff exists. I believe it's nothing more than an old folktale."

"Well, I believe it exists and I'm going to do everything I can to find it," Aiden declared.

"Me too," Atruss replied. "The time for sitting on the sidelines has passed. We have done that for far too long, and because of that, our enemy is strong. I am going to put out an open call for all nations to join us in this effort if they so wish." Arguing followed for several seconds until Shavrok let another roar escape him.

"You will be destroyed if you do not join forces as these two suggest! This nation will soon join the ruined cities that cover this earth." The Gogs left with Aiden following right behind them. Atruss watched relief flood over the other's faces.

"Finally we can have a civilized meeting now that the hideous creatures and Aiden are all out of here."

"I support them fully," Atruss answered.

"If you support them fully then we do not wish to have you here either."

"You do not have the authority to take the leadership from me."

"Will you step out of the room Atruss? We would like to discuss this amongst ourselves for a few moments."

Atruss took a deep breath and bowed his head as he stood. He walked out of the room and let the door shut behind him. He stood in the silent corridor for several minutes, waiting to be asked to come back in. The time passed and no one ever came out to speak with him.

He turned from the hallway and walked through the palace to his chamber where his wife was waiting for him. Her face showed her surprise to see him back so soon. He didn't speak until he was in and had shut the door. She came up to him.

"What should we do?" Gabrielle asked. Atruss shrugged his shoulders.

"This is all we've known, yet the feeling that this is the end of one chapter but the beginning of another keeps going through my heart. I think we must leave, and travel far away from this place."

"Don't worry about how things will unfold, it was meant to happen this way," she answered.

"I know it was, but I struggle to see why. I can't imagine being able to do as much good as we did from the throne."

"Maybe that's where we're wrong in our thinking," Gabrielle suggested. "Wherever we end up we will still stand up for everything that we know to be true. We will still fight for the slave that's beaten by the master for no reason, or the widow that sleeps in the slums with her children. This is not the end my dear." Atruss looked into her eyes and smiled.

"Every day I'm reminded of why I fell in love with you."

"Something's bothering you," Lily said. Ellizar had been silent for nearly an hour as he stared up at the ceiling as though it had some great answer in it that Lily couldn't see. The comment took a couple of seconds to register with Ellizar but finally, he looked in her direction.

"Nothin's botherin' me," Ellizar replied.

"You're lying Ellizar and I know it. I've known you long enough to know when you're lying."

"Okay so I am, but I know there's somethin' botherin' yeh as well."

"How did you know?"

"Yeh called me Ellizar, even if I was lyin' yeh would usually call me Ellie just teh drive me up a wall and distract me from my thoughts." They both laughed lightly, looking at each other from across the room. "I just wonder what will be after the war."

"I'm not sure I understand."

"It's been long since I've seen any number of Dwarves. After being removed from that culture for so long, I suppose I feel like I don't fit in with them anymore. I'm glad to see a large number of Dwarves in Ariamore. I just feel like I'm different."

"You are different. I for one am glad," Lily comforted. "I'm grateful for that day I saw you at the port. Without you, my life would be rather boring you know?"

"Oh, I know! Now you're stuck with me! "

"I haven't objected yet and I never would. Despite the teasing we give each other I've always enjoyed your company if you can believe that."

"Strange, isn't it?" Ellizar asked with a laugh. "A dwarf and an elf, friends. Who would've thought of such a laughable concept?"

"All our friends are laughable when you think about it," Lily answered. "We are friends with both Elves and Humans, and my brother is an elf giant. I guess there's just nothing normal about us."

"Maybe we were never meant teh be normal," Ellizar replied. They laughed again. "I think it's how Lathon wants it. Now yer turn, what's botherin' yeh?"

"I just keep thinking about Fiori and what happened. I feel like I have to go back at some point. My heart tells me that there's something there that we forgot or missed the first time. I've lost countless nights of sleep trying to figure out why, but I still haven't come any closer to a solution."

"Maybe when this war ends we'll go back and figure out this mystery once and fer all. Fer the first time, I'll probably receive a warm welcome. Albeit because everyone's dead."

"Whatever happens I'm looking forward to the future, when the war's over. I dare to dream that there will be another life. I don't know what our life will be like or what we will end up doing, but I look forward to it."

Silence passed between them and they allowed themselves to slip into their thoughts and then their dreams as they wondered what the future would hold.

LEAVING BELVANOR

Atruss and Gabrielle walked briskly through the palace. They carried a couple of bags on their backs and walked with confidence despite everything that had unfolded.

They entered the main dining hall to find everyone else waiting for them. The food on the plates was untouched, and each one of them was nervous about what was going to be said. Shavrok and the Gogs stood behind everyone else, sure to intimidate anyone who walked in.

"It seems that this will be the last meal that we eat in Belvanor," Atruss announced.

"They're kicking us out?" Drake asked.

"They have officially banished *all* of us from the land. To enter again after today is punishable by the sword. They want all of us, even the Gogs out."

"Good luck enforcing that one. I'd love to see those little rats try and force us out of anywhere," Shavrok said. "When the war is over, we are returning here to live."

"I completely understand how you feel," Gabrielle replied.

"So this is the thanks we get after everything that we've done for these people?" Gwen asked. "We've saved them twice, so they're getting rid of us."

"Yes, they are. Before last night no such law existed for them to do this, but after they got rid of Aiden and me, they made a new law allowing them to do such a thing."

"This is terrible, we must do something!" Lily exclaimed.

"We must leave," Aiden told them.

"Why must we leave?"

"We cannot force anyone to do anything; that is not the way of Lathon, that is the way of the Sorcerer. If they want us to leave then we bow out and move on, always seeking to do good in this world full of turmoil."

"So we're not going to stop doing something even though we are on our own?"

"Correct," Aiden answered. "There is still work to be done. This nation has chosen its path, let them live with their decisions. I have everything arranged and know exactly the course that we need to go by."

"I wish I could see the end as clearly as you could," Gabrielle said.

"You just need to have faith about these things," another voice said from the doorway. They turned to see Isabel coming towards them with another piece of paper. Her appearance now didn't change every few seconds but instead stayed constant. "They kicked me out too. Big surprise there. I've already got the things I need packed. I've left the rest of it in my house. It'll be safe there, I'm sure they'll be too afraid to clear it out. Even if they do go snooping, they'll find a few surprises waiting for them."

"Is there anyone we know who hasn't been kicked out of the city?" Drake asked. As if they had heard his question Willard and Miles came casually walking around the corner.

"*They haven't kicked us out, but neither have we felt the desire to stay. We feel as if there's something more for us to do beyond these walls,*" Willard answered.

"Indeed there is," Aiden said. "I have a plan for all of us, one that will not be easy, but it must be done. *We* have to march forward and find the Wizard's Staff before the Sorcerer does. This nation may not want to do anything but our nation will."

"Our nation?" Drake asked.

"The followers of Lathon are called to step forward and take the lead when no one else will. Our time is short on this earth and we must always keep working to save the world."

"*What did you have in mind?*" Miles asked.

"Maybe I'm wrong in assuming this but are there more than two talking wolves in the world?" Aiden asked.

"*Perhaps,*" Willard answered. Isabel couldn't help but hide a chuckle.

"It seems I'm not the only one with secrets," Isabel said. Miles laughed.

"*There are more talking wolves, or at least there are more wolves that we can get in contact with. Some of them can't talk the way we do, but we can still communicate with them. Do you have something specific in mind?*"

"I might, but mostly it's your knowledge I'll need. Being wolves, you have probably gotten into places that most of us have never been. It could prove to be quite valuable when we go to war."

"*We'll round up as many as we possibly can and wait for your orders. Is there anywhere specific we're supposed to gather everybody?*" Miles asked.

"The Rock of Petron, in Idumea?" Aiden asked. Willard shook his head.

"*That many wolves in the open will scare everyone and then we'll likely be attacked, and there's too many cities in the southern half of Idumea to risk gathering in such large numbers. I would suggest the northern forest of Epirus, there isn't much up there and we shouldn't arouse suspicion by doing so.*"

"That will work just fine, gather as many as you can until we join up with you," Aiden said. The wolves dipped their heads and darted out the doors, past Isabel who watched them curiously.

"I suggest that even though Gabrielle and I have been banished from the land like everyone else here, I think we should stay and wait for Rohemir to return. I've sent an owl to find him, warning him of everything that's transpired," Atruss explained.

"Shavrok is your navy ready to sail?" Aiden asked.

"On your command my lord," Shavrok answered doing a bow.

"Calamar itself isn't very large, there's only one major city on it. The city is called Havet, it's a seaport and it runs the entire width of the Northeast shore. We need you and your ships to attack the city while we go around the island in another boat, land on the southwest side of the island, and begin looking for the Wizard's Staff. Do you think your soldiers are up to the task?"

"We will do what we can, a little city should be nothing for the Gogs who are happy to go to war."

"Now, we just need to find us a ship that can sail around the island. We should probably take a normal ship, that way we won't be noticed as unusual because we all know that the Gog ships are unique."

"There is a ship you can take, it's sitting in the harbor and you won't have to steal it. There's an independent sailor that brings supplies to us now and then," Atruss explained. "As I understand it, some of you may have met him previously."

"What's his name?" Drake asked.

"I believe he said his name was Barnabas?" Atruss asked, looking towards Gabrielle who nodded in agreement. "He seems to be rather upset because he missed out on a paycheck that someone had promised him in Revly." They all smiled and lightly laughed.

"We will pre-pay him this time. I'll go talk to him and we will leave as soon as possible," Aiden said. "Shavrok prepare your troops and ships and sail immediately. We won't depart the harbor until you go by."

"As you wish my lord," Shavrok answered, bowing again and then disappearing from their sight.

"Isabel, will you be coming with us?"

"At the moment I will have to decline. I have some business to attend to somewhere else."

"Don't suppose we'll find out what it is?" Lily asked. Isabel shrugged her shoulders and smiled.

"Eventually, if you listen hard enough you'll figure out the answer. I've got some personal things to attend to."

"And with that, I won't ask any more questions," Skander said. The others chuckled.

"It would usually take us a week to get Calamar, but the seas are unusually calm, no doubt the work of the Sorcerer," Aiden started. "The Sea of the Spirits isn't going to be an issue this time. We should arrive at the shore of Calamar in about three or four days, and then we'll see how things unfold."

"Very well, I wish you the most luck that I can," Atruss said, embracing him.

"Luck is for fools. May Lathon be with me. Before I leave there is one thing that I must ask of you."

"Name it my friend."

"Do you know how to get in touch with Rade and Cerin? I have something for them to do."

They gathered their supplies as well as all the belongings they could carry and were forcibly removed from the palace shortly after. Drake looked back at the palace, saddened to see it fading into the distance.

This had been the first place that Drake had ever been able to live without fear and now they were being thrown out as though they were nothing more than a pack of wild dogs.

They camped out on the shoreline, waiting for Shavrok and his ships to appear in the harbor. To their left, a hundred feet the large ship they had tried to charter several months ago, stood tied and ready to depart at a moment's notice. The conversation with Barnabas, when they had arrived, had been one of the most hilarious ones Drake had ever been a part of.

They had paid the man in advance and were now waiting to set out on this next great adventure that was before them. Drake couldn't help but feel a little nervous or apprehensive about setting out again. Every time they had left someplace it had ended with them barely hanging onto their lives and then running for the next week or two, and here they went again.

Drake knew that everyone else was feeling the same thing even if they didn't say it. Elohim and Destan flew overhead, so high and so distant they were nothing but black dots against the rising sun.

Drake had wished they would use the Taruks to get to the island, but Aiden had pointed out that if the Taruks were spotted the Sorcerer would know in an instant where they were headed. So they would take the ships, leaving the two Taruks to follow them and offer assistance if they needed it.

"What's the history of Calamar?" Drake asked, the others talked lightly and Isabel had vanished altogether.

"In this part of the world, it was the island that the Taruk's first lived on. Wild Taruks as well as hundreds and hundreds of tame Taruks lived there in perfect harmony with each other. Time passed and eventually, Men from the west sailed in and inhabited the island. The thing about Taruks is, they can be seen when they want to be seen, and invisible when they want to be. They hid themselves from the settlers hoping that they would turn away and leave the island. They didn't and the Taruk's peacefully revealed themselves. Their intentions were good but they scared the poor men out of their minds. Then it became a war, and the island was ravaged. It's now a barren wasteland. You'll notice when we get there, that there's a certain smell to the island. Everything looks and acts like it's burned. Ashes are everywhere and the entire island is ready to catch fire again, should something spark it.

"The Sorcerer will have likely reached the island by the time we get there and who knows what he will have done to the place," Lily commented.

"Do you think that it's possible to face the Sorcerer and win?" Gwen asked, joining the conversation. "It's supposed to be winter right now and it feels more like late summer. He seems to have more power than he knows what to do with it. My hope fades with each second that passes."

"We must not lose hope, even if the world crashes down and is destroyed all around us, we will have each other. Remember we have something that the Sorcerer doesn't," Aiden said.

"Love?" Drake asked.

Aiden nodded. "We need only to gain an advantage against the Sorcerer and he will lose all of his power in a second."

"Really?"

"All who gain power are afraid to lose it. They're even more afraid when they weren't given the power but instead, have taken it by force. Sherados is very close to coming forward, even now."

"You know who Sherados is?" Drake asked.

"I've always known," Aiden answered.

"I wish I knew who Sherados was," Drake replied. Aiden smiled.

"Look inside your heart, Drake, and you'll find the answer, I promise you that." Aiden patted him on the shoulder and walked away towards the shoreline, picking up a flat stone and skipping it on the water.

"Do you think you're Sherados?" Gwen asked in a whisper.

"I'm not sure," Drake answered. "You would think I would know it right?"

"That's what I would think. Lathon was very humble, maybe you're not supposed to know until the right time, that way you don't come across as a person who knows everything."

"Maybe," Drake admitted, dread filling him moments later. "The more time that passes though I feel as if somewhere along all of our travels we met him. I just can't figure out who it is. I don't think that it's me."

"I'm sure everything will work out the way it's supposed to," Gwen said, embracing him and giving him a light kiss on the cheek. "No matter what you do, I'll be by your side, as will the rest of us."

"That means a lot," Drake replied looking back to the city in the distance. "Belvanor was such a bright light, now its light has been affected."

"If only they would stop turning on each other the city might still be shining brightly. I fear by the time we get back from our trip that the city will be gone or taken over, I'm not sure which," Aiden said.

Loud deep horns echoed in the distance. They turned to their left seeing hundreds and hundreds of ships beginning to appear on the coastline. They were still off in the sea a mile or so, but their horns blew and the note radiated through the evening sky. Drake looked at each of the ships, overwhelmed by the number of them.

"I've never seen that many ships, not even while we were staying in Negev," Drake said as they began boarding their ship.

Aiden smiled. "Shavrok said that there were three Gog cities. Probably around two hundred thousand Gogs are on board the ships."

Drake looked at all the ships, unable to see the end. For miles and miles both wide and long, ships filled the sea. Chills rippled through him as they left the dock and joined the procession. The Gog's were going to war.

Isabel had always liked the spring, but this time it made her uneasy. It should be winter and they should be buried under ten feet of snow, yet none remained.

She had always done whatever she could to hinder the Sorcerer's plan but this time she felt powerless as his armies loomed on the horizon. She looked behind her where Belvanor was shrinking in size until finally it vanished altogether. The sun was setting and before long it would be gone completely, leaving her in darkness.

Her soul was stirred and curiosity peaked as she thought about Calamar. She knew a little about the island, but she had never been there herself. She searched her memories and, for the most part, was able to predict what the others would find when they arrived.

Isabel knew many people and many secrets from all over the earth and there was no secret greater than the one that Calamar was hiding. She had read hundreds and hundreds of ancient scrolls over the years and had finally discovered something that had given her hope. After she had read it, she had burned the scroll and willed herself to forget the information until the right time.

She walked for another couple minutes and then entered a large clearing that looked down into an open valley. The sound faded and then came back as she walked through an invisible shield that she had created with Elven magic so many years ago. Anyone else who walked through this part of the forest wouldn't see a thing, but to those who opened their eyes and took their time to look at their surroundings, another secret of hers would become visible.

She listened to the forest, for a moment whistling a little tune her father had taught her when she was a child. The tune was carried through the air and echoed as though they were in a great hall. Immediately after the sound stopped, she heard movement in the forest. Her heart leaped inside of her chest, always excited to return here.

A roar went up into the air, but Isabel was the only one who heard it. Finally, a large shape became visible in the setting sun. It grew in size as the creature extended its wings and then leaped into the air, taking flight. The massive Taruk let a roar of pleasure escape her as she swooped down out of the sky and landed gracefully.

The Taruk rested on the ground and closed her eyes, enjoying the touch of Isabel's hand. The Taruk was nearly twice the size of Aiden's Taruk, Elohim, and far larger than Drake's. Its dark green color had made it easy to hide her in the forest for as long as she had. The Taruk had both experience and youthfulness. A Taruk could live as long as a hundred years so even this Taruk was still young.

"It's good to see you Aspen," Isabel greeted. The Taruk let a joyful rumble escape her, almost like a cat when it purred. "I have good news. We don't have to hide anymore." The Taruk turned its large head to look in her direction. "Sherados is close and so is the one that will make a way for him. It's time for us to show ourselves and wage our war against the evil that is taking over this earth. Maybe then people will like us. However, I doubt that. There's just one thing we have to get before we go home. You know what that is?" The Taruk nodded and she climbed on Aspen's back.

Without a moment's hesitation. the powerful Taruk pushed off the ground and left it far below. Isabel reached into a large bag that she had brought with her and pulled a cloak out of it, wrapping it around her.

They passed beyond the barriers she had set up. People would be able to see them again and there was nothing she could be happier about. Aspen flew gracefully through the sky, heading towards the southeast, where if they continued too far, Belvanor would come into view. Finally, a pit came into view and Aspen landed in the clearing next to it.

Isabel willed herself to take the next breath as the stench of rotting flesh reached her nose. The smell crippled her for a moment, occupying her thoughts. She slid off the Taruk, reaching into her bag for a large cloth that was several times the size of her.

She spread it out on the ground and looked at the mass grave that had been created after the battle at Belvanor. The pile was nearly ten feet high and at least a hundred feet wide. She knew this wasn't the only pile of dead bodies, after all, they had been attacked by nearly a hundred and eighty thousand Borags and she doubted they were all here. She climbed the pile of dead, shoving dead Borags aside.

A couple of hours later Tremin's body was found and his head was scattered a few yards away. Emotion threatened to overtake her as she tossed the head back towards the white cloth she had brought. She dragged the body down the pile and wrapped it up in the cloth.

She tied the bag to Aspen's back and then climbed on. The Taruk pushed off and soared into the sky heading northwest as Isabel finally let the tears fall. For so long she had held them in.

She was tormented by the memory of what her husband and Tremin had done, yet she still felt something for them. The time faded and turned into days as they flew towards the northwest. Epirus appeared on the horizon beneath them. She was almost home.

They flew north for hours over the town of Bucklebeary, which looked as though it had been fortified many times over. They followed the river to the west and south, coming to the ruins of Fiori, which still smoldered and let off a foul stench.

They continued west until the sea came into view and they landed on a set of hills that had long ago been cleared of trees. Isabel slid off and grabbed the body bag, carrying it up the hill, behind the old house that stood on top of the hill.

She laid Tremin down and she moved away while Aspen used her massive claws to easily dig a grave for her son. She left the area for a few moments, long enough to walk to a large crate sitting on the porch of the house. She opened it up and picked up one of the tombstones that she had carved many years ago, just for this occasion. Tremin's name was on it as well as a small paragraph about the person he had once been.

Tears welled up in her eyes as she put the stone to her chest and held it tight. She sobbed and cried wishing that she didn't have to bury her son.

It wasn't right, it went against the laws of nature, and never in all of her life had she thought she would be doing it. She had been in many situations over the years where her life was nearly spent, now she wished she could trade places with Tremin and allow him one more chance to come back to the good side.

She stood and made her way back to the grave, lowering Tremin's body bag into the ground. She stepped away and Aspen quickly filled the dirt back in. Isabel put the grave marker in place and then stepped back, falling to her knees and sobbing.

Aspen lowered her head and also seemed to feel her pain, which was more than Isabel could ever ask. The two of them had been through a lot together and only Aspen knew the true story.

Aspen extended her head over the grave and let a tear fall out of her massive eyes. The tear hit the fresh dirt and it gently spread over the entire grave. Within seconds new life was beginning to form and a unique variety of lilacs covered the area. All different colors grew over the dirt and made the grave something beautiful.

When she finally was able to stop her crying she noticed that she was leaning over Aspen's large neck. Aspen lay next to her, tears also coming from her eyes.

At last, Isabel found the strength to stand and then walked away from the grave with Aspen following a few feet behind. She reached the porch and sat down in one of the old rocking chairs. It creaked and groaned as she looked out to the horizon.

She sat in the chair for what felt like an eternity, before entering the house. The inside was both spotless and much larger than should be possible seeing the house from the outside. The kitchen stood to her left with a small fireplace and a table and chairs to her right. Ahead of her, a long hallway extended out in front of her, with a dozen different rooms to both sides.

She moved to the kitchen and made herself some food, reminded of the countless nights she had spent here. She had lived many places in her life, Grimdor, Belvanor, Laheer, and this very house. She had lived in all of them for many years, going back and forth between the two. Now she didn't feel like she had any reason to go back to Belvanor.

Ever since she had left her husband in Grimdor her life had been about secrets and hiding, and trying to hinder her enemies. No more. From now she would tell all of her secrets, and love her former husband for who he had been.

She finished her food and then walked back into the hallway and looked through each of the different rooms, each of which was unique and special in its way. In one of them, the sun was shining brightly and in another, was completely dark with the objects in the room giving off the light as opposed to the other way around. It was those two rooms that she enjoyed the most.

Time passed and she found herself finally making her way to her room. In the center of the room, with one end pushed up against the wall was a bed and a small night table and then a closet and dresser on the next. The entire wall was filled with dozens and dozens of Trayvens. Some of them were large and others were no bigger than her hand. She looked at all of them, hoping to gain some wisdom from them.

One of them told her what day of the week it was going to be tomorrow and some of the others showed her the things she wished she could do something about. Her attention was grabbed by a fairly sizable Trayven that showed a man riding a horse through an open field surrounded by woods.

Joy leapt through her and she quickly changed into a nicer dress and then ran out to the front of the house. Isabel stood in the kitchen, watching the woods for any sign of the rider. Finally, he appeared in the distance, gracefully riding up to the front of the house.

His horse reared for a moment when Aspen came around the corner, but the rider comforted the horse and they continued. He dismounted and tied his horse. Isabel unable to contain her excitement any longer, threw open the door and ran out to him, jumping into his arms and kissing him.

They separated and Morgrin smiled, joy radiating from his eyes as were hers. This was just another secret she had kept over the years and for good reason. They embraced again, wishing they wouldn't have to hide any longer. Loving each other may be a risk to both of them but neither of them cared anymore.

"It has been far too long since you've been here." Isabel couldn't hide a smile.

"I know. Unfortunately, some things needed to be done in Belvanor."

"I see there is a new grave," the man commented after a moment.

"Alas, there is a new grave. It pains me, but he made his choice, though that doesn't do much to ease a mother's heart."

"Indeed not. But, it's over now." They embraced. "What I would give to be able to spend the rest of my days with my wife and not have to be pulled away to war."

"What I would give to be able to tell everyone that I have a husband," Isabel answered reaching into a pocket and pulling out an emerald ring. She slipped it on her finger, the memory of that day bringing her a feeling of peace and satisfaction that was unequaled by all but one day of her life. The emerald was in the shape of a rose, with the different pedals radiating different colors and changing every hour or so. She loved all the colors.

Morgrin pulled out his ring and slipped it on his finger, just a simple gold band, perhaps a little more ordinary, but that had been how he had wanted it. They kissed each other again and then separated, staring into each other's eyes knowing how much they had missed this.

"I think it's time we don't try to hide this any longer. For too many years have we done that, and being separated from each other is something I cannot bear much longer."

"Well said my dear!" Morgrin exclaimed. "So, tell me what the plan is. I know you must have some ideas and certainly must know things that I don't know."

"I certainly do. Have you eaten?"

"Yes I have, I left as soon as I was off duty."

"How many towns or cities in Epirus are still free of Grimdor's armies?"

"Only one that I know of and that's the one I was stationed in. Bucklebeary was taken long ago, despite all the effort we put into trying to make the city secure. I'm stationed a couple of hours away, a town called Ur. Nice, but we can't hold out much longer, the armies of Grimdor are far too strong."

"I'll be coming back with you and I won't take no for an answer."

"You can't come back, it'll be too dangerous."

She shot him a look of amusement. "Morgrin. You know my past, nothing's too dangerous for me. If my husband is going to be at war then I will be standing right by his side. Until death do us part." They both smiled and laughed.

"Can't argue with that. Did they finally kick you out of Belvanor?"

"Me as well as everyone else who wanted to do something. The Farsees and the Council have taken control of the city now."

"It's quite a shame, Belvanor was such a beautiful city."

"And it will be once again, though I fear the road the city has chosen will be darker than they care to acknowledge. Anyway, the end of the age is near and Mera Runa will be returned to the former glory that it once was, and on its throne, the king of kings shall sit and rule the land as it once was."

"So Sherados is close then?"

"The time is coming when he will step forward. It's coming sooner than we might have guessed. Most of the world will not believe him, but the time is right and now we must take a step of faith."

"Together we will stand against the armies of Grimdor and march to the gates of Iscariot if we must."

"My heart tells me that we must. How many people in Epirus believe in the ancient scrolls about Lathon?"

"Last count, there were nearly three thousand of the cavalry and five thousand of infantry that were true believers. Not much of a force compared to the hundreds of thousands that Grimdor has, but it's something. We've been serving the king, but we've been serving the wrong one."

"Let's gather all the faithful troops. Willard and Miles are rounding up all the wolves. Have all the men join up in the ruins of Fiori, no one will look for us there, I would then send the three thousand cavalry to the Rock of Petron in Idumea. Split the force, half of them staying there and the other half heading to Revly. Friends will soon be attacking there and will need all the help they can get."

"I will send the word out immediately my dear. It'll take then three or four days of hard riding to reach Idumea, even longer to reach Revly."

"It's okay, we still have time, but it is running short."

"Do I have enough time to love my wife for the evening before we head off to war together?"

Isabel smiled. "Yes, I believe you do."

He took her in his arms and the night wore on, seeming as though it was something from a dream. To be able to love her husband without worrying whether they would be discovered was a dream come true.

The world was changing and excitement filled Isabel. She had longed and waited for this day to come and now it was nearly here. They woke the next morning and began preparing for the battle that lay ahead.

THE BRINK OF WAR

Isabel was awakened by the smell of a campfire just outside their tent. Morgrin's side of the bed was empty, telling her that he was likely already up and preparing all the troops for what the day would bring. The response to his call had been far greater than they could have hoped for.

Altogether nearly six thousand horsemen had arrived. Many of them were part of Epirus's infantry who had managed to get their hands on a horse, meaning their travel would be much faster than anticipated. She dressed and then walked out into the sunshine.

The pale sun drifted through the forest and over the ruins of what had once been Fiori. She had been to this village numerous times over the past twenty years and to see it in the shape it was in left her with great sorrow. Skeletal remains had been cleared from the sight, but other than that nothing had been done to clean the village up.

Morgrin greeted her good morning with a kiss. He handed her a plate of food and a cup of coffee. She accepted it and together they sat on the ground looking out at the sea of tents and horses that had arrived. Some were farmers and others were merchants, either way, anyone who had owned a sword and knew how to fight had arrived here.

The Borags still occupied most of the towns and villages and how all the troops managed to get out of their cities without being seen or noticed was beyond her knowledge.

A man came riding forward, dismounting his horse and then bringing an envelope to them. Isabel put her food on her lap and took the envelope opening it and reading what was inside. Her heart dropped and her hope began to dwindle for just a moment.

"It seems we have a thousand people who want to leave," Isabel told Morgrin. His face showed concern but not as much as she had expected. "I'll finish my dinner and then we'll go talk to them."

"The men are anxious and scared."

"I suspect your right, but they shouldn't be afraid."

"Try telling that to people who have never been in a battle before," Morgrin responded. Isabel knew he was right. She had been trained and taught to fight, these people hadn't been.

She quickly finished her food and they mounted their horses, riding through the camp to the far edge of the village ruins along the river. There they found a thousand horses with riders ready to depart. Isabel spurred her horse forward and gracefully rode to the front of the group. The leader looked down at the ground, clearly ashamed of wanting to leave.

"What's going on?" Isabel asked. The group looked at each other for several seconds, each of them trying to get up the courage to speak, finally the person at the head of the group, Matthew, spoke.

"We have decided to leave the force," Matthew replied. "It's not that we don't support everything you are doing or are going to do, but we are just a little overwhelmed and scared you see. We are only farmers, what can we possibly do against all the forces of Grimdor? We think of our families, our wives, and children, and wonder what their lives would be like if they didn't have a father or husband to come home. That is a situation we cannot put them in."

"You aren't seeing the whole picture," Morgrin answered. "Yes, there is a chance that they may lose their fathers in this war. They might lose their friends, but if we do not fight in this war, far more than just us is going to be lost. The Sorcerer marches on the Earth with anger and hatred that is unmatched. He does not fight to contain us, or to herd us around like sheep. He fights to kill every last one of us until the ground is soaked in our blood and the vultures feed on our flesh. This battle that you are leaving will come to you one way or another. Don't you understand that?"

"Your words ring true in our hearts, but our heads are having a hard time coming to that conclusion. If we all worked together we might be able to protect our lands and hold them off."

"Perhaps, but for how long?" Isabel asked. "It may be hard to fathom, but the Sorcerer will not be satisfied until every last person has been slaughtered like animals. We have to pull together and have faith that he can be defeated."

"Faith in what though, that's the question," Matthew replied. "We are aware of your Elvish beliefs but we are Men, not Elves. This is not our battle to win. According to your ancient scrolls and based on my knowledge of your beliefs the Elves are the chosen people. Not men. Not Dwarves. Just the Elves."

"I follow your thoughts and your process but I'm afraid you've made an error that people make all too often. Although the Elves are the chosen people of Lathon, the scrolls say he will go first to his chosen people and lead them out of darkness, and then all others who believe will be saved just the same. We were all made in his image. We are different, yes, but it's our differences that make us complete. If we were to exclude one race and say we didn't need them we would find that we were the ones that suffered. Sherados has come to save the world, but first to unite it. Long has there been a separation between the Elves and Men. The Giants have kept to themselves and the Spirits lurk in the shadows. The Dwarves and Gogs have been in hiding. While we were hiding and separated from each other, the Sorcerer has grown strong and has now launched a campaign to do away with us. Sherados comes to all, his heart full of love for those who recognize him as the rightful heir, and anger for the enemies that have driven us apart. He has come to unite what was once united and make the world as it once was." Matthew's horse shifted beneath his weight as Matthew pondered her words.

"Is Sherados with us now?"

"He walks the earth the same as we do. I've met him and even I missed him at first. He embodies everything Lathon ever was. He has humbled himself, not to come into this world as a king, but as one of us. He has shared in our suffering and seen the world as we see it, now he's longing for us to see the world the way he sees it." Matthew looked at the men with him.

"I'd be a fool to argue with that. We shall not protest anymore, we will follow you to the ends of the earth."

Don't follow me to the ends of the earth, follow Lathon." Matthew nodded. Isabel smiled and turned her horse around. "Morgrin. Spread the word for all riders to be ready immediately. The time has come for us to unite and destroy the enemies that occupy these lands. We ride to Idumea and then to Revly!"

The smell of salt water greeted them. The sea opened up in every direction, welcoming them and inviting them into the unknown. The sea churned as the ships sped towards the island at a rate faster than Drake would have thought possible. They were only a day away from the island of Calamar, despite having left only three days ago.

The sun was beginning to rise above the horizon, breaking through the light cloud of fog that had settled over the water. As fast as they were going, Drake wished they could go faster. The uncertainty that plagued the future occupied Drake's mind.

"Good morning Drake." Drake looked to see Aiden coming up from the lower deck where the others were sleeping. Aiden's sword was strapped to his side. Looking at him, Drake could see nothing that was out of the ordinary. No matter what they had gone through, Aiden hadn't changed at all. In some ways Drake envied him.

"Good morning Aiden," Drake answered. Aiden joined him at the bow of the ship.

"By tomorrow morning we should be landing on Calamar," Aiden replied.

"How are we supposed to win against the Sorcerer?" Drake asked. "He seems to be so strong and so powerful, it seems hopeless at times."

"I suppose it does, yes," Aiden answered. "But, we have Sherados on our side, as well as you."

"I don't know what I'm doing Aiden," Drake started. "I'm supposed to recognize Sherados when he comes forward, yet I don't know how I'm supposed to do that. I'm just a person who-"

"Talks way too much when in fact listening might answer your question," Aiden interrupted. "If you want to find Sherados, first you must look for him. Think of it this way, you can't see the shore unless you come up to the main deck and look out over the water. Similarly, you must come and look for Sherados, there are signs of him throughout the world if only our minds and our hearts are open to finding him. Many in this world don't want him to come forward, their hearts are hard towards Lathon.

"After that, you must feel Lathon. At first, this is going to be the strangest part, but after you look for him you must follow your heart to know that this person truly is Sherados. You must feel his presence guiding your life and pulling you towards him.

"Then, the last and probably the hardest part is you have to trust him. Trust that he has a plan for you that goes beyond the next battle, and trust that everything the ancient scrolls say about him is true. It's the hardest step because whether we're human or elf-kind, our hearts like to think that we have control when in reality we can't control anything but our reactions."

"You make it sound so simple," Drake replied. They both chuckled lightly. "Are you sure that Lathon has a plan for me beyond the next battle? During my time here, that's all I've known and it's hard to imagine anything else. People expect me to be a good fighter and if I'm not, I feel like I fail them."

"Don't worry about trying to win their approval or meeting their expectations. You are a good person, but failure to win in battle does not mean failure in life. There is a purpose greater than the next battle, or even the war that lies ahead. It's more than a mark on your hand."

"What do you think that is?" Drake asked, Aiden shrugged.

"Only Lathon knows, that's between you and him, but there *is* more for you beyond the battle. Remember that."

"I will." Silence fell between them for a few moments. "Aiden, why do the Farsees hate you so much?"

"I don't go along with the mindless rituals they called religion."

"Didn't Lathon create the religion in the first place?"

"No. He created a relationship."

"I'm confused," Drake said.

Aiden smiled lightly. "Nowadays it is a *religion*, but that's not how it started. Have you never heard of Erathos?"

Drake's mind flashed with light for a moment. When his vision returned he could recall having heard of Erathos in the past, though the rest of his memories were still muddled and unclear.

"It's just myth and tale?" Drake said.

"Is it?"

"That's what I've been taught."

"Perhaps it's time to relearn," Aiden said, taking a seat. Drake joined him. "When the world was created it was a land that knew no evil. It was called Erathos, which means paradise. It was within the bounds of that land that the nations of the earth were with Lathon, and walked with Lathon."

"The people of the earth were deceived by the Sorcerer and with that deception, the world was broken. Things that should not have happened, did. Things that should not have been forgotten...were forgotten. The people strayed and left the land of Erathos, which had wilted into the barren wasteland that it is today."

"People once lived with Lathon?"

"Yes, but in a world that was now filled with sin, there was a great divide that took place in their hearts. They could not be with Lathon, for their sin separated them.

"But, Lathon devised a plan. Far beyond the imagination of the Sorcerer. He created a religion. It required sacrifice, remembrance, devotion, and above all else it required love."

"How does religion help fix the problems?" Drake asked.

"Religion can never fix the problems. If you look at the Elvish beliefs today, it is nothing like it should be. It's filled with traditions and rules that no one can ever hope to keep. In addition, the Farsees have made so many *extra* rules over the years, that quite frankly, it disgusts me.

"But behind the scenes, Lathon is using the religion for the purpose he intended. He used the prophets to call attention to something that was beyond them. To the one that would save the world."

"Sherados!" Drake said.

Aiden nodded. "You want to know why Lathon sent an heir to save the world? I think it was because he wanted to end religion. For thousands and thousands of years, people have made religion, changed religion, and wandered farther and farther from where they should be. I believe Lathon looks down at the world and is saddened by how far we've strayed. So he did the one thing that no one expected of him. Through his great power, he influenced the world forever by sending Sherados to save the world and by doing so, give all a chance to be reunified with him."

"So Sherados will fill the void? So to speak," Drake replied.

"Yes. By doing this, he would not only fulfill the purpose of the religion, but the people, if they believe in him, they will get to live with Lathon at the end of the ages. Religion would no longer be able to exist."

"Why not?" Drake asked.

"Religions follow someone dead or gone, but a relationship is with someone alive."

"You speak of Sherados and Lathon as if they're the same person, how is that possible?"

"If Lathon can create all that is around us, how much more can we trust him? Are you familiar with how Sherados came into this world?"

"No. I must admit I would've expected him to come into royalty. How else would he be able to save us?"

"That's the biggest misconception about Sherados. When you study the ancient scrolls and prophecies, you begin to realize that Lathon was a humble person, if he was to return he would not come into royalty, he would humble himself and come into the world as an ordinary person, that way he could truly live with the people he wanted to save. Plus it would be the last thing that the Sorcerer would expect."

"How did Sherados come into the world?" Drake asked.

"Find it inside yourself," Aiden answered. Confusion swarmed Drake's mind at first, but then peace overcame him and he looked for the answer, searching through all of the knowledge that they had gained while living with the Gogs.

They had read the ancient scrolls and had been educated in all the ways of the world. The more he thought about and surveyed the situation, the more he realized that Lathon was far different from what Drake had first thought. Chills swept through Drake.

"Aiden. You are Sherados aren't you?"

Aiden smiled weakly. "What does your heart tell you?"

"It tells me that you are Sherados," Drake replied. "I can't believe it! All this time and you've been right in front of us. Living with us, eating with us, fighting with us, and we've missed you."

"Until now," Aiden pointed out.

"I can't believe it."

"That's why you missed me for so long because you didn't believe it. I am right in front of you Drake Thomas, I've been right in front of everyone. I came into this world as a normal person so that *I* could get to know the people that I love. Any fool can have a religion but I wanted something more. Something greater, something the Sorcerer would never understand. Even he has missed me. He thinks you are Sherados. If he truly read the ancient scrolls he would have seen the truth."

"I'm not sure what to say," Drake concluded. "You are right by our side waiting for us to come to you and most of us don't ever do that."

"True again. But know this Drake. You have found the truth, now what are you going to do with the time that is left?"

"Make sure that I tell everyone I can who you really are."

Aiden smiled. "If I may say one thing. I'm not looking for fans…I'm looking for followers. I warn you ahead of time, some people will not like what you have to say, and you will likely be thrown into prison or persecuted for what you believe in the days ahead. But if in your heart you believe, then you will not care about what happens to your body, the worst they can do in this world is kill your body."

"Are you saying there's another?"

"I'm saying there always has been. Something beyond what you can see or reach with your hands. There is something else and you will see it someday, but only when your time here is done. Death is just another part of life that we all must take."

"Do you have the mark as I do?" Drake asked, showing his hand to him. Aiden pulled off a glove and held out his palm, showing him the scar of three slashes. "Incredible."

"If you've had this scar all along why didn't you show anyone before this? Why didn't you come in and just save the day before there was pain and suffering?"

"I didn't want to come until the time was right. Until people could see that there was a line drawn. I wanted to make sure that those who loved me, truly did love and believe that I could save them. If I had come too early people wouldn't have believed I was who I said I was because the evil wasn't as clear to them. I wanted there to be no mistaking it when I came."

They fell silent.

"So what happens now, the end of the world or something?"

"That's what people have always thought, but no, that's not the case. The world will not end anytime soon Drake. This age is about to end, but a new one is just beginning. We will march against the armies of Grimdor and the Sorcerer and we will defeat him and then this portion of the world will be as it was meant to be before the time of the Sorcerer."

"I worry about the future."

"The future is not yours to worry about. Worry does nothing but cause a headache, I'm not worried about the future."

"You're not?"

"I can beat the Sorcerer in an instant if he chooses to show himself."

"What if he doesn't show himself?" Drake asked, dread filling his heart. Aiden just smiled.

"More likely than not he will just stay in his castle and command his thousands and thousands of troops and we'll never see him. He's a coward and that's the simple truth. After we get the Wizard's Staff, we will march directly to the gates of Iscariot and wage our war, forcing him to come out of hiding and fight us head-on."

"Ambitious plan."

"That's why we have to pursue it. The Sorcerer wants us to feel powerless, as though we can't do anything to stop him. We need to rush forward with our swords drawn and storm Iscariot's gates, restoring it to its former glory."

"Have you ever seen the walls of Iscariot?" Drake asked.

"I have and trust me it's not going to be an easy battle. Each second that we don't act is another second that allows the Sorcerer to grow stronger yet. We cannot delay."

"I'm afraid to run head-on into the battle."

"You have to have faith about these things Drake. You must trust in the prophecies and that Lathon has a plan for you."

"See, feel, trust, I know."

They looked out into the ocean as it churned before them. Their attention was diverted to a commotion coming from the stairwell that led to the lower level of the ship. Ellizar and Lily came out with Gwen and Skander right behind. Lily had a smile on her face while Ellizar mumbled under his breath.

"Good morning everyone," Drake greeted. Ellizar looked at him and then shook his head, turning to look at Lily.

"Blasted elf kind!" Ellizar exclaimed.

"What did you do to him this time?" Drake asked. Lily shrugged her shoulders.

"She didn't do anythin' teh me in the real world, but in my dream...oh in my dreams, she did outrageous things!"

"Such as?" Gwen asked.

"Such as hidin' my ax on me and givin' me a wooden sword teh storm the Borags with. I believe she also hid all my food. It was a terrible dream."

"I'm so sorry Ellizar," Lily started. "I tend to find it amusing how easily Dwarves are bothered by the threat of food."

Ellizar laughed and turned to Aiden. "Blasted elf kind! So what's new? Are we preparing to land and battle on Calamar?"

"Not yet, we have another day before we get there. We should be there by dawn," Aiden answered.

"Before anyone says anything else I must tell all of you something," Drake said. "Aiden...is Sherados." Everyone looked at him.

"You're certain?" Skander asked. Drake nodded, and Aiden showed them his palm. Immediately they all fell to their knees and bowed to their king. Drake did the same and he couldn't help but notice that the Gogs were watching their ship with curiosity. Aiden looked at them and reached down and grabbed Lily's hand, bringing her back to her feet. The others did the same.

"You may bow if you wish, but if you are the chosen ones of Lathon you can prove it by how you live. If you put others first then the whole world will see just how much you are like me and thus have an eternal impact on their souls."

"Yeh Elves are lucky!" Ellizar said. "Yeh are the chosen ones, the rest of us are left teh our own demise." Aiden looked at him funny.

"I don't think that's true my friend. That may have been what you have been taught all these years, but that's where the Farsees have it all wrong. For years they have thought that only the Elves would be saved and maybe the race of Men if they were united once again. In reality, one is not made a child of Lathon because of their ears, or their height, it's the heart that matters to me. Nothing else.

"It's not all the rules that the Farsees tell you. Religion is dead and it will stay that way for the rest of time as far as I'm concerned. I wanted a relationship, a chance to fight and love and then demonstrate my love for all the world to see. It's part of why I came to live among you, so I could set the record straight once and for all. I may have come first to the Elves, but the life I bring is for all nations."

They talked and chatted for several more minutes until a horn bellowed to their left. They looked to see one of the Gog ships coming towards them. The massive ship pulled alongside. Without stopping or slowing, a wooden plank was extended from the deck of the ship, connecting to theirs. Shavrok walked down the plank and soon joined them at the bow. The two ships continued on a parallel course.

"Greetings exalted one!" Shavrok greeted. Weapons were strapped to his back and his waist and it appeared as though the spikes that protruded from his back and his shoulders, as well as his hands, had been sharpened and polished.

"You don't know the half of it," Drake exclaimed. "He's Sherados." Shavrok's face showed surprise at first but then a smile spread across it.

"Long have the Gogs suspected this great news and now it is finally confirmed. Our troops are at your disposal, your majesty!" Shavrok bowed for a moment before standing and looking back to the other ship. "We will be honored to fight against the Sorcerer with Sherados. Never did we expect that the great one himself would come and live among us. I tell you the truth, a love like this speaks louder than the opposing voices and would destroy the Sorcerer in a second."

"And destroy him it will," Aiden said. "Are there some new developments that I should know about?"

"Our scout ships have sent several messenger birds to us, saying that they have spotted a convoy of twenty ships or more heading to the coast of Calamar. We've confirmed that they are Grimdorian vessels. We believe them to carry reinforcements, and that a main force of Borags is already on the islands looking for the Wizard's Staff. Our ships are far superior to theirs and we are certain that if we extend the top sails we will be able to catch them before they can get word to Calamar. Probably around midnight or so."

"We cannot let them reach the shore or get messages of any kind to land. Have they spotted you?" Aiden asked.

"It's unlikely," Shavrok answered. "Our scout ships are far ahead of us. A couple of them have already landed on the island and are putting together an attack plan and scouting out the city."

"Very good. Prepare your troops for the battle ahead."

"We will do our part!" Shavrok exclaimed with enthusiasm. He bowed again.

"When we reach the island this ship will go around the island while the Gogs attack the main city. This should draw all the troops to you allowing us to wander the island and look for the Wizard's Staff. I'm sure Barnabas wouldn't want to damage his ship."

"You've got that right!" Barnabas yelled from the back, coming near them. "I've heard what you said and I know who this man is. Many won't believe, but I do and this ship is yours for as long as you want it, though I would like to keep it in one piece."

"It's much appreciated," Aiden replied.

The topsails were extended, increasing their speed by twice what it had been. The Gogs came over with the proper supplies and fitted Barnabas's ship with a sail that was similar allowing them to keep up with all the other ships. Drake held onto the railing unable to comprehend how fast they were traveling.

They would be soon landing on Calamar and Drake had no idea what to expect. Gwen caught his gaze. He smiled and took her hand, the two of them remained at the bow for a long while. Time passed and it seemed like they were the only two in the world. Drake's fear vanished and he found himself ready for the battle.

Atruss walked out into the forest that he and his wife now called home. For the past ten years, they had lived in the palace and now they were living in the wilderness. A white horse and a rider appeared over the hilltop.

Rohemir came into their camp and dismounted his horse before it was even brought to a stop. They embraced for a moment before taking a seat next to the fire.

"I hear some interesting things have happened since we've last seen each other," Rohemir stated.

"I take it you got my letter?"

"It was most intriguing. I had a hard time believing they actually kicked you out of the city or the nation for that matter, but now I can see they were serious."

"They were serious, let there be no doubt about that. Thankfully the high and mighty haven't figured out that we never left. We wanted to talk to you first."

"That's probably a good thing, I would have been very confused when I walked into Belvanor."

"They have kicked us out as I told you in the letter and they have also elected you to be the new leader if you want the position. I'm not sure if that's a good thing or a bad thing."

"I'm not sure I'm the right person to lead the nation, but yet I feel an obligation to lead them. Do you have any advice for me?"

"Remember Lathon, and then stand up for what you believe no matter what the cost. You know as well as I do that they've hated Aiden and me for standing up to them."

"I think the word hate is a little extreme," Rohemir replied. "They might dislike the two of you, but for good reason, you've opposed them at every turn."

"And for good reason," Atruss defended.

"If you and Gabrielle are the only ones left in the nation, where is everyone else?"

"On their way to Calamar to find the Wizard's Staff, if there's any chance of defeating the Sorcerer, this is it."

"The Wizard's Staff?" Rohemir asked. "Can't say I was expecting that. Many people believe that it's a legend and doesn't exist. However, you and I both know differently."

"Yes indeed," Atruss answered. "What are you going to do my friend? I can't stay here forever, we must be on our way. If we're going to confront the Sorcerer then we need all the help we can get."

"I don't mean to sound discouraged but do we really think that we can stand against the nation of Grimdor? The Sorcerer has brought the Borags and Spirits together and he is far stronger than he ever was in the past. We're just one nation. We don't stand a chance."

"No, we don't stand a chance; however I will be riding into battle nonetheless. The time for action has come and I shall respond. Furthermore, I received a letter from Drake and the Gogs this morning saying that Sherados has come forward, which means he will unite the races of Men and Elves once again. The small force we have built has now become much more dangerous."

"I'm not sure what's more terrifying, Sherados having come forward or going to battle against Gogs. Are you sure they exist? Once again they are said to have been extinct."

"Aiden and I have known differently for some time and now they have finally gone to war. They will all be landing on the shores of Calamar by tomorrow morning."

"Keeping secrets from your best friend? That feels nice."

"Only three of us ever knew about them, and Aiden was the one who revealed them to me."

"Figures."

"There is one more thing you need to know," Atruss started. "Aiden is Sherados."

"Aiden? The Tarukai? The one that the Farsees and the council hate with a passion?"

"The same one. It was surprising to me, although in my heart I've always known there was something different and unique about him. I never guessed he was Sherados, but even so, I feel terrible that he was in front of me the whole time and I never saw it coming."

"You just made my job a hundred times more difficult. I may be able to get the council and Farsees to cooperate with me, but I can't even hope of getting them to follow or assist Aiden in any way. I could very well be killed for suggesting that."

"I know it's a tough spot but it's the only option we have. We can't hold off attacking the Sorcerer any longer. We have to attack now and try our best. All nations have to come forward and try to stand. We have people all over the place rounding up loyal troops."

"You do?"

"Yes, we have some people in Epirus and I'm sure there's some in Idumea. I don't know all the people personally, but I know people are willing to take a stand, especially when they find out Sherados has come forward."

"The Sorcerer might be caught off guard by an attack on his own city but still, he's the most powerful Sorcerer to have ever lived in the world, I'm sure that he knows about what's going on and will be ready for you. I've lived inside the walls of Iscariot for many years and I know those walls will not be easily breached."

"I know that as well. Aiden didn't seem to be overly concerned about that. He seemed to think he had a way to get into the city. I can't imagine what that might be."

"I'm not sure I want to know," Rohemir replied pacing. "I'll take the job of leading this nation, but I cannot guarantee that I'll be able to do anything helpful. As you said, the council and the Farsees are more controlling than they used to be."

"Yes, but nothing says you couldn't break the rules and take charge regardless of what they said."

"That would be treason."

"Would it be better to let the Sorcerer's armies come crashing through the gates?" Atruss asked. "You know as well as I that's what's going to happen eventually. The other nations have already been attacked and for the most part, conquered. Epirus, Idumea, Giahon, I'm sure Farndor, and Calamar have been invaded. He doesn't need to go into Vernal because he's forced the Spirits to work for him. He will reach Ariamore, it's just a matter of when."

"I will do what I can, but I can't make any promises. You understand don't you?"

"Yes, I understand."

Rohemir stood up and began to walk away, his horse came to him. "What are you going to do?"

"We're going to stay hidden, but ride throughout Ariamore where it is safe and tell people the good news that Sherados has come forward. That alone should scare the Sorcerer a little bit."

"Perhaps." Rohemir mounted his horse and wished Atruss goodbye spurring his horse and disappearing into the forest. Atruss's heart shuddered in his chest. There was something in the air that warned of trouble, yet as hard as he looked he couldn't see it.

A while later Atruss sat in silence, carefully watching the woods. The world was headed to war and what lay on the other side no one could know. Gabrielle came up over a distant hill with a couple of rabbits in her hands and her bow on her back.

She reached their campsite and put the rabbits on the ground, sitting next to Atruss and then looking towards him. Questions filled her eyes and unfortunately, he didn't have any of the answers. They lightly talked for a few minutes, while they cooked the rabbits and had a tasty meal. When they were done they sat talking for a little while longer before putting the fire out and packing their supplies. They had too much to do to sit back.

They mounted their horse and rode off into the forest with Gabrielle hanging onto him. An owl flew overhead and then screeched, catching their attention. They came to a stop and the owl swooped down to them, landing on the horse's head.

Atruss grabbed the envelope in its beak and then it took off, flying over to a tree several feet away. Atruss read the words on the paper his heart jumping for joy at the words he read. He wrote a response, sending the owl off to the destination. They remounted their horse and sped through the forest knowing full well what would happen.

They rode into several small cities and outposts telling everyone the good news and telling them to be ready to depart at any moment. The men agreed and the word spread quickly as Atruss and Gabrielle left and continued to the next town or city.

They put all their faith into Aiden, Sherados. They didn't know how things would turn out, but they rushed into battle, hoping to defeat their enemies. Regardless of how things played out, they were grateful to have been kicked out of Belvanor. Sherados was now with them. Who could stand against them?

XIII   A PROPHECY FULFILLED

The mansion was silent and the stars shone down on Marion and Joseph as they lay on the ground looking up to the heavens. Joseph looked at his wife, more in love with her now as he had been when they had met. The servants had finished their work for the day and were now fast asleep. Beyond their mansion, Grimdor lay in complete darkness.

The world had changed a lot in the past few months and somehow they had been overlooked by everything. They could hear Borag armies walking throughout Grimdor and into Epirus, but they had never seen one Borag. It was as if no one knew they were here and they could live in peace because of it.

As much as Joseph was grateful they could live in peace, he hated it. Why should they be so lucky to have been forgotten while hundreds of thousands of other people were being hunted like animals? The question had plagued them both for the past couple of months. They had thought of leaving and going to war, but something had whispered inside their heart that they were supposed to be here for a little while longer.

Marion looked at him and smiled, holding his gaze for several seconds. Every day that passed Joseph was more and more grateful that they had been brought together even if it had been through some unusual circumstances. The night faded and eventually, Marion fell asleep, her head on his chest. His arm was around her and it seemed like there was nothing else in the world than the two of them.

The air was warm even though they knew during this time of year it should be winter. How long could the Sorcerer continue like this before Sherados would come forward?

His mind drifted to that night so many years ago when the elf kings had come to visit. He and Marion had known that the child was not their own and that he was Sherados, but it was the elf kings that had visited them that had made him even more curious. Did everyone who looked at their son know that he was Sherados?

The flapping of wings rippled through the sky and the shape of an owl became visible in the faint light provided by the fire. Joseph gently kissed Marion on the head and moved her head off of his chest. He covered her over with a blanket and then walked to the owl which had landed on the far side of the fire.

Joseph grabbed the letter from the owl's beak and quietly opened it, reading the words that were written inside. He smiled and his heart leaped for joy as he read the words, at the bottom of the page was his best friend's name.

He moved over to Marion and shook her awake. She smiled at him as though she was in a dream she didn't want to wake from. He helped her sit up and waved the letter in his one hand. Her eyes displayed confusion at first, but soon she knew what he meant.

"He came forward?" Marion asked. Joseph shook his head.

"Yes, he did. Aiden finally revealed himself to the world. The one to make the way for him has been doing just that. The word is spreading quickly. The end is not far off. Did you ever imagine that we would see this day?"

"Only in my dreams!" Marion exclaimed. "We have to tell Bethany and Sedric."

"They're the ones who sent the letter. They know. They said that Aiden and his company would soon be coming and that we should come immediately."

"I'll second that motion," Marion said standing up. They turned and ran into the house. Though the rest of the mansion was silent and dark. Marion and Joseph wasted no time in lighting every candle that they could, waking all the servants, and having them meet in the main living space. Marion and Joseph ran up to their room and pulled out a couple of bags, stuffing them with a few sets of clothes and food.

Smiles spread across their faces as they walked into the main living space where their sleepy-eyed staff of servants stood or sat, trying to wake up. The servants immediately stood in a line when they walked in.

"The reason we have called you here is nothing to be afraid of," Joseph said. "Instead I have good news that is for all people. Sherados has come forward and is now preparing to defeat the darkness once and for all." At that, a light entered all the servants' eyes and they looked at each other, smiles on their faces. "The moment we thought we might never live to see has at last come. What I'm going to ask you to do is nothing short of crazy. Marion and I are leaving. How long we do not know, but we are filled with so much joy that we cannot help but leave. I can see in your eyes the very same emotions even now.

"You've known about this day for as long as you've worked here and my next job for you is to leave this mansion and home you've known for so long and go everywhere, telling everyone you meet, that Aiden is Sherados. Marion and I were blessed enough to have been chosen to be the parents of this child, even though at the time we didn't understand. Now everything is clear and the end is nearing." Marion moved from his side and took a picture from the wall, revealing a small chest in a hole. Together they removed the chest and then grabbed a key and unlocked it revealing numerous bags of gold. They motioned the servants forward one at a time.

"This is all I have to give you," Joseph told them. "This is your salary for the next ten years. It may be a long time till we are here together, so we will pay you accordingly, and may Lathon be with you all in your journeys."

"But, before we go, a toast!" Marion went into the kitchen and they all followed as she broke the seal on a bottle of wine and poured them all a glass. They drank and celebrated for a few minutes until Marion and Joseph took their leave. They wrote a quick letter of reply to Sedric and Bethany and then gave it to the owl that was waiting. The owl flew off into the night and vanished from their sight.

They walked to the stables where Marion and Joseph found their horses ready and waiting for them. They mounted and waved to their servants who all said their goodbyes. Before they were out of earshot they could hear all their servants mounting their horses and heading out into the nations.

Time passed as they rode at whatever speed they could, the only light coming from the pale moon and the stars above. Grimdor's border was pitch black, with not a single star or light to be seen. Joseph had been in Grimdor on only a few occasions and it was something he would rather forget. They turned and headed east.

Bethany and Sedric had been in his thoughts and prayers for many years. Within a couple of years of the events in Masada, Bethany, and Sedric had left for the East. They had only come back a year ago, searching for something that had been lost.

They rode hard, taking only a quick break for breakfast before continuing forward. Their son occupied their mind, each of them knowing that even though he was their son he was just as much not their son. He was special and Marion and Joseph knew in their hearts that they were only his earthly parents.

Even so, they couldn't be more proud as the horses galloped through the countryside, the wind blowing through their hair and the sun beating down on them. Time faded and now they found the skies darkening and the smell of rain drifting in on the breeze. They weren't entering Grimdor but they were entering a place that was similar in many ways.

The spirit nation of Vernal stood before them. It always rained in these mountains and today was no different. The nation was unmarked on all the maps because people feared it. They didn't speak and slowed their horses to a walk as they picked their way through the mountains.

Time vanished and so did their thoughts. Joseph and Marion found themselves deep in a twisting maze of mountains. They looked all around, noticing a light in the distance. Several hours later they stopped their horses next to the opening in the mountain.

Scrambling was heard in the cave and the lantern was left on even though they both knew the people were hiding. Joseph helped Marion off the horse and put his arm around her as they walked into the cave. They were ripped from each other, Marion shoved up against the wall and Joseph thrown to the hard floor a sword to each of their throats.

The world spun for Joseph and when it finally stopped he found himself looking into the face of his captor. He smiled and then his captor began to laugh as Sedric put his sword away and helped him off the floor. Bethany also put her sword away, both of them embracing their long-lost friends.

"Way to give me a scare," Joseph said. "I thought for a second that we had wandered into the wrong cave."

"I don't think there's any danger of that. To my knowledge, we are the only humans hiding in these mountains. It's a wonder that we've been able to remain hidden for this long. We've been here for six months now and no one suspects a thing. It can be a challenge to stay isolated for this long."

"I can certainly imagine," Marion replied. "It's so good to see you again. We got your letter and we couldn't help but set out right away."

"I'm not sure what the future holds but something big is going to happen," Bethany said. "I'll bet you will be happy just to see your son again."

"It has been a long time. I wonder who the person with him is."

"Person with him?" Sedric asked.

"The person who will make the way for Sherados. The note you sent didn't say anything about the other person."

"That's because we don't know anything about the other person," Bethany replied. "We only know what we were told and we've told you everything we know. If the word is spreading as quickly as you say it is then the time for war is near."

"I'm a carpenter and not much of a warrior. I'm not sure how I'll hold up in a battle," Joseph admitted.

"That is something you cannot worry about," a voice said from behind them. Marion and Joseph turned to see a dark silhouette standing just outside of the light. His hair was longer and a cape trailed behind him as his features came into focus.

"Who are you?" Marion asked.

"A person you should be grateful to have on your side. My name is Cerin I am a Spirit who has dwelt in these mountains for many years."

"Don't worry, we can trust him," Bethany said. "He is the one who gave us this cave to hide in."

"Don't the Spirits work with the Sorcerer and Grimdor?" Joseph asked.

"There are a few of us who have found a loophole and decided to act on it. I will not say more on this subject except that the majority of us are on your side and seek to wound the Sorcerer in any way that we can. Once I knew what they were hiding, the decision for me was quite simple."

"The Wizard's Staff?" Marion asked. Cerin nodded.

"Some might say it was foolish to hide the very thing the Sorcerer was looking for in a nation that's supposedly loyal to him, but I think there could be no better place than right under his nose. Turns out I was right."

"We're very grateful for being able to hide here," Sedric answered. "It won't be long until they arrive and then I'm not sure what we'll do."

"How about we start by cooking dinner?" Marion suggested.

"Excellent idea," Cerin agreed. "However, you will find food rather scarce in this nation."

"Then it's a good thing we brought some of our food." Marion and Joseph unstrapped the bags of food that had been tied to their horses and they cooked it and celebrated. They invited Cerin to join them, but he only watched for a few minutes before leaving and turning into a cloud of blue mist, racing off into the rainy world somewhere beyond.

XIV CALAMAR

The crew of the ships were silent, while the churning of the sea surrounded them. The wind had died down a little bit, allowing them to make a quieter approach on the ships that awaited them. Fog rolled in, further hiding them from their enemies.

Shavrok surveyed the greeting party they had put together. The Gogs had been thought to have been extinct all these years and now they were ready to reveal themselves and destroy their enemies.

Their massive ship moved ever closer to the Borag ships which looked puny compared to the Gog ships. They would take out this convoy of ships and then they would storm the main island providing a proper distraction for Aiden, Drake, and the rest of them to move around to the other side of the island. Shavrok glanced to the left where Barnabas's ship drifted off into the dark murky waters, moving away from the main fleet as planned.

Nearly fifty ships were being sent to destroy the fleet of twenty ships. The deck of the Borag ships had some torches lit. The Gogs had gotten rid of all their torches, only planning to light them after they had announced their presence.

"Grovarich!" Shavrok yelled as quietly as he could. The person at the wheel of the ship stood at attention. "Turn our ship directly into the side of the nearest one. With our size difference, it'll be like walking through a field of flowers."

"Yes sir," the reply came as he and the men with him made the proper adjustments. The other ships followed his lead. The ships moved closer and still, there was no sign of their presence having been detected.

Shavrok grabbed his horn and blew it into the air announcing their arrival to everyone on the Borag ships. The call was echoed by the other Gog ships on either side. The decks of the Borag ships immediately came alive. The Gogs lit torches, revealing themselves to their enemies.

The first Borags drew their weapons and yelled out orders to turn the ships, trying to avoid being sideswiped. The effort was useless as the Gog vessels raced forward and collided with the ships. Crunching wood was heard and then the sound of screaming, cursing, and water as their reinforced bow cut through the middle of the ship.

The bow separated from the back of the ship. The Borags tried to grab onto the Gog ships but they weren't fast enough as they were soon by them and they were left to sink with their wreckage. Shavrok turned his attention to the next group of ships.

"Turn the ship and run parallel with them!" Shavrok yelled. The men did as he instructed, turning the ship but doing it a little slower than the Borags had expected. The two ships raced towards each other and finally struck side to side. The hull of the Borag ship was cracked and shattered, but not as badly as the last ship. Shavrok's men leapt off the deck to the Borag ship below.

Shavrok jumped onto the mast and then dropped down to the main deck where everyone was landing. The Borags drew their swords. He roared and raced forward, backhanding the first Borag he came to. The spikes on the back of his hand caught the Borag and sent him flying through the air.

Another Borag moved to attack Shavrok but soon found himself floundering in the ocean as Shavrok picked the man up and threw him over the side. Torches were thrown at them but Shavrok and a couple of others caught them in midair. They touched them to the tarps and sails, consuming them in fire. They threw the torches into the lower deck of the ship and blocked the entrance as the ship burned from the inside out.

Despite the peril to their ship the Borags didn't try to save it and instead raced towards them with a hatred that was deep-rooted beyond Shavrok's comprehension.

The back of the ship spewed black smoke into the foggy air as the flames began to come up through the boards. Another Borag ship turned towards them, forced to do so by a Gog ship on the other side.

The ship was forced into them, colliding with the blazing inferno that the Gogs had created. The Gogs rushed forward and spanned the gap between the two ships, grabbing onto the railings and then pulling themselves over the edge, spearing the Borags with the spikes protruding from their backs.

The soldiers of the ship were defeated and soon the fires began to spread on this ship as well. Shavrok blew through a different horn, this time calling one of their ships towards them. The ship moved by and the Gogs jumped from the deck of the ship, grabbing onto nets that had been dropped over the side. They climbed onto the deck and pulled the nets up watching the ships burn and sink to the bottom of the ocean.

A cry of celebration was heard as Aiden and Drake came flying in on Elohim and Destan. They flanked one ship, each of the Taruks letting out a plume of fire that consumed every part of it. The Taruks twisted around the next ship, narrowly missing arrows fired by the Borags. Destan's claws wrapped themselves around the mast, ripping it off and dropping it into the ocean. Elohim swooped low into the opening that had been created.

He climbed back into the sky for a brief second before dropping down and wrapping his claws around the side of the ship and the shattered deck. Elohim pushed off and with it ripped the side of the ship apart. Shavrok smiled as the two Taruks sunk ships just as fast as the Gogs did.

Flames spread through the sky and this time they weren't from the Taruks as Rade and the Korazin raced towards them. They swooped low and devastated another Grimdorian vessel. The entire bottom half of the ship was destroyed, sending the ship to the bottom of the sea. The battle continued for several more minutes until, as planned, only three Borag ships remained and these three had been taken over but not destroyed.

Rade and the other Korazin landed on the deck of Shavrok's ship, taking the form of regular people after the flames subsided. Aiden and Drake slid off the Taruks as they flew overhead, only having to fall a few feet until they landed on the deck of the ship.

"I'm glad I don't have to go to war against you guys!" Drake exclaimed.

"They don't stand a chance against the Gogs!" Shavrok exclaimed.

"I'm sure they don't, but still be careful. We don't know how many Borags are going to be on this island and we can't afford to underestimate them," Aiden warned.

"Your point is well seen, and we will be careful. However, I think you need to be more careful than we do. I'm not sure what you'll find on the other side of the island, but I'm sure it won't be a walk in the park.

"True enough," Aiden replied, turning to Rade. "Was your trip successful?"

"Fairly."

"Glad to hear it," Aiden said. "In that case, we'd better be off and we'll catch up later." They said their goodbyes and then dropped into the water. Destan and Elohim dove beneath them and then rose into the sky. Shavrok watched as the two Taruks and their riders disappeared.

"Prepare for assault. We aren't far from the coast. Prepare the landing parties on all ships and prepare the catapults!"

"If you don't mind. I think myself and a couple of the Korazin would like to help in this attack," Rade said.

"Only a fool would turn down help when it's offered. What did you have in mind?"

Pale light filtered through the fog. Shavrok rode on one of the landing barges, following a hundred yards behind the three Borag ships they had taken over. Rade and the Korazin stood on the deck of the ships in Borag form, at least making it appear as though they were still under Borag's control.

Shavrok's barge led nearly a thousand others, each filled with Gogs. There were still more on the ships themselves and he knew they would join the battle once they had taken the ship in as far as they dared.

The fog hid the city from their view until they were only twenty feet from the dock. Beyond that, a dark outline resembling a city stood on the horizon. The men on the ship couldn't likely see the city yet.

Rade and the Korazin looked back and Shavrok nodded. Shavrok put a horn to his mouth. The other ships returned the call.

The commotion of the orders being carried out filled the night as boulders covered with oil were lit and then launched through the air. The projectiles rained through the sky, pummeling the main wall of the city. The wall cracked and splintered. More catapults were launched, while the landing barges picked up their pace running ashore.

They released the gate on the landing barge and charged onto the land, looking for any sign of their enemies. The wall was still being pummeled by the boulders, but so far the bottom part of the wall had been left intact making it that much harder for them to get in.

Fire raced through the sky and then an explosion echoed from the left where Rade and the Korazin had struck the outer gate. Borags poured out, while countless Gogs landed on the shore and rushed forward. The Korazin pulled up into the sky, once against taking the form of fire. They spiraled several times before diving to the ground.

They tunneled into the ground and the whole earth shook and rumbled at the force of the impact. The section of the wall was blown twenty feet into the air, sending flaming projectiles into the Borag army. Shavrok watched in amazement as a crater remained.

Shavrok and the other Gogs rushed into the city, quickly disabling any Borags that tried to oppose them.

Another horn echoed from behind, but this one didn't belong to Grimdor. Shavrok strained his eyes to see the source of the sound.

He let the other Gogs continue while watching as a legion of men came into view. He jumped into their path and the men stopped. The men before him, shrunk back in his presence.

"And whose side are you on?" Shavrok boomed.

"We fight with you great beast. Forgive us, but we do not know your kind. Nonetheless, there is much to do and little time to do it. This city was our home until recent events forced us to the mountain. We seek to avenge the death of our loved ones and fight alongside you!"

"Fulfill your blood-lust and we shall be victorious!" Shavrok let another roar escape him and together they ran into the battle giving chase to the Borags who were fleeing. A few minutes later they found the Gogs assembled in one place. A large wall before them stood nearly thirty feet tall. A quick scan of the horizon told them that there weren't any buildings for them to climb on, or if there had they had been destroyed. The Borags were on the other side and on top of the wall with the stone doors shut and barred.

"Do you know how we can get into the keep?" Shavrok asked. The man smiled.

"There's an entrance on the south side of the island, an underground tunnel that runs to the keep of this city. We have men stationed there and they should be arriving any moment."

"Rade! Couldn't you just destroy the walls again?"

"Probably, but we've still got to have the strength to fight. I saw this wall from a flyover and it's nearly thirty feet thick. It would require an enormous amount of energy."

"In that case, we shall wait for your friends. We can trust you can't we?" Shavrok asked. The man nodded his head.

"Long ago three brothers witnessed the king coming into this world. Now we shall see him seated on the throne as he should be."

"Three kings?" Shavrok asked his curiosity peaked. "I know your stories and prophecies and am a believer and follower of Lathon. Are you saying?"

"Berdin, second eldest of the three sons of Herma at your service." Shavrok trembled. He knew those names as well as anyone who was well-versed in the stories that had circulated in the past twenty years. He had held strong in his faith and had always believed, but now beyond the shadow of a doubt, he knew he was right. His heart leapt for joy.

"We are at your service, my king!" Shavrok announced, kneeling and bowing to him. Berdin just smiled.

"Do not waste your time bowing to me. I am not worthy of anything. I am only an elf, the one who will lead us against Grimdor, however, is far greater than you or I, or the whole world for that matter. If you must bow then bow to him and if you must pledge your allegiance to anyone then may it be to the king of kings!" Shavrok smiled and stood.

"Your words are golden and the truth is easily seen in them. We will serve only the king of kings no matter what this world has to offer us."

"What if your homes are destroyed and your families?" Berdin asked. "What will you say then?"

"I came into this world with nothing and I shall leave with nothing. Blessed be the king who reigns forever."

"You are indeed a follower of Lathon, in both mind and spirit. It will be an honor to fight this evil alongside you."

"As will we."

"For Lathon!"

All the men cried out as they turned their attention to the wall. The cheering drew the attention of all the Borags on the wall, striking fear into all their hearts. When finally the cheering subsided, silence followed, interrupted only by the sound of an explosion. Fire and smoke poured into the sky and debris rained down on their enemies in the keep. Shavrok and his men drew their weapons.

They silently rowed their small boat through the water, clouded by the dense fog that surrounded them. Trees towered in front of them, their outline barely visible. The air was cool and damp.

Aiden sat at the rear of the small boat with Drake and Gwen sitting in front of him, each with a paddle in their hands. Ellizar, Lily, and Skander were in a boat just a few feet from them, while twenty or thirty soldiers were in other boats, slowly making their way to the shore.

"Have you ever been here before Aiden?" Drake asked.

"This is one of the many places I haven't been."

"What do you mean one of the many?" Gwen asked. "Everywhere we go you show up or have been there."

"There's more to this world than what you know my friends. There are many places I have not been yet. I soon will travel to these places though." They didn't ask any more questions, interrupted by the boats running aground. They pulled the boats onto shore and waited for everyone else to arrive. Eventually, all boats landed and the troops assembled behind them. Ellizar stood with his ax in hand.

"Ellizar, why don't you use a sword instead of an ax?" Lily asked in a whisper.

"Why don't you use an ax instead of a sword?" Ellizar countered.

"Okay," Lily replied. She grabbed the ax from him, unsheathed her sword, and handed it to him. He smiled.

"Blasted elf kind!" Ellizar exclaimed as quietly as he could. They silently started chuckling and they changed weapons again. "One of these days I'm going to outsmart you for a change!"

"Just do it before I'm an old lady, okay!"

"You two," Aiden said pointing at them. "Why don't you quiet down? The dead would be awakened by the ruckus you two are making."

"That's Elves for you," Ellizar said, following Aiden and the rest of them up to the forest.

Lily smiled "Good one."

The forest reached high above, inviting them closer, yet also wanting to make them turn and run away. The trees were dark and menacing. Their leafless branches extended into the air, weaving in unpredictable patterns. The ground was black and barren as though it had been scorched by the sun for a hundred years without rain.

"Do you think this place is safe Aiden?" Lily asked.

"Probably not. Then again, if Shavrok's attack distraction worked maybe we are alone."

"It feels like someone's watching us," Gwen said.

"I agree, but we haven't seen anyone," Drake answered.

"It doesn't mean they aren't there," Aiden replied leading them on a little further. Countless shapes moved through the fog toward them. Aiden was knocked down and so were the others. They tried to get back to their feet but they were held down tied and then pulled back to their feet. Their weapons were taken and at once their captors began looking through all the weapons, marveling at Aiden's sword..

Drake walked along, confusion plaguing him relentlessly as they were marched through the forest. They hadn't been captured by Borags, they had been captured by Men.

They reached a clearing that was large but surrounded by the same dark menacing trees that covered the rest of the island. They walked a few feet further and the fog vanished and the forest appeared green and beautiful.

Drake looked behind, trying to figure out what had happened. The sun shone above him, letting its rays of heat come down. In front of them was a small fortress, which was built out of a reddish-colored rock. The fortress was filled with troops. They were marched up to the main gate and then stopped as they stood and waited for something to happen.

The gates were opened and they were led into the small city. The troops paid them no mind as they were led through the streets and up the castle until they came to a small palace at the top of it. Surprisingly the city was laid out almost exactly like Belvanor, except on a smaller scale.

They entered the palace and made their way through the halls until finally they turned a corner and laid their eyes on a man standing at the front of a room. For a throne, it was nothing more than a great wooden chair. It still looked magnificent but it wasn't nearly as glorious as they would have expected. In front of the man was a table covered with food of every kind.

The man was older, his hair grey and his beard much the same. His clothes suggested a rich history while the rest of his demeanor said that he was a humble man. His deep brown eyes invited them forward and put them at ease about their situation. He studied each of them for several seconds, a smile tugged at his lips.

Drake studied the man further, noticing Elvish ears on the man. Tears welled up in the man's eyes as he came forward and bowed to one knee in front of Aiden. The man kissed his hand and looked at Drake, wonder in his eyes. A moment later he moved back to his seat, too weak to continue standing any longer.

"You have brought an unusual sword," the elf stated.

"Unusual to some, but to myself it has always been deeply treasured as have the other gifts I was given," Aiden replied. "I have always been grateful to the ones who welcomed me into the world when no other people did."

"You know this man?" Drake asked. Aiden nodded and smiled.

"Though I may not have ever spoken to him, I remember him in spirit, Drake Thomas. This man is a hero in the world, he and his brothers saw a star in the sky and did the unthinkable. They left their thrones and set course for a destination they did not know. They took a step of faith and traveled unceasingly until they found me."

"We only did what you had done for us," the elf answered. "Such a precious gift."

"Yet so many people will squander it," Aiden replied. "But blessed are those who have opened their eyes and see, for their hearts have been softened."

"Were they hard before?" Drake asked. The elf smiled.

"Some hearts were hardened by Lathon, but only because they refused to let him in. Think of it like a candle, if you are a follower of Lathon, like the flame that softens the wax of the candle, so is your heart softened. For those who choose the other gods that the various races of the earth have created, they have removed the flame leaving them hard and alone."

"Never thought of it like that," Lily replied.

"Few do," Drake concluded.

"Now where are my manners, I am Ishamel, eldest of three Elven-kings who welcomed Sherados into this world many years ago. Long have we waited to see this day and now we shall ride forth into battle and destroy our enemies with one swift blow."

They smiled as Ishamel motioned for all the doors to be opened. A mass of people came into the grand hall and filed around the group of them. The king stood on the throne, looking out to all the people.

"Ladies and gentlemen, dukes and duchesses, masters and servants, fathers and mothers, sons and daughters! I would like to introduce the one and only person we will follow from here on out. Before us, having come to our very halls is Sherados, Aiden!" Cheering rang through the halls and then all at once everyone bowed to one knee. Drake did the same.

Aiden walked to the weapons that had been taken from them and grabbed the double-handed broad sword that had been gifted to him when he was only a baby. He drew it from its sheath, the sound radiating through their hearts and their minds. Drake's own eyes were filled with tears as he watched the sight.

He may have figured out that Aiden was Sherados, but now in his heart, he truly believed it. Aiden thrust the sword into the air, and cheering erupted. Ishamel stood to his feet once again.

"What brings you all the way out to a little island nation called Calamar?"

"Do you not know?" Gwen asked, the elf smiled.

"I certainly have my fair guess. You are here to get the Wizard's Staff am I right?" They nodded in reply. "There have been countless people and Borags roaming the island as of late, trying to find the Wizard's Staff. They have searched in vain, they have not found it."

"Do you know where it is?" Lily asked. "Our sources have informed us that it's on this part of the island."

"I'd be curious to know who this source is, but yes, I have. I found it just about a week ago when I was walking in the forest. I hid it away immediately. I knew there was more at stake than just my life."

"Do the Borags know about this place?" Skander asked. "When we were being led here we were wandering through a dark foggy forest and then suddenly everything became as clear as day and sunny. It was like we had stepped into another world."

"The foggy world and the sunny world you are now in are the same. This place is hidden by the wisdom of Lathon. It is only able to be seen by those who are looking for the truth. Hundreds of people have walked by here and even walked right up to the walls and haven't seen a thing. Though the light was right in front of them they still were blind and continued on their way."

"Sounds like a metaphor for the world," Lily replied.

"More true than you know," Ishamel answered. "Follow me." They walked for a few minutes until they came to a slightly darkened room. A table sat in the center of the room, covered with a cloth.

"I must warn you ahead of time that when I take this cloth off the Wizard's Staff, you will feel something change inside of yourself. You are going to want it, you're going to be drawn into its power and you will not want to destroy it. This is the moment of truth. The moment when you find out once and for all if you have what it takes. This is when you find out whether you are truly a follower of Lathon."

"So if we can't resist that means we're not followers of Lathon."

"Let me rephrase that last statement," Ishamel said. "Lathon can always forgive because, after all, we always screw up. Don't we? But this is the moment that you will either be undone by the power of the staff or resist it. It is what happens afterward that reveals your true heart. If you come to your senses and realize your mistake, then you are not as far lost as you could be, if that makes sense."

The cloth covering the table was pulled away and the Wizard's Staff was revealed. As Ishamel had told them, the air in the room did change and they were left to ponder life by themselves.

Ishamel watched each of them carefully as every one of them was tempted by the power of the staff. Imagine the things they could do with it. Surely they could use this for good right?

Drake dismissed the question a moment later. He turned from the staff and the questions vanished immediately. He took a deep breath, he had survived the test. The others stared ahead, while Aiden looked at it and then around at all of them.

Drake watched as Gwen and Ellizar moved forward inch by inch until they were standing right in front of it. They stared into the ruby at the top, losing themselves to their thoughts. Drake's heart cried out to help the both of them but he could do nothing for them. Aiden watched with interest. Finally, they both looked away and Aiden stepped forward holding his hand out to Ishamel. Ishamel handed him the cloth and Aiden covered it over, relief flooding through all of them.

Gwen and Ellizar fell to the floor, exhausted by the effort it had taken to resist the Wizard's Staff. Drake now understood in his heart why the Sorcerer so desperately wanted to have it for himself.

"You have done well," Ishamel replied. Aiden wrapped the Wizard's Staff in the cloth and then left it on the table. Ishamel handed it to him and it was tucked into his belt. "As good as you may have done, this is not the moment for celebration. The closer you are to the Sorcerer the harder it will become to resist. You will find your heart wanting to see it just one last time, but you mustn't let your heart win. Stand firm in your faith and you will find the strength. If you let your guard down for only a second it will gain a foothold on you."

"Remember, you defeat temptation by refocusing, not resisting. What you resist, persists. Instead, just turn your attention elsewhere," Aiden told them.

"Now if you will follow me," Ishamel led the way, grabbing a torch from the wall. The oily flames flew out behind him a foot or so as they made their way down the darkened hallway. At the end of the hallway was a door that was simple yet seemingly elegant. "Behold a secret force that I and my brothers formed."

Ishamel pushed the door open and entered the room which was flooded with light. In front of them, a cave sat, having been carved out of the solid rock that made up the mountain they had seen. Dwarves milled around in the cave, thousands and thousands of them as well as Men and Elves.

"Dwarves!" Ellizar exclaimed. "I am overjoyed to know that I am not the only dwarf to be fighting in this war."

"Far from it, my friend."

"And I thought I was from a dying race!" Lily smiled and put her arm around Ellizar.

"How long have they been here?" Lily asked, overcome with the same emotion that filled Ellizar.

"They've been coming for nearly fifteen years. It started as just a few here and there. There are other Dwarvish nations in the world, but many of these Dwarves were brought on the White Ships."

"Sounds strangely familiar," Lily said. The tone in her voice intrigued Drake, but Ellizar's expression didn't give anything away. "Do you know where they are from?"

"They speak of strange places beyond my charts and maps. I sense there is a great deal of pain involved in the memories."

"It would be an honor to fight alongside some of my race!" Ellizar exclaimed.

"They have made tunnels that will come up into the middle of the city on the far side of the island."

"This is an amazing gift," Ellizar said. Drake envied him. He was happy for Ellizar, but he also wished that it hadn't happened. How many times had he wished to know his history, to remember the events that transpired before that day on the river? Too many to count and yet he had never remembered anything.

"Where are your brothers?" Skander asked. "According to legend didn't they go with you to welcome the king as well?"

"Indeed they did, and they still serve him in their old age. One of my brothers lives on this island as well. The northern shore. The other still lives in Ariamore. He set out on what we thought was an impossible mission, and we have not heard from him since."

"I am deeply sorry," Aiden said. "The death or vanishing of a loved one is not easy to deal with. Perhaps he is still alive."

"My heart fears the truth, though I cannot see for certain what that truth is. Truth is lost these days. Everyone wants to know what the truth is. Countless people asked me that when I was in Ariamore, I had half a mind to ask them if they wanted me to lie to them or give them a truthful answer, but I didn't. The truth is that Sherados has come to live among us and destroy the evil that ravages this land."

"That is both right and wrong," Aiden replied. "I came to live among my people and be their king again. Evil will one day be destroyed for good, but it is not this day. Instead, I came to defy death and make a way for people to join me in a world far from this one. The end will come, but the world will not end when this war ends."

"Speaking of war! What are we waiting fer?" Ellizar asked. "There's a battle going on upstairs and I want to be a part ov it."

Isabel and Morgrin had led the army from Fiori four days ago. The blistering sun beat down on the horses and their riders. Yet another reminder of the Sorcerer's great power. They were now in Idumea. The hard ground laid out in front of them with the vegetation showing the effects of the dry weather.

Night came and they made their camp and quickly fell asleep after they had eaten, entering the world of dreams. Isabel's dreams let her rest peacefully and the night faded until the morning came. Morgrin lay next to her buried beneath the blanket. Although the day had been hot, the night had turned cold, freezing the land to kill any plants that might have been alive.

The Sorcerer was indeed powerful.

She started a fire. On the horizon, the rock of Petron stood before them. She had to laugh. If she had realized they were that close she would've kept going.

Still, the rest had been nice.

Tremors filled the ground, drawing her attention while everyone continued sleeping. She spotted a cloud of dust to their north. She grabbed her horn and blew through it alerting all the soldiers. She mounted a horse and quickly rode to the north side of the camp. A cavalry approached as the army behind her assembled.

The cavalry brought their steeds to a halt and the man in the lead dismounted his horse and came near to them.

"And who may I ask is camping in a place such as this with a force so large?" The man asked.

"We are on our way to the seaport of Revly to try and free them from the bondage that has held them these past months."

"You speak the words, but my heart fears that they are empty, waiting for me to turn my back so that you can stick me with a knife. We have had several groups come to give us aid only to turn on us and kill our families and loved ones. Why should I believe you?"

"Because if I was going to kill you I would've done it by now. You found us and were ready to take up arms, yet we did nothing. We are people of our word and we only wish to do as we have said."

"Why do you wish to help us? You're elf-kind, and the army is mostly human as far as I can see. What interest do you have in our nation when your own is likely under attack?"

"My interest is that Sherados has come forward. I am stepping out in a leap of faith that he will protect and join us in the battle we are about to wage."

"Your faith is surprising. Have you not seen the devastation that ravages the land? The Sorcerer bogs down our thoughts and affects the weather, we will all die if he has it his way."

"I am well aware of the Sorcerer's intentions, but that is why we must attack now before we attack out of desperation not desire."

"You are full of great wisdom and make me look foolish. I and my company are the only kind of reinforcements or protection that has survived the Grimdorian army. The rest were killed defending our cities and towns, we managed to flee, seven thousand of us is all we have though."

"It's still seven thousand that we didn't have before this moment," Isabel said extending her hand towards the man.

"Aramen of Idumea at your service."

"Isabel of Vonlaus at yours. Your men can make camp with ours and not fear anything, you must be tired."

"Yes but evil does not rest and I do not wish to either."

"What can you tell us about Revly? What has changed since being conquered?" Isabel asked.

"No one has been allowed to come or go since the Borags first invaded. They have killed thousands of people, not even letting the people bury their own dead. The city, though once majestic, is now a living graveyard, corpses rot in the street, while creatures who should die run the city. If the king of the city is still alive it would be a wonder. Realistically, I don't think attacking the city will do any more than kill our troops."

"Still we must do it. Is there an easy way to get in?" Morgrin asked. Aramen thought for a couple of moments.

"It has been long since I've been in the city and unfortunately the Borags have made their own modifications, fortifying it far beyond what it was. We might be forced to postpone our attack and send spies into the city. As of yet, none of our own have come back."

"We ride for Revly at once," Isabel told him. Aramen and Morgrin both nodded. "Though at a more relaxed pace than we've been traveling up until now."

"May I suggest riding near the shoreline? There we will be able to find water and perhaps enough food to feed our armies. We can camp ten miles outside the city and then send the spies in," Aramen suggested.

"Very well, but I will be going in as a spy," Isabel said. Aramen's face showed surprise and concern.

"Are you certain?"

"Don't try to convince her otherwise, my friend. When she gets something in her head she'll follow it to the ends of the earth," Morgrin replied. "That's one of the things I love about her so much."

"I don't have much room to argue the matter," Aramen replied. "I've sent my own men to spy on the city because I cannot muster the courage. I will go as well."

"As will I," Morgrin replied. "If we are lucky, we'll be able to get in and out."

"There's no such thing as luck," Isabel corrected. They sent runners throughout the camp telling everyone to pack up their things immediately. Within ten minutes they had packed up and were ready to depart.

Isabel and Morgrin followed Aramen as he led them towards the shore and then down the coastline. The wind was warm and for whatever reason they made better time than they had planned, making it to their destination a day early. They made camp and sent scouts out, as well as hunters and fishermen to catch what they could. Isabel, Morgrin, and Aramen kept to themselves for the most part, preparing for their mission tomorrow.

They called their First Officers into their meeting and gave them orders should they not return. The men accepted the jobs grimly.

The afternoon faded and the hunters and fishers returned. The entire army was fed with food to spare. They ate, drank, and then said their good-nights as silence fell over everyone. Isabel woke up during the night, her past playing through her head once again. Her heart cried out and Morgrin did what he could to comfort her.

The night passed and dawn came, offering Isabel another chance to forget her past and live her life in the present. Each event played a role in bringing her to where she was today. She followed Lathon with all her heart and she had a husband who loved her as much as he possibly could. She praised Lathon for bringing her through the dark times.

Most people considered the idea of following Lathon to be a religious act, and although the Farsees had made it that way it couldn't be further from the truth. There was nothing religious about following Lathon. Lathon was a real person, who had lived and through his great power had done something the Sorcerer could only dream of.

Created life.

He had sent an heir to live with them and out of all the gifts that could be given, she couldn't think of any greater.

Morgrin walked out of the tent and sat next to her. He greeted her with a kiss as they talked and ate their breakfast, soon joined by their First Officers, and then finally by Aramen.

"You are in charge should we not come back," Isabel told the Officers. "Don't do anything stupid. And be ready when we come back to go to war immediately."

"Yes ma'am."

They dismissed them and mounted their horses. They rode cautiously, trying not to raise too much suspicion should they be spotted by scouts or Borags.

They brought their horses to a stop as Isabel pointed to a cart that was being pulled by several deformed and twisted creatures. A Borag sat at the top of the cart, whipping the animals mercilessly, almost to the point where they would drop over dead. The cart bounced along, covered with a tarp, which would be the easiest way to get into a city.

Morgrin produced a strange whistle from Isabel's childhood and let the shrill and unusual sound permeate through the wilderness. The sound caught the attention of the Borag who immediately stopped the cart, fleeing into the forest when he heard the sound again.

They left their horses and carefully climbed onto the back of the cart, covering themselves beneath the tarp. They had only been lying there a few minutes when the Borag came back and then started again. The cart bounced along uncomfortably, for another half hour.

The cart slowed and the sound of a large city reached their ears. The Borags muttered back and forth in their language. Morgrin and Aramen would likely have no idea what they were saying, but Isabel was fluent in the tongue and understood every word.

Once the cart came to a stop. Morgrin slowly lifted the edge of the tarp covering them and looked out into the city. They carefully slipped out and walked through the streets. Aramen meanwhile tried to count the number of Borags in the street.

"I think someone's onto us," Morgrin whispered, motioning with his head to something behind them. Isabel looked back, barely seeing a group of Borags walking down the street.

"I think you're right," Aramen replied. "We can't exactly take off running without alerting everyone in the city."

"Either way we are running out of time and options," Morgrin pointed out. They walked for a few more minutes, picking up the pace a little bit and then slowing down, only to have the Borags following from the same distance.

"Let's go in there," Isabel said pointing to a large inn called *The Scarlet Rope*, on the left side of the street. They did as she suggested and walked into the main dining room, which was filled with Borags and humans. They looked behind them seeing the same Borags that had been following them entering into the inn.

"I see you have some friends coming to visit you." They looked to see a woman standing behind the bar. She was tall and thin with long wavy black hair that went just below her shoulders. Her smile was simple but would have easily seduced any man who looked at her. The woman smiled knowingly. "I'm assuming they're your friends."

"Some *friends* we would rather do without," Isabel answered.

"You need lodging for the night?" the woman asked. Isabel looked at Morgrin and Aramen.

"Just long enough for our 'friends' to leave," Isabel replied.

"There's a stairwell through the door to the left. It leads to my room. I'll distract the Borag scum and you can get up there."

"Thank you," Isabel said.

"Don't thank me yet. They'll likely want to search the inn for you. If you hear them coming, go to the roof and stay there until I come," the woman advised.

The woman grabbed a tray of drinks and walked out into the crowd, looking behind her and then running into the Borags. Curses rang out from the Borags. Isabel and the rest moved towards the door and climbed the stairwell on the other side.

They reached the top, each of them holding their breath as they looked about the lavishly decorated room. Questions surrounding this woman, (who must be the owner of *The Scarlet Rope*,) filled their heads as they looked at everything. Their thoughts were once again interrupted by a commotion at the bottom of the stairs.

Morgrin led the way up another smaller staircase, a little more concealed than the one they had just come up. They quietly made their way up to the roof and waited for the woman to come.

The day faded and they tried to keep themselves occupied by using the rooftop to hopefully gain more knowledge about how they might breach the walls with the tools that they had. Try as hard as they could, they were having a hard time coming up with any idea good enough to spare hundreds if not thousands of lives on their part.

Night came all too soon and for what felt like an eternity they remained in the darkness. Finally, a light entered the stairwell that came to the roof. They moved to the shadows placing a hand on their weapons, ready to use them if needed. The light moved nearer until finally the figure of a woman in a red silk robe came into view.

"It's just me," the woman whispered. They stepped out of the shadows and into the moonlight. The rest of the city had fallen asleep, leaving the four of them alone.

"We were hoping nothing had happened to you," Isabel said.

"You certainly know how to get the Borag's attention. They turned my place upside down and searched every room in the inn. When they didn't find anything, they left."

"We're in debt to you for hiding us," Aramen said.

"I just wanted to get rid of the Borags," the woman replied. "I'm Chloe."

"My name is Isabel, this is my husband Morgrin and a friend of ours Aramen. It's a pleasure to finally meet you."

"Don't say things you don't mean."

"I meant what I said," Isabel replied.

"You don't have to give me a line. I know you're spies of a sort. Doesn't take a genius to figure out what I do. I'm hardly an honorable person," Chloe confessed.

"You're keeping three spies hidden," Aramen pointed out. "How is that not honorable?"

"You must be a sheltered type," Chloe said. "I'm a prostitute. I work here during the day...and at night. I hate every second of it, but it does keep the bills paid doesn't it?" Chloe stated sorely.

"What is your story dear one?" Isabel asked. As if a magic spell had been spoken Chloe shrunk down to her knees on the rooftop and wept openly. They joined her on the ground and Isabel took the woman in her arms.

"I'm not proud of my life at all," Chloe started. "I never thought I would end up like this. I'm miserable on the inside no matter what act I might put on."

"Tell us your story. We're listening," Isabel said.

"I grew up in the nation of Farndor. One day the king's aids and assistants came to our small town. Me and my sister...I guess something about us was attractive. The men had come to find the king some new women to sleep with. We were chosen. I never saw my mother again. I was fourteen at the time.

"My sister was killed for refusing to submit to the king, and I, fearing the same fate as my sister, did whatever he asked or wanted. For whatever reason the will to live took hold of me. I was disgraced and humiliated in every possible way. Every day.

"Three years ago, the king said I was no longer pleasing and sent me packing. I thought it was the best day of my life.

"A couple days later reality hit me. I would never be able to escape the fate that had been handed to me. In the eyes of the world, I would always be one of the king's play toys. No one would want to marry me or have kids with me. I was unclean, I was a part of their society that they didn't like.

"A few months went by and I found myself a beggar in tattered clothing on the streets. I fled Farndor, for Idumea hoping that I could leave my past behind me. It didn't matter where I went my reputation followed me. Desperation forced me to return to the life that had been forced on me. I became a prostitute and opened *The Scarlet Rope* to ensure that I would always have customers and that's been my life. The real reason I saved you from the guards..." She turned to Isabel. "You are Elvish. I've heard about your beliefs, the Elven kind that is. They preach love and compassion to all people don't they?"

"Yes they do," Morgrin answered. "Are you familiar with the Elven beliefs?"

"Not as much as I would like. I have heard the name of Sherados from Elvish visitors. And now I hear someone named Sherados has come forward. The Borags fear you, I can see it in their eyes. The Borags would not fear somebody unless they were a true threat. If not for any other reason, I am curious about Lathon because the Borags fear him. If they fear him, does the Sorcerer?

"I hate myself anew, for I have spared you for my own selfish desires. I wish to come with you. This city, this world has nothing for me, let me fight against this very world that has tortured me since I was taken from my home. For the first time in my life, I feel as though I must do something."

"That is a good place to start Chloe," Aramen replied. "Everyone needs something to get them going. After we take the city, you may ride with us."

"Won't your soldiers and people be revolted by the sight of me?"

"There are many people in the Elven nation Chloe, but not all of them are Elven. My husband isn't," Isabel said pointing to Morgrin. "The war is not about what we have done, it's not about a race being superior in any way. The war is about the soul, the heart, the things that have been long forgotten by the world and the Sorcerer. You will be accepted into the army because your heart is in the right place. You don't have to have all the answers. As far as your past, there are many of us with pasts that you might never have guessed, I being one of them."

"The words you say sound good, but my head and my heart are telling me different things, one tells me to trust you and the other wants to kill you. I don't how else to say it except that I feel as though I would accomplish nothing even if I was to come with you."

"There's a purpose and a reason for everything Chloe," Isabel replied. "This is one thing we are certain about. We have all been through the fires and bad times. Your past is scarred, yes, but maybe you ended up where you are right now for a moment such as this. When you lay your head down tonight Chloe, know that you have done more for our army than any of us could ever do."

"How though?" Chloe asked. "I haven't done anything."

"You've saved us from being killed, you have spared our lives so that we may rescue everyone in this city," Morgrin replied. "When it comes to faith, you should be in the hall of fame."

"Once again, my head reminds me of every lie I've ever been told. I still doubt, though my heart doesn't want to."

"That's the part that matters," Isabel said. "Your heart doesn't want to doubt. You have heard the prophecies and everything related to Sherados no doubt; you said that the Borags and the people of this city are afraid of us… that's why. Because there is truth in everything we stand for. It's a truth without flaw. It's the only thing in this world that you can rely on."

"The three of you are angels in the darkness of my soul," Chloe answered. "I would like to come with you if I live through the attack."

"You have our word that we will not kill you or any other citizen of this city. We only wish to drive the evil away."

Chloe shook her head. "How am I not a part of that evil? I'm a prostitute!"

"You don't want to be," Aramen observed. "Help us and trust that we'll help you. You will not be forgotten after this battle."

"So you say," Chloe replied.

"I promise you, *I* will not forget you after this battle," Aramen declared. Chloe stared at him long and hard.

"I can get you out of the city in the morning. Though, I have no idea how you're going to breach these walls in any meaningful way. There's possibly one weakness in this city and that's the city gates. Good luck breaking through them, it takes twenty Borags to push them open."

"Are they steel or wood?"

"They replaced the metal gates with stone gates, they covered them with wood to fool anyone who might attack. The way they've built the entrance to the city it's a trap. They get everyone going for the door and then they've got turrets and towers directly overhead and to either side. They don't look to chase an army away, they look to slaughter them. If you could get the gates open, then you would walk through them like tissue paper."

"Now we just have to figure out how to get the gates open," Aramen replied. They fell silent.

"The only way I can see getting the gates open is to have Aspen help us," Isabel said.

"Aspen is a friend of yours?" Chloe asked.

"She is a Taruk, actually."

"I don't know what a Taruk is capable of but would you be able to destroy the gate with the Taruk?" Chloe replied.

"Maybe. Or we could at least do some serious damage to it. When we fly over the city we'll pick you up here and get you out of here and take you back to our camp before returning to the battle," Isabel said.

"No you won't," Chloe argued. "I'm not going to sit on the sidelines. I want to fight and if you think that just because I'm a prostitute means I don't know how to use a blade then you're making a deadly mistake."

"If you want to fight we will gladly let you fight although we might not have any armor for you," Aramen replied.

"I don't care about armor, all I want is to fight the vile creatures and kill as many as I can."

"And that's the opportunity you'll get," Morgrin assured. "Do we have to wait until morning or could we escape now? It seems like the entire city is sleeping."

"Now is just as good of a time as the morning. I have a friend whose house is right next to the city wall, literally five feet from it. I'll grab some rope and then we can go." Chloe disappeared into her room for a moment before she came back in a black dress with a sword around her waist. She grabbed some rope from the roof and they followed her down the stairs and out of the inn. The streets were silent, echoing their footsteps for the first few moments until they took off their shoes.

After a while, they reached a large house near the outer wall as Chloe had said there would be. They moved around back and grabbed a ladder, standing it up and climbing to the rooftop. Once up, they pulled the ladder to the roof and used it to span the gap between the roof and the wall, which would've been too high to get on using just the ladder.

They scanned the wall for Borags, seeing only a few far off in the distance. They walked the gap to the wall and Chloe quickly dropped the rope down the side of the wall and then tied it around an outcropping of rock. One at a time Aramen and Morgrin climbed over and let themselves slide down. Isabel was the last one, embracing Chloe.

"Thank you for everything," Isabel said.

"Thank you. You stick to your word and I'll stick to mine."

"We'll stick to our word. Just stay on the rooftop and I'll get you." They said their farewells and Isabel lowered herself down the long rope until finally she was able to put her feet on solid ground. Chloe pulled the rope up and vanished from their sight.

They walked as fast as their legs could take them, grateful when they entered their camp. The First Officers stood up at attention.

"Back so soon?" one of them asked.

"Yes, and we have work to do. Get everyone ready for battle. We march for the city at once."

"We built a great number of ladders. I know you didn't order them but it seemed like a logical thing to do," one of the Captains said.

"Indeed it was," Isabel replied. "Now have the army ready to go on foot in twenty minutes. We'll assemble and then march for Revly."

"Yes ma'am," the officer said. Each of them ran out of the tent going off in a different direction and waking all the troops with trumpets and yelling.

"Hopefully this battle goes the way we want it to," Isabel said. Looking out of their tent as the troops came alive and stood in formation.

Morgrin smiled and kissed her softly on the lips. "I promise you someday soon we'll be able to leave this war behind us and live up in the hills where no one will seek to do us any harm."

"I'd like that," Isabel replied.

Suddenly a great commotion was heard outside their tent and when they went outside they saw the mysterious person they knew as Michael striding confidently through the camp. The people backed away from him, suspicious for a reason they could not discern. Isabel studied him carefully still unsure of whether he was elf or human.

"Isabel. A pleasure to see you!" Michael greeted. Everyone held their breath in anticipation as he stood before them. "You march to war, but not to victory."

Aramen started to object, but Isabel held a hand to silence him.

"What are we to do?"

"Do not take ladders. Nor machines of war. Walk to the city and surround it on the sides that do not border the ocean. Then raise your horns and blow long and hard on them."

"You can't be serious?" Aramen questioned. Michael's expression was unwavering. Isabel nodded in acknowledgment.

"We will do as you say," Morgrin answered. Some cried out disbelief and Aramen was speechless.

"Anyone who disagrees is free to leave!" Isabel hollered above the masses. "This is a test of our faith. After all we've been through, why should we question Lathon now? Lathon is with this messenger and I will do as he says."

Everyone present fell silent, considering what was being asked of them. Whether moved by Michael's presence of Isabel's conviction, none of the thirteen thousand soldiers turned to leave.

Isabel turned to face those assembled. "Prepare your minds and your hearts for battle because by mid-morning we will be there! I have no idea what to expect, but we will do as we have been told! Beyond that...The enemy we fight will have no mercy and will try just about anything to defeat us. There is no telling what they'll do or what the future will hold, but we will fight the battle that is before us nonetheless. It is not the citizens of the city that we fight against, it is against the Borags. Anyone who kills a citizen of the city will be punished accordingly, so fight strong and stay focused. This battle will wear on our minds and our bodies but this is something that must be done if we are to provide a safe home for our future families. To war!"

The army started moving towards the city, which was still many miles away. Anticipation filled their hearts as the future rushed towards them. Ironically, all those years ago when she had left Grimdor, she now found herself on a road that would lead back to the very place she had called home.

OBSCURE HAPPENINGS

A twig snapped, alerting Atruss to a possible intruder. He remained silent. They had camped in a different place every evening, sometimes choosing to move at night as opposed to day because most people would be sleeping. They usually would've had a fire going to keep them warm, but lately, even that had been risky. Rohemir had returned to Belvanor and they hadn't heard from him since.

He gently laid a hand on Gabrielle's shoulder. She didn't move but opened her eyes and looked up at him. Another twig snapped, and this time Gabrielle sat up, hearing it as well. The sound of hooves echoed through the forest.

In an instant, they sprang from their spots, and mounted their horses, sending the horses into a dead sprint. Arrows flew through the air, embedding themselves in the ground where they had been sitting.

They galloped, orders being yelled behind them. The rustling of armor was heard as their attackers pushed their horses in pursuit. More arrows flew by them in the dark, one of them catching Gabrielle in the side of the arm, only grazing her.

The rest of the arrows missed and either landed in the path in front of them or implanted themselves in the trees. They made their way further into the hills, splashing through several small streams, hoping to lose their tail. Their hearts fell as soldiers appeared in front of them.

They had run right into a trap.

Gabrielle's horse screamed in pain and went down on its front knees, an arrow having struck it in the chest. Gabrielle jumped off and landed on the ground. Atruss extended a hand to her and began to pull her up.

Another arrow pierced the darkness. The arrow sunk into Gabrielle's chest. She screamed out and another arrow struck her. Her body went limp and fell from his grasp.

Atruss abruptly stopped his horse. Gabrielle lay on the ground, arrows protruding from her body. Atruss started to dismount but was forced to leave as another arrow came through the night, this one from behind.

Tears rolled down his cheek as he pushed his horse down the path and through the woods. The sound of hooves increased as the people pursuing him neared. He dismounted and sent the horse free.

The horse ran into the forest while he hid behind a tree. He took a couple of steps and froze in his tracks, seeing twenty dark shapes moving. They were quiet enough that they would hear any movement that he made.

"Go!" a voice whispered. Atruss searched the darkness unable to find where the voice had come from. "Get out of here, we'll take care of these men. Hurry, we can't wait forever!"

Unsure what was happening Atruss started into the forest, looking behind him as he ran. He watched and listened as his pursuers were overtaken, though what overpowered them Atruss couldn't say.

He kept moving for nearly an hour until at last he found a small cave. He slipped inside and then tried to muffle his crying the best he could as he mourned Gabrielle's death.

She had been his wife and best friend ever since they had met and now life without her seemed to haunt him and make the hole in his heart greater still. He cried himself to sleep, but the sleep brought him no rest as her death played through his head again and again.

A sword was the first thing that Atruss saw when he opened his eyes. A group of ten soldiers surrounded him. He remained still, looking into the face of his attacker.

"Grab him." The soldiers rushed forward and picked him up from the ground, taking his weapons and tying him up. They marched him through the forest, coming to a small camp filled with twenty other people, all soldiers from Ariamore.

Several soldiers were sent ahead to alert Belvanor that they would be arriving by the end of the day, while the rest of the soldiers traveled at a more leisurely pace.

As the day neared an end they entered into the Grass Canyons and then an hour later into the open space and meadows that led up to Belvanor's gates.

Horns called out and orders were yelled out as the guards on the wall opened the gates and allowed them to enter. He was marched through the streets and finally to the top level of the city.

He was thrown into a cell and left there, leaving him to sit in the darkness for an immeasurable amount of time. Eventually, Rohemir came to his cell door. Atruss stood and moved towards the gate.

"What's going on Rohemir?"

"I assure you that I did not authorize this. This is no doubt the Council's doing. Since I have taken the throne they seem to have started operating as their own special force, carrying out many orders without my approval! If it was in my power I would release you immediately."

"It *is* in your power. You are the leader of Ariamore!" Atruss exclaimed.

"It's *not* in my power, you have no idea what the council is like these days. If I try to get you out of here, it'll mean the death of us both before we can take our next breath. The fact of the matter is, this might just be the best place for you. You're alive and so am I."

"Rohemir, there is a war happening outside these borders, I can't just sit back and let things happen while I'm not a part of it."

"There's nothing I can do! I'm powerless against the Farsees. Unless *you* have any better ideas on how to get you out of here, I can't help you."

"I do have an idea actually," Atruss told him. "Send an owl to Aiden and tell him what's happened."

"What can he do for you?" Rohemir asked. "The council hates him more than they hate you or me. The likelihood of Aiden coming, let alone being able to do something about the situation is slim to none."

"Just send the blasted owl, that's all I want!"

"Alright! I'll do it for you, I still don't see what he'll be able to do. Do you have any idea where he is?"

"He's out there and I'm sure your owl will be able to find him. He has to at least know what is going on whether or not he comes to help doesn't matter to me, but I do want him notified."

"As you wish." Rohemir finally agreed. "Where did they put Gabrielle?"

"She was killed."

"I'm sorry to hear that," Rohemir replied. The next moment he left, leaving Atruss locked in his cell.

A thousand Dwarves accompanied seven hundred men as they ran down the long tunnel. Even though Lily knew, in the end, they would win and they had Sherados fighting with them, she couldn't help but feel fear as they ran into the battle before them.

Even though their side was promised victory, they weren't promised that none of them would die. Gwen ran alongside Drake, looking conflicted which was curious to Lily.

A large door appeared at the end of the tunnel. The door was opened by the waiting guards and they immediately flooded the streets with their presence. The Borags turned to see them, furiously giving out orders to counter the new threat.

Sounds of war rose from the other side of the gates as the Gogs were still held at bay outside the main gate, unable to do anything to assist.

Lily ducked away from everyone else, Ellizar right behind her. They snuck through the streets and back alleys until they the wall and gates. They scaled the stairs, slaying Borags as they ascended.

Rade and the Korazin changed form and became fire as they flew over the wall and released the locks allowing the Gogs to push the gates wide open.

"I think we are going to win this battle," Lily said.

"Yeh can say that one again. Now we just have a hundred more battles teh go," Ellizar replied.

"A hundred more?"

"Metaphorical'y speakin' that is."

"The Sorcerer is still so strong. It's hard to believe that he can be beaten."

"Even my own heart is troubled, but I also know that we have Sherados with us!"

"Then what are we waiting for!" Lily exclaimed. Without hesitation, they joined the battle. The battle hardly seemed to last ten more minutes as the large number of Gogs as well as the Dwarves and humans that had been revealed overwhelmed their opponents. Soon the city was silent, save for their cheering.

"Do you think the Sorcerer knows we have the Wizard's Staff?" Gwen asked. Drake shrugged his shoulders. They sat on the edge of the wall overlooking the city that had just been taken over.

"Hard to say. He seems to know a lot."

"Do you ever wish that we could leave this war behind us and have a different life?" Gwen asked.

"I would love to have another life or to know what my life was before I awoke on the riverside, but I think I was supposed to lose my memory."

"What do you mean?"

"Everything seems to be centered on Sherados and me, the one who would first recognize him. I'm not sure how to exactly explain it, but I feel as though losing my memory wasn't an accident. It was intentional so that I wouldn't be distracted by everything around me and I could better focus on the task in front of me."

"So, you're saying you were meant to lose your memory?" Gwen asked.

"That's what I feel in my heart. I also feel as if in the future my past will return to me or I'll discover it. I can hardly imagine what secrets it might hold. Was I in love? Married? Who were my parents? All questions that will soon be answered, at least my heart hopes they are answered."

"Do you think you were married before that day?"

"Maybe. I had a dream the other night, I think my parents were in it. I'm not sure who they were, or where they were but the two people in it seemed familiar to me."

"What were they like?" Gwen asked.

"I don't exactly know, it was more like I felt them rather than saw them. My heart longs to see them and move on with my life."

"What are you going to do if you can't remember your past? If your past never comes to you?"

"I must admit I've thought about it quite a bit," Drake admitted "My heart is broken with a past I don't remember. I can't deny my heart has grown rather fond of you."

Gwen smiled shyly.

"I don't know what my past is either," Gwen reminded. "I was found on a doorstep after all. Maybe after the war, we can go on an adventure to find out our pasts together."

"That would be wonderful. Perhaps we could forget our pasts and just live our life together," Drake said. They both smiled.

"Whatever we do, or don't do...just know that I love you," Gwen whispered. She pressed her lips against his and kissed him deeply. Gwen finally separated from him and together they looked over the city.

"There you are!" Skander exclaimed coming towards them. "Aiden's been looking all over looking for the two of you."

"He has?" Drake asked. "I haven't seen him anywhere."

"Maybe you weren't looking."

They followed Skander through the streets until they found Aiden and the two elf kings Berdin and Ishamel at a table with Lily, Ellizar, and Shavrok, talking lightly, taking notice as they showed up.

"Welcome my friends," Aiden greeted. Drake and Gwen both sat down.

"Sorry, we didn't know where you were. I guess we were off celebrating our victory," Gwen said.

"Celebrating is a wonderful thing and it is near and dear to my heart," Aiden started. "But it is not a heroic thing what we did. We only did what we were called to do. Get off our butts and do something as opposed to assuming someone else is going to do it."

"Which battle's next?" Shavrok asked, his deep voice booming even though he was talking gently. "We cannot rest while the Sorcerer is alive."

"Well said," Lily replied. "I feel in my heart as though many more people will die before the day is over."

"Your heart does not deceive you," Aiden said. "You are right. The Sorcerer by now knows that we have defeated his armies on Calamar and from that he can assume that we have the Wizard's Staff. Knowing this, he will try everything he can to try and get us to talk, to temp us."

"How can he do that if he's so far away?" Ellizar asked. "We've all seen him, I'm sure that we'd be able to spot him if he was coming our way."

"Do not underestimate him. He has not shown his true strength yet. While he appears to be weakening, he is secretly preparing for our death. We are dealing with something greater than a human being here."

"What do you mean?" Drake asked. "Something greater than human?"

"How is it, Drake, that you knew I was Sherados?"

"My heart told me. It's a little hard to explain but it was as if there was a voice that was speaking to me."

"When Lathon left thousands of years ago, he left his Spirit to move in the world, to find a place in the hearts of Men, Elves, Dwarves, Giants, Gogs, all of us. That way evil would not win. We may have seen the Sorcerer physically, but we have not seen the true nature of evil. Like the Spirits that are in his service, he can change form if he so desires, ever being able to tempt us and catch us off our guard.

"Like the voice in your heart, this one will seem real, but it'll be something that only you see. Everyone will see something different, it could be something that you love or desire. Anything he thinks will be able to sway you to his side. He will speak many lies. We will all be tempted, and it won't just be us, it'll be everyone he thinks knows where the staff might be."

"What can we do to protect ourselves from this?" Berdin asked.

"Put your trust in Aiden. He is Sherados. If we know what we believe in our hearts then the Sorcerer won't be able to find a foothold," Drake answered. Aiden smiled.

"He will find each of us when we're alone. It'll be at that moment you will have to decide how much you actually believe in me. In the meantime, we must sail immediately for Revly, as I think they will be needing our assistance there."

"Consider it done my lord," Shavrok replied doing a bow.

"Very well," Aiden said. Shavrok bowed again. "The Gogs and those that came with them will sail to Revly."

"Our armies will no longer sit on the sidelines and do nothing," Ishamel announced. "We and our armies shall sail with you."

"This is good news. I would like you to sail north and gather at the rock of Petron. Wait there for the rest of us. Then we will get busy planning our final attack."

"It would be a pleasure and a great honor," Ishamel said.

When the time to leave had come, it seemed as though the entire island had come down to see them off. Children pointed at the Gogs in wonder, having heard the tales and songs of the Gogs around campfires late at night. The Gogs smiled back, as friendly as they could look seeing their appearance.

The Dwarves and the Men as well as the few Elves who had been on the island boarded a fleet of normal ships, numbering twelve in all. Ellizar, although he was disappointed to separate from the rest of his race, took joy in knowing that there were more Dwarves than just him.

They pushed off from the docks and watched as the island disappeared from their view. Destan and Elohim flew high above them and several times during their trip Drake and Aiden jumped off the ships, only to be picked up by their Taruks and carried into the sky.

From up here, Drake realized just how small they were. They were but specks of sand on the beach. Useless and pathetic by themselves but if you put them together you had something great. Drake breathed in the fresh air, glad to have a moment alone with just him and Destan.

He felt a change inside himself. It had felt small and insignificant at first but had been growing stronger since he had finally realized Aiden was Sherados. Purpose had grown in his heart and his soul. It was as if he was looking through someone else's eyes.

Aiden flew just below and to his left, riding as though he was no different than any other person. Drake smiled, wondering just what kind of love a great ruler like him must possess to come to the world like he was. He was humble and far greater than Drake could even hope to emulate. The day faded and they dropped back onto the ships where they talked for a little while before everyone went off to bed.

VISIONS IN THE DARK

The height of the walls still surprised Aramen as the army approached. He had been to Revly many times in his life but never had he seen walls like this, so menacing and overwhelming. The Borags had added to the already large walls, making them nearly forty feet tall, and beyond that, numerous Borags waited.

The Borags had noticed the army approaching and now they were close enough to hear the orders being given. Aramen's chest constricted seeing hundreds if not a thousand Borags coming to the edge of the wall with spears and swords.

And they were going to surround the city and blow on their horns? Did they stand a chance against such an enemy?

Most people would say they were foolish and that they stood no chance, and right now Aramen would have to agree with their assessment. The Borags looked down on them with disgust and hatred and Aramen could only wonder what lies they had been told by the Sorcerer.

From the hilltop he could see Chloe standing on the roof of her house, just as she had been instructed. His heart was stirred and the faith she demonstrated gave him the strength to not waver in his. The men behind him starting to divide, wrapping around the city.

From the walls they could hear a mixture of laughter and confusion as they could not make sense of their strategy. The army continued to wrap around the outer wall of Revly, making sure to stay out of bow range.

When everyone was in position a single note on Isabel's horn, signaled for each soldier to take their horn (if they had one) and blow on it. The city shook and trembled as the note rang out, and immediately each soldier grabbed their sword and brandished it high above their heads.

A rumbling shook the city and they stood in awestruck wonder as the walls of Revly crumbled and fell to the ground. Dust filled their view and when it cleared they could see an entire army of Borags, looking just as stunned as they were.

"Our Lord will deliver us!" Aramen cried. "For Lathon!"

The air was filled with their battle cry and the ground thundered with their footsteps. Aspen, the green Taruk with Isabel on top of it, rose into the sky, leading them into the city.

Chloe had no words to describe what she had just witnessed as the walls of the city fell outwards and the armies of Idumea began to move in. The Borags, though they were plenty, ran and scattered, unsure of what to do next, with their defenses destroyed in such a definitive action.

She quickly moved out of the way as the Taruk with Isabel on it's back landed gracefully on the rooftop. She ran forward and grabbed Isabel's hand which was extended.

"How did you get the wall to blow up like that?" Chloe asked.

"Only the power of Lathon could have done such a thing."

"No wonder the Borags are afraid of you. Are you going to blow up the Keep like you did the wall?"

"We need to see if the king of the city is loyal or if he is on the Borags' side. It'll make things much easier if he's on our side."

She swung herself up onto the massive Taruk and they took off, climbing above the battle, watching as it played out before them. Isabel pointed to the left towards a group of Borags who were running towards the front of the city to assist with the now overwhelmed troops.

"To the Keep!" Aramen yelled, Morgrin repeated the order and within a minute the remaining army swarmed the streets, slaying whatever Borags were in their way. Isabel and Aspen flew overhead harassing the Borags in any way they could.

Finally after twenty minutes of fighting and running they reached the Keep that towered above everything else. Borags rushed to slaughter them. Aramen and Morgrin led their forces against the foes, crushing the first wave of Borags within a few minutes.

The gates stood in front of them, not nearly as large or menacing as the ones that were now a pile of rubble, but something about the sight unnerved them. They were frozen in their fear as they looked behind the thick black gates. The air seemed heavy and hard to breathe, slowing down their movements and their thoughts.

A roar filled the sky as Aspen flew overhead and landed and spewed fire from her mouth. A moment later the gates were knocked from their hinges.

The smoke cleared as Morgrin entered the inner wall.

They rushed forward joining Isabel and Chloe who were now standing to the side of Aspen. Aspen took off into the sky, destroying as many Borags as she possibly could.

Their hope was stolen from them again as storm clouds suddenly appeared in the sky and rain began to pour down. The storm was from the Sorcerer, they knew that.

They finally defeated the last Borag and grabbed a set of keys from him finding the one that fit the door on the keep. The door opened and Morgrin shoved the keys in one of his pockets as they entered into the dark chasm on the other side. Torches flickered on the walls, giving little light as they looked at the dark moist walls of the castle.

"Where do you think we'll be more likely to find the king?" Isabel asked. "The throne room or the dungeons?"

"More than likely the dungeons, I doubt they would've killed him," Aramen answered.

"Why do you say that?" Chloe answered. "The people haven't seen or heard from the king personally in months."

"True, but for the Borags to have a peaceful existence here they would need to have the king order the close officials. I'm sure he's alive in the dungeons somewhere, the question is how long will they keep him alive now that they know we're here?"

"I guess we are going to find out," Isabel replied. "You and Morgrin go to the dungeons and get the king, Chloe and I will head towards the throne room and do whatever we can to hinder the Borags."

"Be careful," Morgrin warned. Isabel smiled and they gave each other a quick kiss on the lips. Aramen and Morgrin took five of the men with them and then sent the other twenty-five with Isabel and Chloe.

They ran through the maze of twisting corridors and passages which rose higher and higher into the tower. Eventually, they came to a large door, heavily guarded by ten Borags. The Borags were quickly defeated and dragged off to the side, where they grabbed their keys and entered the dark dank prisons.

Water dripped from the ceiling into puddles on the floor and no torches were in the long hallway. Small windows in the cells allowed the grey light from outside to come in. Outside, the rain pounded the castle.

Creaking was heard, grabbing their attention as they looked toward the source of the sound. Unable to find it they continued. Their hearts pounded inside their chests and their minds were one hundred percent occupied on their surroundings.

Yelling was heard and torches poured into the dungeons. Borags raced towards them, twisted cruel faces, scarred by the evil that had poisoned their souls. Morgrin drew his sword, only just in time. Their hearts sank in their chest.

A noise came from behind them.

They looked to the ceiling behind them, watching as Borags dropped to the ground, hiding, from holes in the ceiling. The five men with them whirled around, trying to block the blows but were instead killed. Morgrin and Aramen backed up against the cells. They lowered their swords and looked into the faces of their captors.

The Borags gave a confused look, clearly surprised.

"We don't need to fight you. We've already won," Morgrin declared.

The Borags looked at each other confused. A moment passed as the Borags spoke to each other in their foul language. The leader hissed, spat in their face, and drew his sword. A rumble filled the building as the fortress shook and dust fell from the ceiling. The Borags pulled back, frightened by the noise.

Pieces of debris fell from the ceiling as the entire building shook unceasingly. The wall in front of them crumbled in a second, leaving a gaping hole. The rain pelted down and the lightning flashed through the sky.

More of the wall crumbled, the outline of a Taruk becoming visible. The Taruk swung his tail again and smashed more of the bricks away from the wall, this time collecting a dozen Borags as he did. The Borags hissed and yelled as they retreated or fell over the edge.

The Taruk turned around in the sky, using his tail to smash away the roof of the small section they were in. Rocks were thrown on their enemies allowing Aramen and Morgrin to grab their swords. They engaged the troops and fought with a new energy that had come over them.

"Jump on!" the Tarukai yelled. Morgrin nodded.

"What about the king?" Aramen yelled through the sound of the wind and rain. Light and thunder crashed all around them. Rain poured into the open prisons, soaking them to the bone and washing the blood of their enemies away.

"We can't help the king if we're dead!" Morgrin argued.

"That's alright, the king is dead!" a voice said from their left. Standing in the gloom of the shadows a dark shape could be seen. Taller than a Borag, but not as big as a giant. He strode forward, dragging a long dark cloak behind him. The flashes of lightning cast light onto him, but his face was still clouded and mirrored by shadows. "I killed him this morning when the attack began!"

"Who are you?" Morgrin asked. The man laughed.

"Don't you know who I am?" The man asked. "My name is Merderick. I am someone who can bring peace to this land." Morgrin looked out to the Tarukai, who was now slumped over his Taruk, holding his hand. He searched his memory, thinking the Tarukai looked familiar.

"I don't believe you!"

"You don't?" the man asked. Morgrin reconsidered his words for a moment. "Why don't you believe me? Even as strong as I am there are something things that I can't control. I want nothing more than peace on this earth."

"You want peace?" Morgrin scoffed. "Then why do you attack like you do?"

"Because I don't have much of a choice," Merderick answered. "The people hate me, leaving me no option except to work with the filth called Borags, Spirits, and other twisted souls."

"You expect me to believe that?" Morgrin asked.

"It's the truth, whether you believe it or not," the Sorcerer replied. Silence lingered and in the silence, the words began to take hold in Morgrin's mind. Maybe Merderick was telling the truth after all.

"If there's one thing that I am, it is compassionate and understanding," Merderick said. "I'm certain you know the history of the Borags? You know they were cursed by their own kind. That kind of abuse leaves scars. I have given them meaning, purpose, and direction. And those things I offer to anyone who follows me."

Morgrin's thoughts ran wild inside his head. The man's face was still mostly clouded by the shadows but in his heart, Morgrin knew exactly who this was.

This was the Sorcerer standing in front of him and in that moment Morgrin knew he didn't have the strength or the courage to strike him down. Conflict plagued him.

"Following me...you shall not be a slave to anything. Do your enemies rise against you? You shall get your revenge! The evil that runs this world unchecked? Justice will be served! I only wish to help the people. Set them free. The Borags are simply the ones who have wanted my help the most at this point. Are my goals and ambitions really that bad?

"You don't want to destroy the world?"

"No, I don't. I just need some help making it right. It is time for the world to be rid of the evil that has plagued it for so long. Join me and we can do it."

Morgrin fell silent for a minute looking out to the man on the Taruk again. He was slumped over his Taruk holding his hand and facing toward Morgrin. Morgrin shifted his focus to the Taruk who still hovered in the air, seemingly effortless despite the storm. The Taruk looked at him and held his gaze filling his mind and heart with the truth of Lathon.

When the sensation passed Morgrin stood taller and more confidently. He was still standing in the rain. He was still soaked to the bone. His sword was still in his hand. The truth of Lathon revealing the Sorcerer's words to be empty and deceptive.

"You have no power here Merderick!" Morgrin declared. The truth is written in my heart. I will not join you!"

"So you condemn the world to evil?" Merderick asked.

"You are evil," Morgrin declared. "You speak lies. If I were to join you, I would be dead to Lathon. It's in the power of Lathon's name that I stand resolute. You have no power here! Leave."

The Sorcerer narrowed his eyes, uncontrollable malice filling them. The Sorcerer turned and walked back into the shadows, when he was almost out of sight he stopped and turned back around.

"I wasn't lying about the king," the Sorcerer said. "I did kill him."

"Prove it."

Merderick kicked something on the ground and before it even hit the light Morgrin knew it was the king's head. The Sorcerer turned and left, vanishing into thin air, making them all wonder if he had even been there at all.

The man sat up on his Taruk, shaking his hand. The Taruk flew closer and Aramen and Morgrin both jumped onto the back of the great beast. The rain still thundered to the ground, but the sounds of the battle echoed louder.

Morgrin's heart was clouded with fear and mystery once again as he looked to the shoreline, the outline of ships, larger than any he had ever seen, visible when the lightning flashed. The Taruk dropped out of the sky, closer to the ground, allowing them to see Gog's running through the street destroying the Borags with a force and ferocity that Morgrin had never seen.

"What is your name?" Morgrin asked the Tarukai.

"Drake Thomas."

"We have to go back!" Morgrin pleaded. "Please my wife is in there!"

"I can't carry more than you two. She'll be alright," Drake assured.

"How can you know that?"

"You have to have faith, plus Aiden's on his way."

"Aiden?" His heart questioned the name remembering it from his past. Morgrin looked at Drake recognizing him from the village at Bucklebeary.

"Aiden is Sherados!" Drake exclaimed.

The castle was as silent as a tomb. Isabel and Chloe went around corner after corner fully expecting to have to fight their way through the scores of Borags that would be waiting. Yet everywhere they went they found nothing.

Isabel's heart was nearly ready to beat out of her chest.

A presence settled over her, a voice whispering in her head. The voice was strong and seductive, whispering things to her. Isabel found the voice disturbing. None of it matched reality. There was always something with what it said that was wrong. Isabel pushed the thoughts and the voice from her head, having heard that voice many times before.

Her determination was renewed by the voice. She rushed forward and around corner after corner until the main throne room came into view. She and the others rushed forward, running to meet dozens of Borags who were waiting. The Borags stood in their place and didn't even try to move. She pulled back her sword and let it find its target, only to find that her sword passed right through. Her mind was filled with questions as she walked right through the next Borag in her way.

"What is this?" Isabel asked.

"It is something that was added after the Borags invaded, at least that's what I heard," Chloe said. "It's a room that shows you whatever you want to see."

"We want to see the throne room and the Borags guarding it, so that's what it's showing to us?" Isabel asked.

Chloe nodded. "Something like that."

"No doubt this is the Sorcerer's work," Isabel said, Chloe shifted uncomfortably.

"You know that for certain?"

"I'm related to him. It's a union I wish to forget, but the memory haunts me like a bad disease. How do we get out of this room?"

"I'm not sure. We don't even know where this room started. Everything we see though is likely a fabrication of this room. Scary when you think about it."

"So if it shows you what you want to see does it show everyone the same thing?" Isabel asked.

"I don't know, think of something." Isabel thought hard and watched as the objects in the room changed to reveal what she had imagined. She was back in her house, except this time she was with her husband and her daughter. Her heart leapt for joy at the sight as she rushed forward to embrace them. A moment later she found herself embracing nothing as she passed right through the two of them as though they weren't there. She looked back to Chloe who was crying at whatever she was seeing.

"What do you see?" Isabel asked.

"I see my mother and my sister, but I know they are not real," Chloe said. She passed her hand through the open air in front of her, apparently passing through the two of them. Isabel's heart was stirred. With this room, there was power, perhaps too much power. Chloe saw her family and she had seen her own but neither could see the other. Her heart was troubled. People could waste themselves away in this room.

"We should go, and leave this room," Isabel replied. Chloe cried.

"Can't we stay for another minute or so? I haven't seen them in years and even though I know they're not real, the sight is greater than I could ever imagine."

"These are lies, Chloe. Nothing more than fabrications of the Sorcerer's doing."

"But why would he want to fabricate this?"

"To distract you, deceive you, tempt you to keep coming back to this room until you waste away to nothing. This room is evil and we should leave while we still can." Chloe hesitated and tears filled her eyes as she looked at Isabel and then at the open space in front of her. "I can't see them, Chloe."

Chloe closed her eyes and nodded. They as well as the other twenty-five men with them began walking through the room, walking by all the images that had been made in their minds. Hunger gnawed at the two of them. A moment later a table full of food as long as the hall they were in appeared in front of them. The smell of freshly prepared food reached their noses, stimulating everyone. The food looked so good and so delicious, but it was just a fabrication. Isabel reached out to pass her hand through the table of food, surprised to find that this time it hit something solid.

Was this real?

She looked at the others, knowing that for whatever reason everyone *was* able to see this. Her heart cried out for the food, consisting of everything you could imagine.

A bowl of apples caught her attention and she reached towards it, able to grasp it in her hands. She studied it wondering if there was a catch.

"Feel free to eat anything you would like. That's why it's there after all." They turned towards the head of the room where the voice had come from, seeing a man standing in the distance. He walked towards them. His features were clouded and a black cloak trailed behind him. Chills ran up and down Isabel's spine.

"Go ahead, I prepared this food just for you. Isabel, it's so nice to see you again. I've been hoping we could be reunited someday and perhaps come to a mutual understanding."

"You know this man?" Chloe asked.

"He's the Sorcerer, or so I think. For all I know, he could just be creating a vision of himself and he isn't actually here."

"Oh, I'm here, don't have any fear about that. But the food is real enough, however, it's not normal food is it? No, this isn't a normal room so why should the food be normal, but does that mean the food is evil? Of course not! This room is nothing more than a unique gift that I gave the city after the Borags invaded. I have lost control of my empire and now people are paying for it with their lives. There is nothing I hate more than pointless killing. It is because of this reason that I have created this room, as a way to ease the pain of losing loved ones."

"You can walk right through them, how does that help ease the pain?" Chloe asked. Isabel studied the Sorcerer carefully.

"Right now you can walk through them, but for any who eat the food from this table, they become real and full of life, able to interact with you and me. This room is not a fantasy world as you might think, but a way to create a new reality. People often perceive me wrongly, they think I am out to get them but that is not the case. I love this world more than anything else. It is my home and I shall live in it for as long as I can."

"Don't eat that fruit, Chloe. He's lying."

"I am not lying about anything. I am not evil, but tell me is Lathon really good? After all, he walked out and left the world to fend for itself. That doesn't exactly say love does it?"

"The people were led astray by a serpent. You," Isabel said. "Now, Lathon has returned to change the fortunes of the world."

The Sorcerer shook his head. "I must say I'm rather disappointed in you Isabel. I had always thought you were above being brainwashed, but now it becomes clear that is not the case. Will anyone here eat the food I have prepared?"

"No," Chloe replied. The Sorcerer looked to the twenty-five men, some of them eyeing the food, while others held it inches from their mouths. Isabel said a prayer hoping that they would have the strength. One at a time, with much difficulty everyone threw down the food. The Sorcerer's eyes turned hard and cold.

"You don't believe the words I say do you?" the Sorcerer asked. "I shall demonstrate for you the full effect of this fruit. I will prove that everything I have said about this fruit is real. I will eat it and what I wish to see will be visible to you." He took the apple in his hand and bit out of it.

Borags appeared, in front of them, running with their swords drawn, letting a battle cry escape them. They drew their weapons and defended themselves against their enemies who fought much more fiercely than any others they had faced up till now. Isabel looked over the Borags to see the Sorcerer licking his lips and continuing to eat the fruit, with each bite, more Borags appeared.

Desire filled her for only a moment, a desire to eat a piece of fruit and imagine a peaceful world. Then none of this would matter.

The thought lingered in her mind as the Sorcerer held her gaze, finished the apple, and then threw away the core. When she looked again the Sorcerer was gone, making her wonder if he had been there at all.

She looked out the window noticing the sky was starting to lighten and the rain had now stopped. Within a few minutes, the sun was shining, unnerving the Borags who were struggling to fight. Isabel ducked a blade and then spun to her left pulling a dagger out of her belt. She threw it through the air, the Borag easily deflecting it.

The strange call of a bird came to her ears. She looked to see the black featherless bird entering the room. It landed in the middle of the great hall.

Light flooded the area. The top of the tower was destroyed, leaving them fighting on the open tower. They formed a line with the tables the Sorcerer had created and ran the Borags off the top of the tower, letting them plummet to the city below.

Ships had docked at the shoreline and scores of Gog's filled the city, mingling with the humans and some Elves, and the citizens were now coming out of their homes and hiding spots, each grateful to have lived. Isabel thought about what would happen now, unable to imagine what the future held. She knew in her heart that the future was not hers to worry about and that she would be content with whatever life gave to her.

Elohim swooped low over the ruined city to where the people were gathering. Isabel's heart broke when she saw them and wondered how many of their family members had been killed.

Sherados was on their side and she knew in her heart that they could not lose. Too much depended on who won the war. She thought about her past and then the present situation and then about her future.

Rays of red sun illuminated the sky. Lily sat up on the edge of her bed and stretched. Isabel and Gwen were on the far side of the room and the woman named Chloe slept peacefully in a chair in the corner.

Isabel was the next to wake, getting dressed and then stepping outside. Lily immediately followed Isabel until she found her entering a small little shop.

"Good morning Lily, do you want to paint?" Isabel asked. The shop owner was nowhere to be found and yet Isabel picked out some paints and a canvas without paying any mind.

"I'm not sure how to paint," Lily admitted.

"I can teach you if you'd like," Isabel suggested.

"I'd like that, but can we really just take this person's stuff? It must belong to somebody."

"Of course, it belongs to somebody," Isabel replied. "If that wasn't the case I don't think it would be here." Lily couldn't hide a smile and grabbed her own supplies from the shelves, moving to the middle of the room where two chairs and two easels were sitting.

"Have you ever painted anything before?" Isabel asked.

"No. I wasn't allowed."

"That's too bad. It's a great release for me. I love to paint in the silence of the day. It calms my mind for the rest of the day if that makes sense."

"I guess so," Lily said. Isabel pulled out her paints and brushes and started painting, appearing to not have to think about it.

"What and how do I paint?" Lily asked. Isabel stopped.

"Paint whatever is in your heart and don't worry about what people think of it. It's your vision and it's your painting. The approval of others is a useless thing to chase."

"Why is that?"

"Because everyone dies," Isabel answered. "Unless you're already dead in which case I'm not sure how you could die."

"I'm not sure I follow."

"It's okay, most people don't follow my thoughts, and they only follow the ones that make sense to them. They never care for the ones that don't make sense, even though they do make sense if you think them through."

"They do?" Lily asked, beginning to paint.

"Yes, if you listen close enough you hear the meaning. To continue what I said about death, I often think there's a great deal of life after death even though you're dead."

"You see that makes no sense to me," Lily said with a laugh. Isabel smiled and kept painting.

"If you truly believe Aiden is Sherados then it has to make sense, think of it that way."

"You're a real puzzle you know that?" Lily said. They both laughed.

"So people tell me."

"Can't you just speak normally every now and then?"

"I like to speak in riddles and stories and questions, it makes people figure it out for themselves. Then they don't end up feeling like a two-year-old when you correct them on something."

"Explains a lot about you," Lily replied. They painted the vision that was in their minds and their hearts. Surprisingly, Lily found hers coming together much better than she had thought possible, though when compared to Isabel's it was hardly anything noteworthy.

"Have you figured out my riddle yet?" Isabel asked. Lily shook her head. "Well, then I'll tell it to you. If you believe that Aiden is Sherados and you believe that Aiden is Lathon incarnate then you must believe that there is something else beyond death because how else could he be alive? He couldn't have lived that whole time and even if he did, coming back wouldn't do him any good. Therefore if he's something beyond death, we can only logically assume that there's life beyond death and that death cannot harm those who call upon his name."

"Why am I suddenly reminded of a passage I read in the ancient scrolls?" Lily asked. "It was something that Lathon himself had said, 'The worst they can do in this world is kill your body.'"

"You see? You've had the answer to my riddle all along and you just didn't realize it!"

"How about that," Lily replied, thinking and reflecting for a moment. If she had the answer to that question how many other answers did she have and just not realize it? The thought stuck with her the rest of the time they were painting as she began to go through the passages of the ancient scrolls she had read, comparing them with the world around her and then noticing how Aiden seemed to fulfill many of the things in them. Her heart leaped for joy as she painted.

She now knew in her heart without a shadow of a doubt that Aiden was Sherados. She had figured out the riddles and now saw clearly through them. Most people, like herself, would read through the riddles and dismiss them as just that. Riddles.

They finished their paintings without talking. As the sun rose slightly over the horizon Lily found herself enjoying the silence and everything that came with the painting and she realized that Isabel was once again right.

It was relaxing.

They put all the paints back and then left the paintings on the counter with all the supplies along with a note that the owner could keep the paintings and sell them if he wished to make up for having used the paints in the first place. Lily's mind was captured by the unique nature of Isabel's picture. She looked at it and studied it, thinking for a moment that the picture was moving. Isabel was one of the people in the picture while Morgrin was the other. The third however was clouded and mysterious.

Her curiosity was peaked but she didn't say a word as they stepped out into the streets where the city was now starting to show signs of waking up. In the distance, the walls still lay in piles of rubble.

They walked and then met up with the others. Drake, Gwen, Aiden, and Shavrok stood side by side, discussing something important. Skander came up and hugged her good morning, followed by a sleepy-eyed Ellizar.

"Good morning Ellizar!" Lily greeted, a smile spreading across her face. He flinched, startled by her enthusiasm.

"Blasted elf kind, always greetin' us before we're wide awake!"

"That's why I greeted you, to wake you up."

"Good idea," Ellizar said, smiling back. They embraced and then separated. They took a seat at the table, enjoying their meager breakfast.

"So what are we up teh now Aiden?" Ellizar asked.

"We're going to put the Dwarves in a small chamber and see how long it takes before they go crazy," Lily replied.

"He's the king yeh know, I could have him throw yeh into the dungeons if I wanted," Ellizar replied.

"Except none of us own a castle," Skander pointed out. Ellizar muttered to himself as he continued eating.

"There is much to do and little time to do it," Aiden replied. "We are all going to have to split up if we can ever hope of accomplishing all of it before the Sorcerer can stop us. I received a message from Atruss and Gabrielle. It seems they have been arrested for having not left Ariamore. We have to rescue them, and more secrets have yet to be discovered."

"Sounds like a fun time," Morgrin said. Isabel smiled.

"We'll do whatever you want us to my king," Isabel said, bowing.

"We will in time attack the three cities of Grimdor. To start though, I would like for Chloe and Aramen to head into Farndor and try and find as many people that are loyal and then bring them to the Rock of Petron. The Calamarian army is headed there, in fact, they've probably already arrived."

"Morgrin, the Idumean army is not dead, they have taken refuge in a cave system along the coast. Too afraid to stand. Search for the rest of the Idumean army and bring them to the Rock of Petron."

Morgrin nodded.

"Lily and Ellizar, accompany Shavrock and company to the rock as well." They both nodded and Aiden continued. "Drake, Gwen, and I are headed up to Epirus to meet with Willard and Miles who have gathered a great number of wolves. I would like Skander and a few Gog friends to head to Giahon and see if there's anyone there who might be loyal. I highly doubt it, but Skander is the only giant here, and sending extra muscle along can never hurt anything. It should be noted after Drake, Gwen and I go to Epirus we will be headed towards Ariamore to break Atruss and Gabrielle out of prison. We're not going to attack the city so it shouldn't be too dangerous. We will wait until we are all done with those tasks before we decide on any further action."

The fire appeared in the sky and then struck the ground and gave way to mist. Rade and the Korazin stood in front of them, their rings glowing brightly. A moment later Cerin appeared, transforming from a blue mist to take the form of a man.

"When we get to attacking Grimdor, both Cerin, the Spirits, and the Korazin will be assisting us," Aiden said.

"There is a problem with the curse that has been put on the Spirits," Rade replied. "The Sorcerer is too powerful and smart for them to betray him at Grön and then also at Iscariot. Likely after Grön the Sorcerer will realize his mistake and fix the spell. So the question is where do you want them to attack with us?"

"Probably in Grön, but let's not worry about that until we get to that moment," Aiden said. "Everyone knows what they're doing?" They nodded and finished eating before heading their separate ways.

Aiden climbed on Elohim, while Drake and Gwen climbed on Destan. They took off and vanished into the sky.

Skander and some Gogs were the next to leave. Lily embraced her brother one last time and he departed to the southeast. Aramen and Chloe mounted a horse and left to the north. Morgrin also mounted a horse and left, heading up the coast, each taking a small number of soldiers with them.

Rade and Cerin talked amongst themselves before vanishing into the sky somewhere. Ellizar and Lily were the last people from the group to leave. They met up with Shavrok and the Gogs who left their ships and continued on foot, marching with the rest of the army, to the Rock of Petron. Shavrok reached into one pocket of the jacket he wore and pulled out a strange-looking horn.

He blew into it and the note echoed through her mind even though she couldn't hear it. Her curiosity was peaked.

"What is that?" Lily asked.

"It's how the Gog's call for help," Shavrok answered. "Only a Gog can hear this horn. I've called all of them to the Rock of Petron. They will be arriving shortly."

"I thought there was only one group of Gog's and that was in Ariamore?" Lily asked.

"No, there are three different villages in this region of the world, the one in Ariamore was just the largest one."

As night fell they came over the crest of a hill and laid their eyes on a site that nearly overwhelmed them. Thousands of tents were organized in neat rows, extending as far as the eye could see.

The Calamarian army had arrived and had fortified the ever-growing camp the best they could, also contributing food and weaponry to those who might not have very much. Far in the distance to the north, she could see another cloud of dust as a number of Gogs were now joining the camp.

Lily could hardly comprehend just how many people would be marching on Grimdor. The rest of the Gog's, Shavrok insisted would be arriving by the end of the day making their numbers close to eighteen thousand.

She and Ellizar stood on top of the Rock of Petron, looking over the growing camp. Despite the growing number of troops, it wasn't boosting her confidence about the battle ahead. They had been in Grimdor once and they both wished they could forget the experience.

"What do you think will happen after the war is over?" Lily asked. Ellizar shrugged his shoulders.

"I don't think we should worry abo't that. The future will be what it will be. Accordin' to the ancient scrolls and prophets we are promised victory."

"Then why does my head fear what lies ahead."

"Because it's unknown what lies ahead," Ellizar said. "Deep in all of us is the desire teh be able teh control somethin' and here we are unable teh do anythin'. We have teh trust in somethin' greater than ourselves. Not somethin' easily done, even fer a dwarf."

"Ellizar, what do you plan on doing after the war has ended?"

"If I live teh tell about it? I once thought that I would go live in a Dwarvish city again. However, I must admit the thought is a little repulsive teh me."

"I'm shocked to hear you say that, I thought you would love to spend some time with your Dwarvish race."

"I would, but being underground and tunneling all my life, forget it! Show me the sun and the rivers and the tops of the mountains. What can I say, you seem to have rubbed off on me in the past few years."

"You've rubbed off on me too," Lily replied nervously fidgeting with her skirt. "Truth is after the war, the thought of getting married to you had gone through my head a couple of times."

"What did you say?" Ellizar asked.

"I was asking you if you wanted to get married after the war."

"Ha, what a ridiculous notion, imagine a dwarf and an elf gettin' married? I've never heard of such a thing!"

"So, is that a yes?" Lily asked. Ellizar smiled.

"Of course, it's a yes. Imagine the looks on Drake's and Gwen's faces when they hear this one."

XVIII — THE TEMPTING OF DRAKE

Drake was both sore and stiff when he finally was able to slide off of Destan and put his feet on solid ground. Gwen was the next to slide off the Taruk and Aiden had already landed and had bounded into the forest gathering some brush and sticks to use to light a fire. He returned a few minutes later and put them in a neat pile. Elohim and Destan opened their mouths and lit the fire with ease.

The three of them sat around the fire, their minds filled with memories. Each in their own way, vividly remembered everything that had transpired here. Below, the ruins of Fiori sat silent, and even the sight of it sent chills up and down Drake's spine.

The buildings lay in twisted messes. Most of them were nothing more than rubble, yet somehow, trails of smoke still drifted from all the buildings. Unusual, but nothing about how the village had been destroyed had been ordinary.

They had found the Wizard's Staff but now what were they supposed to do with it? The question had plagued him since Aiden had wrapped it up and placed it in Elohim's saddle bag.

They talked a while before Aiden and then Gwen fell asleep. meanwhile, Drake remained awake, unable to do anything but stare into the village. He walked away from the campfire, wandering through the remnants of what had once been a town.

"It's a tragedy isn't it?" a voice asked from beside him. Drake turned to see a man with a long black cloak flowing behind him. Drake's heart beat a hundred miles an hour as the bald man stood there with so much conviction that Drake never questioned how he had been duped so easily. They hadn't seen anyone else when they had landed.

"Yes," Drake replied, unsure what to do.

The Sorcerer smiled. "Life is so fragile. So many people take it for granted. They struggle to realize that they have more than some people will ever have. My heart always goes out to those who are less fortunate than myself. They struggle to get by while other people make so much money they don't know what to do with it."

"I highly doubt you'd do anything about the situation, otherwise you would've done it by now."

"I wish I could have, but I am powerless to do anything."

"You're not powerless, you're the Sorcerer. If you want to do something you can do it. It's as easy as that."

"If only," Merderick replied. "The world is a much more complicated place than it once was Drake. It's full of twisted people, all of whom jump to conclusions about people before they gather all the facts. Even you and I have both come to conclusions at one point or another and both times we've been wrong.

"The fact of the matter is I am powerless to do anything because the people of the earth have made me powerless. My heart cries out to help those in need, yet, because of events that are long in the past, I cannot do anything. For the most part, people have decided in their hearts that I don't deserve a second chance and that I am vile and evil. The whole thing saddens my heart."

"It does?" Drake asked. Merderick nodded.

"Do you think all I want to do is kill people and rule with an iron fist? No! I want to become the ruler of this world so I can use my power to do some good. How great would it be if no one ever went hungry again? I have perfected spells that would make all the crops in the land flourish unceasingly. Thousands of people have died from incurable diseases, but I have found a cure. I do not want this throne for myself, I want it for the people of this earth to help *them* find a new beginning."

"It sounds like that world would be a nice place to live," Drake admitted.

"It certainly would be, but if things don't change then I doubt any of my dreams will come true. The nations ride against me, seeking to destroy the very things that I offer them. It's hard to accept that they don't want any help. The ultimate irony in the whole situation is that now they are marching against me. They say that I am evil and that I've killed thousands and thousands of people, but the only reason that I've ended up having to do so is because they oppose me. Sure my armies might have killed thousands of people, but how many have they killed? In standing against me they have become the very thing that they seek to destroy."

"Never thought of it like that," Drake admitted as they walked through the ruins.

"Most people don't Drake, most people don't."

"So why are you here? Shouldn't you be off preparing yourself for the battle that lies ahead instead of talking to me?"

"Yes, I should be going soon, but I came because I knew you would be here. I was merely going to try and prove to you that I am who I say I am, and that I'm not a bad person."

"How are you going to do that?"

"How would you like me to do it?" Merderick looked at him, his eyes gently studying Drake as if he was a long-lost friend. Drake hid his emotions.

"Well, I've never,-"

"Remembered your past?" Drake didn't reply. "Many things reach my ears, Drake, I know all about you and in this area, I find myself quite well versed. Your past is very much like this."

The Sorcerer waved his hand and the world around them changed. First, it grew dark, and then the wind came and within moments a new world was in front of him. Drake studied the town with interest.

He had never seen it before.

People went here and there and he watched the scene as it played out before him. He cautiously walked forward, expecting the ground to give way beneath him. Nothing happened.

"Can these people see us?" Drake asked.

"No, they can't see or hear us. This is a memory of mine. I loved to come to this village when I was a young boy and I still travel there when I get the chance. It's real enough though, go on, try." The Sorcerer motioned to a tall cedar tree that towered far above them. Drake reached his hand out and touched it, feeling the bark beneath his fingers. The wind blew through his hair; he felt the warmth of the sun.

"What do you think so far?"

"It seems so real I'm not sure what the truth is anymore, but at any rate, you've said this is a dream so it's not real. I'm still unconvinced."

"This is a dream," the Sorcerer said motioning his hand around him. "That," pointing to the village, "is not a dream. I think if we make our way down there we will find that it is *very* real."

Drake thought about refusing as he knew he probably should, but they were here and the Sorcerer had been honest enough up to this point. They left the area and walked down the hillside to the base of the village which bustled with the ins and outs of everyday life. Together they walked into the village moving past dozens of people.

"Drake!" a voice cried out from behind him. He turned around and saw a brown-haired woman running into his arms. Her figure was perfect and her dress was exquisite. She leaped into his arms and laid a sloppy wet kiss on his lips in the middle of the street. Drake's mind swirled in the emotion that rippled through him.

Love, mystery, intrigue, and desire consumed him in a way he had never felt before. The kiss ended after only a few seconds but to him, but he didn't want it to end. They held each other in the street looking deep into each other's eyes.

Drake looked briefly for the Sorcerer, finding it hard to deny the truth that was in front of him.

He was loved.

People knew him.

This woman was all he had ever wanted.

"You are just who I wanted to see." Her eyes shone like diamonds. He smiled and held her close.

"Me too," Drake replied. He studied her eyes, her name coming to him.

Rachal.

"I just wish we never had to leave each other's company."

"Just a little longer and then we can waste away the day making love in the green meadows just over there. The world will be ours and nothing will be able to take it away."

"If only we didn't have to wait," Drake said, surprised that the words had come from his mouth.

"You tempt me," Rachal said, kissing him deeply. "Soon enough my dear, soon enough. We'll be free to do whatever we wish."

"Sounds like you have everything planned out."

"Just two more days and we'll be free of my father who for whatever reason has never liked you, then it's just you, me, and the wilderness, and a new life and a love deeper than any ocean in this world." Drake smiled as they embraced in another passionate kiss that stimulated every part of Drake's mind. In all his life he had never felt a love like this, something so real he felt as if it *was* a part of him.

"I love you, Drake Thomas," she whispered, her warm gentle breath moving into his ear.

"I love you, Rachal." They leaned in for yet another kiss, but she stopped him short putting a finger on his lips, smiling seductively.

"Not yet Mr. Thomas." He smiled as she pulled away and began walking backward, still holding eye contact. "Two days, noon at the sleeping willow."

"Looking forward to it, my love."

She smiled again and then winked playfully before turning and running like a little kid who had just received the best news in the world.

The world spun and soon Drake was back in the ruins of Fiori, standing with the Sorcerer.

"How did that feel Drake?"

"Real," Drake admitted. Even now the memory of the kiss was with him.

"It is real Drake. Ever wonder how you fell over the falls? It seems Rachal's father had never approved of you and certainly not of the marriage that was going to take place. He sent some men to kill you when you were on your way to the sleeping willow. You were crossing over the bridge and they confronted you. It was four to one odds. You lost."

"So the village where is it?"

It's a village called Turndale, in the far north. Beyond my knowledge. To think that you had almost made it to the sleeping willow and could have the love of your life in your arms. Unfortunately, her father's men caught you. Likely he hired people from Epirus because only they would've known where the sleeping willow was."

"I'm not sure what to say. Ever since I woke up I haven't been able to figure out what my past was."

"And now it's been told to you. I would love to help you find it after this war is over. To find this woman and see you happy with her would bring so much joy into my heart."

"If I make it through the battle," Drake pointed out.

"I can guarantee that you can make it through the battle," Merderick replied.

"You can?"

"Of course I can, there's just one thing that you have to do and that's join me. Has Aiden ever told you or shown you anything about your past? No, he hasn't. Instead, he's dragged you all across the earth, fighting a war that may not be yours to fight. Maybe you are actually from the far northern lands. You must certainly have family there who wish to have their child back. What do you say, Drake? Will you trust me, or are you going to stay with Aiden?" Drake's mind reeled.

"This is what you want isn't it? To create a vision so real that you can get me to come with you. Is there any part of the vision you showed me that's actually real?"

"I suspect at this point no matter what I tell you, you likely won't believe me. Am I correct?"

"Go Merderick. You're a thief and a liar and I will march against you in this war. When this is over then I'll worry about my past." Merderick held his gaze for a moment before bowing slightly and turning to walk away.

"By the way, I found this near the falls shortly after you fell over." He reached into his pocket and pulled out a small object tossing it towards Drake.

Drake reached out and caught it, his heart racing and mind swirling as he grasped a golden ring with one diamond and a blood-red ruby to either side of the diamond. None of the stones were large but they seemed to shine even despite the darkness. He looked at the ring and then at the inscription on the inside.

To my wife, Rachal.

He looked back to the Sorcerer who moved away and then vanished into the night, making Drake wonder if he was even there. Drake struggled to believe that the ring was a fabrication. Something meant to trick him into joining his side. Finally, he slipped the ring into his pocket and sat among the ruins, his mind too occupied to sleep.

Aiden lay next to the fire watching the smoke and the sparks as they rose into the sky and then vanished from view. The stars were out and the heavens spoke to him. A twig snapped to his left and he turned to see a man donned in a black cloak stepping into the light.

"Well, well, well, what do we have here?" the man asked pleasure in his voice. "It seems in my being lost I've come across the very man himself. Sherados."

"Good evening Merderick, come to pay homage to the king?"

"Maybe I did, maybe I didn't. Do you mind if I sit?"

Aiden motioned for a fallen log near the fire. Merderick sat down. "What can I do for you Merderick?"

"Nothing. I merely wish to get warm by your fire before I head back."

"You are a terrible liar."

The Sorcerer looked taken aback for several moments. "I must admit you had me fooled. Not many can. All these months and I thought Drake was Sherados. Seems I made an error or two, we both know Drake's past don't we? You came into the world in a way that no one expected. Not even I saw that coming. Congratulations."

"Why are you here?"

"Right down to business, that's what I admire about you Aiden, you waste no time in getting to the point. It frustrates me beyond belief when people drag the truth out and prolong telling you the important things. I was merely concerned about you, Sherados. I know it's probably strange, me being concerned about you, but I do feel emotion you know? What I wanted to ask is, do you really think you can win against the Borags?"

"There's not a doubt in my mind that we can and will defeat both the Borags and you," Aiden answered.

"I wish I was as certain about that reality as you were. I know the number of Borags that live in Grimdor and all around the world. They are on their way now towards Grimdor to defend their homeland, they outnumber you almost four to one."

"But it's not five to one."

"I don't think you're quite seeing the big picture. You are Sherados, you should end the war right now before people die in the battle. You say you came to this world out of love for your people. Forgive my doubt, but what kind of love is that?"

"A love you don't understand," Aiden said. "You are forced to live with the people you do. I chose it. I chose to come and suffer through the hardest and darkest time in history with my people. That's the difference between us." The Sorcerer fell silent for a moment or two.

"Still the thought must cross your mind every day that something could happen that you couldn't stop. You could be killed in battle, after all, no one in this world is perfect. Death is just as much a way of things as life is. Here the two go hand in hand."

"Not for much longer," Aiden replied. The Sorcerer's face went white for a moment before it went back to normal. "Soon you'll be dead and with it, death won't be as powerful as it is now."

"If you insist," the Sorcerer replied. "Can I show you something?" Aiden got up and grabbed his sword, strapping it on his waist. Merderick stood and led the way. They walked a few feet and the world around them changed to that of a desert. The desert was hot and dry and Aiden recognized it immediately as the nation of Farndor.

Hunger consumed him. His mouth was dry and bits of sand blew through the air. Everywhere he looked on the horizon was the same. Just sand. Lots and lots of sand. The sun beat down on the two of them, and perspiration instantly formed on their foreheads and soon drenched their clothes. Rocks lay scattered here and there.

"Are you hungry Sherados?" the Sorcerer asked. "You can try to hide it all you want but I can see it in your eyes. You are growing weak in this sun. Can you really last much longer?" Aiden watched the Sorcerer carefully, unable to deny that his hunger seemed to be unquenchable.

"I am hungry," Aiden replied. The Sorcerer smiled.

"As am I. For most people, being lost in a desert-like this without food or water would be a problem, but you are Sherados, correction; you are Lathon.

The rules are different for you, are they not? You could speak to these stones and have them turn into bread without having to work at all. I know you could. Do you deny this?"

"I don't deny this. I *could* speak to these stones and turn them to bread in a second, but this food...won't quench any hunger. No water I could make could ever quench your thirst. We would be better off to trust Lathon than we would be to turn these stones into bread."

"Very impressive answer. Even now when you're so weak you are strong. It's a wonder I didn't realize you were Sherados before recently." They fell silent and walked through the desert, still feeling the effects of the heat as their bones ached almost too sore to move. Still, Aiden pushed on, not complaining or saying a word. Out of the corner of his eye, he caught a glimpse of Merderick looking at the ground muttering.

A moment later the scenery changed and they were back in Belvanor. The sights and the sounds of the city met Aiden like a long-lost friend. They stood on top of the palace looking over the surrounding lands.

"So, if you are Sherados, actually I correct myself, if you are Lathon himself, as you have claimed to be. Jump off this cliff. In the ancient scrolls and prophecies does it not say that your angels will come to your rescue and you won't even stub your toe on the ground?"

"It does indeed say that, but I do not wish to test anything, that is forbidden."

"A very noble answer. Okay, how about this your highness? How about you just bow to me and I'll give you everything? I will surrender to you unconditionally if you just bow. The water, the air, the cities I have conquered will be yours in a second."

"Merderick I have two things to say to you," Aiden started. "Number one: Everything on the earth is already mine, and number two: you will be bowing to me by the time this war is over."

"I can assure you that I will do no such thing, I don't care who you are, I am the ruler of this earth."

"But who's the ruler over you?" Aiden asked. Merderick didn't answer and walked away into the darkness. The surroundings changed and Aiden found himself standing next to the fire just as he had been. Aiden turned and laid back down on the ground and fell asleep.

Drake came back into the camp, where the others were fast asleep around the campfire. Drake envied them at the moment. His mind still buzzed with the things he had seen and experienced with the Sorcerer.

Drake pulled out the ring and read the inscription again. Was there a chance the Sorcerer had told him the truth? According to what he had known about the Sorcerer before this moment he would say that everything he had seen was a lie.

Yet, here in his hands, in front of his very eyes was tangible evidence that perhaps it *could* be true. He had a ring, a wedding ring and somewhere his soon-to-be wife had waited for someone who had never shown up. Remorse rippled through Drake wondering what she must have suffered through waiting for him to arrive.

Unless she was a lie.

He moved over next to Aiden and shook him awake. They moved away from the fire so as not to wake Gwen who still seemed to be sleeping peacefully. Aiden's eyes invited him to tell him everything he wished and that his secrets would be safe. Drake found himself trusting more than he probably wanted to, but he had to have answers.

"Something on your mind Drake?"

"Yes," Drake answered pausing for a moment. "You know how you said we would all be tested by the Sorcerer? I think I just was."

"He showed you something?"

Drake nodded. "He showed me my past, or at least what he wanted me to believe was my past. There were parts of it I didn't believe yet some of it felt so real I could have sworn I was living there and not here. Do you know my past?"

"A good amount of it," Aiden answered. "Enough to put some questions to rest I reckon. You see Drake, the Sorcerer is very smart. He could tell you a million lies to get you to join him, but he's smarter than that. Instead, he takes parts of your past that he *does* know and blends them with lies so that you won't know which was true and which wasn't. You might be able to guess at first, but after a while the lines would become blurred and he would end up controlling you because of it."

"Makes sense. I just don't know what's real and what isn't. He showed me a town, named Trundale does it exist?"

"Trundale?" Aiden pondered the name. "It exists, but not around here."

"Not around here?" Drake repeated. "So is it another planet or something."

"The world is a very big place, much larger than you can imagine. Have you ever wondered what lies to the north? Or to the East and even past the western ocean and the southern sea? There is much to be discovered in the rest of the world Drake.

"If you spend any amount of time in a library you will notice that it is very hard to find a complete map of the earth. The nations have drifted and now wander in darkness. Trundale *is* a town and it is far to the north, in one of these other sections of the earth."

"Do you know who lives there? You are Lathon you have to know right?"

"Yes, I do. What did the Sorcerer tell you?"

"Nothing for certain, but this woman came up to me and embraced me in a way that I couldn't explain. It wasn't strange, it wasn't awkward, even if we were in the middle of the street. It was beautiful and intoxicating. I still have a hard time telling myself it's a lie."

"Who said it was?" Aiden asked. "If the Sorcerer's built lies around some truths then it could be a possibility. That could be the truth."

"He also gave me this," Drake reached into his pocket and pulled out the ring. Aiden took it and inspected it carefully.

"This is a nice ring," Aiden replied. "I especially love the inscription on it. Just makes it that much more meaningful you know?"

"But is it true? Is the Sorcerer telling the truth?"

"I thought we went through this."

"We did, but you never gave me the answer."

"I gave you the answer if you had listened to what I had said. I said some of it is true and some of it is lies. I know the truth, but you have to figure it out for yourself. That's something the Sorcerer doesn't want you to do. You see, I could just as easily lie to your face, tell you what you want to hear, and then what? You'd be gone in a second looking for this woman that you were apparently engaged to. Trust Lathon, listen to your heart, and see what it says. The human heart is the most deceitful of all things, and desperately wicked. It starts rumors and causes inner turmoil. It inflicts wounds in anger and devours the weak. But there is also a part of it that will give you insight if you trust in something greater than yourself. Listen to Lathon and figure out the lies from the truth."

"But what if-"

"I might also warn Drake, that you shouldn't pay attention to what the Sorcerer said right now. The Sorcerer is tricky. He tempted you not to show you something that was or wasn't true. He did it to distract you from the task at hand. If you are focused on something completely different he can rush in and kill you much easier. Truth or no truth, forget for the time being. There will be plenty of time to consider all these things after the war is over."

"I'm not sure I can forget now."

"As it is with all who are tempted, which I'm sure will be many in these next few days. The Sorcerer knows who we are and knows what we will do to him, he has no hope but to distract other people so he can kill them easier."

Aiden handed him back the ring and Drake looked at it for a moment, slipping it into his pocket and out of sight. They made their way to the fire and laid down, resuming looking up into the heavens that called out to him.

Drake wondered if everybody else was being tempted in the same way, or if he was the only one that felt like reality. Perhaps every person was tempted differently. They were each unique and different and Drake couldn't help but wonder if they all had something different to accomplish in their lifetime.

Drake fell asleep, his dreams finally taking him. They played out in front of him, the woman Rachal kissing him endlessly. Then water and the sound of the thundering falls. In an instant, the dream was over and his heart was restless, wishing for answers.

LONGING AND DESIRE

Farndor was the one place Chloe dreaded more than any other. It was the place where her life had both begun and ended. Now she found herself on the border, with people that she didn't even know. She couldn't help but rejoice at the events that had transpired in the past couple of days. Never before had she done something honorable or good. She had hidden the spies, and as a result, she now got to go with them.

Her life had changed and now she wished to remove the memory of the past self from her. She doubted that she would be able to completely move on. After so many years of the same lifestyle, turning a new page and starting over would be difficult, but it was a challenge she was willing to try.

Farndor was near, and her heart was more afraid than ever before. Would someone recognize her? Would she be kidnapped and taken to the king again? Would her fate be the same as her sister? Her mother's face flashed through her mind and she wished she could see her again but she knew that it wasn't possible, her mother had died trying to keep them from being taken in the first place.

She closed her eyes and opened them again, seeing a lone horseman riding through the moonlit land. He reached them, slowed his horse to a walk, and then dismounted altogether. He looked at the four of them and then smiled at Chloe, knowingly.

Aramen drew his sword. The man who had been riding the horse threw his sword to the ground and backed up with his hands in the air. They studied him carefully before approaching.

"Who are you?" Aramen asked.

"My name is Jeremiah," the man answered. "I know what it is you're going to do. I can help you."

"Explain yourself," Aramen demanded.

"You're going to take troops from this nation and use them to march against Grimdor. I am a general in the army of Farndor. Getting the army to join you will not be a problem, but you will stand a much better chance at winning their approval if you get the approval of their king. I know it's a little out of your way but it's not more than a day to Masada. I will even ride with you. Talk to the king and see if he'll side with us. I highly doubt he will, but if he doesn't I'm still loyal to Aiden, Sherados."

"You know the name of Sherados?"

"I do know the name, as well as many other things, but that is the only one that makes a difference. I want to see the Sorcerer destroyed and this land made back into everything that it once was."

"How do we know we can trust you?"

"I will hand you all my weapons and all my money. I will be completely at your mercy, if you find a reason to not trust me then kill me and leave me for the vultures." Aramen thought for a moment and then looked at each of them waiting for their input. The others nodded and then he looked at Chloe.

She struggled with herself, knowing that she had to do it, if not for her but for the rest of the world. There were more things at stake here than just her reputation or her dignity and this was her chance to prove it.

"We must go," Chloe answered quietly, emotion staining her voice. Aramen nodded and turned back to the man.

"It seems we are in accord on this matter," Aramen answered. "Be warned though that we will be carefully surveying everything and if there's one thing that's wrong, your head will roll in the desert sand."

"It is well understood and accepted. I simply wish to try and persuade the king to see a new point of view. If we cannot persuade him, we shall shake the dust from our robes and head out, riding for wherever you wish."

"You are welcome to join us by our fire," Aramen invited. The man dipped his head. Everyone was formally introduced and they all sat down on the ground.

"What can we expect from the nation of Farndor? Are they under as much restriction as the other nations?"

"As of now, we are still free of the Borags," Jeremiah replied. "Likely, this is due to the king of Farndor, who for the time being, has said he will not attack the Sorcerer. I suspect that news of this has reached the Sorcerer's ears and he has had mercy on us. Unlike the king though, I do not think it'll last forever."

"I agree with you on that," Aramen replied.

"The question is how long will peace in Farndor last?"

"Word has reached you of who Sherados is. With that being said, I would expect the Sorcerer's armies to attack immediately. He wouldn't want any hope to spring up in a nation if you understand me."

"I understand you perfectly," Jeremiah replied. "The world is a fascinating place, and it's about to become even more interesting. There's no telling what this war will look like."

"Sometimes, I think we'd be better off just to pull everyone loyal to Sherados and set sail for a distant island where the Sorcerer isn't," Chloe said.

"That could be done, but how would we live with ourselves knowing that we abandoned the good people of the earth who simply hadn't learned the truth yet?" Aramen asked. "Some people might not have even heard of Sherados or Lathon. We have to at least try and give them a chance, right?" Chloe nodded. "It's all about love."

"What does love have to do with war?" Chloe asked. "I understand a fine line between love and hate but I'm not sure I follow your reasoning."

"If we love this land, these people, so much that we are willing to die for them, how can they not see the truth in our convictions? Am I right?" Jeremiah asked.

"You are right. It takes a special kind of love to stand in front of someone who wants to kill you," Aramen replied. "I've always wanted a chance to show people how much I love them and this is how I do it; by standing when others fall, running towards the battle when other people walk away. We have to be strong and stand our ground. Only when we take a step of faith will Aiden, Sherados, be with us in the battle."

"So we have to make the first move?" Chloe asked.

"We have to have faith. Without faith, every effort is useless." Aramen held her gaze for several seconds after the words drifted off. In his eyes, there was so much that Chloe could see. She could see the love he was talking about and realized that she could feel it as well.

Love was intoxicating and all her life she had chased what she had thought was love, but now as she looked into his eyes she knew that she had never known love. Love was justice acting in public and her heart longed to take a stand. In her own way, she already had.

The night faded and so did her attention as she let the conversations continue around her and she slipped into her dreams, so real, so vivid she could have sworn they were true. Then she saw a man coming towards her, her mind went cold and her thoughts vanished. When finally the torment passed she was able to sleep. She had just been tempted and she had survived.

She fell asleep, her mind at peace.

"Good morning Gwen." Gwen's eyes fluttered open as she looked to the east where the sun was just now starting to rise over the trees. She turned her attention to the space next to her where Merderick the Sorcerer sat looking at her. Her blood ran cold and her mind ceased working.

"Sleep well?" Merderick asked her. His words leaked into her mind acting like a poison. Each one repelled Gwen more and more, but yet she couldn't escape them. They ate away at her mind and clawed at her conscience, forcing her to pay attention.

"Fine," Gwen answered. "Why are you here?"

"I'm here to tell you that I'm sorry about the way I treated you when last you were kidnapped. I was mad at Tremin and I took it out on you. I should have killed him right there and then. I am sorry."

"I don't believe you."

"That seems to be the common theme lately, but it's the truth, Gwen. At first glance, we might be very different but in reality, we are very similar."

"That's a pretty screwed-up reality isn't it?" Gwen asked.

"You want to know what we have in common Gwen? A fact that neither of us has truly appreciated. For all your life you were a slave, and seeing who you were a slave for, that couldn't have been very enjoyable. I'm a slave also, a slave of Grimdor. I can't escape it. Not now."

"That doesn't mean we're similar in any way, it's just a coincidence," Gwen replied.

"I'm not so sure about that, you were horribly mangled when you went through one of my mirrors. Remember that? We might be more similar than you think. They seem to only affect my family members. Somehow you are related to me."

"I can assure you that's not true."

"I would love to tell you you're wrong, but I don't have proof one way or the other." He paused. "However there is a way to know the truth, once and for all. Are you interested in learning about yourself, your past, and how to fix it?"

"No," Gwen lied. The Sorcerer smiled, seeing through her in a second.

"Everyone wants to know things, Gwen. Everyone wants to be loved and to feel like they belong. You deserve the same treatment as the person in the richest land in the finest castle. You could be my queen Gwen. These people you have lived with, do you really think they love you? Do you think they accept you?"

"Yes," Gwen replied, finding the answer in her heart. "I do believe they know me and love me. I know they do."

"And how do you know? Drake may have kissed you but that doesn't mean love. He may say he's willing to give his life up for you, but is that true? Over the centuries I have come to conclude that people like him are as shallow as they come."

"You're lying."

"No I'm not," the Sorcerer replied. "It merely sounds like a lie because of what they have said. Truth is different. It's what a person defines as truth for themselves, regardless of what everyone else says."

"I don't agree with that?"

"You don't? Well, then I guess there's no hope that you'll ever amount to much of anything. By disagreeing with the statement you have insinuated that a slave is always a slave and can never improve. If people can change, why wouldn't the truth? Now about this matter of Drake, Aiden, and everyone else accepting you, doesn't true acceptance equate to trust? That might not have been said before this moment but it makes sense doesn't it? I can't see that these people trust you at all, they haven't put you in charge of any armies or anything special. You're the tag-a-long and they're the leaders. They are afraid of your skills, and losing their position, so they keep you on the bottom where you've been your whole life."

Gwen didn't reply. As much as she hated to admit it, there was some truth behind the Sorcerer's words. Her heart cried out for relief from this nightmare, wishing for it to be over so she could live her life the way she wanted.

"As I said before, there is a way to fix this. Do you perhaps remember hearing anything about the Wizard's Staff?"

"Yes," Gwen answered. The Sorcerer smiled.

"I thought you might have. It's something I desperately long to have because then I would be able to fix the world. It would elevate the slaves to be masters and teach the masters a lesson or two when they're at the bottom of the totem pole. I never thought I would have to use the staff, but the time has come and there are no other options. I haven't been able to find it though. Do you know where it is?"

"No."

"Too bad. It could fix many things. If you should come across it...look into the red gem at the top of it. It has powers beyond my comprehension. You can then become the greatest you ever want to be in the world. With it, you can alter your reality and create your version of the truth and everyone will know it and adore you for it. You could be accepted and loved."

"How is that possible?" Gwen asked. "You made it, I can't think you could have made something good."

"Once again good is a point of view," the Sorcerer pointed out. "When you look into it, you will not only alter what the people you know think, but what everyone else around you thinks. The possibilities are endless. First and foremost, peace would radiate from people's souls. No one would disagree, so how could there be a war?

"The choice is yours and, of course, you would have to find the Wizard's Staff first. But it could end once and for all. You could still have Aiden as Sherados, but you would be as great as he is. You could get Drake to love you the way you've always dreamed. Do you follow?"

"I follow."

"Wonderful. In that case please accept my apology and I shall be on my way." The Sorcerer turned and walked away, vanishing into thin air as though he had never been there. Gwen sat up and looked at the dawn and then at the bag that she knew the Wizard's Staff was in.

Maybe the truth she had been told all her life and even in the past few months was nothing more than a lie that she had believed to be truth. The thought astounded her as she realized that using the Wizard's Staff just might end the war as she wanted. She would be accepted, and she would gain great knowledge. She could live the perfect, normal life she dreamed of.

Drake and Aiden still slept by the side of the fire as she pondered everything. Drake slept peacefully and she studied him, suddenly wondering if everything was the way she had thought it was. Her parent's identity had always been a mystery to her and even though Isabel had mentioned them once before, she had never told her anything else.

They didn't trust her, accept her, or love her. With each second that passed her doubt of the things she had called truth multiplied, while her understanding of what was happening shrunk. Was she actually agreeing that the Sorcerer was right and that there could be peace in this world?

Her thoughts were interrupted by a shape appearing on the horizon. Moments later another shape appeared. She struggled to make them out, noticing within a couple of seconds that it was Willard and Miles who looked as if they had seen a ghost. They walked cautiously, with their noses to the ground.

'Hello Gwen,' Willard greeted, speaking through their thoughts as they always did.

"Hello," Gwen answered.

'Interesting night wouldn't you say?'

"I guess so."

'He's been here,' Miles said sniffing the ground carefully. 'I can smell it, it's faint but he was here.'

'It's a good thing he's not here now or else I might have to have a few words to say.'

"Are there more wolves than just the two of you?" Gwen asked, the Sorcerer's words crashing through her head.

'Why don't you come to see for yourself?' She got up and followed them out of the village to the river as she had walked many times. Her mind flashed with images and the sensation of being struck by the dagger as she had. She felt the place the knife had pierced, pain searing through it.

She continued, determined to outlast the pain. Within a moment it passed and she found herself standing on the side of the river with the two wolves. In front of and around them was the forest, with no living being to be seen.

"How much farther do we have to go?" Gwen asked.

'We are here,' Miles replied. Willard stood up and lifted his head to the sky letting a howl escape. The sound frightened her for a moment, but it carried through the forest and echoed inside her heart.

Slowly it seemed as if the trees began to come alive, whispering the message back and forth to each other. Within seconds dark shapes began to come out of the woods. At first, there were only ten or twenty, but soon they were surrounded by well over two thousand wolves. The sight nearly overwhelmed her as Willard and Miles looked at her knowingly.

"I had no idea."

'We're ready to do our part in the attack no matter what that may be,' Miles told her.

"There are more than I expected, and I know you guys just as well as anyone," Aiden said from behind. They turned and smiled at Aiden and Drake, both of the wolves ran to greet them. Aiden pet them gently and they all walked to the edge of the river, watching the wolves still gathering.

'What do you think?' Willard asked. *'Do you think we stand a chance of catching the Sorcerer by surprise?'*

"I think he was already caught off guard by the Gogs, I think this will topple him," Aiden answered. They all laughed.

'That it will my lord, that it will,' Miles replied. *'The ones who couldn't talk didn't come because they didn't hear us. Nonetheless, we will make our war.'*

"Why do some wolves talk and some wolves not?" Gwen asked.

"They were treated like dumb animals for too long and that's what they became," Aiden answered. Willard and Miles nodded their agreement. "It's the same way with people. You treat someone a certain way long enough they won't be able to get out because they think they can't do anything else. It's one of the sad things about this world. Yet another that I am trying to end."

'So what would you have us do my lord?' Willard asked. *'I know you must certainly have something in mind for us.'*

"I do, but I don't quite have everything in order yet," Aiden replied. "Is there any way to keep in touch with you?"

'There is one that might be of use to us, and we can secure it easily enough if you take my meaning,' Miles hinted, Aiden smiled.

"In that case get to it, we have a lot of work to do and little time to do it. The workers are few but the harvest is plenty. We will be in contact in a few days."

'As you wish my king,' Willard replied, turning to face all the wolves.

'Alright, let's move out and make haste! Evil does not rest and neither shall we!' Willard and Miles crossed the river and then led the way, running into the forest and to the northeast, with two thousand wolves following behind them. Aiden and Drake watched the sight until the last wolf vanished from view. They looked at each other and then alarm spread across Aiden's face.

"What is it?"

"Where's Gwen?"

Drake looked beside him where she had been standing, only to find empty space no matter where they looked.

"Where do you think she went?"

"I'm not sure, but if you were tempted by the Sorcerer last night and I was tempted by the Sorcerer that can only leave us to conclude one thing." They ran into the forest.

Aiden sprinted through the forest just as quickly as Drake, as they ran through the woods back to the ruins. They finally broke free of the forest and then sprinted past the large ruins of the mansion that had been Lily's parents' house. They wove their way through the debris in the streets until they came to their campsite, unable to see any sign of Gwen and her belongings.

"Where do you think she is?" Drake asked. Aiden looked around carefully studying the horizon.

"I'm not sure but the faster we find her the better."

THE WIZARDS STAFF

wen looked over her shoulder. She clenched Aiden's bag in her hand, struggling to keep from looking at the Wizard's Staff this very minute. The thought of power captivated every thought and desire. It wasn't power she wanted, it was acceptance and love and those were both things that power could buy. Her heart cried out to be held in a man's arms long into the night and not have to fight in a war if she didn't want to.

The Wizard's Staff could do that for her. She was convinced.

She pushed forward, faintly hearing Drake and Aiden calling out her name. They were looking for her, they cared about her right? As much as there was probably some truth to that, she knew in her heart the real reason they were looking for her was because she had taken the Wizard's Staff.

Any notion that she was doing the wrong thing now seemed distant and foolish. As Merderick had said, the truth was a point of view, which in turn also meant that good and bad were a point of view, and in her opinion what she was doing wasn't bad. There would be peace in the world and she would be forever known as the person who created it. Drake and Aiden's voices were now very distant, with each of them being no louder than a light whisper that could only be heard if she listened for it.

Gwen stopped next to a couple of downed trees that were covered with moss. Up above, even though it was supposed to be winter the trees were in full bloom, completely still in the waking land.

She opened the pack and then pulled out the Wizard's Staff, unwrapping it and looking at the beauty that it held. She was mesmerized by the sight, unable to remove her eyes from it. Somehow it seemed to look more significant than it had the first time she had seen it. It was made of polished gold. Fit for a queen.

The staff captured her attention and she was drawn into it as she sat staring at it. The world slowed until it felt as if she was the only person that was in the world.

She looked at the gem at the top, and her interest peaked. At first, there was nothing unusual about it, just something that tickled the back of her mind, drawing her forward even more. She studied the gem, more intently now.

She was the only one who mattered.

The gem slowly shifted and changed, remaining the same as it had been, but in her mind, it looked different. Her heart was captured by the sight and the desire for more, as she kept on looking into the gem. Images flashed in her mind as the gem seemed to probe it for what she wanted to get out of life.

Peace, a lover, comfort, to be a wife and not a slave. Her heart desired to have all of these. She could feel the Sorcerer's presence and even though in the past it had repelled her, it now drew her closer.

Merderick had been seriously misunderstood.

Anyone who could create something as powerful as the Wizard's Staff couldn't be all that bad.

At once, she jumped back and released the staff as it became too hot to hold and her mind was filled with fire. She landed against a tree and slipped to the ground, the world fading from her. Still, she looked to the Wizard's Staff, wanting to use it to fix the situation she was in. The Wizard's Staff seemed to fight her more as the fire burned inside of her. Her clothes and her hair began to show the effects of the heat and her mind ached with pain.

She stumbled forward, grabbing the Wizard's Staff and staring into the gem at the top. Her heart nearly stopped as ice flooded through her veins and then fire flashed through them. She was thrown backward and landed on the ground.

She sat up and looked around, unable to see anything in the new world that had been created. Was she blind or was there something else happening? Slowly through the darkness of her mind, she heard sounds that she had never heard before. Whispering, and then laughing. It wasn't a light-hearted joyful laugh. but instead a sinister one. Chills ran through her heart as she knew it was the Sorcerer laughing at her.

She pried her eyes open to see the world around her, but there was nothing she could see, she was alone and in the darkness. She started to move, fear consuming her realizing that she was now naked, her clothes gone. She groped around in the darkness, wishing she could do something to help her situation but she was hopeless. She had thought she was helping herself, but now she realized that it had all been a trap and the Sorcerer had won.

She had been tempted and she had given in and now she had been stripped away to nothing but the pathetic excuse of the person she was. She had never felt more alone in her life. She groped around in the darkness for a while longer finally able to grab the Wizard's Staff.

Certainly, this was just part of the process. She would look into the staff and fix all of this. She crawled to the nearest trees, slipping into the brush, hiding in it, and trying to find some dignity. She held the Wizard's Staff close to her chest and began to cry realizing that she had been deceived. The Wizard's Staff could do nothing for her and now it had destroyed her beyond hope.

Drake and Aiden's voices were once again heard in the forest and fear filled her. They would never be able to love and accept her once they learned what she had done. She had to keep it a secret from them, but how? She was powerless to help herself, she was blind and had no way of protecting herself against anything, and hopelessness flooded over her.

She crawled further into the forest, able to come across a couple of bushes that would offer coverage so that if they did find her she wouldn't be exposed. Her heart cried out and her sobbing filled the forest as she hid from the two of them. If she hadn't been beyond hope before, she was certainly beyond hope now.

Footsteps were heard nearing her and she knew that Drake and Aiden had likely reached the part of the forest where she was hidden. She silently hoped that they would never find her and she could live her life in misery and shame as she deserved.

Her hopes were dashed as Aiden approached. Her heart pounded inside her chest as he looked for her, stopping and listening carefully to the surroundings. Gwen held still, hoping to not make any noise.

"Gwen, where are you?" Aiden asked. The question seemed simple enough but she knew it was a deeper question. In her heart, she knew that Aiden wasn't asking where she was as in location, but where her heart was. What she had done.

"Not where I should be," she finally replied. Her voice was frail and weak.

"Would you like to tell me what happened?"

"Don't you know?"

"Yes, but it is better to openly admit your wrong, as opposed to keeping it hidden inside. In the end, all secrets will be brought into the light."

"Why though must I say it?" Gwen asked, tears flowing down her cheeks.

"It's a matter of trust, Gwen. I trust you and I know what you did and I know you are sorry for it, but what will happen when your friends and family find out what you did? They will be surprised yes, but they will be more hurt that you didn't confide in them in the first place."

"I was deceived Aiden. The Sorcerer tricked me. I thought I was... unwanted."

"Everyone is important in my eyes," Aiden answered.

"I understand that now," Gwen admitted bitterly. "What happens now, I can't be a follower of yours anymore can I?"

"Of course you can. In fact, you have more reason to be my follower now than ever before. You see if a person asks for forgiveness and they change their ways then I will gladly welcome them back into my kingdom."

"So there's still a chance for me."

"For you and everyone in the world. Now we get on with life and figure out what to do next."

"You know what we have to do next," another voice exclaimed from the trees behind Gwen. Chills ran up and down her spine as Isabel's pleasant voice rang inside her ears. She could hear two people, she assumed Drake was another one.

"I'm blind and naked," Gwen told them. "My selfishness has blinded me and left me naked. The Sorcerer used me and then left me."

"As he does to many people," Aiden replied. "However, I think that is something easily remedied!"

"It is?" Drake asked.

"If you have faith anything is possible, even restoring sight," Aiden answered. Gwen felt him looking towards her again. "Do you believe that I can?" A moment of silence passed before Gwen nodded through her sobs. Aiden put his hands on her eyes and then removed them.

"Your faith has made you well." Gwen looked out on the world that looked so familiar to her and felt like she was on top of the world. She could see again! She looked down at her body realizing that she was once again fully clothed. She had been given a second chance. She looked at Aiden and Drake and then at the mysterious woman named Isabel who always seemed to show up when things were unusual.

"Thank you," Gwen replied, hardly able to find the words.

"You're welcome Gwen," Aiden said. "Let us learn from this mistake; this is what becomes of those who follow the Sorcerer. He takes away everything and will not give anything back. He leaves you naked and blind on the inside which is the worst thing that can happen in this world."

"Now what are we going to do?" Gwen asked.

"We have to head to Vernal, some friends of mine are tucked away there and they have some things we need," Aiden answered. "Plus, I wish to put the Wizard's Staff where it can do no more damage." They got up to leave and make their way back to the Taruks noticing that Isabel, if she had been there at all, was already gone.

They baked in the midday sun as they rode through the unforgiving desert. Chloe watched the desert landscape go by. Fear still gripped her as she hoped that no one would recognize her, especially the king. Finally, after a couple more hours they crested a hill and the city of Masada came into view. Soldiers were everywhere.

They pushed their horses up to the front gate, bringing them to a stop. The guards on top of the wall assembled and strung their bows, the guards in front of them drew their swords while one of them came forward.

"What business brings you here in this dark time?" the man asked.

"We wish to ally with the king of this land. We seek to march on Grimdor and now have a great army assembling in Idumea," Aramen said.

"A great army you say?" the man waved his hand through the air and all the weapons were lowered or put away. Silence fell between them as the men exchanged glances with their leader. They nodded their heads and the man came forward removing his helmet. Long grey hair fell to his shoulders and his face was hard and tanned by the desert sun.

"We understand your concern, but the king of the land may not side with us. We however believe in Lathon and would gladly fight against the Sorcerer side by side."

"That is good news," Aramen replied. "Still we would like to speak with the king, out of courtesy."

"Yes of course," the man replied moving closer and whispering. "Many soldiers have been brought to Masada because the king fears Sherados! Do not expect him to be receptive."

"I understand."

The guards moved out of their way and the heavy gate was opened. They were given an armed guard and paraded through the streets.

The palace came into view, far less majestic than it had been when she had lived here. Chloe followed everyone else's lead and dismounted her horse, her heart beating a hundred miles an hour.

The guards that had been with them at the gate closed in around them. She looked at the guards, recognizing one. Her mind flashed with the memory and she could see the same thing in his, as he remembered her immediately. He had been the one who had taken Chloe and her sister back to the palace, pulling them away from their mother.

She forced herself to stand tall and proud, hoping that she was appearing stronger than she felt. In the darkness of her heart a small, still voice spoke to her. Maybe she had been brought here for this moment. Maybe she did have value and purpose in this world.

They were led through the various chambers and hallways, all of which Chloe could have walked blindfolded. Then they came to a stop in front of the doors.

"Be wary of the king," the guards warned. They nodded and Chloe took a deep breath as one of the doors to the throne room were opened and they walked in.

The king sat up a little straighter, and it was clear the room had lost its luster in the years since Chloe had left. A dozen guards stood stationed all around the room and from the throne. The king's eyes bored through their skulls.

Relief flooded through Chloe's veins as she realized that the king she had been forced to make love to was no longer on the throne. The relief however was short lived and she recognized him as the son of Erode the Great.

"Welcome weary travelers," the king greeted. "Visitors are a rare thing in such dark hours. I naturally assume that you have a legitimate reason for this visit."

"You would assume correctly your majesty," Aramen answered.

"Come let us talk," the king motioned and a tray of food was brought to him. He ate as he looked at them. "What is it that brought you here my friends?"

"Sherados," Chloe said. Every head turned to look at her. The king stared at her and immediately she knew he recognized her. His eyes scanned her body up and down several times. Chloe held her breath reminding herself of how Lathon thought of her.

"Well, well, well, it seems we have been reunited with old friends," the king said. "I must say the years since you have been here have served you well. Perhaps we could talk later and discuss some details....overnight. I would gladly accept you as one of my wives."

"That is not why we came!" Aramen defended.

"Oh, that's right you came to have me send my small but powerful army to march against Grimdor, our only ally. This city was fortified to protect it against Sherados. I know who it is that rides at the front of your army and I will not bow to him. He is the devil incarnate."

"He is?" Morgrin asked.

"I have heard tales from the north. He goes around casting out demons and doing things just to get people to follow him. I hate him and if he ever steps foot into my kingdom he shall pay for it with his life."

"So you think he's a demon?" Morgrin asked, the king nodded. "I'm sorry, Your Majesty, but I have to disagree with you on that because after all there's no way for that claim to logically be true. A nation divided by civil war cannot stand against itself let alone its enemies. If Aiden was a demon and he was casting out demons he would be weakening himself would he not?" The king trembled.

"Say his name again and I will have you all arrested!"

"Aiden is Sherados. Even I have come to know that in my heart," Chloe replied. Aramen couldn't hide a smile.

"I should have you all arrested!" the king exclaimed.

"Then why don't you?" Aramen asked. "Aren't you just the slightest bit afraid of what the Sorcerer might do? An alliance with someone is only good until the terms of the agreement are met, after that who knows what could happen? He might decide to crush you as well. Then he's the king and doesn't have to share the throne with anybody."

"Get out of here and leave without talking to anyone. Guards! I want them escorted out of this country, we can't have their poisonous words leaking into the wrong hearts."

"Don't worry your majesty we will do as you ask, and we would like to formally thank you for the jobs you've provided us for the past years. We have been very grateful to you."

"You speak as if you're leaving?"

"We are," the guard replied. "It is clear this nation does not function the way that it needs to survive this war. You have gone to great lengths to keep the Elvish beliefs out of this nation, but we have heard the name and message of Aiden and we accept that in our hearts and our minds. We cannot sit still while the Sorcerer runs free and kills at will."

"You are fools and are marching to your death."

"Aiden is Sherados, that's all the hope that we need." The guards from around the room followed them out. When they finally made their way into the outside world tears nearly filled their eyes to see many soldiers standing in rank, a thousand horsemen behind them.

Chloe straightened and swiftly moved to one of the horses, admiring it.

"These are fair horses!" Chloe said. "Where did you find them? I have never seen horses like this in all of Farndor, or Idumea."

"It's hard to say where they came from, truthfully. We had just decided to fight with Aiden and we stumbled across these horses."

"A strange coincidence?" Aramen asked.

Jeremiah shrugged his shoulders. "It's something. Horsemen ride with Aramen and Chloe, the rest of you follow me!" the army cheered as they left the city.

"Make your way to the rock of Petron in Idumea, by the time you get there I'll have orders and Aiden will have told us the plan."

"Yes sir."

The horse's hooves thundered through the desert.

The ever-darkening skies loomed overhead. Drake and Gwen flew on Destan, following behind Aiden and Elohim who seemed to know the way they were going even if Drake had never been here before. They had been flying for nearly three days and as far as what was happening in the world below them, Drake hadn't a clue.

Instead, they flew east.

The world was shifting and was steadily becoming darker and darker until no thought of light existed. If the growing darkness continued, people might forget that there was light that overcame the darkness.

All the sounds that they had come to love about the land had vanished from their ears, sometimes it was because they were too high to hear them, but at other times it was as if the land was dead or sleeping.

Along with all of the other things Drake had noticed, he couldn't help but feel as if someone was following them. He had tried several times to glance over his shoulders and study the sky and the ground, looking for whoever might be behind them, but he was unable every time.

Dark mountains began to appear on the horizon, the black jagged rocks jutted into the sky making them want to run and turn back at a moment's notice. Drake had looked at a map or two and there was only uncharted space beyond Epirus, Grimdor, and Ariamore.

Drake looked at Gwen, still seeing conflict etched on her face. He thought for several moments, wondering what was going through her head and if he could do anything to cheer her up. She stared straight ahead lost in her thoughts.

"We're going to be hitting rain pretty soon!" Aiden yelled from Elohim. He pointed to the distant mountains, which were now beginning to grow in size.

"Where are we?" Drake asked back.

"Right where we're supposed to be," Aiden replied. "Those are the Rainy Mountains. We are in Vernal, the nation of the Spirits. It's unmarked on most maps, but in these mountains is a secret that we need."

"Why can't we just destroy the Wizard's Staff and be done with it."

"In due time my friends, in due time," Aiden replied. They flew in silence, the mountains growing in size. Drake and Gwen put on cloaks and prepared for the rain which could now be heard pounding the horizon.

They entered into the rain and soon they were drenched to the bone. A light fog filled the mountain range, hanging in the lower valleys. After a while, the rain lightened but continued to fall consistently. The mountains were vacant and empty, with no vegetation. Instead, just dark black rock mountains, laying in a mixed-up pattern with no clear path through.

Drake strained his eyes to see what might be hidden in the fog, his heart lifting when he spotted a light in the distance. The two Taruks moved towards the light, which grew to the size of a cave. Once again, the feeling that they were being watched came over Drake.

The Taruks swooped down and then landed twenty feet above the light they had seen. They carefully started to make their way down the slope and through the rain. Aiden walked in front.

They reached a small outcropping of rock, maybe three people wide that led up to the mouth of the cave. The light that had once shone out of the cave and into the darkness was now dimmed; they had been seen.

They approached the mouth of the cave, jumping back as the light glint of a sword blade came rushing through the air. Aiden drew his sword and blocked the man's next blow, a smile soon came across Aiden's face.

"It's okay everyone, it's just our long-expected guest," the man said. The light from the cave grew and they were welcomed into what appeared to be someone's home.

Four people stood before them. Two of them Drake recognized, Marion and Joseph. The other two were strangers to him. He studied them, thinking the woman looked familiar.

Everyone stood, studying the other people, each of them looking distantly familiar to Drake. Gwen on the other hand turned white. Drake put his arm around her and kept her close to him, each of them feeling increasingly nervous about the situation.

"Long have we waited for this day to arrive," the woman Drake recognized said.

"What day is that?" Gwen asked. The woman looked at the two of them displaying through her eyes everything she was feeling in her heart. Darkness, joy, light, and hope all flickered and burned, but also love and that one seemed to be greater than the others.

"The day when all would be made right," Marion said. "Long ago my fiancé and I were promised something that we did not ask for, and could not dream of. A chance to change the world through our son."

"Who is your son?" Drake asked. Aiden looked at them and smiled.

"These are your parents?" Drake asked. Aiden nodded.

"My name is Marion and this is my husband Joseph. It's such an honor to meet you again Drake Thomas, we've heard a lot about you."

"You have?" Drake asked, surprised. They nodded and then bowed to Aiden, Gwen, and Drake followed suit. They stood and Aiden embraced both of his parents, a new light in his eyes.

Drake once again found himself envious wishing he could have a family that would love him like that. The ring the Sorcerer had given him burned a hole in his pocket as he wondered where Rachal was or if she even existed. Drake caught himself mid-thought and then shoved the thoughts further from his mind. The last time he had been envious he had been tempted. He didn't want to go through that again.

"Do you have the Wizard's Staff?" Joseph asked, Aiden nodded and pulled it from his bag, leaving it in its wrappings. Joseph took it with care and then placed it on a wooden table that had been crudely constructed. He removed a cloth that covered the objects and Drake's mind came alive as memories flashed through his head.

One dark black blade sat on the table, the blade of it in pieces. Next to that was the Wizard's Staff, or at least a nearly identical lookalike beside it. The Wizard's Staff they had brought was placed with the real one.

"And who are you?" Gwen asked, referring to the other couple. The woman shifted anxiously, while the man appeared to be in great thought.

"Do you not know?" the woman asked. Drake stared and recognized her, but knew not from where. An uneasy silence fell over them.

"My name is Sedric and this is my wife, Bethany," the man said. Bethany came forward, her dusty blond hair gently cascading over her shoulders. Tears were in her eyes as she shook Drake's hand. Drake's heart was conflicted as he looked into the eyes of this woman.

"Isn't this a lovely sight," A familiar voice said from behind them. They turned and saw only a shadow of a person standing at the mouth of the cave. He walked forward, followed closely by a long flowing black cape. Drake's heart was chilled.

Merderick came in closer and then paused as if waiting for a 'congratulations' on finding them. When he didn't receive any welcome he moved to the table and carefully studied the contents. He looked at Gwen and then at Drake, pacing in front of the table.

"You have all done very well, I must admit that. How you did such a good job at creating a copy of the Wizard's Staff in such a short amount of time is beyond me, but either way, well done," Merderick complimented.

"Short amount of time?" Gwen asked.

"Yes my dear, you see I merely needed you to look into the staff for me to know at all times where it was. The fact that you have had this for three days and made such a convincing copy is quite a feat and you should be very proud of yourself." Merderick turned his attention back to the two staffs, and the rest of them exchanged glances.

He stood there and studied the weapons, and they watched him as the time passed and grew into minutes. The sounds of a horse riding up outside the cave entrance came to their ears and the Sorcerer perked up as well.

"Good my brother is here, he should be able to cast some light on this great mystery," the Sorcerer said, moving his eyes to the black blade at the other end of the table. He reached out to touch it and immediately recoiled his hand as if it had burned him. A man appeared in the cave entrance and walked in without a moment's hesitation.

Rohemir.

No one spoke as the pair moved past them and to the table, still unsure of which was the real one. Gwen and Drake exchanged glances and then they both looked at Aiden who didn't seem overly surprised by the revelation.

"After all this time you are on his side?" Drake asked, breaking the silence. Rohemir paused mid-motion and turned around to face Drake and everyone else. Ice flowed through Drake's veins and anger streamed through Rohemir's eyes.

"Of course I'm on his side, he's my brother, why wouldn't I be?" Rohemir snapped. "Family must stick together don't you know? Oh that's right you don't have any family."

"I had suspected there may be dark thoughts in your heart Rohemir," Sedric said. "I only wished I had seen it earlier."

"Have you really joined the Sorcerer?" Bethany asked. "How?"

"When my brother came to me a long time ago it became clear that he had found a way to become the most powerful person in the world. There is nothing I wanted more than to make sure that he was the king that he deserved to be. We went to great lengths on our quest for power and they all paid off."

He turned to Drake. "When you awoke on the side of the river and I found you, my heart was torn. I wanted to kill you right there and then, but the

Sorcerer had told me to leave you alive. He thought you were Sherados and he wanted to kill you himself. Unfortunately, he never got the chance and I was forced to take you to Belvanor, despite my efforts to lead us into trap after trap."

"So every moment we spent with you was a lie?" Gwen asked. Rohemir's face hardened when he looked at her.

"That's correct my darling, let there be no secret that I wanted you dead just as much as Drake here, or Aiden, I had never gotten along with Aiden."

"Now we know why," Drake said. Silence fell as the Sorcerer turned to Rohemir his eyes silently conveying whatever he wanted to say.

"It seems that you did such a good job creating a copy that we don't know which one is the real one," Rohemir started. "Which one of you will tell us?" Several seconds of silence passed. "That's what I thought, but I think we can all come to a mutual agreement here, don't you? We're civilized people and I know that people act differently when their life is on the line."

The Sorcerer came forward holding both Wizard's Staff in his hands. He pointed one of them at Gwen while the other hung by his side. Gwen took a deep breath and Drake clutched her hand.

"I will try them both, whichever one kills you is the correct one," the Sorcerer said with a smile. "The only way to save your life is if you tell me which one is the real one."

No one replied and the Sorcerer pulled back one arm slightly, getting ready to cast a spell.

"Touch her and you are dead!" Another voice yelled from outside the cave. Everyone looked to the cave entrance.

Isabel.

She wore a sword and a dagger around her waist, her clothes soaked from the pouring rain. Outside the cave, lightning flashed and the thunder rolled. Drake looked at the Sorcerer and Rohemir, both of them looking as if they had seen a ghost.

"Sedric, Joseph, a pleasure to see you again," Isabel said as she walked to face Rohemir. He stood before her, unable to speak.

"Impossible," Rohemir whispered, barely loud enough for them to hear.

"Sorry to disappoint you, *dear*, but I am alive. I always have been. I've just kept myself from your view and reach all these years."

"I should have killed you when I had the chance!"

"Once again I'm *so* sorry that you didn't get the chance," Isabel said.

"What are you talking about?" Bethany asked. Isabel looked at them briefly before holding eye contact with Rohemir.

"Everyone here must certainly know that I have many secrets in my past and this is just another one. Everyone I would like you to meet my former husband...Rohemir."

"Your husband?" Sedric asked. Drake watched their interactions, able to discern that everyone here knew Isabel in some way.

"It's a long story, so I'll give you the shortened version," Isabel started. "Over twenty years ago a girl fell in love with a boy that she had been attracted to for a long time. They got married and lived happily ever after, for a few years anyway. They lived in Grimdor, which at the time wasn't such a bad place to live. I thought it was kind of unique and different, and I was with the man I loved and so I loved it.

"The time passed and we had our first child a son named Pargin. You've met him before, he was later renamed Tremin by his father and his uncle Merderick. A little bit more time passed and Rohemir and his 'brother' Merderick started changing and spending more time together. Before long it became evident that the man that I once loved and married no longer existed.

"I tried everything I could think of to get us back to a place where we were in love like we once had been, but all that got me was a death threat. Not taking it seriously I stayed for another couple of months. Only when Rohemir and Tremin tried to murder me in our bedroom did I know for sure that I had to get out and get out fast.

"So I left both my son and my husband in the wasteland that they, along with Merderick, were creating. I made several trips back in the next couple of years, first to curse the Sorcerer's mirrors, then to steal the seeing stones, and then finally to steal and create a copy of the Wizard's Staff. I didn't know what was going to happen but I knew enough that those three things would be very important in the future. I've lived in Epirus near Fiori for the past twenty years. My husband Morgrin and I have been very happy ever since."

"So you're the one who stole everything?" Rohemir asked. "I suppose you also know the location of my Taruk?"

"And I suppose you know the location of my horse."

"Horse?" Drake asked.

"A white stallion named Fastfoot. He was mine when we moved to Grimdor, but Rohemir wanted it for himself and took it from me. So I took his Taruk." As if on cue a green Taruk stuck its head into the cave, smoke slowly coming from its mouth, its eyes hard and judgmental as the Taruk looked at her former master. A growl filled the cave.

"What lies have you told my Taruk?" Rohemir asked. The Taruk growled louder.

"I told her the truth, by the way, I gave her a name unlike you who made her feel like she was nothing. Her name is Aspen and she has been a great companion since we left Grimdor." Rohemir looked at Isabel, anger and hatred spewing from his eyes.

"Fiori?" Rohemir asked. "Did I hear you correctly or are my ears playing tricks on me?"

"You heard me correctly. I was right under your nose the entire time. I had to stay close to Fiori to keep a close eye on one other thing that you don't know about."

"And that would be what my *dear*?"

"I believe that it has been decided that Gwen is somehow related to your brother correct? She's our daughter." Surprise rippled through everyone's soul.

"Daughter?" Gwen asked, a smile tainted with confusion stretched across her face.

"Yes Gwen, you are my daughter," Isabel replied. "I had no idea when I left Grimdor that I was pregnant with Rohemir's and mine second child, but when I found out, I knew I had to come up with a way to keep you safe. I gave birth to you and then a few weeks later I left you on the doorstep of some wealthy people in Fiori. I hated to do it, but all my life I would be on the run and I wouldn't be able to raise a daughter like I wanted. I left you with some people hoping and praying that I was doing the right thing. All those years you felt alone, I was watching you, Gwen. I even had the chance to meet you several times. Although my outward appearance was altered, we did meet in the streets." Smiles spread across everyone's faces except Rohemir and the Sorcerer's.

"Are there any other secrets we don't know about you?" Merderick asked.

"About me? No. However, I do believe there is still one more thing that has not been brought into the light here."

"And what might that be?" Rohemir asked, anger evident in every word that he spoke.

"Drake, do you remember long ago when I said that your cousin had come into my shop on several occasions? I just couldn't remember his name."

"Yes."

"Your cousin is in this room."

"Your cousin is Aiden," Bethany said from behind him.

"How do you know?" Drake asked.

"Marion and Joseph are Aiden's parents, and my late husband Malachi, is Joseph's brother. I am your mother." Drake was stunned.

"Well, well, well, after all these years this is what it comes down to. The two people that the elf kings helped escape from Masada so many years ago, and the people who assisted them," Merderick said. "Hasn't this been a fun family reunion? I almost hate to see it end."

"So you're my father?" Drake asked Sedric.

"Step-father. It seems when Malachi and I helped your cousin and their family escape Malachi was killed and I fled the city with Bethany. Neither of us knew at the time that she was pregnant with you."

"If I had known then the power that you two would have I would have you slaughtered in your cribs, I assure you," Merderick replied. "But unfortunately, I was too weak to carry out the task. Now though I am here and I will see the end of this rebellion and then I will be the king of this world and no one will be able to touch me." He raised one of the Wizard's Staff slightly and then flicked it at Drake.

Light flashed from the end of it and Drake never expected to open his eyes again. Thunder filled the room. Then screaming. He opened his eyes, having not felt any pain like he expected. The Sorcerer had been thrown against the wall his skin looking charred and burned as though he had just walked through a fire.

Rohemir helped him up to his feet and his eyes darted around the room coming to a rest on Isabel who stood a little ways away from all of them. The Sorcerer raised the Wizard's Staff he had used above his head and threw it to the ground. The impact although it had been small, was enough to shatter the weapon. The pieces flew to the wall with such force that they embedded themselves there. In front of them, they watched the Sorcerer seethe.

"Well done Isabel. Well done." He pulled back the other one and sent a light flashing from the end as he had done with the first. The light raced at Isabel's chest but never touched it, hitting open air a couple of inches away and spreading as though it had hit something.

The light changed colors and formed into a ball again just next to Isabel's left hand. She threw it back at the Sorcerer and then stepped out of the way allowing Aspen to put her head in the cave. The Sorcerer quickly dodged the energy ball, which hit the wall of the cave and exploded sending chunks of rocks through the air.

Aspen opened her powerful mouth at the same time and released a stream of flames from it. The flames flooded into the room and wrapped around everyone as the Sorcerer and Rohemir both deflected the flames with their magic. The others were surrounded by flames but not consumed as the fire wrapped around all of them.

The fire continued without ceasing and Drake's mind went wild as he watched the Sorcerer and Rohemir in the fire, trying to keep it away. Finally, they muttered a spell of some kind and the fire recoiled. Aspen finally ended the flame and before long they stood in front of each other once again.

"I don't need to beat you here, instead I'll humiliate you in the pathetic excuse of a battle you are going to wage on Iscariot!" the Sorcerer exclaimed. He reached into his pocket and pulled out a horn, blowing it. No sound was heard at first but slowly they became aware of a note that was so low and so revealing they could hardly stand to be in its presence.

"We'll be waiting." The Sorcerer replied. Rohemir followed behind and they left the cave, the Sorcerer jumped on his red Taruk and Rohemir mounted Isabel's horse that he had stolen so many years ago. The two of them vanished from sight as the rain continued to pour down, complimented by the lightning and thunder.

"I'm not even sure what to say after a display like that except that Gwen has a very smart mother," Joseph said.

Isabel smiled. "Forced to be this way because of the treachery of my husband. It's quite sad."

"So all this time and you were Gwen's mother?" Drake asked.

"Although I may have left her with strangers when she was just a baby, I did love her. I've been watching her all these years."

Drake looked to Bethany and Sedric, his mind filled with hope. "After all this time I've actually figured out something about my past. Do you have any idea why I was near the Charenella Falls, where I fell over?"

"Why you were so far west we couldn't say," Bethany answered. "You had been missing for quite a while. At first, we thought Zebethar had killed you, but we couldn't accept that. We came west to search for you. I am unsure of the events that took you to the falls, but it was the will of Lathon for things to unfold this way."

"Why were things meant to unfold this way, Aiden?"

"Some things are not for you to know," Aiden replied. "There will be time to learn about ourselves later, right now a war lies ahead of us and we will rush forward and destroy the Sorcerer and Grimdor before they have a chance to do any more damage."

"Why was the Sorcerer attacked when he tried to use the Wizard's Staff?" Gwen asked.

"He tried to use the fake. I had placed a curse on it," Isabel replied.

"Of course you did," Gwen replied with a smile. They embraced and then Drake embraced Bethany and Sedric, hardly able to explain the emotions that were raging inside of him. Never in his life had he felt so loved. He held their embrace, the Sorcerer's temptation coming back to him. He embraced it for a moment and then pushed the thoughts away, contentment filling his heart.

"What's next Aiden?" Isabel asked. "I'm sure there must be some kind of a plan."

"There certainly is," Aiden replied, even as he finished his statement flame and blue mist came flying towards the cave and hit the ground, taking form into Rade and Cerin who walked forward. Aiden waved his hand and an opening appeared in the bare rock wall. Several people appeared in the distance, Morgrin, Aramen, a woman Drake didn't recognize as well as Willard and Miles. Stood waiting for them.

"Time to prepare for our war on Grimdor and the Sorcerer."

XXI ALLEGIANCE

One by one, they made their way through the opening in the wall. They stood and shielded their eyes for a moment as the vast amount of light overwhelmed them. When their eyes focused they found themselves at the Rock of Petron in Idumea, with all that had gathered.

Ellizar and Lily ran up to them and embraced them, questions in both of their eyes. Skander had also returned the night before but had only been able to persuade a handful of the giants to fight with them.

Aiden led them through the camp, bringing them to a large tent, three times the size of the regular tent with a dozen chairs and a table in the center. A map of Grimdor was spread across the table as well as some rough plans of Dhuma that Isabel said she had drawn from her memory. Shavrok stood over the map, with another couple of Gogs alongside. They sat down at the table while Aiden remained standing.

"So what's the plan?" Ellizar asked.

"The plan is Isabel and Morgrin will take every troop present and crush Dhuma with one swift blow," Aiden started.

"Is there any easy way to get into Dhuma?" Shavrok asked. "The Gog's are certainly willing to do their part in this battle."

"I think there is much that the Gog's can do. Do we have any catapults' and large-scale assault weapons?" Isabel asked.

"The Gog's have been busy disassembling the ships that we built and are creating battering rams, ladders, and siege towers to use. Anything you want us to do can be done."

"I have an idea but it's a little bit extreme and I don't know if it *can* be done or not," Isabel said. "I think I can get us into the city and take it over without losing a single life."

"What did you have in mind?" Shavrok asked

"I've lived in Grimdor for many years and when Aspen and I took our leave we spent a couple of years searching the land for anything that might prove useful in a situation like this in the future.

"I snuck back into Iscariot several times and one of those times I buried myself in the library reading everything I could find about the true Grimdor. If you remember there are only three cities above ground, but multiple cities and passageways are connecting them beneath the surface. This makes it possible to go to any city they want without having to ever come to the surface. It was mentioned in one scroll, the possibility of tunneling to other cities outside of Grimdor. If that was ever accomplished I don't know about it.

"Dhuma is unique in that it sits in the open on a large hill of stone. There are mountains by it, but only a few and nearly a half mile away.

"Aspen and I searched and found a reservoir on the mountain. It might as well be a lake for all the water and size it is. At its narrowest point, it's three miles across, and at least a mile deep. The Borags have built and added to a large retaining wall, circling the entire mountainside to hold as much water as they wish. It doesn't make sense for them to store so much water when the Sorcerer can make it rain at will, but my best guess as to how they will defend the city is that they will allow us to approach the city and then let the water loose, wiping us all into the city or killing us on the sharp jagged rocks that are one mile to the southeast. That would be their best bet and I'm willing to put money on the fact that they will do that."

"That's fine, but how on earth are we supposed to get into the city and take it over if they're just going to wash us away?" Chloe asked.

"Now you've even got me curious hon," Morgrin replied. "How?"

"We use their defense against them. We're going to send a small force to attack Dhuma, probably Gog's. When they see the small force they will think that either we're cocky and think we can take it without even trying, or they'll think that we are trying to save our numbers to fight at Iscariot. Either way, it's in our favor."

"How many troops should we send?" Drake asked.

"A small number of what we have, but big enough to get their attention," Isabel answered. "I suggest sending ten thousand troops, with the knowledge that they will be swept away."

"If that's going to be the case send the Gogs. We are good swimmers and won't have a problem dealing with any kind of a wave they send at us," Shavrok said.

"Make sure your troops have minimal weapons we don't want any of your troops to get killed by accident. Inside the city, there are two different ways you can get beneath the ground. First, there are the drain tunnels which I believe, if I've heard correctly, Ellizar and Lily have had some experience with."

"You can say that again."

"There are two tunnel systems in Grimdor, one for water and one for citizens to come and go. The tunnels are miles long and they go deep into the ground. However, there is a powder that covers the walls, the Borags put it there intentionally because they like the smell of it better than they like the smell of themselves. I've tested this several times and it explodes violently when it contacts water. Our job will be to get people inside the city to keep the drain tunnels closed and to open the other tunnel system. The water will rush inside, hopefully igniting all the powder on the walls, blowing it to kingdom come."

"So, by doing this we could wipe the entire city off the map with one small effort?" Aramen asked.

"Yes," Isabel said.

"The only problem is, how are we going to get that main gate open?" Lily asked. "They want to wash us out to those jagged rocks."

"The Gog's will have no problem avoiding the rocks," Shavrok assured. "If you can get the gate open I don't see why this plan won't work."

"Willard and Miles," Aiden called. The wolves looked at him. "Take your friends and wait on the northern side of the mountains by Iscariot. When you hear our horns come and assist in that attack."

Willard and Miles nodded, exiting the tent immediately.

"What about me?" Drake asked.

"You, Gwen, and I will be coming from the east and with the help of the Korazin and Spirits, take out Grön. But first, we will do what we can to aid the people of Belvanor. Atruss may still be inside and no doubt Rohemir will have become very hostile towards the people. We can't afford to take too long, but we must try."

"After Grön is taken out, we'll march to Iscariot. The Sorcerer will have a war on three fronts.

"I'm scared to think of what the Sorcerer will have waiting for us," Lily admitted. "I'm still trying to rid the thoughts of the past from the last time we were in Grimdor, and now to think that we're headed there willingly, it's almost too much."

"Except this time we're goin' teh put an end to it," Ellizar replied. "Either that or die tryin'."

"Aiden tells me that you've lost your memory," Bethany said, coming up to his campfire. Drake nodded miserably. Everyone had gone to sleep for the night and only Drake's fire still burned. Gwen lay on the ground sleeping peacefully.

"Yes, I know it might be hard to believe, but whatever my life was before the past six months I don't remember."

"Nothing?" Bethany asked.

"Not one thing," Drake admitted. "I recognized you in the cave, but I couldn't put a name to your face. I hardly even remembered you were my mother, as strange as that is."

"It is strange, but it is what it is," Bethany said plainly. "This mother's heart is just happy to see that her son is alive. Sedric and I had feared the worst."

"I'm sorry, you've suffered," Drake finally said.

"In time we'll see why things were meant to be this way," Bethany said confidently.

Drake sighed heavily. "I suppose. I just wish I understood why."

"Let me tell you a story," Bethany started. "Once upon a time, there was a young girl who married a man, her knight in shining armor."

"Is this a story about you?" Drake asked with a smile.

"Yes. I loved Malachi very much, and then one night we were called on to help Marion and Joseph escape with Aiden. Sherados as we now know him." Bethany paused for a moment. "In the events of that evening, Malachi was killed. I was forced to flee.

"I was pregnant with you," Bethany continued. "To save me the shame of being a widowed mother, Sedric took me as his wife. And it's worked out rather well. That being said. I was once like you are. Always wondered why some things were. Why did Malachi have to die? Why was I not able to save him? Why hadn't I died with him that night? How could I possibly marry Sedric and be a good wife, while I was still grieving the loss of my husband? How would I raise a child who would never know his true father?"

"How did you do it?" Drake asked.

"One day at a time," Bethany answered. "Always trusting that Lathon had a grand design and that something good would come out of all my sorrows. In some way that only Lathon can explain, he did bring something good out of all of it. He's reunited us, and helped me see more clearly the events of the past."

"But what about the future?"

"The future is not ours to worry about," Bethany said. "Lathon will bring good out of this yet, my son. You'll see." Drake smiled, taking comfort at the thought. They fell silent.

"How do you know Isabel and Rohemir?" Drake finally asked.

"Never knew them together, that's for sure!" Bethany exclaimed. "Everyone has their secrets. Joseph and Sedric helped her with an odd job years ago. Rohemir was one of Sedric's friends in Farndor. We had kept in touch for years, off and on. We came west looking for you, and then figured we should try and find him while we were in the region."

"I'm glad we were reunited, even if I still don't have a clue about life," Drake said. They both laughed.

"I would say you've found a nice life," Bethany said, motioning towards Gwen. Drake couldn't hide a smile.

The land was silent beneath them. From high up in the sky, the land flew beneath Drake and the others as they sped towards Belvanor. Drake tried to catch up with everything that had transpired in the past twenty-four hours. He had gone from having no past to having a family that loved him.

Aiden and Gwen rode on Elohim. Drake and his mother, Bethany, were atop Destan. Together the four of them raced toward whatever would be waiting for them.

It felt like an eternity since Drake had last set foot in the city and now they had no idea what to expect or what they would find. Rohemir had betrayed them and was now in charge. The strength of the Sorcerer was intimidating, but by the small little skirmish that had taken place at the caves, it was obvious that he was beatable.

They flew onward, dropping out of the sky slightly, the forest now visible to them. Finally, the Grass Canyons appeared in the distance, and beyond that, faint lights. Fortified walls came into view. A few Borags walked through the city.

They landed in the Grass Canyons, for the moment hidden from view. Aiden motioned for them to get off and they began walking through the silent land.

They came around the last corner and felt their blood run cold. Merderick stood in front of them. His eyes filled with hatred.

"Merderick," Aiden said casually.

"I thought you might be stopping by," the Sorcerer greeted. His eyes bored into Aiden's eyes. The two seemed locked into a silent duel.

"How are you tonight?" Aiden asked.

"Don't waste my time with flattery you fool. You want to kill me and I want to kill you so let's just come out and say it."

"I don't want to kill you Merderick," Aiden answered.

"You say I'm a deceiver? I think you should look in a mirror and take a good hard look at yourself. You want to kill me."

"I want justice!" Aiden exclaimed.

"And that means killing me doesn't it?"

"No, that means fighting for all that is good in this world, which you clearly don't believe in."

"I must admit you are audacious I will give you that. You walk in here and accuse me of not wanting justice when I have no choice but to be with this slime? Do you think I like the Borags? They're a waste of my time as they are yours."

"They are not a waste of time," Aiden answered. "At least they once weren't, but their thoughts were twisted and morphed into something no one had ever wished. If they are a waste of time, you have made them that way!"

"I've had enough of this!" Merderick exclaimed. "I know you want this city and Atruss. But, I want another chance!"

"You have a proposition for us?" Aiden asked. Merderick smiled.

"Yes," Merderick said with a sly smile. "I want another chance to tempt Gwen. You cannot help her in any way. If I can get her to curse you, then I win and you surrender to me and my army. If you win and she does not curse you as I desire, then I will take all my Borags from this city at once!"

"There is no promise you can make that we can trust," Gwen replied. "You would never keep your word."

"My dear Gwen...if there's one thing I am...it's true to my word!" Merderick said.

Aiden and the Sorcerer held eye contact for a moment before Aiden looked at Gwen.

"I'm not ready," Gwen replied.

"Have faith, Gwen. Stand true to what you know. Temptation will come, regardless if you are ready or not."

"So it's agreed then?" Merderick asked, grinning. Aiden looked up.

"Yes, it is. Test her how you wish, but you must not physically harm her!"

"Deal," the Sorcerer said shaking Aiden's hand. Aiden moved behind the Sorcerer to Atruss who watched with interest. The Sorcerer stood in front of Gwen and slowly began circling her, like a vulture about to devour fresh meat.

Gwen took a deep breath and calmed her breathing, trying to steady her nerves. Could she stand up against this temptation? Last time it had been too much and she had given in. Her heart cried out and her mind went blank as the Sorcerer continued to circle her, muttering in an unintelligible language.

Within a second the world changed and she found herself lying on a beach on the edge of the ocean. The sun was setting and the light glistened off the water. She could smell the ocean and taste the mist that drifted through the air.

It was paradise.

As if her thoughts had been discovered, the sun turned blood red before finally turning black. The light vanished from the land and the stars even went dark. Only the sound of the ocean remained and even that was fading. A few seconds passed before she began to grow uncomfortable, suddenly aware of the sounds all around her.

She stood to her feet and then walked forward. Her mind drifted as she walked into the darkness. The waves crashed up onto the shore and touched her feet. Even in the darkness, she found comfort. She knew this was nothing more than a fabrication. A very real fabrication. Her mind tried to figure out how exactly this was supposed to be a temptation when she didn't feel like she was being tempted.

Fear grew in her as she wondered what was making all the strange noises in the forest. Her fear only increased as the sound of crashing was heard from behind her. The ground shook and trembled. She instinctively took off running but soon tripped on something that was lying across the ground.

She groped around in the darkness hoping and wishing that she could find cover from whatever the beast was. She found none and her heart began to panic. The booming footsteps came closer until finally, she felt as if they would crush her with their next step.

She screamed out and light appeared. It shone a brilliant white and in the light was a person. He came forward shining brightly, causing apparent pain to the creature who backed away from her. Soon the man stood between her and the monster, keeping him at bay.

The light increased and the creature moved away further and further until the light was as bright as day. Everything around them was cast in white light. The man turned around and revealed himself. It was Merderick. The conflict raged inside of her.

"You see Gwen, on first glance this 'temptation' if you must call it that, seems as if it's simpler than the previous one I gave you, but the truth of the matter is neither one was a temptation but rather something that *could* be if you made the right decisions. Right now you're swimming in the middle of the ocean with no land in sight and I am the light that can save you. I did not lie to you in the vision I showed you previously, your life could be like you saw in the Wizard's Staff, but not if you choose to stay with Aiden.

"He has no power. He's afraid of me. If he thinks he can beat me with the armies then he is delusional. This life is short and power will rule without a doubt.

"I think it's time for you to choose which path you will be on. Aiden seems content to let people suffer. I will make sure you never suffer. The choice is up to you Gwen."

Gwen shivered in the darkness and when she blinked she was right where she had started. The room was the same and her heart was still aching from the pain she had experienced.

"What's your choice Gwen of Fiori?" the Sorcerer asked. Gwen looked down and then back into the Sorcerer's eyes, seeing nothing but lies in them.

"I will not curse Aiden or anyone who fights with him. I see things clearly now. You are a deceiver, you are alone in your castle and you will never know love. I do not wish to help you now or ever. You can surrender right now."

"I'm afraid I can't do that," Merderick answered, starting to walk away. "I guess the next time we meet will be in the middle of a battle."

The Sorcerer turned and walked away from the both of them, disappearing into thin air moments later.

"You did well Gwen," Aiden congratulated.

"Thank you. I didn't think I would have the strength."

"Everyone who believes in their hearts that they can be saved are saved, this is the same sort of deal."

Without speaking another word, they walked up to the gates of Belvanor, which were now open. Borags marched out of the city, and Merderick could be seen on his horse leading them into the wilderness. The people of the city watched in wonder and great confusion.

The word of what happened spread quickly throughout the city and when morning came so did many people who wished to join in their attack against Grimdor. Not long later, Atruss was released from the prisons and joined them.

To their surprise, Berdin, the third of the elf kings, who had visited Sherados so many years ago, arrived in the city near midday, bringing with him almost two thousand warriors. Anticipation filled the air. Many voiced their allegiance to Aiden and were gathered at the gates of Belvanor.

At once, Aiden rode up beside them. Drake mounted his horse and anxiously gripped the reigns. Yelling echoed from behind them as a couple of Farsees came running forward, standing in their way and preventing them from leaving.

"What is the point of this?" the leader asked. "I am a very powerful man Aiden, perhaps you've forgotten. I should kill you right now and do all of us a favor. If it hadn't been for you, none of this would have ever happened. Our fields would still be full of crops and our lives would be plentiful. We had everything under control until you came into the picture. You and your followers should leave right now."

"We will, and I promise you we won't return to this nation until the war is over."

"War? Why does there have to be a war in the first place? If we respect our enemies they will not breach these borders, it was only because of you and Mr. Thomas that they were breached in the first place!"

"Our enemy is strong and will move swiftly to destroy all that is good in this green earth if we don't do something. For years you have called yourself the religious leaders of Lathon. You set the bar so high that no one, not even you can reach it. You've burdened the people with religious demands that were never intended. You are nothing more than hypocrites in my eyes."

"We're not interested in your eyes," the leader replied. "You are a criminal."

"He's Sherados!" Drake exclaimed. The leader looked stunned.

"That's not possible. You are not Sherados, because Sherados would not associate with such scum like you do."

"Scum?" Aiden asked. "Look in a mirror and you'll find the majority of the scum in this world. I didn't come here for people who think they can save themselves, or think that they don't need help. I came here for people who are defenseless and feel worthless. Cursed are those who put their trust in mere humans, who rely on human strength, and turn their hearts away from Lathon. They are like stunted shrubs in the desert, with no hope for the future. They will live in the barren wilderness, in an uninhabited salty land. But blessed are those who trust in Lathon and have made him their hope and confidence.

"They are like trees planted along a riverbank, with roots that reach deep into the water. Such trees are not bothered by the heat nor worried by long months of drought. Their leaves stay green, and they never stop producing fruit.

"The human heart is the most deceitful of all things, and desperately wicked. Who really knows how bad it is? But I, Sherados, search all hearts and examine secret motives. I give all people their due rewards, according to what their actions deserve. You are worthy of no rewards, you have led these people off in directions that Lathon never intended. You think it's right, you think you're better than everyone else. You are like white-washed tombs, nice and appealing on the outside but inside you are a rotting corpse that doesn't begin to understand anything about life."

"How dare you accuse us of these things? We have only wanted to be like Lathon."

"No, you did these things so that if Sherados came forward he would look at you and say, 'I like how you did things'. It was always about you and now at the end of all things you find that you've had it all wrong. I've been living among you and people have failed to see me until recently.

"You loved to sit in the seat of honor at feasts and banquets when you should've been out helping people. I honor those who honor me. If you had truly read the ancient scrolls you would have discovered the true message of everything I am trying to say and do in this earth. Love Lathon and love other people.

"There is no better thing in this world than when a brother helps out another brother. The world is changing and will never be the same but there is one thing that is the same in all instances. Love. Love is the thread that is woven through the ancient scrolls, history, and the present and future.

"It is because of love that we will march forward and fight the Sorcerer. For the Sorcerer holds no love in his heart and he is not capable of doing so. Instead, he is filled with lust for power, greed, and every other thing that will drag you down. He seeks to destroy this earth and we fight for our families and our friends." Aiden turned to face the army that had assembled, as well as all the citizens.

"If you think that I have come to bring peace to this earth you are wrong. I did not come to bring peace but instead to divide a family, with two in favor of me and one not in favor of me. This world will be made new but you will still have to choose for yourself whether you're going to stand with me or not.

"Those who do will find a life of joy and peace no matter what they are going through if only you cast aside yourself and love other people. If that is what your heart wishes to say then let it sing the song and live the life you are called to. Tonight we ride for war and the future. We will destroy our enemies. Who's with me?!" The people let a cry escape and the Farsees exchanged glances not knowing what to do.

"By whose power do you have the authority to do these things?"

"If I have to tell you then you are completely lost," Aiden replied. The Farsees moved out of the way and Aiden led his horse out of the city. Drake, Gwen, and Berdin followed suit leading the army of now nearly seven thousand horsemen out of the city and into the night. They rode for many hours. Destan and Elohim were up in the sky watching over them. The sun was now beginning to peak up over the horizon and the signs of the coming dawn appeared.

Drake followed Aiden, wondering where they were headed. The great host had been traveling north for a while when finally Drake's mind was filled with a memory. He looked over at Gwen whose face was covered with fear. This was the invisible castle that they had visited previously.

The memory of the mirrors, and Gwen being attacked overwhelmed Drake's mind and he knew it must be haunting her as well. Still, she rode forward, pointing something out to Drake. He followed her finger and noticed soldiers on the wall. Horns announced their arrival.

"Open the gates!" Someone yelled from the wall. "Make way for the king!" The gates were opened and they rode into the large courtyard. In the distance, the keep stood. Drake looked around noticing that several walls between here and the edge of the keep had been torn down. Now, one could see into the deepest part of the structure.

"What happened here?" Drake asked. Berdin rode forward.

"Me and my men have remained hidden for some time. Having heard the name of Sherados being spoken in the wide world, my men and I attacked this city before riding to Belvanor. We have also made special modifications to the Keep, to ensure a speedy arrival at our destination."

"How does that work?" Gwen asked. Berdin smiled and Aiden turned to them.

"Instead of traveling on horseback the entire way, it would be much faster to ride our horses through the mirror that will take us wherever we want. We can end up right at Grön if we want to."

"The last time I did, I nearly got killed, and I'd rather not relive that," Gwen admitted.

"Isabel has since changed the curse she put on the mirrors, it still affects Rohemir and the Sorcerer, but you can walk through without any difficulties," Aiden answered, turning to Berdin. "Are your men ready?"

"They will fight for Sherados. We will follow our king into battle!" Berdin drew his sword and all the other men with him did the same thing. The men cheered as Aiden led the way through the now-open halls until they reached the mirror. He rode his horse forward and then vanished to the other side. The rest of them followed as fast as the space would allow, entering in one after the other. Drake and Gwen both entered, and the world spun around them. In an instant, they found themselves standing before the city of Grön in Grimdor as the army continued to come through the mirror.

Morgrin sat behind his wife, nervously gripping Isabel. He had only ridden on Aspen once and it hadn't been the most relaxing ride he had ever experienced.

They flew high above the ground and despite his anxiety about flying, he couldn't help but feel as though nothing could top this moment. Isabel studied the ground, not noticing that he was watching her and falling in love with her all over again. Often he wondered how he had been so fortunate as to end up with a woman like her.

She had her quirks and her flaws, but he loved every one of them in their own way. Even though they had been secretly married all these years he still didn't have her completely figured out, and he doubted he ever would.

The sky and the ground below were lit only by the moon as it shone down. It would be daytime before the army arrived, but the cover of night would help them get in position without being noticed. The bulk of the army would travel around Dhuma while ten thousand Gogs, led by Shavrok, would head straight for the city.

In a few hours, the city would be rubble.

Aspen rode an updraft of wind that carried them further from the ground, causing Morgrin to hold his breath for a split second. Finally, they leveled out and flew ever closer to the city that was somewhere below them. Isabel pointed the city out to him and he focused in on it, amused by the fact that from this high up it looked like nothing more than a speck of sand. How she had spotted it was beyond him.

Aspen flew until she was directly over the city and then went into a steep dive which suddenly reminded Morgrin why he didn't like flying. He closed his eyes, unable to stand the sight of the ground rushing towards him. At the last possible second Aspen pulled up and they let themselves slide off as Aspen kept on flying. They landed on a rooftop and then ducked out of sight, as they quickly moved down to the ground.

Isabel had tried to make a map of where they needed to go, but no matter how many times she had tried to explain it to him, he hadn't been able to make any sense of it. She led the way, careful to keep her weapons from rattling around like they normally would have. Morgrin did the same as they checked every alley and street before they entered it.

The city was silent, the only sound being the occasional guard that stood at the wall that surrounded the entire city. The houses and buildings were all dark, making it feel more like a ghost town as every sound echoed through the open space.

They walked until they came up to a large building. Isabel tried the door and found it unlocked and they moved inside. Torches flickered on the wall, illuminating the complicated mechanism that was before them.

"What is this?" Morgrin asked in a whisper.

"It's the locking mechanism for their drains. Through this building, they can open or close the drains that lead to their water supply. They're shut right now and we need to keep them shut otherwise this whole idea of mine will be for nothing."

"I'm not sure how this is supposed to work."

"I've never actually seen it myself, all I know is there are a lot of gears and it's simpler than it looks. Now all that we have to do is take it apart."

"You never cease to amaze me, you realize that?"

Isabel smiled as they began working, using tools that were strange and foreign to disassemble the mechanism in front of them. The longer they worked on it, Morgrin came to figure out that it really wasn't that complicated, and that the Borags weren't nearly as sophisticated as the other races. Within a half hour, they had taken all the gears and easily moved parts off and piled them into one of the corners.

"Do you think that they'll open the civilian tunnels if they're just going to wash the troops away?"

"Yes. They'll still bring out some soldiers, or at least try to bring them out. If for no other reason, they'll do it just to bluff our army. They don't know we are aware of their reservoir and they don't know what we are going to do. I imagine they will have many more soldiers ready to defend their city."

They left the large building and carefully crept near to the front gate where they hid in a back alley that was within a hundred yards of the wall. The city was still unaware and slept peacefully for another hour or so.

Dawn came and with it a horn sounded from the wall and Isabel and Morgrin both stood to their feet, keeping themselves hidden. As Isabel had predicted Borags came running from every direction including tunnels that came up in the middle of the streets. When the soldiers came out they left the passages open. Morgrin held his breath.

The moment of truth.

Shavrok carried his sword in hand and let a terrifying cry escape him. The army behind him did the same, drawing the attention of the Borags on the wall. Horns were sounded and more and more Borags appeared. Aspen flew in the sky, now clearly visible to everyone, including the Borags.

Shavrok halted the army when they were just within the area Isabel had instructed. From here the water would rush at them and from here they would also defeat their enemies. The Borags yelled out on top of the wall. The Gogs returned the challenge and rushed at the wall, some of them moving aside to make way for Gogs carrying ladders.

The Borags made no move to defend themselves, instead a horn echoed through the rocky barren land. The call was answered by another horn behind them to the northwest.

Thunder rolled through the rocky landscape. As planned, all the Gogs turned and ran to the northeast where the ground was higher.

The sound of rushing water shook the area as it thundered toward Dhuma. They sprinted for the high ground, all of them breaking rank and sprinting as fast as they could. Aspen dove towards the city. The water rushed towards them but it was no longer of any concern as it passed by them for the most part. Aspen dropped out of the sky.

Isabel and Morgrin waited. They heard the horns, they heard the Gogs, and now they heard the water rushing towards them. The tunnels were open and Borags stood in them, eager to destroy their enemies if they survived the wall of water.

Aspen roared and then dropped out of sight. Moments later, thunder shook the area in front of them as Aspen thrust her full weight against the large gates. The gates were shattered and so was the wall. Aspen stood to her feet, sending fire spewing from her mouth and swinging her tail at a couple of Borags with enough courage to attack her.

The rest of Borags turned and fled, now able to see the fast-approaching torrent of water heading towards them. Morgrin and Isabel jumped on and Aspen immediately pushed off the ground, her tail just getting brushed by the wall of water which had risen to nearly forty feet. The Borags were swept from their feet and carried through their cities as the water shattered houses and buildings and the wall of the city itself. Then the water entered the tunnels.

An explosion devastated the area as the entire city was blown to pieces sending rock, flame, and water in all directions. What was left of the Duhma fell to the ground, only to be thrown up by another explosion more powerful than the first, as the water worked its way further into the tunnels.

Isabel and Morgrin watched the city as it continued to explode and send chunks of rock and flame into the air. Finally, the explosions stopped and steam was all that could be seen as the water quenched the flames that had erupted. Morgrin pointed the Gogs out to her, standing on dry ground and cheering. She hadn't expected them to try and outrun the wall of water, but it had been a far better idea than she had come up with. They landed and watched as the water carried away the city and all of its contents, leaving only shambles of the city that had just stood.

"I think the Sorcerer will think twice about how he fights his war from now on," Isabel said. The Gogs let out a cry of victory.

"Everyone's through," Drake told Aiden. Cerin and Rade stood next to him. A thousand other Spirits were waiting for the order to attack. They were cleverly disguised as horses and riders, so they wouldn't raise any suspicion.

The city lay ahead of them, with little movement on the walls.

Aiden spurred his horse forward a few steps, the others all did the same thing. Slowly they gained speed until finally they were galloping towards the city. Drake searched the city wall for any sign of life, but he could only see a couple of the guards who stood at the wall.

They pressed forward, following Aiden's lead, who seemed not to notice the strange situation that was in front of them. Aiden looked at Drake and then over at Cerin and Rade who nodded at him and then raced ahead.

"What's going on?" Drake asked.

"Spirits are guarding the city," Aiden answered. "That's why no one is particularly concerned about us."

"They are waiting longer than I thought they would," Gwen said, riding up next to them. "You think there are Spirits in there?"

"No," Aiden replied after a couple of moments of thought. "They're not *in* the city."

"Then where are they?" Drake asked. Yelling and fighting were heard from behind. Rade and Cerin as well as all the other Spirits changed form, Rade and the Korazin into fire and Cerin and the rest of the spirits into blue mist.

The Spirits raced overhead and towards each other. The sound of explosions and magic being used by the Spirits thundered through the air. Though Drake wanted to watch, none of them had a chance to see what that battle would look like as Borags came out of the city and headed straight for them. Drake's heart cowered in fear but found courage as Aiden took the lead and rode his horse toward the coming enemy.

The two sides collided, but many Borags were trampled as their steeds pushed through the defenses. Drake swung his sword as much as he could, grateful for the armor that had been gifted to him and the horse. He brought his sword down on one of the Borags, the sword bounced off his helmet harmlessly.

The Borag glanced a little further back and then made a mad dash for Gwen. Gwen was pulled from her horse, her sword thrown from her grasp. She cried out as the Borag thrust his steel boot into her hand.

Drake threw himself off his horse, knocking the Borag to the ground, and allowing Gwen to grasp her sword. They held their swords at the ready, never having to use them as the Borag was slain by another soldier of theirs.

"Is your hand okay?" Drake asked.

"I'm perfectly fine," Gwen said holding her hand up for him to see. Drake looked hard not seeing any sign that her hand had been injured.

"How is that possible?"

"Unclear," Gwen replied. They looked out to the battle, slightly unnerved as they noticed the skies above the battle were now silent. The seven Korazin stood before them, their rings glowing brightly.

"Call a retreat," Rade told them.

Drake and Gwen both exchanged looks.

"What do you mean?" Gwen asked.

"Call a retreat," Rade said calmly. Aiden rode up to them.

"Do as the man said Drake," Aiden said. Drake blew his horn and signaled the retreat. Their army at once began pulling back. Drake and Gwen followed Aiden in retreat, while Rade and the Korazin remained. The Borags looked at the situation in utter confusion.

In a fit of rage, the host of Borags charged toward the Korazin.

Everyone watched in wonder and horror as the Borags dropped dead twenty feet from the Korazin as if they had hit an invisible wall.

Rade and the Korazin looked towards the city of Grön. In unison, they held their hands towards the walls of the great city. Their rings glowed brightly and the walls shook and began crumbling.

This continued for several minutes as every building crumbled and fell to the ground. In a matter of minutes, the city was raised to the ground. The last Borag was crushed by the collapsing city, and they were left with nothing but the silence of the dead to accompany them.

Aiden marched to the center of the ruined city and sat down. Everyone made camp and they soon all fell to sleep.

"Rise and shine everybody!" a cheerful voice greeted them. Gwen knew that voice and she loved it more than ever before. She looked up to see her mother, Isabel, walking through the camp, greeting everyone she came to.

Gwen shook Drake from his sleep and they quickly enjoyed a light but satisfying meal that had been provided. The food was different from what she had thought it would have been. No matter how many times she took a bite she still couldn't come any closer to figuring out what kind of meat it was.

"It's a wonderful day isn't it?" Isabel asked, taking a seat at their makeshift table. Gwen and Drake exchanged glances.

"Wonderful? It's war. How can that be wonderful?" Drake asked.

"I still count almost a hundred thousand people ready to march on Iscariot," Isabel said. "How did you manage so well?"

"The Korazin helped greatly," Gwen answered. She looked around, wondering where Rade and the others had gone.

"Fascinating," Isabel said. "I shall have to find Rade later and see what he knows."

Morgrin came up and joined them.

"Hurry up and eat we have a lot of planning to do if we are to end this war quickly."

They finished their breakfast and then made their way to Aiden who was waiting for them. In the distance, high in the mountains were all three Taruks. Ellizar and Lily wasted no time in embracing them.

"How did you get here?" Drake asked.

"We found another invisible fortress in Idumea and used the mirrors to our advantage," Lily answered.

"That's right, if there's Dwarves that are goin' teh be attackin' the cursed city, then I want teh know what's goin' teh happen!" Ellizar exclaimed.

"You are nosy," Lily teased.

Ellizar shook his head. "You came with me." Lily smiled. "Pay her no mind she's only jealous because *I* found the invisible city."

"The fact that you found anything is shocking," Skander said coming up from behind them.

"I would never guess that yeh two are related!" They laughed and then Aiden came forward.

"How-"

"Yes," Aiden said. They fell silent.

"How-"

"Yes," Aiden interrupted. "You don't understand do you?"

They shook their heads.

"The answer to 'How' is 'Yes'. Think about that for a moment, there's a lot of truth behind that isn't there?"

"Yes," Sedric answered. "There is. Funny how I've never thought of it before though."

"Most people don't," Aiden replied. "You would ask *how* are we going to defeat the Sorcerer and all his strength, which is now gathered at Iscariot. In my mind there is no question; no doubt. To ask *how* is to suggest even slightly, that the Sorcerer will win. I promise you that we will not lose. *We* will win.

"This battle has been brewing for some time now, but the Sorcerer has yet to admit his flaw. One cannot give what he does not have. I have love, and I love this world. That is exactly why I came, to show a love that people could not understand, in a world that does not know what love means.

"The Sorcerer has no love, and for that matter, he will never be able to give it. The world serves itself, when it should be serving others. To be a true follower of Lathon you *must* love others. The two commands go hand in hand, even though people often try to separate them.

"Only people driven by a love for others will stand on the front lines and offer their lives to protect those people. Those people will be affected by the choices of others and their hearts will be stirred by that love. They will see, that in a world where no one has done anything, you stood and tried to do something, even if victory is not in the picture."

"Are you saying we'll lose?" Gwen asked.

"I'm saying, you do the natural and I'll do the supernatural. We all have skills, abilities, and things we're gifted in. The only great battles that are remembered in history are the ones where people stepped out and took a step of faith against incredible odds. Those are the stories that people remember. To attack a smaller force with a large one takes no courage. But to stand in the face of death and risk it all. Now that's courage. That's faith. That's audacity! That is what a follower of Lathon has to be made of. We cannot sit back and pray that someone else will do it when it is fully in our power to get off our butts and do something.

"It is only with an audacious faith, that we will prove who we really are. What we're made of. Only with an audacious faith will people's lives be changed. Only with an audacious faith will our enemies cower before us because they know who rides with you. Only with an audacious faith, will people's hearts be stirred by what they see, and then be driven to investigate until they find what is different about us. The love you demonstrate for the people of this good earth will change the world. I ride for Iscariot, now I'm asking if you want to ride with me. Even if the battle should go ill, I have already saved the world."

"How?" Ellizar asked.

"Since the corruption of Erathos, evil has had a foothold in the world. Evil will always be present on this earth. The true battle of the ages does not require a sword, it just requires a heart filled with love and compassion for the people of this world. Having a heart of love will repel the forces of darkness until no trace of it can be found. I have given you the keys to save this world if only people would be brave enough to use them. But know this, those who seek to change the world for the better *will* be the first ones the Sorcerer will attack, but the rewards are far beyond anything on this earth. It is now your turn. I have shown my love for you, but will you show it for me?

"Tell me my friends, who here has all the traits and qualities that will give you the right to say that you are a follower of Lathon?" Silence followed as they each searched their hearts for the answer. Drake stood up and drew his sword, laying it at Aiden's feet and then bowing.

"I will ride with you to Iscariot and not because of a mark on my hand, or because I feel like I'm supposed to. I want to do this."

"You're emotions are well understood, my son."

"Son?" Drake asked.

"Anyone who is a part of the kingdom of Lathon is a son, daughter, brother, sister, mother, or father of each other. Any who do my will is my son or daughter."

"I will ride with you to Iscariot, my king," Lily said laying her bow at his feet.

"As will I." Gwen and Isabel both said at the same time. They laid their weapons down.

"Don't forget teh count this dwarf in!" Ellizar exclaimed, putting his ax on top of the weapons. "This dwarf knows the truth when it's right in front ov him."

Everyone else who heard the call bowed before Aiden, who Drake realized was much more than just Sherados. He was Lathon.

Chills ran up and down everyone's spine as Aiden told them to rise and they moved back to the places they had been standing previously. Aiden stood, looking into each one of their souls, touching each of them on a different level.

"You ask how?" Aiden asked.

"Yes," Morgrin answered. Aiden smiled.

"And now a special weapon for all," Isabel said. Shavrok came forward bearing a great trunk.

"Where did these come from?" Drake asked.

"A few knick-knacks I picked up from some less than reputable people I once knew in The Dead Mountains."

"Did you steal these?" Lily asked. Isabel thought for a moment.

"I don't think so. At any rate, no one knows they are missing, and they've been gone for many years!" Isabel said. The trunk was opened and a dagger was given to each of them. They were deep burgundy red, with black gems in the handles.

"What do they do?"

"Use them well," Isabel answered. "They're only going to work for one attack."

XXIII ISCARIOT

Sweat rolled off every member of the army as they pressed closer and closer to the one place they feared to go the most. The skies were black and seemed to be getting darker. The wind had stopped, making them uncomfortable.

Lily tried to calm her nerves as she wondered what this final battle would look like. Everyone had gone through the plans countless times but still, she felt unprepared. The Sorcerer's presence was growing in their minds.

The events of the past played through her head, reminding her of everything that had happened since that day on the side of the river. Her parents and the entire town of Fiori had been wiped out. They had traveled for almost two months, all while nearly getting killed every step of the way. Everyone had finally figured out who their family members were and now they were marching to battle with Sherados himself leading the army.

The sun was hidden behind the clouds dampening their spirits and the heat seemed to radiate from the ground. It had been two days since the victory at Grön and now they were nearly at their destination.

Aiden would be approaching from the east with his troops, while Shavrok, Isabel, and everyone else would be marching from the west. Willard and Miles although they hadn't been seen in quite a while would be coming from the north and would do what they could.

The excruciating heat continued to build. The skies were ever-darkening, but in the darkness, they were finding strength and determination.

Isabel and Apen flew above the stormy clouds, immersed in the bright, warm sunshine. The sunlight glistened off the clouds which were all white when you were this far up. Even when the rest of the world was at war and the storm was coming, there was still beauty to be seen. You just had to know where to look for it. Aspen let a pleasurable roar escape her.

The sound would never reach through all the clouds, but if it had she hoped that it would strike terror into their enemies. The war would take its toll on all of them and it would probably be the hardest for her.

The conflict raged inside her, not wanting to face her former husband but acknowledging that she may have to. Morgrin had comforted and supported her the most he could before she had left and even the small effort that he had tried had been enough to lift her spirits and give her strength.

Isabel clung to Aspen as she went into a steep dive, nearly straight down. They entered the clouds. Her skin and her clothes were soaked by the rain that was held within the clouds. The clouds vanished and the heat hit the two of them like a plague. Directly below was a large tower, which rose above all of the others. This tower was special and until the other day, she had been the only one who had ever known why.

This tower was invisible from outside the city and when you were at the top of it you could see further than was humanly possible. Several guards would be posted on top, keeping watch for their arrival, but they would never get the chance. Aspen continued her long steep descent until she had no choice but to spread out her wings and dig her claws into the roof.

A commotion was heard beneath them as several of the guards below looked up to see Aspen. Isabel slid down the roof sending herself feet-first into one of the guards. He was knocked unconscious as his head struck against the wall. Another of the Borags rushed her but was easily dispensed of. She pulled out her sword and slayed the last of the Borags.

Isabel pulled the Borags into the tower and then came back out, locking the door and sitting on the edge of the wall, with her feet dangling over open space. No one inside the city would be able to see her and now no one would be able to see the army until they were a normal distance away. Aspen made herself comfortable as best she could, while still sitting on the roof of the tower.

The skies became darker yet. Torches were lit in the city itself as the Borags prepared for the battle. She could see the army approaching from this tower, but she knew that everyone below couldn't see a thing. Torches from the approaching army came closer, smoke lifting high into the sky. Thunder and lightning now crashed through the sky, but still, there was no rain. She moved to the other side of the tower, seeing Aiden and his army beginning their approach. She looked to the north where the mountains towered over her.

She thought she could see Willard and Miles as well as the rest of the wolves, but if she did, they could likely be farther off than they appeared. It would be her job to let the wolves into the city and they would only enter the battle after everyone else had started attacking.

The lightning and thunder became more frequent, the lightning illuminating the landscape and the coming army which she knew could probably now be seen from the main wall. A sea of torches and armor descended upon the city, the sound of their footsteps echoing through the otherwise silent land.

Finally, the rain thundered down, this being the hardest rain she had ever been in. The wind picked up, threatening to destroy her just from sheer force. Isabel put a hand on the pommel of her sword.

Shavrok called into the sky, the surrounding army echoed him. The rain pelted down and pinged off their armor. The advancing army stopped, well out of bow-range of the archers on the walls. The walls were as tall as Isabel had said they would be, easily reaching up to forty feet at the lowest section. He looked up and down the long row of troops, Gogs, Dwarves, Men, and Elves. All of them ready to take a stand for Sherados.

Siege towers had been built and the catapults were ready to be released at any moment. The Spirits floated somewhere high up in the sky, each side getting ready to do their part. Lily and Ellizar came up next to him, standing in front of the army. Torches illuminated the faces of their opponents, their rage and malice biting into their hearts like daggers of ice.

"How long do you think we should wait to attack?" Lily asked.

"What the elf means teh ask is when should the chosen Dwarves take their positions?" Ellizar corrected.

"Take position as soon as the line starts moving. I'm sure the battle will begin shortly," Shavrok answered.

"How will we know when it starts?" Ellizar asked.

"We'll start rushing towards the wall with troops and ladders Ellizar, I thought that would be obvious," Lily teased.

"Blasted elf kind!"

"We will wait for Aiden's signal, whatever that may look like."

"It will be a fire in the sky," Morgrin answered pulling his horse to a stop just in front of them. He dropped off and the water splashed beneath his boots. "Rade has just informed me that he and another of the Korazin will signal in the sky that we should begin our attack."

"In that case, I'd better go get the Dwarves ready now, that way we aren't caught off guard."

"That would be good," Morgrin replied. "If I may say a few words before you go. There is no other group of people that I would rather fight and die with. All of you. Here, in a world that is crumbling, we find all the races united against the common foe that has divided us for so long."

"The world may still be divided, but we aren't," Lily said. They embraced and then Morgrin mounted his horse, heading back to the section of the army that he and Aramen were in charge of, which included all the men from Idumea and Farndor. Most of the men had been forced to walk on foot, but a cavalry of two thousand horses waited at the back. Horses would do no good in the opening stages of this battle.

"Now, the Dwarves go teh war!" Ellizar said with a laugh and a smile unlike any they had ever seen.

"Ellizar?" Lily said. Ellizar turned to look at her and she leaned down and kissed him on the cheek. "Don't get yourself killed."

"Likewise elf!" Ellizar replied, winking and then running off as fast as he possibly could, vanishing inside the army where more Dwarves were gathered. Shavrok looked at Lily with an amused smile.

Lily smiled and shook her head. "Shut up."

Drake's heart was filled with fear as he looked at the dark menacing walls and the Borags that waited to kill them. They had traveled far, and now they were finally here.

Aiden moved his horse ahead a few feet and then turned to look at the army that was behind him. Everything was set and everything was ready.

"Stand now!" Aiden exclaimed "Fight for all that is good on this earth. Fight for your families, your land, and your country, and fight for Lathon who is here among you. The world will never be the same after this battle, but that is the reason for us to rejoice. When a person stands alone they are not a threat, but when they stand united with brothers and sisters then they are a mighty force.

"Today we will be the stone wall that breaks our enemies. The Sorcerer's walls may be rock but his heart is empty, and soon his city will be too. Followers of Lathon on the other hand, have full hearts and strong wills. We will be victorious!" Battle cries echoed through the rainy air. The army pounded their feet on the ground and shook their shields as Aiden turned to Drake.

"Catapults!" Aiden yelled. The order was repeated until finally a barrage of projectiles flew ahead of them, striking the walls of Iscariot. The walls trembled and shook. In some places, the top five feet of the wall were completely demolished as they were struck. Fire streaked across the sky, two of the Korazin signaling to the other armies to begin their attacks. The fire formed a cross.

"Are you ready?"

Drake searched inside himself for a moment.

"Yes," Drake replied.

Aiden drew the sword that the elf kings had given to him so many years ago. He raised it into the sky. The army let out a great shout. Two more times Aiden raised his sword high and each time the cry from their army grew louder. From where they were they could hear the echo of the battle cries from the other side of the city. Though they were far away Drake could see the fear growing in the Borags atop the wall. The deep horns of the Gogs and the horns of all other races present were blown throughout the army and the roar of their army rose far louder than it had previously.

The Gogs went first, rushing towards the walls with massive ladders.

"Archers ready!" Drake yelled. The archers came forward and pulled back their bows. "Fire!" A volley of arrows sailed over the walls of Iscariot, taking out many.

The armies now rushed towards the walls. Within moments arrows came from the walls of Iscariot. They raised their shields. Many warriors fell, but countless arrows bounced off shields. Their archers released another volley of arrows.

"Ladders! Ladders!" Aiden yelled. The Gogs hoisted their ladders upright, the points on the edge of the ladders were razor sharp, cutting deep into the hard rock.

Aiden didn't break his stride, becoming the first one to climb up the ladder. Drake took the ladder next to him, his heart racing as the catapults of Iscariot were released.

Aiden reached the top of the ladder moments before Drake did, drawing his sword and slaying the first Borag. Drake dodged an attack from the Borag in front of him. Drake grabbed the Borag by the wrist and pulled him forward, he stumbled and fell over the wall to his demise.

More soldiers made their way up the ladders and onto the wall as the Borags continued to fight them. Drake turned, striking another Borag. As soon as one opponent fell, it seemed two more would attack him.

The battle wore on and the effects of the battle became evident. He looked to their army, seeing that the Gogs had now moved the catapults closer to the walls. Drake flinched, but the Borags cried out as flaming projectiles came through the air and landed deep within Iscariot.

Drake looked to the nearest catapult that the Borags were preparing to launch. He ran along the edge of the wall, jumping the gap if he needed to. Before the Borags knew what was happening, Drake jumped and tackled the Borag next to it. He grimaced in pain as he was struck in the gut by a Borag sword.

The Borag grinned before Drake stood revealing chain-mail beneath his clothes. The contest continued as their swords clashed furiously. To Drake's dismay another Borag, having seen what was happening, came forward and released the projectile. It sailed out over the massive army.

Blue mist dove out of the sky and intercepted the bolder, smashing it into a thousand harmless pieces. The Borags looked at each other, scared. Drake quickly dove out of the way. The catapult was demolished as the Spirits crashed into it.

The cries of Taruks filled the air. Elohim and Destan flew overhead spewing fire into the city. They landed on sections of the wall, using their powerful tails to destroy everything within reach.

More ladders were raised and more of their soldiers came up. Gogs now raced to the top and rolled off the top of the ladder, spearing their enemies with the spikes on their backs.

Heat seared Drake's back as a blade grazed him between the armor. He yelled and then spun around, effortlessly slaying the Borag. More of the wall was pummeled by the Taruks. The wall where Drake stood was now only ten feet tall.

"Get back from the wall!" Drake cried. He grasped the dagger Isabel had given him. "Get back from the wall!" The soldiers who heard his voice obeyed and repeated the orders, pulling the ladders down and running away.

Drake thrust the dagger that Isabel had given him to the stone. From the point of the impact, a shock wave went out, ripping through the wall and throwing the Borags a hundred feet into the air. They crashed down onto their troops. A gaping hole, twenty feet wide, stood in front of him. Drake threw the dagger away, where it shattered like glass.

The army flooded into the city, splashing through the water, and overwhelming the stunned Borags inside. Drake stood to his feet and led the charge as anyone who entered the city split up and fought the Borags. Horns filled the air once again. Then it was followed by howling.

Drake could vaguely see a mass of grey descending from the mountains behind the city. There was no wall at that point, as the city merged with the mountainside. The wolves flooded into the city. From where he was, the sound of the Borags panicking was evident.

Up above, lightning of many different colors and thunder crashed through the sky as the Spirits battled each other. Every few seconds an explosion would rock the city as one of the Spirits died and would fall to the city below.

Ellizar waited nervously, the other Dwarves with him ready to do their part in the battle. He gripped his ax and checked his other weapons as the siege tower was pushed toward the wall. Ellizar heard arrows being released, but due to the Dwarves' short height, they weren't even seen. The arrows were instead aimed at the great beasts who pushed them forward. The arrows noisily, but harmlessly, clanged off their armor.

He tried to spot Lily in the darkness but was unable. Most of the Gogs had now moved around to the south side of the wall, putting ladders up and also trying to take down the massive gates that were keeping them out of the city. He had heard the wolves announce their presence.

The Sorcerer was now surrounded.

The tower was pushed to the wall and Ellizar released the gate, rushing forward, surprised to find no one waiting for them. A pile of bodies, filled with arrows lay at the bottom.

Ellizar led the way down the stairs and the other Dwarves behind him split up, some of them moving towards the other ladders and offering their assistance.

Ellizar and those with him turned, heading for the Borags on the other side. Surprisingly they didn't move or defend themselves. From somewhere behind, the sound of rock scrapping reached their ears. Doors opened up on the buildings. Borags poured out, now having all the Dwarves surrounded.

Battle cries sounded through the city, but not from the Borags or the Dwarves as all the Borags that surrounded were killed from behind. Ellizar looked towards the new line of troops that had appeared. He smiled when he noticed that it was Lily and the Elves under her command. She smiled at him as she came forward. He shook his head.

"You totally get credit fer killin' these blasted Borags!"

"We have to hurry to the gate and try to let the rest of the army in if it's possible." Ellizar didn't argue and followed her through the streets, having to fight the entire way. Fire streamed in front of them and they ducked out of the way as it wrapped through the street like oil being lit. They looked up seeing a dark burgundy Taruk flying through the sky and breathing fire down. They were held at bay by the flames. Lily and Ellizar both pulled out weapons that Isabel had given them. They faced the flames and touched the blades together. Suddenly, the entire area was filled with white light.

The fire recoiled and dispersed itself upwards and forwards, rushing past them and colliding with the Borags who were in front of them. The fire moved up into the sky, reached up, and consumed the burgundy Taruk. The Taruk shrieked in pain but wasn't taken down as the fire went out a couple of seconds later.

Finally, they reached the main gate, prevented from going any further by the Borags. The gates of the city trembled and splintered as the Gogs used their battering rams.

With the gates finally broken, the Gogs flooded into the city. Within a couple of seconds, the Borags rushed to meet their enemies. Lily was knocked down by a blow to her helmet. The Borag stood overtop her, his foot on her chest, her sword just out of reach.

Ellizar moved as fast as he could but in his heart, he knew he would never reach her in time. A roar shook the sky and the tail of a Taruk brushed by them both, collecting the Borag and then impaling enemy troops. They both stood, acknowledging the Taruk, Elohim, who flicked the Borags off his spiked tail before diving back into the city.

Rumbling filled the city a moment later.

Drake felt the ground shaking before the rumbling had begun and now his entire body was filled with terror. The fighting in the city stopped, even the Borags seemed interested in the ground shaking. Drake made his way back to the wall where Aiden came up next to him, standing and looking out to the surrounding lands. Nothing out of the ordinary could be seen.

"What do you think it is?" Drake asked.

"Something the Sorcerer thinks can defeat us," Aiden replied. "Probably not the answer you were looking for, but I prefer to wait until I see what it is before I make judgments of any kind. My prediction could be wrong."

The rumbling grew. The ground, a half mile beyond the city walls, was torn up in several sections around the entire city. Even the mountains had now been filled with holes that likely could've swallowed an entire village. The rumbling ceased and for a moment everything stood still, smoke rising from the newly formed craters.

Hideous screeching filled the air as creatures began to claw their way out of the earth. Flames were visible as fires started wherever the gigantic creatures stepped.

Drake grabbed his sword and Aiden did the same, each of them staring into the eyes of the approaching beasts. Six legs supported the giant creature, which stood easily forty feet tall from the ground to the top of its head. Each had a long gangly neck, covered with spikes, both big and small. Atop their necks three heads were connected, each of them with four eyes atop their head. Their legs were consumed with flames.

"What is that?" Drake asked.

"A demon of the underworld."

"What can it do?"

"Get the catapults aimed at those vile beasts!" Aiden yelled. Drake quickly moved to the other side of the wall, getting everyone who could be spared to aim the Borag catapults at the oncoming beasts. The fighting resumed in the city and those on horses formed a line and rushed towards the beasts, doing their best, but in the end, dying. The archers released dozens and dozens of arrows at the creatures, but no matter how many arrows they put in them, they wouldn't die. Instead, they inched forward, undeterred by the seemingly small people who were attacking it.

Wherever the beasts stepped, fire billowed out like someone pouring water from a jar. Within a couple of minutes, the fires had gone out due to the torrential rains, leaving the remains of whatever had been caught in the fire.

"Drake!" Aiden yelled. Drake turned to look in his direction. "Get some Gogs up here immediately and have the ground army aim their catapults at the beasts too!"

"Catapults ready!" Drake yelled climbing off the wall and running through the streets carrying out the orders, while also looking for familiar faces. Finally, he spotted someone fighting in the middle of the streets.

It was a woman, of mid-height, with long brown hair. She fought vigorously, but Drake could tell she was new to the art of sword-fighting. In an instant, she was slayed by the Borag she was fighting. He rushed to her aid, quickly dispensing of the Borag. He dropped to his knees and rolled the woman onto her back.

He did recognize her!

Blood flowed from her chest and he knew she wouldn't live too much longer. She turned to face him, her eyes coming alive when she saw him.

"Your name?!" Drake exclaimed. "Tell me your name."

"Verah," the woman replied through labored breathing. The ring the Sorcerer had given him burned a hole in his pocket.

"How do you know me?" Drake pressed. "I know your face but nothing else." The woman smiled weakly, her strength fading.

"Search for her Drake Thomas," Verah said weakly. Drake wanted to press her for more information, but she went limp in his arms before he was able. He gently lay the woman on the ground and closed her eyes. He was pulled from his thoughts by his name frantically being called out. Aramen and Chloe rushed up to him.

"What's going on?" Aramen asked.

"Get the catapults and fire them at those monsters."

"I'm not sure how our catapults are going to help," Aramen answered. "Nothing seems to stop them."

"That's just what Aiden said, I'm sure he has a plan."

"He always does."

Without another word, Drake rushed back up to the top of the wall, where Aiden was already putting a plan into place. Gwen stood alongside Aiden.

"Ballistae fire!" Aiden yelled. Drake and several others repeated the order and all around the city the ballistae that at one point had been used by the Borags were used against the beasts. The javelins pierced the monsters which let out roars of frustration. The creatures jerked backward, held by the ballistae, many of which were anchored to the ground. Gogs rushed forward and grabbed the massive chains that were connected to the javelins that had pierced the beasts and began to pull. Slowly the creatures were pulled towards the wall.

"Load the catapults!" Aiden called out. Drake's mind tried to make sense of what he was seeing as the Gog's began climbing into the places that would normally hold the rocks. Shavrok ran past him and got into the one nearest to Drake.

"What are you doing?" Drake asked. Shavrok smiled.

"Showing these pipsqueaks who is boss."

The command was given and the catapults were released, sending Gogs flying through the air. Drake watched, inspired and amazed as the Gog's turned in the air, using the spikes on their backs to stick themselves to various places on the beast's body. Then from there, they could use any of the spikes on their hands and arms to climb their way up to the head where they could then use whatever weapons they could to slash and cut at the animals.

The demons bellowed in pain and frustration, several of them jerking their heads and breaking the ballistae off the wall, sending them hurtling through the air, before they crashed into the ground.

The creatures rushed forward, but Drake and Gwen didn't move. The Sorcerer wouldn't likely permit any of them to enter the city and destroy his own buildings. The demon stopped in front of the two of them, allowing them to look in its eyes.

Drake swallowed hard as his temptation was brought back into his mind. Everything stopped, as he embraced it for a moment before remembering that although there may be shreds of truth ingrained in it; it was a lie.

The three heads all rushed towards them at once. Drake darted out of the way while Gwen let out a fierce yell and leapt into the mouth of the middle head of the beast. The mouth closed over her and Drake yelled until he noticed a blade protruding from its snout. The mouth opened and Gwen sat, pulling the blade out and sticking it through in as many places as she could. The creature roared in pain.

Drake jumped the growing distance as the creature pulled away from the wall. Drake flailed, finally grabbing one of the teeth. The mouth of the creature began to close. He reached to his belt and pulled out a knife, sticking it into the upper mouth that had been closing. The creature opened its mouth fully again and Drake grabbed another knife using them to pull himself up on top of its snout, which was filled with dozens of holes from Gwen's sword.

Drake put his knives away and moved to the top of the head and thrust his sword into the beast. The creature shifted and swayed as it staggered and toppled over. Drake grasped his sword as the creature fell sideways. The ground raced at them and Drake could think of no other way out of the situation.

The impact jarred him and sent him down onto the hard rocks. The wind was knocked out of him for a moment, but his energy quickly came back to him as he heard cheering. Drake stood up and gained his bearings noticing that the other creatures were beginning to fall as this one had. The Gogs stood on top of them, toppling them like a tower of stones.

Drake rushed to the mouth of the beast, laying his eyes on Gwen who was motionless and covered in blood. He pulled her out of the mouth of the beast and checked for a heartbeat. He pulled her sword from the mouth of the creature and motioned for a pair of Elves that were fighting nearby.

"Take her and make sure she is well." Even as he finished his statement, Gwen began to stir, holding her head.

"That didn't feel good," Gwen said. Drake smiled, and the Elves smiled as well.

"That was quite a fall, my lady," one of the Elves told her.

"It was worth it though. I finally defeated the darkness in myself. I didn't give in to the temptation."

"The one thing that many don't have the strength to do," the other elf said. "You should be proud."

"I am," Gwen said a smile on her face. Drake helped her up and handed her sword back to her. She wiped the pommel off and then looked towards the city. Drake stood next to her as did the Elves.

"Are you ready?" Drake asked.

"I've never felt more ready in my life." Together they bounded through the army and into the city, joining in the battle again. Above them the Taruks continued to fight each other, creating rubble and roadblocks that coincidentally seemed to help them and hinder the Borags.

A green Taruk had joined the fight and Drake knew that it was Aspen. The magnificent Taruk twirled and flipped in the sky, outracing her opponent and then when the burgundy Taruk least expected it, she would attack.

Drake climbed to the top of the nearest building. and looked through the confusing maze of bridges and buildings towards the citadel, where a dark shape came out of the tower. From here he could barely see the Sorcerer's bald head.

In an instant, Drake was surrounded by Borags, and before his mind could comprehend what happened, Aiden had come and slain all of them.

"What do you say we end this war?" Aiden asked.

Drake checked his sword and they started making their way towards the Sorcerer.

THE SORCERER'S WAR

From atop the tower, Isabel watched the battle. The city had been ravaged and shaken by the battle thus far but still she refused to join. Instead, she searched the city. Watching for one person.

As of now, she had no sighting of Rohemir but she knew that he would soon be coming out. The time passed and she searched below, finally seeing something that caught her eye. A man came out of the tower below her, wearing a black cloak and appearing to be bald.

The Sorcerer was too smart to come out right in the open at this stage. She reached to her belt and dropped a dagger, letting it fall from the top of the tower. She hadn't aimed it at his head, as he would likely have some kind of invisible protection against things like that. Instead, she had aimed it just to the side. The dagger struck the ground.

The bald man's appearance changed, revealing his true identity as the spell that had been put on him was broken. Rohemir was lifted into the air and then thrown against the building. The dagger had shattered into a million pieces but now they all came back together and the dagger came flying back up to her hand. She threw it at the tower and the spell that kept it from being visible was broken allowing everyone in the city to see it.

She looked down and caught Rohemir's gaze. She raised her eyebrows at him and then smiled and waved. Rage spread across his face. He got up to his feet and sprinted to the base of the tower, entering and vanishing from her sight. She called Aspen with her mind and the powerful Taruk came and settled down on the roof of the tower, just out of sight. Isabel sat on the edge of the wall, facing the door.

A few minutes later, she heard pounding as Rohemir tried to break through the door, unable to do so. Several magic attacks were heard, but she had put enough protection on them to keep her safe for the next two years if she wanted to. She listened to him scream and curse in his frustration.

Both she and Aspen were filled with sorrow. It was clear Rohemir wasn't the same man that he had once been and certainly wasn't the one she had loved. Still, the thought of having to kill him plagued her mind. She stood and drew her sword, ready to fight.

Aspen flicked her tail at the door knocking it in. Rohemir cursed loudly before he came out looking a little worse for wear. Having been in an enclosed area while releasing all his magic attacks hadn't done him any favors. He stumbled through the gaping hole and looked in her direction his eyes filled with malice and rage.

"Hello, Rohemir!" Isabel greeted, flashing a smile at him. Rohemir paused when she smiled and she took the opportunity to swing her sword first. Rohemir ducked the blade, but not completely as her blade caught his cheek. He cursed and threw a dagger in her direction.

She spun and caught the dagger by the handle, then she twisted herself around throwing it back at him before she touched the ground. Rohemir hadn't seen the dagger coming and it buried itself deep in his thigh.

He grabbed his sword, swinging it wildly. She easily sidestepped his attack, allowing his sword to hit the ground. She brought the pommel of her sword down on his head, hoping to knock him out and leave him be. Instead, he hit the ground, cursing and remaining still for a moment.

"First rule of swordsmanship Rohemir, keep control of your emotions, or else your opponent may be the one to manipulate you to do what they want." He cursed and stood back to his feet pulling out his wand.

"Second rule of swordsmanship," Rohemir replied. "Kill your wife before she has a chance to put a knife in you."

"I don't want to kill you Rohemir!"

Rohemir didn't speak directly to her but muttered endlessly under his breath. He unleashed attack after attack. To Isabel's surprise, the magic attacks bounced off her, ricocheting in every direction. Before long, much of the top of the tower had been destroyed. Rohemir seethed, blind to Apsen who watched from the ever-weakening rooftop.

Isabel methodically attacked him with her sword, swinging at his hands. Finally, she struck his wand, breaking it and rendering it useless. The wand fell over the edge, broke into a thousand different pieces, and caught fire. By the time they hit the ground, they were nothing but ash.

The rain had now stopped altogether and Rohemir looked at her, years of anger manifesting itself.

"The only one who is going to be winning this battle is Lathon," Isabel told him. "Aiden is more than just Sherados, he *is* Lathon. You helped him escape so many years ago, but at what moment was your heart bought? You are not the same man that I married."

Rohemir lunged at her, swinging his sword wildly. She swung at him, striking his other hand. His sword clattered over the edge. He pulled a fist back to strike her, but when he did, Isabel wasn't there.

She had twisted out of the way, and Rohemir in his rage had fallen headfirst over the edge of the tower.

Aspen breathed a torrent of fire, consuming Rohemir. Isabel looked away, unable to watch as he burned and struck the ground far below.

Isabel wiped the tears from her eyes and then jumped off the tower. Aspen quickly swooped in below and caught her. Isabel sat upright looking out over the battle that seemed to be getting more and more fierce. She dried her eyes and focused her attention on the battle, looking ahead to where Destan and Elohim were fighting the burgundy Taruk.

They charged forward, the three Taruks each coming from a different direction. The burgundy Taruk twirled and flipped in the air, hoping to go into a dive and outmaneuver his opponents. The Taruk wasn't fast enough, slowed down by fire that was sent from Elohim's mouth. The fire went out a moment later but they could still see the damage the fire had done. The skin that had been burned was discolored and seemed to bubble.

The Taruk flipped in the sky, trying to climb higher but was unable to do so as Elohim dug his razor-sharp claws into the Taruk's belly. Destan and Aspen soon joined in, Destan grabbing the Taruk's head and Aspen grabbing the backside of the Taruk.

The burgundy Taruk roared in frustration and from the distance Isabel could see a white stream of light coming towards them. No doubt the Sorcerer was trying to protect his Taruk. Isabel looked at the white light for a second and it changed course heading back the way it had come. It struck the tower that it had come from, destroying the entire side of it.

Meanwhile, they continued to tumble out of the sky, the three Taruks, still holding onto their victim. All at once the three Taruks let fire spew from their mouths and they released their enemy who was now consumed with so much fire that he was powerless to do anything.

The burgundy Taruk crashed into the ground, creating a massive crater and a deafening boom as the fire consumed their enemy. Up above, some of the Spirits still fought each other, although it was significantly less than before. Korazin streaked through the sky, grabbing the attention of the evil Spirits while Cerin and those loyal to Lathon came from behind and took down their enemies. Aspen landed and Isabel got off, soon joined by Cerin and Rade as well as Willard and Miles.

"We can't do this much longer," Cerin said. "The Sorcerer knows what's going on and he's almost figured out the loophole. If he finds it and swears us to his protection then there's nothing we can do. We will be a slave to his will."

"Is there anything you can do to prevent it?" Isabel asked.

"There is one thing," Rade said, looking at Cerin knowingly. "I wouldn't normally suggest it."

"I know what you speak of. The time to surrender ourselves for the sake of our friends and family has come," Cerin replied.

"Are you sure?" Isabel asked.

"There can be no better display of love. It's one I know Sherados will display one day."

Cerin raised his head towards the sky taking the form of the blue mist. A strange note bellowed in the skies. The Spirits that were loyal to him, flew away from the city until they were beyond the walls. Then, they turned and raced toward each other.

Then they struck.

Drake followed behind Aiden, becoming more confused as time passed. Aiden had said that they were going to get the Sorcerer, yet Aiden had gone off to the left. Drake watched the Sorcerer look out over them, his fear growing.

He looked away for a moment and when he looked again the Sorcerer wasn't in sight. Drake studied the place he had been looking for a few moments, before seeing Rohemir climbing up off the ground. His mind asked a thousand questions, but they all fled out of his head as he followed closely behind Aiden.

Aiden jumped over the edge of the first bridge they came to, landing in front of a company of Borags that were rushing towards them. Just beyond the Borags was a large tower, taller and cruder than any that Drake had seen up to this moment. The walls were rough and jagged and the top of it was completely open, with no roof to cover it.

The Sorcerer was waiting for them.

Horns were blown behind them, forcing Aiden and Drake to both turn around and see who was coming up behind them. To their relief, it was the three elf kings and a force of fifty soldiers.

Borags rushed towards them. Aiden and Drake raised their swords into the sky, and everyone within sight let a shout escape them, rushing towards the oncoming Borags. Drake and Aiden both fought their way through and sprinted toward the base of the large tower, leaving the men behind to fight.

They reached the tower and pulled open the door, slaying the Borags that were waiting for them. Drake sprinted, right on Aiden's heels, eager to be rid of the evil that ravaged the land. Time passed as one second flooded into another and still they never seemed to get any closer to the top.

At last, they set their feet on the hard black rocks that made up the last level of the tower. The Sorcerer stood in their view, circling, showing his surprise as he looked at them. Aiden and Drake both came to a stop.

"Welcome my friends, at last, we get to talk formally with each other," the Sorcerer said. "Here we are, all together. Sherados, and the one who will make the way for Sherados, and then me. I have you both right here and I can kill you and make this world all that it was meant to be."

"And who gives you the power to do that?" Drake asked. The Sorcerer looked at him knowingly.

"You give me the power to do that Drake Thomas. Every person who walks the face of this earth gives me the power to make my reality the way it's supposed to be. Do you know what you would find if my reality came to fruition? You would find that my reality isn't evil."

"That's because there would be nothing better to oppose it," Drake fired back.

"You are correct, but then again isn't that a better point of view?"

"So you, as a good king would strip people of their choice, keeping them as slaves for the rest of their lives?" Aiden asked

"If it would keep them safe," Merderick answered. "I love the world too much to let them be harmed. Are you going to tell me that you don't seek to destroy me?"

"I seek to destroy you, but until this earth is no more and I take my people back to the place where the lands are undying and unstained with the filth you've created, people on this earth will always have a choice."

"Are you saying that you can't beat me here?" Merderick asked. "That *is* what you are saying. You are saying that even if you destroy me, I will be more powerful."

"No. That is not what I'm saying," Aiden replied. "I am saying that your poison has leaked into this world long enough and now it shall be made right. This is why at the end of all things the earth will be destroyed."

"Such a pity we don't see eye to eye on these things, it could be a great partnership," Merderick said his eyes dancing back to one of them and then to the other.

"It is not a partnership I would accept," Aiden said. A flash of light appeared to their left. Drake could only look for a moment but he saw fire falling to the ground. The Sorcerer seemed to take notice but hid his emotions as he drew his sword and held it at Aiden.

"You might reconsider if your life was on the line."

"Kill me if you wish," Aiden said. "There's one more thing that you haven't clued into yet Merderick. In all these years you have been trying to wipe out the Elves, carefully planning this day and waiting for the moment to be right. You assumed Men to be the weak race. You assumed the Elves were too reserved to do anything of significance, too wrapped up in their religious beliefs to be a threat. You assumed the Dwarves would hide in their mountains and the Gogs were extinct. You assumed the Spirits would all fight for you when in actuality they don't. Every race is stronger than you thought."

"If I kill you, their hope would be gone and they too would become slaves to me," Merderick declared. "No man, elf, gog, dwarf, or any other kind of living beast could ever stand in front of me and not serve me. You too are proof of that. You've been standing here all this time and you haven't killed me yet."

"Let us put aside our words and fight with the sword?" Aiden suggested. Merderick smiled.

"The moment I've been waiting for."

Drake drew his sword first and rushed at the Sorcerer, who appeared stunned by the move. He easily defended his attacks. Thunder streaked overhead as blue mist raced towards each other. Drake was distracted by the sight and was thrown to the ground by the Sorcerer's sword a moment later. It dented the armor across Drake's chest and knocked the wind out of him as he struggled to catch his breath and collect his thoughts.

The Spirits collided in the sky. The sound was louder than any he had heard, a shockwave ripped through all the Borags in the area. A third of them were wiped out and the clouds flashed with color and lightening as the spells that had bound them were shattered and broken by the force of the explosion.

Aiden drew out a dagger which was promptly knocked away by the Sorcerer. The dagger clattered on the floor as the Sorcerer looked at them both.

"What a shame. You are supposedly the chosen ones, yet you can't do anything to stop me." He turned to Drake and stared into his eyes, holding his gaze. The memories of the temptation flooded back over him and Drake shivered in fear. Was there truth to anything the Sorcerer said? Drake reached deep into his pocket, pulling out the ring with the inscription on it.

The Sorcerer watched, suddenly interested as time seemed to stop. Drake looked at the ring, his heart torn. This could be the secret to his past, but it could also be a trap by the Sorcerer, something to hold his attention and occupy his time and energy.

Drake laid the ring on the tower and struck it with his sword. Light flashed and Drake's mind burned for a moment as fire consumed it, his sword was ripped from his grasp. The Sorcerer flinched and then the light was gone. The Sorcerer glared at him, but Drake smiled.

He had defeated the darkness in himself.

Aiden was up on his feet and sprinting towards the Sorcerer. In an instant Drake found courage and gathered his sword, engaging the Sorcerer. The Sorcerer blocked him, but never got a second attack as Aiden thrust his dagger into the Sorcerer's chest.

Light radiated from the Sorcerer as the dagger continued to glow brighter and brighter as though the blade was on fire. Aiden held the dagger in place, though Merderick screamed and tried to pull it free. Slowly the Sorcerer in front of them began to change. His skin turned grey and became flakey, and soon looked no different from any of the Borags. Drake cringed at the sight.

This is what happened to those who gave in to all the temptations and dark things in the world. This was what you looked like on the inside. The dagger Aiden held glowed brighter and brighter until finally, it burst into flames.

Drake looked away as the Sorcerer was consumed. The light vanished seconds later and Drake looked at Aiden, confusion clouding his mind. Aiden stood with the dagger in his hand, smiling at Drake weakly.

"That's it? It's over?" Drake asked.

"Not quite," Aiden said. He helped Drake up and then threw the dagger at the air surrounding the tower. The dagger flew and cut through the air, which acted like an invisible wall. The dagger stopped in the air as though it had hit a target and the light that radiated from the impact overwhelmed Drake.

Fire raced around them as Aiden rushed Drake toward the edge of the tower. They both jumped, their Taruk's catching them and carrying them away. The city rumbled and pieces of debris fell to the ground as the Borags below panicked. All those who had stood in defiance of the Sorcerer, retreated out of the city as it crumbled and fell apart around them. Elohim and Destan landed outside the city, the rest of the army joining them as bright lights filled the sky.

"What's happening Aiden?" Drake asked. Aiden smiled again.

"The end of the Sorcerer as we know it. Just watch." The pieces of debris that were crumbling off the buildings, burst into flames as they fell, but when they hit the ground sparks floated up into the sky. The sparks seemed harmless, each of them was a different color. Some were blue, some were orange, and others were green, purple, and red. The sky was filled with thousands and thousands of sparks.

They floated towards Drake and he reached out to touch one. It was surprisingly cool to the touch. Moisture began to mist down to the ground, cooling them off as the city and all the Borags in it began to spark away. The city vanished from view and so did the dark menacing mountains. The sky was gradually filled with sparks that seemed to not die until finally, they could see nothing but the vast swirling cloud of colors that rotated slowly around them.

Everyone felt joy rippling through their soul as the hard rocky ground beneath their feet changed. A spark would hit the ground and grass would be growing in the area moments later. Slowly, the sparks began to spread out and the members of the army began to run around and celebrate as though they were kids playing in the streets.

Gwen came and jumped into Drake's arms and they exchanged a kiss as the cloud of color whirled around them. The world faded, and for a moment it seemed like they were the only two. The Sorcerer's temptation flashed through his mind, but he found it easier to silence now.

The sparks began to thin and retreat and slowly they became aware of the changes that had taken place. Sunlight began to shine down on them when it wasn't veiled by the sparks.

Beneath their feet was lush green grass and in the distance, Drake even thought he could see a forest. The sparks faded out even more and warmth flooded over them. The forest grew and they became aware of a city sitting in the distance.

The city was different from the one they had been fighting in, and as hard as Drake looked around he couldn't even remember where Iscariot had been. The city in front of them looked far grander than any city that Drake had ever seen and certainly seemed worthy of a king.

The sparks disappeared and they were left in a world they didn't recognize as they began wandering in different directions, exploring all the new things. Drake and Gwen stayed behind with Aiden and the others, each of them waiting for an explanation.

"What is this place?" Skander asked.

"Don't you recognize it?" Aiden asked. They shook their heads.

"It feels like an entirely different world altogether," Lily commented.

"I suppose some people might think that, but that is not the case. What you see in front of you is none other than what the land looked like before the Sorcerer came to power. Mera Runa now stands before us in the glory that it once did. Just like nothing has changed."

"That's because you never change," Drake said. The others shook their heads in agreement. "All this time and you're still the same caring, loving person."

"Only love would compel me to go to such great lengths to save the world, for I could just as easily destroy this world and create another, starting over."

"With the way things were headed I wouldn't have blamed you if you did," Ellizar said.

"This world was falling fast, but there was still hope. I will do whatever I must to save the people who call on my name."

"That's a love the world doesn't understand," Lily said.

"How would they when no one shows it to them?" Aiden asked. Drake pondered it for a moment.

"You didn't save us and this world just so we could live in peace did you?" Drake asked. Aiden smiled.

"If I had wanted that, then I would have taken you all to my lands without question or delay. But that was not my purpose."

"What are we supposed to do then?" Skander asked.

"Live. Demonstrate the same love that I have shown you, for I will not always be with you."

"Are you saying you're leaving us now?" Gwen asked.

"I will always be with you Gwen. Maybe not physically, but I am in your heart if you will have me. I know this may be hard for you to understand, but by me being in your heart and you in mine...none of us can ever be robbed of that. If you should die, then we will be reunited in the undying lands."

"I don't understand. What are we goin' teh do now?" Ellizar asked.

"Have you never wondered what lay to the east or the south? Have you ever wondered what lies to the north? This part of the world has seen me and has been saved, but there is much more of the earth that has not yet heard of me. Grimdor has been saved, but the other parts of the earth, are in chaos. The Sorcerer's grip on them is strong and that is something I cannot stand for. It is to those places I will travel. When the whole world has been given the chance to hear the good news, then the end of this world will begin."

"What are we to do?" Drake asked.

"How are people going to hear about me if no one ever tells them about me?" Aiden asked. "Go out into the world and make disciples of all nations, teaching them as I have taught and shown you. If there are two things that best describe what I have shown you it's that above all else, love Lathon and love each other. Everyone is welcome no matter their past. If they hear you and believe then, you should welcome them and then teach them, and then they will tell their friends, and their friends will tell their friends. Together we can save the world. Tell them your story, tell them about me, and then teach them. And surely I am with you always, to the very end of the age."

"How are we supposed to convince people that you can save them if they never see you?"

"But they will see me," Aiden answered. "*You* will be the light. They will look at you and notice how you are different, and although many may hate it, many will want to be like you. You must live your life in a way that is pleasing to Lathon, and lives will be changed as a result. Love is what I offer to them. I have shown them. Now it's your turn to show them. You've been given a wonderful gift and now it's up to you what you do with it."

XXV   A DISCONTENTED HEART

The following days brought so many changes and exciting new things that Drake could hardly keep up. The land in front of them continued to change and shift for many weeks. It seemed more trees sprouted and the signs of war were erased by some other means than their own.

Drake puzzled over all the great changes, admittedly, feeling a little out of place with the flawless landscape that now surrounded them. Each leaf, each tree, each blade of grass seemed so perfect that Drake became afraid of stepping on one for fear that he would kill it.

At the end of the first day, the armies that had marched against the land of Grimdor felt as if it was already a distant memory. Aiden had kept them from entering Mera Runa as of yet, warning them against it. As hard as they could, none of them could come up with any practical reason why they had to be kept out. Some people claimed they had seen strange people going in and out of the city gates, but those accounts were deemed to be nothing more than rumors.

Soon fires were lit and the people and nations enjoyed their first night in the shadows of Mera Runa, which they had not yet entered. The songs and stories that were told went long into the night. Gwen and Drake lay next to their campfire, looking up at the stars above, feeling uneasy about the uncertainty before them.

"I'm not sure what to do with myself now," Drake admitted. "Ever since I woke up on the side of the river, I've been on the run, or trying to bring down the Sorcerer. Now, there's nothing."

"There's this," Gwen said, kissing him. "And I think that counts for something."

"That it certainly does. Don't you wonder what's next though?"

"Yes, I do," Gwen replied. "I wonder very much. I also wonder what it's going to be like having Isabel as my mother." They chuckled. "Still trying to adjust to that news."

"I understand. I'd ask where your mother is in all of this, but it's Isabel, so who knows?"

"She's on the other side of the city, carefully studying a rare vining plant that glows in starlight," a voice said. They turned to see Aiden coming up to their fire.

"I was just about to guess that," Drake said. They laughed.

"Sure, you were."

"I don't know how she has time or energy for half the things she does," Drake stated.

"You always have time and energy for something if you make time for it," Aiden said. "The things she is studying or takes an interest in might seem strange or pointless, but they do have a purpose far beyond just making her 'interesting'."

"Like what?" Gwen asked. Aiden thought.

"For one, she's spending time in the great outdoors. Lathon's playground. He didn't create all of this just so we can take it for granted."

"I guess you would know better than anybody," Drake said with a smile. "I like what you've done with the place." Drake motioned to the city. "Hardly looks the same."

Aiden smiled proudly. "It is a fine piece of land, which from now on, shall be called Rhallenin."

"What does that mean?" Gwen asked.

"It means 'delivered.' For this land was ridden of great evil and much that was at risk of falling shall stand strong for ages to come."

"You'll make a great king if I do say so myself," Drake said. Aiden looked at him, with a quizzical expression.

"I am not going to rule this city," Aiden said. Drake and Gwen both felt their mouths drop open.

"You're not going to rule Mera Runa?" Gwen asked.

"No. That is not the purpose of this city. I will rule a city one day, but it will not be this one."

"Then what are we going to do next?"

"This nation will become a great nation, devoted to the teaching of great leaders. Teaching about Lathon and equipping people to go out and spread the news about Lathon and myself. People will come to Mera Runa from all corners of the world for the knowledge and wisdom that will pour out from here. Even though many may take it for granted."

"Who's going to lead the city?" Drake asked.

"A person named Drake Thomas," Aiden said. Drake and Gwen once again showed their surprise. "Don't worry—you won't be alone. I will stay with you for many months, teaching and equipping you so you can do the job."

"I don't know what to say," Drake admitted. "What do I know about being a king?"

"It's not about being a king; it's about being a leader and thinking of others first," Aiden said. "Just know that the time of peace is coming, but peace does not mean inaction. There is a plan for you, even after the last soldier goes home."

"I never imagined this," Drake said. A look in Gwen's direction conveyed the same thing.

"Do you trust my judgment?"

"Yes, but you must understand it is still a shock."

Aiden laughed. "Yes, I certainly understand that! Trust me though, we have much time to get you ready and I know you both have it in you, even if you don't see it in yourself yet."

Drake smiled to himself, taking delight in the compliment and wondering just how everything would work out. They talked for several more minutes before Aiden excused himself, leaving them by the fire as they had been.

The next morning brought a sense of merriment and joy that Drake hadn't felt in many months. The sunrise covered everything in dazzling shades and hues of reds and purples. The people rose and assembled at the gates where Aiden stood to address the masses.

"Welcome one and all! Behind me is the city of Mera Runa, and I can hardly wait until I can take you in to see the magnificent city, just as it was at the height of its beauty and power. But today is not about this city. It will not be until the evening of tomorrow, the third day, when we will be allowed to enter it.

"But do not fret about this, for about you is a great land flowing with riches and wonders that you have never seen before. Explore. Enjoy the land. After we have entered the city there will be time for allocation of property and the makings of homes and building a life in the land of Rhallinen."

To Drake's surprise when Aiden had finished speaking, nearly everyone did disperse and go exploring in the new land. Drake and Gwen were joined by Sedric and Bethany, and together they walked for many miles and even took turns flying on Destan to look over the vast and beautiful nation.

Already forests and rivers filled the landscape as well as pasture lands for the grazing of animals. Drake's mind was boggled in every way as they walked among the trees. Most of them he didn't recognize and even though they had only sprouted yesterday, they were as large and majestic as any trees he had ever seen.

Isabel and Morgrin joined them during the afternoon, and together the six of them had a merry time, as they explored everything that they could. Finally,

when they were spent, they made their way back to Mera Runa and enjoyed a long supper and a time of telling tales or recounting everything they could remember.

When the dawn of the third day came, everyone stayed within walking distance of the city, not wanting to miss the moment that the gates were finally opened. The excitement and anticipation only grew as the day progressed until finally, great horns bellowed from inside the city walls. The massive gates, which appeared to be made of solid amethyst, began to open. They strode up to the gate, stopping for Ellizar, who was admiring the gates.

"I have never seen anythin' like this!" Ellizar exclaimed. "How and what skill must have carved these gates?"

"There are more than just a few mysteries for you to enjoy," Aiden said, beaming. "Please, come in!"

The entire assembly filtered in through the gates, each of them speaking no words after they were in. They were beyond words. They walked through the city, exploring and finding a great deal to marvel at. Time faded and each of them walked as though they were in a dream, though none of them could accurately put their finger on what it was that captivated their attention so fully.

All at once, horns once again echoed through the city, though this time they came from the citadel. Everyone immediately made their way up the three levels until they reached the top, once again speechless.

The vast space in front of them was filled with chairs and tables and food, fully cooked and prepared. Beyond all the tables a large palace reached into the sky.

They took a seat and waited for everyone else to sit. To Drake's surprise, everyone present was able to find seating and had food to eat. Aiden stood, with his cup raised and everyone followed suit.

"Dear friends, welcome to the city of Mera Runa. A city with a long and storied past. What is history? History is our story, and though small it seems at times, there is hope once again. This city shall be a great reminder of the heart of a follower of Lathon. For once you were as this city was, dead, lost, and broken, but now you can stand tall and proud once again.

"Those failures and hurts, that have seemed pointless and unnecessary up until now, will now be used to bring glory to Lathon. For Lathon is a God of restoration. What was once lost and broken is now restored to glory."

Aiden gave thanks and they ate the feast that had been prepared. No matter how much they ate, they never ran out, and curiously enough the large platters and serving trays seemed to fill themselves. If someone was doing it, no one could see them.

When the meal was over, Aiden addressed them again, telling them of all the things that would happen in the coming days. Before the allocation of the property was to begin, anyone who wished to leave and go home would be allowed, and by the same token, anyone who wished to come and live in Rhallenin would be allowed to send for their spouses and children to join them.

Though they were given advance notice of the events that were to transpire, Drake was more nervous than ever to wake up the next morning. The dawn was just breaking over the land of Rhallenin. Drake went into the palace and closed the door behind him, sitting alone in a chair.

The sun grew brighter outside and a great assembly could be heard and the sounding of trumpets, signaling the people, rang out. After a while the palace doors opened and Aiden strode through them.

"Morning Drake," Aiden greeted. "It's almost time. What are you doing in here?"

"Hiding. I'm nervous," Drake admitted. Aiden sat down next to him.

"Why? Do you not trust me?"

"I trust you, but I never thought of myself like a king before."

"Being king is at the heart no different than being a servant. To those who handle well what they've been given, even greater responsibility shall be given. You have done well with what you have been given."

"What about my past?"

"What about it?" Aiden asked.

"Will I ever be able to remember it?"

"Whether you do or don't is not for you to worry about. You need only look ahead and towards Lathon. Serve him with all your heart. That is what makes a man a king."

"What about my parents? They said they need to be heading back home," Drake said. "I thought I would be going with them."

"No. Your road does not lead there. Though it may one day."

When they finally came out of the palace, the sun was high above them and a gentle, cool breeze moved through the air. A large platform had been built, overlooking the entire citadel where the masses were waiting for the ceremony to begin.

The ceremony itself was a blur to Drake, who even afterward only half-remembered everything that had happened. Aiden gave a long and powerful speech and then Drake was brought before the fellowship. He was presented to the people, to which everyone cheered and then Gwen came forward carrying a beautiful crown.

The crown was made of bronze, but inlaid into it were a great number of gems, gold, and silver. It was in many ways a simple crown, not big and outlandish like some that Drake had seen during his time.

It was set upon his head, and the assembly once again cheered and bowed before their new king. Aiden looked at him with smiling eyes and even his friends looked at him differently than they had before. There was a great feast for the midday lunch, and then work began.

Aiden and Drake worked side by side, which Drake was very thankful for. They began making a list of people who wished to stay in Rhallenin and would be allocated the proper land, according to the works they had completed.

The next morning started with Ellizar and Lily meeting with everyone just after breakfast had been finished. The two were smiling and it didn't take anyone long to figure out what they were going to say.

They were married that same evening and allocated land less than a mile from Mera Runa, along a peaceful river that sparkled in the sunset. Although they had no house as of yet, they threw up a tent, while arrangements were made.

To the surprise of many, they had a house built in two days, largely because Shavrok and his friends, who had grown so fond of them while they had lived amongst them, had offered their services. By the end of the second day, a modest house of stone and wood had been finished for the happy couple.

Their marriage surprised many people and just as many disapproved of the union simply based on the fact that they were of vastly different races. Drake knew this was a matter of the heart though, and eventually, many people came to discover that for themselves. For that matter, Ellizar and Lily didn't care.

As for Drake though, once the allocation of land was done he continued to learn everything a king had to know under Aiden's guidance. Isabel and Morgrin took their leave and headed back to her shop in Belvanor, but promised to return often.

Three months later Drake and Gwen were wed and she was crowned queen of Rhallenin. The ceremony was large and saw delegations and parties from all the surrounding nations. Even the nation of Farndor was represented by their new king and queen. The festivities went on for a couple of days and all the nations paid tribute to the Queen and Rhallenin. After everyone had left and gone back to their home, it seemed that everything returned to normal.

Six months later saw the departure of Aiden, who by now, had taught Drake and Gwen everything that they needed to know to do what had been asked of them. His departure was bittersweet for both of them and in the silence that followed their hearts grew restless.

The days passed and slowly Gwen's thoughts turned to their pasts, which they still did not fully remember or understand. The pattern of thoughts took root in Drake's heart and the thoughts and desires were allowed to swirl around in their heads and hearts. For many nights, they were tempted to leave the throne to follow those desires.

Two months later, Drake was finally convinced that going north would satisfy their longing for the past. A great council was called to order and eventually, everyone else also became convinced that Drake and Gwen should leave.

Ellizar and Lily, though reluctant, were appointed the temporary king and queen of Rhallenin. Drake and Gwen set off to the north, having every intention of returning once they had discovered the past that had eluded them for so long.

Aiden watched from the distance as Drake and Gwen climbed on Destan and flew off to the north, his heart saddened. The darkness of night settled in. Suddenly, a rustling in the trees was heard behind him and a shadow of a person stepped out. He wore a long black cloak and his hood was up.

"Merderick." Though his disguise would fool many, Aiden was not surprised.

"I didn't think you could see me."

They stood in silence watching the Taruk fade from the sky. "You may be physically dead, and there are some who would be able to see you as I see you now, but I assure you that you will never be invisible to me."

"You must certainly be saddened at Drake's departure?"

"Of course. Any time a person listens and then acts on the dark thoughts you whisper in their mind I am indeed sad."

"You might as well give up now," Merderick said. "If I can get Drake to neglect what he's been given, certainly I can pull the wool over other people's eyes. There are people much easier than him."

"You have little faith, and absolutely no foresight," a voice remarked. The voice was strong and powerful, full of both love and gravity. The Sorcerer, Merderick, seemed to shrink in size, slowly backing up to the edge of the clearing.

An awkward silence fell between them as a great rustling was heard. From the overgrowth that surrounded them, Elohim stuck his head out, his eyes filled with malice and rage as he looked at Merderick. To Aiden's left, a man bearing a great staff came forward. His eyes pierced every darkness, and the very ground he walked on seemed to shudder beneath his feet.

Aiden watched the surprise on the face of the Sorcerer. Without warning Elohim let out a fierce roar, but it was only heard by one person. In an instant, the shadow of the Sorcerer vanished.

"The difference between us and him...the real difference," Aiden started. "He sees a failure; we see an opportunity."

"Drake has followed bad council, yes, but if he opens his heart...I can use that to transform much more than he has thrown away," the man with the staff said. The trees around them seemed to tremble with pleasure at the sound of his voice. "Drake has faltered, but even so he left the nation in the hands of Ellizar and Lily. They will not fail. Nor is the story of Drake Thomas close to over. For life does not start and end with the drawing of swords and the roar of battle. The battle worth winning is what you do when the sword is put away and you put your guard down. There are many more who need to learn this lesson."

Aiden smiled and looked down at Mera Runa. Elohim joined him. The man with the staff walked down the slope to the fields before the city. Their hearts surged with joy. Elohim once again roared up into the night sky. Everyone heard the sound this time. Those who heard it were encouraged. Aiden quickly mounted Elohim and took to the sky.

The Adventure Continues...

DRAKE THOMAS

-BOOK 3-

THE DEAD MOUNTAINS

TYLER SVEC
JORDAN SVEC

EPIRUS
VERNAL
GRIMDOR
GIAHON
Idumea
Farndor
CALAMAR
ARIAMORE
Tyre
Ruins of Fiori
Buckleberry
Chanella River
Nariven
Nathon
Masada
Grön
Dhuma
Iscariot
Tel-Amor
Negev
Rock of Petron
Dav
Omar
Remnda
Maril
Revly
Ruins of Temnar
Havren
Belvanor
Lake Ross
Negev River
Kesinr River
Sea of the Spirits
N
E
S
W

STORIES/REFERENCES

Stories & References

Pg: 190-195 – Rahab hides the spies. Based off Joshua 2:1-8

Pg: 207-208 – The walls of Jericho fall. Joshua 6:20

Pg: 233-237 – Tempting of Jesus. Based off Matthew 4:1-11

Pg: 254 – Genesis 3:9

Pg: 255 – Jesus healing the blind man. John 9:6

Pg: 258 – Luke 11:17

Pg: 278-279 – Begining dialog loosly based off acount in Job.

Pg: 324 – Matthew 28: 19-20

Pg: 330 – 1 Samuel 10:22

About the Authors

Tyler Svec is a farmer in Northern Michigan who first started writing in high school. In the years that has followed, he has written 7 novels. He is happily married to his wife, Jessica, and they have four kids together.

Jordan Svec lives in Northern Michigan with his wife and two children. By day he works along his brother (Tyler) and together they collaborate on the ideas that go into the Drake Thomas series.